THE LAKE

The Lake Series, Book 1

by

AnnaLisa Grant

THE LAKE

ISBN: 978-1482066302

Cover art by Cover Me, Darling

For more information, visit:
www.AnnaLisaGrant.com
Facebook.com/AuthorAnnalisaGrant

Dedication

For Donavan

who has always believed in every

crazy dream I've ever had.

So much.

What lies behind us and what lies before us

are tiny matters compared to what lies within us.

-Ralph Waldo Emerson

Chapter 1

I went to bed last night praying the nightmares wouldn't come, but they did. It seems the pain of my parents' death is destined to be with me forever.

I tossed and turned, as I have most nights for the past five years. Sometimes I wish I could sleep forever, but that would mean dreaming forever…and I just can't risk that.

As I finally give up on sleep and open my eyes, I have to wipe the tears in order to take note of the time: 7:30 a.m., thirty minutes before the annoying buzzing is set to go off. I turn off the alarm so it won't bother me later.

I'm surprised I didn't sleep longer, considering how wiped out I was from yesterday's packing. Now that Gramps has passed, I am moving from small town Florida to small town North Carolina to live with my dad's only brother and his wife, people I barely know. I barely knew Gram and Gramps when I came to live with them five years ago, so at least I know how to handle myself in unknown situations.

So far my uncle and aunt, Luke and Claire, have shown me more kindnesses in the last 24 hours than my grandmother did in the two years I lived with them before she died. They remind me of my parents in this, which fills me with more excitement than I know how to express. Years of stuffing down every feeling like a puppet in a Jack-in-the-Box will do that to you.

With all the arrangements that had to be made, we've had very little social conversation in the 48 hours since Luke and Claire arrived, but at least they're here and ready to fulfill their duty as my new legal guardians. And while I'm nervous, my gut tells me that living with them is the fresh start I've been starving for, that this last year of high school will be my chance to reset my path.

Gramps' passing was inevitable. It's just the way he died that seems unfair. Gramps took a hard fall down the stairs last week. The booming sound of his body landing was the second scariest sound I've ever heard. Luke was listed on Gramps' emergency contact information with Medicaid, so the hospital called him once Gramps was admitted.

"Layla! Are you almost ready?" I hear Claire call as I unwrap the towel from my wet head. "We're leaving for the funeral home in forty-five minutes."

"Yes, Claire. I'll be ready," I call back. I have yet to call either of them Aunt or Uncle. The term implies a relationship we don't yet have, and while I'm grateful for their presence, I can't bring myself to it, even out of obligation. My time with Gram was a lesson in building walls. I've become quite adept at it.

Today is Gramp's funeral, and I'm giving his eulogy.

Suddenly the full weight of everything is hitting me. Who in their right mind would let a 17-year-old girl give a eulogy? Isn't a eulogy supposed to reflect on the departed's life? I don't know much about life, although I certainly understand death. I'm the only one who's been here for him since Gram died, so I suppose I'm best suited for the job, and after everything he did for me, it's the least I can do. I only hope I can get through it without having a complete meltdown.

I was 12 when I moved in with Gram and Gramps. I had only met them a few times at Christmas and once when my parents took me to Disney World. They didn't seem to think much of mom, which was fine with dad because of whatever falling out they had when he was younger. The tense status of their relationship made for short, infrequent visits.

Living with Gram and Gramps was not the life I would have chosen had I known what it was going to be like. My grandmother made her opinion very clear that the accident that killed my parents was my fault. I really couldn't argue the point, so my days were spent making restitution for my transgression. This meant giving up everything that brought me joy. I didn't have friends outside of school, I never had anyone over, and I certainly never asked to go anywhere. I learned early on that Gram didn't mince words. She said what she meant, and she meant it when she said, "If you think you deserve anything good after what you did, you're sorely mistaken."

To be honest, when Gram died two years after I came to live with her and Gramps I was pretty relieved. I know it sounds terrible, but I was. She reminded me daily of my transgression. Sometimes it was a statement about what they could be doing now as retirees if they didn't have to take care of me, and when my father's birthday came around, well, that was another level of guilt altogether. "Another birthday John will never have!" she'd say, followed by hours of sobbing. As hard as I tried, there was no making up for how I had wronged her. After a while I just stopped trying. I did what I was told and kept to myself.

But…my days with Gramps were entirely different. Never once did he even remotely imply that I was to blame for my parents' death. In fact, he never mentioned my parents at all because Gram would not allow it. When I first came to live with them, he filled the role of loving grandfather immediately. His affection, so opposite of Gram's, was exactly what my heart hungered for from the moment I moved in with Gram and Gramps. He let me sit on his knee, or cuddle with him on the couch like grandparents do with their grandkids. He told me he loved me almost daily, an act of affection that Gram did less than infrequently. He would also quietly slip me a five here or a twenty there. We never went anywhere or did anything, and I couldn't buy anything with it either because then Gram would know. So, I squirreled it away…all $640 of it.

After a few months the affection Gramps gave me ceased when Gram informed him that I no longer needed his doting. His displays of affection were reduced to a wink here and there and a hug when Gram wasn't looking. Gram said it was time to grow up. And grow up, I did.

I finish drying my long, brown hair and pull it up into its usual ponytail. The Florida heat is too much for me to wear my thick hair down. It's grown down to my shoulder blades since I haven't had it cut in almost three years. I have no plans of chopping it all off, so I suppose I'll be ponytail girl forever. I put on Gramps' favorite blue dress of mine because I refuse to wear black, and the nicer of my two pairs of sandals. Before I make my way downstairs I take a long look at myself in the mirror. I stare at my father's hazel eyes, his small nose and chin, too. I've waited so long for this day to come; the day that would be my official discharge back onto the path to the life I was supposed to have. I look to see if this newfound release has changed me. No, nothing yet, but for the first time, I see something I haven't in a long time: a glimmer of hope.

I descend the stairs and find Luke waiting at the side door dressed sharply in a black suit and blue tie. He reminds me so much of my dad. He has typically short brown hair and is handsome by anyone's standards. When I reach the bottom of the stairs I finally notice just how tall Luke is – probably 6'1". We've been so scattered these last few days that I never really stopped to look at him that much and in the light streaming from the kitchen window I see clearly that Luke and I have the same eyes. I think we must all look like Gramps.

"The car is here. Oh, Layla, there you are. You look lovely. Everyone ready?" Claire says as she comes in from the carport. "*Wow,*" I think, "*Claire is so pretty.*" I remember thinking so the first time I saw her when I was a child. She's classy, wearing her hair shorter than I've seen on any grown woman under the age of 60, and next to Luke, her stature is exquisite. They both seem to tower over my average frame. I'm definitely more bronzed than Luke and Claire. Not because I spent my days sunning at the beach, but because there have been weekly yard chores since I came here. I didn't mind those chores so much after I saw them transforming my stick-like arms and legs into strong, defined limbs.

"Thank you," I say meekly. Claire responds with a soft, sweet smile. Luke and Claire rented a Lincoln Towne Car limo to take us to the funeral home. It will surely be the nicest vehicle I've ever been in. They're both lawyers so I guess they can afford it. Gramps said they weren't the high-powered ones you see in the movies, but still well off. They don't have any kids. Maybe their jobs are more important than having a family. I don't know.

There must have been a similar falling out with Luke, too, because as far as I know he didn't talk to anyone in the family either. Dad never spoke of Luke, and never explained why he and his brother didn't talk. I guess just because you're family doesn't mean you have to be friends. Gram and Gramps never spoke of them either. I guess that bridge got burned, too. Hell, Gram probably poured the gasoline and lit the match herself! But I like them. I don't care what happened between Luke and my dad or grandparents. That was their business, not mine. All I know is that my gut tells me I'm headed into a life with a real family and I'm not going to do anything to mess that up.

When we arrive at the funeral home I'm surprised at how many people are already there, with more pulling into the parking lot behind us. I think back to Gram's funeral and am certain there weren't half this many people there. This comforts me in an odd way. Something about it lets me know that I wasn't the only one Gram treated poorly, and the kind and generous man I knew to be my grandfather was the same man all these people were coming to pay their respects to today.

"It's time, dear," the funeral director says thoughtfully to me after we've been seated for what seems like eternity. "Are you sure about this? I knew Jack, and I'd be happy to speak on your behalf."

"No. I want to do it. It's…important," I tell him. I stand up from the front row and step up to the podium. My hands are shaking so I grab a hold of the cold, brown lectern to steady myself. I'm breathing so deeply I think they can hear me at the back of the room even before my mouth nears the microphone. The room smells like overly scented flowers. It's unnatural. I am momentarily distracted by the obnoxious scent and blinding glare the sun streaming through the window is causing as it reflects off the bright white blooms. Then I notice Gramps, lying there in the open casket. Peaceful. Happy. After what seems like a long time, I take a final breath and begin. "Thank you all for coming today. I'm Layla Weston. Jack was my grandfather. I called him Gramps. I was going to write something down, but I wanted to speak more from my heart today, so I hope it's ok if I just wing it." I chuckle nervously. "To be honest, now that I'm here, I'm not really sure what it is that I should say."

So much runs through my mind. I'm kicking myself and wishing I had at least written down some bullet points. How am I going to do this? How do I sum up life with Gramps? For the last three years I took care of him. I washed his clothes, cleaned his house, and made his breakfast before I went to school. He was ok with cereal or toast, which was good because I had neither the time nor the inclination to put out the spread Gram did for breakfast every day. On the weekend I would make pancakes and bacon, though. I would prepare his lunch and leave it in the fridge before I left for school. When I came home I did my homework, cleaned the breakfast dishes and Gramps' dish from lunch, and then made dinner. Sometimes Gramps and I would go out for dinner, but not too often because it took a lot out of him and he got tired very quickly. I was tired a lot, too. Life was emotionally draining, but I loved Gramps and could never have left him. He was the only light I had in a prison of darkness with Gram.

As I think of the brightness that Gramps brought to my life, I know exactly what I'm going to say.

"Jack…Gramps…was the greatest person I've ever known. He was kind, generous, and loving. I watched him love Gram with a passionate love that most only dream of. After 50 years of marriage, he looked at her and still saw the blushing bride of his youth." I pause to collect myself and need to lighten the mood as much as possible in order to keep myself from crying. "He…was a terrible driver…but never minded taking me anywhere I wanted to go." *Which wasn't anywhere, but no one here needs to know that.* "He and Gram took me in when I had no one and nowhere else to go. When they should have been enjoying their retirement, they were raising a teenage girl. After Gram died, Gramps never faltered in being there for me. How he handled three years alone with a teenage girl on his hands is beyond me. But I will forever be grateful to him for all he did for me. I know that there's a special place in Heaven for Gramps – a place where Gramps is finally with his bride again." That's all I can say. I know it should have been longer, but I'm afraid I'll start talking about Dad and Mom, which will lead to uncontrollable crying and I just can't do that. I wasn't allowed to say anything at their funeral. People thought it would be too traumatic for me – as if I didn't know what trauma was. I've never talked about it before, why start now? So I just leave it at that.

The service is being held at the cemetery, so we don't have to follow in some depressing funeral parade across town to bury Gramps. The crowd of about thirty walks the path from the building while they put the coffin in the hearse and drive it to the gravesite. By the time we get there, they've already got everything set up for the graveside portion of the service. It's June, almost the hottest time of the year in Central Florida. I can smell the freshly turned dirt from where they dug Gramps' grave. It's raw and musty and my gag reflex reacts in just the smallest of heaves. There's a green tent with chairs set up under it but it's still hot even in the shade. The sun is blazing and I think I saw that the high is supposed to be 98 degrees. It rained yesterday, so that makes today both hot and humid. This is good only because I can pretend that my tears are really beads of sweat rolling down my face. I don't like to cry at all, let alone in front of anyone.

The funeral director says a few words, and then the priest from the church that Gram and Gramps attended on Christmas and Easter gives a short message. Several people lay flowers on his coffin, with me leading. Then it's over.

"He was such a good man," one woman says to me as she passes by and pats my shoulder. I'm glad that was all she said.

"Yes, he was," is all I can squeak out.

I stay to the very end. Some suggest I go home and relax, but that's a ridiculous idea since all that waits for me there is the stress of packing up a house where two people spent their entire lives together. I spent the last five years there, but did not *live*.

I insist on staying to watch them lower Gramps' coffin into the ground. I'm watching this beautifully ornate box with my grandfather's body inside inch its way into the earth and all I want to do is jump on top of it and go with him. Through everything, he never made me feel guilty. I suppose he knew that Gram was dishing out enough. He was the only ray of light I had in five years and now he's gone.

In this moment I feel so alone. Life is crumbling around me. I'm headed into a multitude of unknowns, so torn between what my heart is screaming at me to do – *Go, Layla! This is your chance to start over!* – and clinging to the only ill-fitting life I've known for the last five years. I've spent so long being strong and now there's no one left to take care of – no one but myself.

This has to be it though. I'm tired of living in this place of eternal misery. I woke up every day knowing it was just another day in a prison sentence of undetermined years.

I see Luke and Claire in my periphery and I know that this is the opportunity I've wanted for so long. My penance has been paid and I am now free. I may not know much about Luke and Claire, but what I do know is that they are my only shot at getting my life back.

"Layla? Are…you ready to go? I don't want to rush you, but we've still got a lot to tackle in the next few days," Luke says in a hushed, reverent tone. I feel the warmth of his hand as he starts to rest it on my back, but then he seems to change his mind because he steps to the side and puts his hands in his pockets.

I wipe the tears that were welling up in my eyes, and then wipe my forehead too so it looks like I was just sweating. "Yeah. I'm ready."

I declined the idea of having some kind of reception after the funeral. I hated the idea of everyone mingling around, eating casseroles and pie, and talking about Gramps in a steady stream of past tense phrases and stories. Gramps' death didn't need to take up everyone's day either.

When we arrive back at the house I don't even bother to change my clothes. I dive in immediately to a stack of papers on the kitchen counter. There's so much to file through that everything is starting to blur together. Most of it is old junk mail that just never got thrown away and miscellaneous papers that were shoved into random drawers around the house. When I reach the bottom of the stack I find a manila folder with Gracehaven Boarding School for Girls written on it. I open up the folder wondering when Gram and Gramps entertained the idea of sending me to boarding school. *Whoa this place is expensive!* I can only assume they would have used my college fund to pay for it. It's not much, but probably enough to pay for a few years. I scan the application and see that it's dated for three days ago and signed by Luke and Claire. My heart stops.

"Ready for a break? Luke's going to run out and pick up some food," Claire says as she and Luke enter the kitchen. The visual of this application is rolling around in my head like a pinball and I haven't had to time to process it at all.

"Are you…sending me to boarding school?" I ask abruptly.

"Oh…Layla…" Claire says in quiet shock. Obviously this is not how they planned on telling me. "We were going to talk with you about that tomorrow." Claire is nervous, her voice faltering.

"You don't want me to live with you," I stutter out. It's not a question but an observation. I feel so stupid. I actually believed that they were riding in like knights on white horses to free me from the prison I'd been living in, but the reality is that they want to send me to another prison.

"No, Layla. That's not it at all," Luke protests. He takes a step forward and it's the most emotion I've seen from him since they arrived.

"What is it? I'm too old? You're too busy? You don't want a kid around?" How could my gut be so wrong?

"It's not like that. We…" Luke stammers.

"I'm not going to be any trouble. I promise. I just…I need to get out of here. I need…I need a real home." I pause as I watch Luke and Claire look at each other, not knowing what to do now that I've interrupted their plan. "But…if that's not what you want, I understand. I don't want to be anywhere I'm not welcome anymore."

"It's complicated, Layla. Claire and I…" Luke begins but Claire cuts him off.

"We didn't think you'd want to live with us," Claire explains awkwardly.

"Well…don't I get a say?" I plead.

"Of course you do," Claire says softly. There's a surprised smile on her face.

"I'd…like to come with you…if that's ok." I squeak out the first declaration of my own desire in five years and beam with pride on the inside.

Claire steps forward and takes me by the shoulders. "You are *more* than welcome to live with us. We want you, Layla." Claire's tone is soothing and evokes a feeling of belonging in me that I haven't felt in a long time. Her words echo in my ears and I think I'm going to cry.

"Ok. Thank you," I say after a moment. I watch Luke and Claire smile at me and then at each other.

"Good. No more talk about boarding school or living anywhere but with us. Ok?" Claire says brightly. I nod in reply and smile as best I can.

We spend the next two days cleaning and packing up the house. Luke handles the items in the attic. I've never been up there, and won't have a clue what I'm looking at, so I let him decide what should be kept. I figure it's probably stuff he'll recognize from his childhood and will know better. Luke and Claire take just a few things from the house and let me decide what to do with the rest. I determine that donating it to the church is the best thing. I'm keeping only a few things. Old photos, the blanket Gramps used to snuggle up in with me when I was little and both Gram and Gramps' wedding rings. It doesn't seem right for them to go to just anyone.

And just like me, the rest of it is being set free from this place.

Chapter 2

When everything is finally either packed or donated and the house is completely empty I stand in the living room where Gramps' favorite chair used to be. I breathe a few deep breaths and inhale the last lingering scent of Gramps' aftershave and the muskiness of the furniture that Gram picked out when they got married. I close my eyes and listen to the walls creak, as if they're releasing me, saying goodbye. I nod in silent thanks in return for the shelter they provided, and I thank my lucky stars that I won't have to live in this house for another second. I adjusted to life here and paid my penance for what I did. The time has come for me to live my life again. I take one last look around and then leave through the front door, never looking back.

I walk slowly to the rental car. This is my moment to be free, to find myself again. As I watch Luke and Claire my heart begins to beat faster, pounding so hard inside my chest that I'm sure they can hear it. They have no idea how they are changing my life. More than anything right now I want to make this work. I'm ready. I had been old with Gram and Gramps for five years. No more. Gramps' death has pardoned me, and Luke and Claire are carrying me into a new life where everything I have dreamed of is finally coming true. Step one of this process is getting as far away from this place as possible.

I get in the car and find myself lost in thought. I think about Luke and Claire and wonder what life will be like with them, remind myself of what my mom always told me. "Your gut will never lie to you, Layla," she'd say.

"Layla, you need to buckle up, dear," Claire says.

"I'm sorry. What?" We're on the plane when I wake from my haze and come back to reality.

"We're about to take off. You've got your head in the clouds a little early," Claire says sweetly. I echo her smile and buckle my seatbelt before the flight attendant comes by to reprimand me.

We arrive in Charlotte and Claire and I wait outside baggage claim while Luke gets the car. The weather is warm, but not like Florida. Still, we ride with the windows up and the air on full blast. Both Luke and Claire ask me if I enjoyed the flight. It was my first time flying and they seem genuinely interested.

"It was good," is all I say.

The drive from the airport is pleasant and beautiful. The highway is lined with trees and peppered with shopping plazas, gas stations, and restaurants. I've never seen so much green. Then, like a gift in my tragic hour, there is water on either side of the highway in the form of a behemoth size lake. The sign reads "Lake Norman" and I wonder how close to the water my new custodians live, reminding myself just how much I miss the ocean.

My days spent at the beach as a child were the most wonderful of my life. Most of the best days we had as a family were spent playing in the sand and the ocean from morning until sunset. My parents taught me to appreciate the kind of peace, comfort, and joy that only the ocean can bring.

The drive off the highway to Luke and Claire's house is beautifully different from anything I'd ever seen in Florida. The town I grew up in is pretty much one big city. There are neighborhoods, but no real suburbs separate from a big center-city. As we get farther from the interstate Claire tells me they live in an area of town that is very nostalgic. "It's a cute little town with mom-and-pop shops and restaurants. Oh, and there's a library," she says excitedly.

I hope the library is a good one. If there's one trait of my mother's that I never let go of it was my love of books. When I was little we used to take the stories we had read over and over and play the "What if…?" game. *What if…Old Mother Hubbard found a million dollars in the cupboard?* I feel a smile creep onto my face at the thought of her.

Their neighborhood streets are lined with tall, leafy trees, and I think I just saw someone actually pick up after their dog. As we drive up to their house I suddenly feel like Annie arriving at Daddy Warbucks' mansion. Gramps seriously downplayed Luke and Claire's success. It's the biggest house I've ever seen. *Why do they have such a big house if it's just the two of them?*

It's much nicer than the houses I lived in. The house is white, two stories, with a front porch that extends the length of the house, and dark shutters. Blue, possibly black. It looks like it belongs on the cover of a Martha Stewart magazine, except I think Martha reserves the cover for herself. The steps to the porch are wide enough that we can all walk up together…*with* our luggage. The big, red door has a window on the top half covered by a small curtain on the inside with little blue flowers. They're slightly open and I unsuccessfully try to get a peek inside before Luke unlocks the door and lets us all in.

The house is beautiful and decorated exquisitely. The fragrance filling the room is just the right scent of flowers. Clean, not overwhelming. The like-something-out-of-a-magazine theme continues with elegant furniture and accent pieces strategically placed throughout the room. I want to ask Claire if she decorated the house herself or if she had a professional do it, but I think that might sound rude, so I don't.

"Well, here we are. Would you like to see your room? Then I can give you a tour of the house, if you'd like," Claire asks as I nervously stumble to set my luggage down. She turns just as she's asking and I think she's trying to catch me before I drop my bags and possibly disturb the room. Too late. The wheels of my suitcase catch and flip the corner of the rug, and my backpack knocks a few pillows off the couch. Luke catches a falling vase and I freeze. *No, no, no Layla! This is not part of the plan. In fact, it's the opposite of the plan! You're trying to make this work, not make them regret taking you in from the first second you walk through the door!*

Luke smiles as he places the vase back on the table. "I should've let it break. I never liked this piece," he whispers to me with a crooked smile. I smile back at him as relief floods my body.

"My room, yeah, that'd be great. Thanks," I say politely as I clumsily pick up the pillows and straighten the rug. I watch for Claire's reaction to my disturbance of the perfection of the room. She doesn't seem upset at all. In fact, she joins me in picking up the last pillow and gives Luke a teasing nudge at his not-so-subtle comment.

Claire leads me upstairs to a huge open loft with floor to ceiling windows on the backside of the house. There are no curtains or blinds on the windows, but it's getting dark and I can't really see what's out there. There is beautiful designer furniture filling the room, and an impressive media wall.

The most impressive feature in the room, a wall made entirely of built in bookshelves, catches my eye and makes my heart leap. There are books and perfectly placed vases and picture frames with people I don't know stylishly placed on each shelf. I'm in heaven at the idea of spending hours reading selections from this library.

I follow Claire down a short hall to the only room on the second floor. It is, like the rest of the house, absolutely beautiful. My room at Gram and Gramps' was small – big enough only for a single bed, a tall 5-drawer dresser, and a small desk. The chair to the desk barely fit between the bed and the desk itself, and the closet door never closed completely. This room is huge. There's a white, four-poster queen-size bed with beautiful white bedding with blue flowers and green accents. The windows that face the front of the house are fitted with curtains that coordinate with the bedding perfectly. There is a white desk with a pale blue chair on one wall, and a wide dresser with six drawers and a mirror hanging above it, all also white, on the opposite wall. The room is painted the perfect shade of pale blue, although it probably has a trendier name. I imagine it's called something like Pacific Ice. I love everything about this room.

"I made some calls and had a friend come in and decorate. I hope you like it. It's all yours. The closet is there, and the bathroom is the door next to it," Claire says as she points to a door with a little porcelain sign on it that reads "The Toilet" in pretty script.

"It's perfect. Thank you…so much." I add the *so much* to let her know that I really do appreciate all she's done to prepare a place for me on such short notice. My appreciation runs deeper than she may ever know. To say the introduction to my room at Gram's was anticlimactic would be an understatement.

"Are you hungry? I can make something, or we can order Chinese. Do you like Chinese food?" Claire asks.

"Whatever you want to do is great, but Chinese is good." I love it, actually. I'd had a standing date with my dad since I was nine. We got Chinese at this little hole in the wall near our house every Friday night for almost three years. They died on a Thursday. I haven't had Chinese food since.

"Ok, then. I'll order Chinese. Any requests?"

"Um…General Tso's Chicken…if they've got it. If not, sweet and sour chicken? Thank you." I can't remember the last time someone asked me what I wanted for dinner. I feel like I'm in some parallel universe.

Claire nods and excuses herself. I survey the bathroom and closet. Both are a good size. I'm sure I don't have enough toiletries or clothes to fill either room. I unpack, putting delicates in the smaller drawers at the top of the dresser and quasi folding my other clothes into the rest of the drawers. I don't really have a lot to hang in the closet. It looks pretty sparse even after I'm done hanging items I don't usually hang. I put my suitcases in the closet and decide to take a shower before dinner. It'll save me time later, and I could use the time in a hot shower to relax.

I throw on my pajamas – an old t-shirt of my dad's and a pair of lounge pants – and go down stairs to find the kitchen. As I approach the swinging door I can hear Luke and Claire talking.

"Are you sure about this?" Luke asks.

"Only time will tell," Claire says softly. "I didn't think I wanted this, but…when she was standing there I looked in her eyes and…"

"I know…I saw it, too," Luke agrees.

Saw what, my desperation?

I stand there on rickety legs, having to steel myself so I don't fall. They're hesitant. I don't hear anger and resentment in their voices like I did Grams. It's more like…fear. There's something different about their qualms. Maybe it's just the idea of having their lives interrupted, but I will do everything I can to reassure them of their decision to take me in.

When I push the door open the food has arrived and Luke and Claire are serving the plates. My plate has a generous helping of General Tso's Chicken, which makes the corners of my mouth lift a little.

"So you found the towels in your bathroom! Great! Was the shower ok?" Claire asks as if she's looking for my approval. She's got the situation flipped, but I tell her, "Yes, they were easy to find. Thank you. And the shower was great." She's straightened herself out and there are no signs of the distress I overheard a moment ago.

"We know this is…difficult," Luke starts. "It's hard for all of us, but I'm sure the hardest for you. I know you were close with Gramps, and we want you to know that you can talk to us if you need to." I don't know if that is supposed to be my cue to talk, but I'm silent as I'm still considering the exchange I overheard. "Or…we can…find a counselor for you. Whatever you want."

"Really, it's ok. I'm fine. I appreciate you taking me in. I know you weren't prepared to, and you're not used to having kids around, so I'll do my best to stay out of your way." I'm overwhelmed by their generosity, especially after hearing their hesitancy.

"You're family, Layla. We honestly didn't want it any other way. We're overjoyed that you would want to live with us." Claire has a way of speaking that is so fluid, like an angel. It matches her stature.

Luke agrees with Claire and adds, "We hope that you'll be happy here…with us. I'm sure it seems strange, being here and not knowing us, but we're really looking forward to getting to know you. Like Claire said: family."

We make it through dinner with small talk about my few friends from back home, and Luke fills me in on the school I'll be attending. Luke also tells me that they've already added me to their car insurance so I can use one of their cars to drive to school. Luke and Claire work at the same law firm and can ride together. Sometimes they work from home, so it will work out just fine. I don't really know anything about cars, but what I do know is that it won't be Gramps' 1984 Buick. That hunk of metal was a real adventure to drive. Start? Not Start? Each day was a crapshoot.

"How about that tour?" Claire asks cheerily.

"That sounds good." I say as I take my dishes to the sink. I begin to do the dishes out of habit but Claire stops me. I'm puzzled for a moment, but Claire insists and I do as I'm told.

Claire leads me through the house and I'm in awe with every step. The colors, patterns, and placement are meticulous. There are warm browns and cool blues throughout the open living and dining rooms. "Your home is beautiful," I say sincerely.

"She's a natural. This place would be filled with milk crates, cinder blocks and plywood if I had anything to do with it," Luke says with a smile as he joins us. He and Claire look at each other and smile as Luke wraps his arms around Claire's waist from behind. It's easy to see that they're in love. I like that Luke dotes on Claire. Dad was like that with Mom. I didn't realize how much I missed that until now.

I yawn and Claire notices. "It's been a long few days and we could all use the sleep."

"Are you sure you don't want me to help clean up in the kitchen? I really don't mind."

"Don't worry. The chores are coming," Luke smirks and Claire gives him a playful jab in the ribs.

"I'm going to go to bed then. Thank you for dinner…and everything," I say.

"Of course. That's what family is for," Luke says just as much with his piercing eyes as with his words. It's in this moment, with this one honest look from Luke, that I know now that my gut has been right all along. I'm exactly where I'm supposed to be.

Chapter 3

I'm exhausted but don't sleep very well. My eyes open in the early hours of morning. I want to go back to sleep and wish myself into a pleasant dream, but every time I close my eyes all that appears is terror. I'm not surprised. I certainly didn't think that one night in this wonderland was going to make the nightmares end. At least my nightmares aren't so unexpected like they are for other people. I can pretty much count on them.

I watch the darkness of early morning transform from dark blues to oranges and finally to streams of bright light spraying through the crack in the curtains. When I see the clock reads 8:30 a.m. I give up and pull myself out of bed. I took a shower last night, so I *could* get dressed, but I want to leave dad's t-shirt on a bit longer.

I pull my hair back into a ponytail, make my bed, and head downstairs. Before I reach the stairs I finally see what is beyond the wall of windows in the loft and I can't believe my eyes. It's like a dream. Not like the kind I have, but the kind that make you look forward to sleep. The house sits at a perfect distance from a lake, separated only by a few dozen or so deliberately placed trees, with an equally perfect flagstone path cutting between them from the house to a private dock. I approach the window in an attempt to get an even better view. As I step forward I see that it is just as breathtaking as my first look, and for some reason hope it's the lake I saw yesterday. I'm overwhelmed by this amazing twist of fate. That the one place I felt true peace would be represented here is more than I could have ever asked for. I know it's not the same as the beach, but it's the closest I'm going to get and I'm happy to receive it.

Looking down from the window there's a patio, or because it's so big maybe it qualifies as a courtyard. I hadn't taken enough notice last night during dinner to see which doors lead to this outdoor space, but I assume it's off the kitchen. Luke and Claire are at the table eating breakfast so I redirect myself to join them. My exploration of the wall of books will have to wait until later.

When I get to the kitchen Claire is refilling their coffee mugs, still in her pajamas: a t-shirt and lounge pants. It is in this small commonality that I take one small step forward in feeling at ease here.

"Good morning," I say in as chipper a tone as I can muster. My goal is to have a clear perspective today, so I want to have a good start, a clean slate.

"Good morning, Layla! Can I get you some breakfast? We've got eggs, bacon, fruit…anything sound good?" Claire asks cheerily.

"Actually, I'd love a Pop Tart…or some toast," I say with some level of bravery. I once asked Gram for a Pop Tart and was swiftly told I wasn't being appreciative of the time and effort she takes in providing a hearty most-important-meal-of-the-day.

"Got 'em! Strawberry or Cherry?" she says joyfully having met my first need.

"Um…Strawberry. Thanks." Amazing that a toaster pastry could bring me such joy.

"Luke's out on the patio. Go ahead out," she points to the French doors I hadn't noticed last night. "I'll bring your breakfast out in a minute. Would you like some coffee or orange juice?"

"Orange juice, thank you," I say as I pull open the doors to the patio. The view is just as magnificent from here as it was from upstairs. There's a beautiful breeze blowing that rustles the leaves in the trees. I love this sound.

Luke sits with his back to the doors, facing the water, reading the newspaper. He must have heard me answer Claire as I opened the door because he addresses me directly.

"Good morning, Layla. How did you sleep?" he asks.

"Like a rock," I lie.

"Great!" He folds the paper halfway down toward his chest so that he can see me.

"This view is amazing," I say.

Luke smiles and takes in the view for a moment before responding, "Yeah, it's pretty spectacular. That's Lake Davidson. You should see it from the dock."

"Do you have a boat?" Even though I'm not the best swimmer, I'm itching to be out on the water. I went a couple of times with a friend from school on her dad's boat when Gram was feeling generous. It could have been being out on the water, or maybe it was just because I was away from home and acting my age, but I had the most incredible time.

"We used to." His answer is slow and thoughtful. "What would you like to do today?" he asks, bringing his attention back to me.

"Well, I'm not really sure. You've got a pretty impressive library up there. Do you mind if I borrow a book?" I don't feel like going anywhere. There will be plenty of time for exploring later. I've got nothing but time.

"Of course not. It's your library now, too. You can read anything up there. Although I doubt you'll find the law books very interesting." Luke seems different this morning. He's lighthearted and open. Our conversation doesn't feel forced like it did last night. This is the real Luke. He isn't coddling me like Claire, not that I mind her treatment of me. It's been so long since I've been on the receiving end of care that I'm not sure how to respond to her, but I appreciate Luke's attempt to make my life here normal right from the beginning.

"Aren't you two going to work today?" I ask.

"No. We've arranged for the whole week off. We've planned to be home more often than not for the next several weeks. We want to make sure that we're here for you as much as possible while you…transition and get settled," he says.

"That's not really necessary…" I say. Luke looks at me with serious eyes and I know there is no point in arguing. "…but thanks." I could tell him that I spent the last three years being caretaker to an old man. I washed dishes, did laundry, and handled all of the finances, so I'm pretty sure I can handle being home by myself, but I don't tell him that. I am doing my best to be 17 not 70. "What do *you* have planned for today?" I ask changing the subject from my perceived neediness to Luke's plans for the day. I'm also wondering how much time I might get to myself today. I play with my hair, tightening the ponytail, sectioning it off and braiding skinny braids in the locks. It gives me something to do with my hands while I wait for Claire to bring my long-awaited toaster pastry to me. I'm not used to having idle hands.

"Not a lot, really. I'm getting ready to start a project down in the basement, but I'm still working up the plans, so I'll probably spend some time down there. The town puts on a summer concert series, mainly local musicians. It's tonight and Claire and I always go. We'd love for you to come with us," he says hopefully.

Claire's exit from the kitchen couldn't have been better timed. "Oh, yes, Layla! It's a lot of fun! Everyone sits on the Village Green in front of the library with blankets and picnics. Please come." She nudges me and seals the deal when she tells me it's the best place for people watching.

"That sounds…really fun," I say trying to show my excitement. I think about it for a moment more and then it sinks in. They *asked* me to come. They didn't demand it or even just assume that I would go with them. I suppose I could have said no if I wanted to, and by the looks on their faces, they're actually really happy that I'm going. I pick apart my breakfast as I try to digest this realization. This is perhaps going to be the biggest adjustment. I don't think I can recall a single time Gram gave me a choice.

Luke smiles so big that his eyes almost disappear. "Great! We don't need to leave until 5:30, so if you want to go out, I know Claire is dying to show you around."

"That's ok. I think I'll just hang out here for now…if that's ok," I answer, testing the waters of their flexibility. Do I really have the ability to choose? Am I *allowed* to say no?

"Really? I was hoping to take you shopping, maybe get some new summer or school clothes, but if you don't want to go today, we can go another time…whenever you want. No pressure." Claire is disappointed. I must have looked terrified when she said *shopping*. I can be just as girly as the next girl, but shopping is definitely not my thing. Mainly because I wore a uniform to my old school, and Gram and Gramps never had an excessive amount of extra funds for things like new clothes. Gram was handy with a sewing machine so she mended anything that started to get worn. I didn't have time for a job, so I never had the money either, except for what I squirreled away from Gramps.

"Oh…er…thanks, Claire. You don't really have to do that. I'm sure I'll find something to wear when school starts." I haven't soothed Claire's disappointment so I quickly amend my statement. "But I know I don't have any winter clothes, so maybe we can go then?" I really will need winter clothes and Claire's willingness to let me decide certainly deserves a good deed in return.

Claire smiles and I swear I can see her eyes actually sparkle. "That'd be great. It'll be nice to have a new shopping partner, someone with a fresh perspective!" She's in for more disappointment because my perspective on fashion is anything but fresh.

I eat my Pop Tart and enjoy every morsel of this breakfast that was five years in the making. Even after Gram died, I felt like I would be disrespecting her in front of Gramps if I totally abandoned *all* that she had done. I push down the twinges of guilt that begin to emerge and I decide that part of my clean slate will be to do my best not to compare anything. It's not like I have an old life that I could go back to, so any comparison would be completely unfair. This is my life now and, while it is only hours old, I am optimistic.

"So, Luke," This is the first time I've called him by his name since the funeral and I wonder if he'll correct me to call him *Uncle* Luke now that we're here, on his turf. He doesn't. He just lowers the newspaper again and gives me his full attention. "You said there'd be chores. Did you have anything particular in mind?" I'm not sure I'll know how to exist here without something to do.

"Well," he says, putting the paper completely down. "Now that you mention it…"

"C'mon, Luke! She just got here!" Claire says in cute protest.

I really want, no, need, something to do. If they don't give me some chores, I know I will spend every waking hour of the next eight weeks upstairs reading in the loft, which, I guess, really isn't the worst thing.

"It's ok, Claire, I really want to help." My insistence is followed by her chagrin, which is followed by her sweet smile. With every passing moment I feel like I'm diving deeper into this parallel universe. I was met by Gram's harder expression at any hesitancy in my obedience, but here I get quasi chastised for *wanting* to do chores.

"Well, as I was saying…" Luke continues, winking at Claire. "Yes, I did have something in mind. How do you feel about handling the dinner dishes?"

"That's great. What else?" I say, agreeing to the start of his list.

"Well…uh…" Luke stumbles having clearly not thought of anything else for me to do. "What did you do…at home…in Florida?" He has a hard time finding the words that will be the least painful for me.

"I did…everything…especially after Gram died. Gramps wasn't able to do much, so I pretty much just handled it all." I'm surprised by my own honesty. I feel like I'm tattling on Gramps, but it's the truth. I did everything because he couldn't. I once caught him trying to trim his fingernails with a pair of scissors. Later that day it occurred to me that Gram must have helped Gramps with his grooming. Which made me think that maybe she wasn't a mean and hateful person; maybe it was just me she hated.

Luke and Claire give each other an apprehensive look and I can't tell what they're thinking. It's been so long since I've seen two people work together on anything that had to do with me. Gram took the reins on the "parenting" stuff. Gramps did his best to help me when he could tell she was tightening them, but it never changed anything. Knowing he was there for me helped a little. It helped make me feel not so entirely alone all the time.

"Layla, with all due respect to Jack and Carol, we know you had a lot of responsibilities there…more than you should have. We don't want it to be that way here. You're 17-years-old and we want you to really enjoy your senior year." Claire's words are soft, like her. I can tell that she and Luke have already talked about this. It's definitely the kind of thing that has to be decided ahead of time. I think they would have given me no chores if it weren't somehow the "right" thing to do.

There was no disrespect. I understood what they were saying and I really appreciated it. I'm just not sure how to exist without having to hurry through a list of chores so I can get to the only leisure activity I have in reading. It seems I'll no longer have to use my contraband flashlight to read after lights out. It will take some getting used to, but this is what I have been longing for. To be…considered.

"That's really nice of you. Thanks, but please don't hesitate to ask me to help out with anything around here. I definitely want to pull my weight, and it doesn't have to be all inside work either. I used to cut the grass and pull weeds for Gramps. I actually enjoy that kind of stuff." I smile awkwardly. Staying busy or burying my head in a book are my two preferred options for occupying my mind. With Luke's non-list of chores, it seems I'll have time to do the latter.

"I'm sure there will be plenty for you to do," Luke says agreeably with a bit of a wink.

I try to help Claire with the breakfast dishes, but since Luke said the *dinner* dishes were my responsibility she won't let me help any further than clearing the table, and that's only because I had the dishes gathered before she could stop me. Luke has made his way down to the basement while Claire finishes in the kitchen. With nothing but time on my hands, I excuse myself to wander the house, exploring.

The furniture is all so beautiful and perfectly designed. It isn't a hodge-podge of mismatched thrift store furniture like I had in my room or the circa 1960's décor I'm used to. Everything is so well thought out, so strategically placed. Two light blue wingback chairs are flawlessly flanked with their backs to the front window so the view is unobstructed when you sit on the brown, tufted couch facing them. I sit there a moment, feeling the soft material of the couch, looking at the view of the trees and landscaping on the other side of the circular driveway, lost in the silence, watching the leaves rustle in the wind.

I have to force myself to break my gaze. I go upstairs with the intention of choosing a new book, but once there I decide it would be unfair not to finish the current book I'm reading first. So, I find what will become my permanent reading spot in the oversized celery green chair facing the wall of windows and open up to the page where I left off and begin to read. I haven't gotten far when I'm struck the character's words. She talks about it being hard to be the one left behind, being the one who stays when everything you knew as your reality is gone.

I put the book down with her words echoing in my head. I know how she feels because I'm the one who stayed. Mom. Dad. Gram. Gramps. They all left me. I understand her loneliness. You can be strong but sometimes the loneliness is so overwhelming that you don't know if you'll be able to take another breath. The pain in your heart is so excruciating that it can't help but spread to your stomach, eventually overtaking every fiber of your being. You cry until you're sure you've dehydrated yourself, so you compensate. You throw yourself into mind numbing activities where you don't have to think about anything. You find an escape, a way for you to be fully present somewhere your loneliness doesn't exist. But for Clare, at least she has some hope that Henry will return. He isn't gone forever. He will literally always be somewhere in time.

At 5:15 we pack the car with a blanket, a few camping chairs, – which I'm pretty sure have never been used for actual camping – some sodas, and snacks and make our way to downtown Davidson. I hadn't gotten as much as a glimpse of the perimeter of town on the way here yesterday, so I'm looking forward to seeing how accurate Claire's description is. The weather is warm so I'm wearing my traditional ponytail, along with khaki shorts and a striped t-shirt and sandals. I am completely and utterly plain. We round the corner onto the main drag of town and I'm pleasantly surprised. Davidson is lovely and quaint. It's like something out of story that begins "back in my day" and I half-expect June Cleaver to pop her head up from behind a rose bush and wave. Davidson College is nestled right in the middle of this nostalgic little town, and there are stores and restaurants on one side of the street. They're contained mostly in one long building, but with different roof heights distinguishing between vendors. The exterior of each merchant's store is different than his neighbor, which only serves to add more charm to this picturesque little town. The Soda Shop has huge windows with a few metal café tables and chairs out front, while the bridal store next door is adorned with hanging flowerpots and an awning that makes it look like a house. Luke tells me there is a bookstore right on the strip that I should check out. I make a mental note to do so sooner rather than later.

A wide two-lane road runs through town on, of course, Main Street. We drive slowly since the speed limit is twenty-five and there are a hundred people making their way to the Village Green. I can see the Green where the Public Library is when Luke makes a few turns and parks the car. We gather our things and make our way across the grass, which I can tell has been freshly cut by one of my favorite scents lingering in the air. Luke and Claire say hello to several people on the way to finding a good spot in the middle of the crowd at the center of the stage. I use the word *stage* loosely since it's really just a raised platform set up in front of the steps to the small Davidson Public Library.

Claire wasn't kidding when she said there'd be some good people watching. There are so many people who reminded me of home. They're dressed and ready for summer, having fun with no regard for who sees them. There are parents with babies and some dads with toddlers on their shoulders. Older kids are running around playing tag and screaming at the top of their lungs. Most of these townsfolk don't have folding chairs. They just sit on their blankets eating homemade sandwiches and chips and drinking soda. I feel comfortable here.

Then…then there are others who are distinctly different than the rest of the crowd, which is to say they are distinctly different than me. The first thing I notice is that they have positioned themselves almost exclusively to the right center of the stage. Their blankets are bigger and they all have chairs. Not a single one of them is sitting on their blanket on the ground. Several of them even have little folding tables for their food. There is nothing ordinary about the way any of them are dressed either. No t-shirts with silly characters or sayings. Nothing sloppy. They're all very put together, crisp. I take closer note of a few families in particular that seem to be sitting together about six yards away from us. There are three older couples and I assume they're the parents of the younger ones sitting with them who all look to be about my age. The parents are clearly uninterested in what's going on around them and focus as they pour themselves another glass of wine. There are three boys and two girls. I can't tell who belongs with whom, but all five of them are very attractive. The girls are stunning and the boys are better looking than any guy I knew back home. They all look like they just stepped out of an Abercrombie and Fitch ad, but one of the boys in particular stands out to me. I don't know why. Maybe it's his smile, or that he is, in my opinion, the best looking of the three boys. His posture is different, more open, and he engages with those outside of their circle with waves and nods of recognition and a brilliant smile. I shake my head out of my stare and can feel my eyebrows crease together. It isn't like me to take notice of anyone, let alone a boy like this. I dismiss any attraction I'm having since I already know that I undeniably belong with the left of center concert guests and make a move for a soda.

"That's funny," Luke chuckles. "Of all the people for you to hone in on, you pick the families of our law firm partners. See the guy with the silver hair and blue Polo? That's Gregory Meyer. He's the senior partner at Meyer, Fincher, and Marks. The woman to his right is his wife, Eliana. The man in the plaid shirt is Josef Fincher, with his wife Marie. Next to them are Daniel Marks and his wife Alice. Josef's son is Chris, the blonde, and Daniel's son Tyler has the buzzed dark hair. The other boy is Gregory's son, Will. The girl with the short hair is Caroline, but I don't remember the other girl's name."

"That's Gwen Kestler, honey," Claire adds, jogging Luke's memory.

"Oh, yes, that's right. We met her last year at the bar-b-q. Do you want to me to introduce you? You'll be going to school with all of them at Heyward Prep," Luke offers.

"No! I mean, that's ok, another time." So, the boy I had been staring at was Will Meyer, son of the senior partner of Meyer, Fincher, and Marks. How is it that I gravitated to the most unfeasible option of all the guys there? Not that I'm looking, but still. Yes, there will be plenty of time to embarrass myself in front of them and the rest of their rich and fashionable friends once school starts. I'll keep my distance for now and delay that humiliating experience for another day.

Just as I'm about to release my gaze from the league of models, Will turns and catches me by surprise. I guess I had been boring a hole into the side of his head and he couldn't take the pressure any longer. He smiles a remarkable smile, one like I've never seen before. I want to look away but I can't. And it's not just because of his god-like features. There's…more. Will's face changes, his eyes grabbing hold of mine, and it's like I can hear him say, "*Have we met?*" My heart starts to race. I give him a weak smile and snap my head to the left and force myself to break the lock between our eyes. It was the strangest, most exhilarating five seconds of my life.

The concert is about an hour in and I need to find a restroom. Claire points me in the direction of the library, but I need to go around to the right side of the building to the entrance on Main Street. She offers to go with me, but my independent self wants to find it on my own. I open the door to the library and a gust of air is sucked outside to mingle with the fragrance of grass and exhaust. The smell of old books is intoxicating. I close my eyes and inhale deeply, exhaling so slowly that I let out the last breath in time to keep myself from seeing stars. I wander just a few aisles as I make my way to the bathroom and recall the mental note I made when we arrived at the concert tonight to check out the bookstore. Finding the bathroom was easy. Finding my way back to our blanket proved to be another thing. I must have exited through the back of the library because I am definitely not on Main Street. I start walking in the direction I think I hear the music coming from but I quickly realize I'm hearing the echo of the music on the buildings. I cross the street and discover I'm now on Main Street and going in the right direction back to the Green. I need a GPS installed in my brain.

Looking in the direction of the Green, and not watching where I'm going, I literally run into someone coming out of the coffee shop. I feel awful because our collision has knocked his drink right out of his hands and into an icy mess on the sidewalk.

"Oh my gosh! I'm so sorry!" I say looking down at the pool of soda on the ground.

"It's ok. Not a big deal, really. It's only Coke," he says with a chuckle of complete coolness.

I look up to see that I have collided with Will Meyer. He's even more beautiful up close. He's tall with light brown hair, worn in a messy, gelled mop and has eyes that are a deep crystal blue. My view of him earlier did no justice to his heavenly good looks, but I need to stop my inventory of his physically amazing qualities before I forget my place. I draw my attention back to the icy puddle on the ground. Each piece of ice lies there, mocking me, reminding me of my awkward existence here.

"Hi. I'm Will Meyer," he says smiling dreamily.

"I'm Layla Weston. It's nice to meet you." I shake his hand fearfully aware of how sweaty my palms are.

"It's nice to meet *you*. You're Luke Weston's niece. He said you were coming to live with them. Sorry about your grandfather." He's so articulate and smooth that it catches me off guard. I'm not used to boys his age being so well spoken.

"Uh…yeah," I say a little surprised that Luke would have told anyone I was coming. "I'm really sorry about your drink. I'd buy you a new one, but I don't think I have any money on me." I feel around in the pockets of my shorts as if I'm searching for some loose change knowing full well that there isn't so much as a piece of lint to be found.

"It's really ok. I promise. I'll dig up another $2.65 somewhere," he laughs. "In fact, I'll even buy one for you, just to show you there are no hard feelings. What d'ya say?" His smile is perfectly infectious. As much as my heart is pounding with embarrassment right now, I can't help but smile back at him.

"That's ok. I've got an unfinished soda back at our spot. Now if I could only find Luke and Claire." I look across the street to the huge crowd of people, both to search for my destination and to keep myself from staring at Will.

"C'mon, I remember where you were sitting. I'll walk you back," he says stretching his arm out inviting me to take the first step with him.

Will leads the way back to our picnic spot, navigating through the crowd without stumbling, knowing exactly where he is going at all times. I'm either right next to him or just a step behind as we weave through the crowd.

Luke teasingly chides me as we arrive. "There you are! I was about to send out a search party, but it looks like you found someone to rescue you. Will, I see you've met Layla."

"Yeah, funny that we would *run* into each other here." Will emphasizes the word *run* and looks at me from the corners of his eyes, pleased with his corny joke. "I gotta get back, but…we should hang out this summer. I'll introduce you to my friends."

"That sounds great," I lie. The idea of spending time with Will and his prep school socialites makes my stomach churn. I know I don't fit in, and finding Will as attractive and charming as I do is a recipe for one embarrassing moment after another. I'm sure he's just being polite in the moment in front of Luke, so I agree happily, knowing I won't have to worry about it.

"Great. I'll see you later then," he says walking away. After he's taken several long strides around people and over blankets he turns around and calls to me. "Hey, Layla!" I lift my chin to acknowledge him. "I changed my mind. You owe me a Coke!" He smiles as I chuckle nervously and turns to make his way back to his family and friends.

"What was that about?" Claire asks.

"Oh, nothing…just the worst first impression in the history of man." I say while I watch- no, stare- as Will walks back to his camp. As I begin to talk myself out of this strange nervousness fluttering inside me I find myself now on the receiving end of a glare. Will's father, Gregory Meyer is staring at me. His face is hard and expressionless. His silver-gray hair reveals years of stress from high-stakes plea-bargaining. The lines on his long face are a road map of the secrets he holds under attorney-client privilege. It's clear that this man does not play games. I meet his gaze and respond with a forced smile, but there's something about him that has my gut twisted into knots. He echoes my feigned smiled with one of his own and turns away. At least if I ever have to meet him in person I'll have already had this creepy experience and won't turn our first face-to-face meeting into a career crushing incident for Luke or Claire.

The concert and Green festivities were over by nine, but we didn't get home until close to ten. The traffic getting out of there was insane. It was a fun night, though. Good music and a chance to get to know Luke and Claire a little better. I'm glad I went despite my tragic first encounter with Will Meyer. I want to, but I can't stop thinking about him. He is, by far, the most charismatic boy I've ever met. He's eloquent and polite and funny. I still can't put my finger on it, but there is something about him. Still, I'm a realist. I'm not his type, so there will be no pining. I won't see him again until school starts anyway, so that's that. I have all summer to pretend I never met Will Meyer.

Chapter 4

I sleep much better in the days that follow. No more nightmares, for now. I'm getting comfortable here faster than I thought I would. Each day I feel a little less like a guest. Luke and Claire correct me every time I ask permission to do something they've already given me carte blanche to do, like use the computer or watch TV in the loft. They are constantly reminding me that this is my home now, and little by little it's beginning to sink in.

Although Claire has offered to take me anywhere I'd like, there's nowhere I really want to go. I'm not quite ready to go exploring yet, so I spend most of my time reading. Well, I try to spend my time reading. Every time I sit in this gigantic chair in front of the windows in the loft, I get lost in the view and my mind wanders. I think a lot about mom and dad and wonder what life would be like if they were still alive. I think about the last Presidential election and am sure they would have been more involved in that one than any other in their lives, and they would both still be teaching. That was their biggest passion. I think about Gramps and realize if he were still alive I would be doing pretty much the same thing that I am now: sitting and reading a great book…in between chores and tending to him, of course.

Next to homework and housework, reading is the only thing I ever did on a regular basis. I used to read the classics over and over again. I must have read *The Chronicles of Narnia* ten times, but last year something happened. I don't know how or why, but a switch got flipped and an interest emerged for what I used to call "girly books." Ok, I didn't call them that as much as I mocked them. They're books about life, relationships, and romance. The classics were safe and dependable. Many were so fantastical that I didn't get emotionally involved because I knew there was no way any of the characters could be real people…mostly because they weren't *people*. They were hobbits, ice queens, and animals, but this new genre is different. I don't know why I started reading them. Maybe I was trying to find out about what I knew I had no one to teach me. I'm levelheaded enough to know the stories are fiction, but they've helped me understand the idea of love in a way I never had. Love can be wonderful and romantic, but it can also be the hardest thing to encounter. Somehow, I connect with the characters and trust them.

My contemplation is interrupted when Claire calls to me that it's time for lunch. I've been lost in my thoughts since after breakfast and it's time I rejoin the cognizant. I collect myself and walk downstairs to the kitchen where Claire is standing at the island chopping what I assumed are salad ingredients: cucumbers, carrots, lettuce, onions, tomatoes. "Can I help?" I ask eagerly. I figure if I phrase it as I'm helping, rather than working, she'll let me do something.

"Definitely!" Claire smiles really big. "Do you enjoy cooking, Layla?"

"Yes." I hesitate before I continue, weighing my options. Do I tell her that I was my mother's sidekick in the kitchen or not? Will it conjure up the bad blood between my father and Luke? If it does, will she take sides? I decide I have to put it out there sooner rather than later so I know what the expectation is. Gram made it clear early on and, while I didn't like it, at least I knew where the lines were drawn. "I used to help my mom in the kitchen all the time. She taught me how to cook. I'm no gourmet, but I'm pretty good," I say and wait.

"Well, maybe we can add that to your list of chores," she says, smiling and making air quotation marks at the word *chores*. "I love to cook, but Luke thinks I make spaghetti too much. I bet you could teach me a few things!" she chuckles.

Not so much as a flinch at the mention of my mother. Not that she would have rolled her eyes or been disrespectful; Claire's too classy for that, but I could have been talking about anyone. Maybe it wasn't as bad as I thought it was, or maybe it's Luke that will lay out the perimeter for conversation about my parents. I will test those waters soon. I have to know if I will continue my silence, or if the ban on discussing my parents has been lifted. *Oh, how I hope it's been lifted.*

As I'm getting some left-over chicken from the fridge, Claire informs me that Luke's assistant on the basement project is here and asks me to get four plates from the cabinet. Luke comes in hot and sweaty from the door to the basement with his apprentice close behind.

"We meet again," Will Meyer says as he emerges from behind Luke.

I'm going to pass out. This can't be happening.

"Will, you remember my niece, Layla," Luke says.

"How could I forget? It's nice to see you again." He wipes his hand on the side of his pants and reaches out to shake mine, flashing his irresistible smile. Even dirty and sweaty, he is still handsome and charming. His hands are strong, like they've seen their fair share of work. I'm surprised to see him here. I hadn't pegged him for a blue-collar-work kind of guy. I thought his people *used* hired help, not *were* the hired help. I can't help but be both confused and impressed at the same time.

"It's nice to see you, too." Too bad no one gets two chances to make a first impression. I'm positive I was the worst first impression he ever had of anyone. As much as I'd love to run from the room right now, I'll just have to roll with it.

"So, Mr. Weston tells me you're going to be a senior at Heyward. Me, too. It's a pretty small school so I'm sure we'll have some classes together. I'll have to introduce you to my friends," Will says continuing.

"Oh…yeah. It'll be nice to know someone there before school starts." This makes twice that I have lied to him. I've already planned on becoming the weird, reclusive girl at school and I won't be changing that strategy any time soon.

"Ah, food! Yes! I'm starving!" Luke gives Claire a quick kiss as he passes by her on his way to the sink to wash his hands.

"How's it going?" Claire asks.

I interrupt before Luke can answer. "What are you doing down there…if you don't mind me asking?"

"The basement has been unfinished for years, but we've been working on getting it to a livable condition." Luke smiles an almost sinister smile, like he's hiding something. "It's…a surprise…for you, so don't go down there until its ready. Ok?"

"For me? Oh…uh…sure…no problem. There's plenty of house to explore…and books to read. I'll find something to occupy me until then." I say, completely perplexed as to why the basement would be a surprise for me. Surprises are for people you care so deeply about that the idea of giving them something so unexpected is more exciting that the thing itself. How could I possibly fall into this category? I want to ask why but Luke is giving me the same look he did when I told him they didn't need to stay home with me. I know it will be a lost cause to argue, and in all reality, it'll probably be just a glorified TV room.

As the days go by, I maintain my homebound status. I'm not spending much time alone with either Luke or Claire, but enough time to know that I really like them both…a lot. Claire and I cook together and have discovered that we work really well as a team. I fix dinner once or twice a week and the other nights we work together. It's nice to feel like I'm a part of something rather than the glue holding it together, and mealtime with Luke is never boring. When I first moved in, I had him pegged as being straight-laced and serious. I'm finding out that he and I are more alike than I thought, starting with our sense of humor.

I've mentioned Mom and Dad several times around Luke and have received the same response that I got from Claire, sometimes even better.

"Your father could barely boil water…" Luke jokes.

"But he could rebuild a car engine!" I say, matching Luke's laugh. It's such a relief. I haven't talked about my parents in five long years. With Gram, it was like I had to pretend they never existed. It feels so good to say their names, to talk about them as they were.

I'm grateful for how Luke and Claire are taking care of me, and they aren't trying to be my parents. Not that anything eventful has happened where they've needed to step in and "act" like parents. Claire has been working from home every day. She doesn't hover, but I'm glad she's here. I can be alone without being alone. Luke goes into the office periodically but is home most of the time. I think they're still waiting for the proverbial shoe to drop and for me to have an emotional breakdown. I guess that's kind of parental of them.

Will is at the house almost every day. Sometimes he works with Luke and sometimes he's on his own when Luke is at the office. My plan of pretending I never met Will Meyer has swiftly been abandoned out of necessity. He eats lunch with us every day; climbing out of the box I put him in with each conversation.

"You definitely want to get Mrs. Dishowitz. She teaches Civics and is great, really fun," Will says as he gives me the low down on the teachers at Heyward Prep. "And you'll definitely have Mrs. Houchens for English Lit and Mr. Regan for Science. He's a crotchety old guy but knows his stuff."

"Thanks! Not that I have any control over it, but at least I know what I'm headed into," I tell him as I refill our drinks.

"I'll see what I can do," he says with a wink. I wish he wouldn't do that. I had been uncomfortable with Will at first, but all that has been disappearing. Those giddy butterflies have migrated and no longer take residence in the pit of my stomach. When he looks at me that way, the butterflies start flying back.

Will and I are becoming friends and that makes me happier than I would have expected. Will is smart and funny, and he's a legitimately nice guy. He makes me feel at ease. I'm not concerned with impressing him…not that I could begin to have the first clue as to how to do that. Will isn't at all like I thought he was going to be. He doesn't *act* rich, and he's been doing manual labor for Luke – a very *un*rich thing to do in my mind. I did to him what I accuse his class of people of doing to me: I judged him, and feel badly about that. I'm glad I've had a chance to see this side of him. Perhaps I won't be so alone at Heyward after all.

I finished reading my book during my first week here, but still haven't picked out anything new. I find myself sitting at the edge of the dock for hours at a time most days. I take in the beauty of the lake, breathe deeply, lie back on the dock, and close my eyes. In all my life I have never known a more peaceful place, geographically or mentally. I feel…alive…which makes me feel guilty. Didn't I feel alive and at peace in Florida with Mom and Dad, or Gram and Gramps? No…well, yes and no. Living with Mom and Dad was truly living. Living with Gram and Gramps? I wasn't meant to feel alive then. That was Gram's point. Penance.

This is so different. This is the first time I've ever really thought about me. What am *I* feeling? What do *I* want? Mom and dad always supported any activity I wanted to participate in, but the more I think about it, the more I realize that I flew wherever the wind blew *them*. Dad's units on kinesthesia volleyed me into soccer, lacrosse, and tennis. Mom's semester of Shakespeare and play adaptations led to my auditioning for every local play I could. I was never cast into anything – I was terrible, but mom joyfully helped me prepare and took me to each audition. If it was an election year, well…Dad and Mom were more passionate about politics than anyone I knew. They had strong opinions about everything and never hesitated to make them known. They rallied and joined campaigns to support both local and national candidates, and they were the first ones at the polls on voting day. Naturally, I ran for class president during the 2004 election. I lost to Amber Riley.

Reading, though…that was a shared activity that was genuinely mine. Mom always said that reading a book was far better than watching any movie. I loved going to the movies, but she was right. A book can tell you all the emotions and subtext that are so rarely aptly portrayed in film. You understand the nuances of each character. You breathe every breath with them and cry every tear. Yes, reading. That is something special that I shared with my mother, but something I owned totally and completely in my own heart.

Chapter 5

I've put it off long enough. It's time to appease Claire and give her some girl time and go shopping. She has been so patient with me and seems to have really been looking forward to it. She was definitely disappointed when I shot her down the day after I arrived. She's been so kind and generous to me in the time she's given me to be alone. I don't feel like I can deny her any longer and she is thrilled when I make the suggestion.

We make our way through the neighborhood and I finally see how beautiful it is. The streets are lined with maple trees, flowering bushes, and sidewalks. I hadn't noticed how huge the neighborhood is when I first arrived. Since I've spent the last weeks being a hermit, this is my first real opportunity to see where I've been living. Each home is huge and completely different than the next. Some are brick, others wood. Whatever the materials are, it's clear that they are all custom, made to order homes. There is nothing cookie-cutter about this neighborhood – nothing but, perhaps, the neighbors.

When we arrive at the shopping area I see a Borders bookstore, which I am eager to go in. There are also shops I've never heard of. Either they are independently owned, or they are too expensive for my blood…or both. It's July so the winter clothes aren't out yet, but I promise Claire I'll be a good sport.

We both try on clothes, which actually turns out to be kind of fun. Claire looks good in anything that she puts on, of course. I stick with shorts and skirts since everything is always too long on me. Claire offers to have anything shortened, but I don't want to be an inconvenience. Gram always shortened my pants for me, so all the pants I have are already exactly the right length. We shop a little more and I settle on a two tops and a skirt. I stopped looking at price tags after the fiftieth time Claire told me to not worry. "I've never had a sister…or a teenage daughter. Let me have my fun, ok?" she'd say.

I don't really need new clothes right now, but I'm grateful. Not for the clothes necessarily, but for the time she's given me to be alone these last weeks, and for the time she's giving me now. This month has brought a lot of reflection on the things I had given up over the last five years. I didn't look at it like a sacrifice at the time because it was what I had to do. I spent the majority of my time with my grandparents so I didn't do shopping or movie outings with my friends. Maybe shopping *was* my thing and I just didn't know it. At any rate, I'm allowing myself to enjoy being with Claire.

We grab a late lunch at another place I've never heard of. I get a salad with chicken, cranberries, and Gorgonzola cheese. I feel so exotic.

"How's your salad?" Claire asks. She's staring at me as I lift the fork to my mouth, excited to hear my answer.

"It's good. I didn't know I liked Gorgonzola." How could I know that I liked it? Gram never bought it, so I didn't either. The extent of eating out with Gram and Gramps was limited to the early bird dinner at Denny's on the occasional Sunday. "How's yours?" I look at her salad and think I recognize some nuts and berries in hers, too.

"Delicious! I get the same thing every time I come here. I really should try something else, but it's just so good! Do you want a bite?"

"Oh, no, but thanks," I pause to take a sip of my Diet Coke. "Do you mind if we go into Borders before we go home? I just want to look around for a little bit."

"Sure! I could spend hours in a bookstore. How do you think we ended up with so many books in the loft? Luke gives me a hard time because I bring books home and never get around to reading them." She chuckles like it's become an inside joke between the two of them, something I'm sure he now considers cute and quirky about her.

We finish lunch, talk about the clothes we bought, and debate if we should go back so Claire can get one of the tops she put back. It's almost three o'clock and we both want to go to Borders, so she decides the top can wait until another trip and we head to the bookstore.

There's something about a bookstore that is so calming. It's a place where I feel like I belong, like everyone there is part of a special family or fraternity that other people don't understand. Avid readers are a breed of their own, and we're often accused of being heady. I don't care. I love books and can devour one in a whole day if I'm allowed.

Claire and I split up and saunter each in our own direction. The store is laid out well with signs hanging above each section indicating the genre or subject matter for that area. I make my way to the fiction section. I always prefer fiction. Anything else feels like homework.

The first aisle I pick at random is filled with trashy harlequin novels. The covers always make me laugh out loud. As I reach the end of the aisle I turn right to make a U-turn down the next row, but I cut the turn too close and bump into the end-cap, which sends me stumbling headlong toward a table of books displaying celebrity autobiographies. Instead of crashing into the table I'm caught by two strong arms. I get my bearings and look up to see that I'm being cradled in Will's arms.

"Are you ok?" he asks in his same smooth, unfaltering voice.

"Yeah…thanks…sorry. I guess I wasn't watching where I was going," I say, staggering my words and my body into an upright position most ungracefully.

He notices the books in the aisle I've just left, gestures to them and asks, "Find anything interesting?"

I'm mortified but do my best to recover. "I visit this aisle for a good laugh. I mean…seriously?" I pick up one of the trashy novels, "Who looks like this?"

We both laugh and Will gives his best smoldering look and puffs his chest out. I'm taken aback. If this is his *fake* smoldering look, I can't imagine any girl not being putty in his hands with his real one. His eyes are the prettiest blue I have ever seen, and when he puffs his chest out I can see how fit he is. I wonder if he's an athlete or if Luke has him on retainer for manual labor that keeps him in shape. He's tall and towers over me, like everyone else. I can't take my eyes off his bronzed face. His cheekbones and jaw line are in perfect harmony. He is so obviously handsome.

"So…you decided to leave the compound, eh?" he says.

"Yeah, Claire wanted to go shopping, so I let her drag me out. We just had lunch and were hitting this place before we went home." I have to make myself look away a couple of times. I've been staring at him and do not want to be *that* girl. I'm sure he's got plenty of girls after him and the adoring gaze probably gets old. Besides, I am not an option in Will Meyer's world so why torture myself.

"Oh, cool. Well...I'm meeting some friends for a movie and then a late dinner. This would be a great chance for you to meet them. Do…you…want to come?" He hesitates over the last part. I wonder if he's just being polite, but he didn't have to say anything to me in the first place, so maybe he really wants me to come. "What d'ya say?"

Claire approaches us before I have a chance to reply. "Hey Will! What d'ya say to what?"

"Will's meeting some friends for a movie and dinner, and asked if I wanted to go with them. Is it ok if I go? I don't have to. I mean…they weren't planning on me being there, so I don't want to impose." I'm rambling, but I want to give him an out if he needs one.

"You're not imposing, Layla. I invited you. I want you to come." He says my name and I lose focus for a split second. "Mrs. Weston, I can drive her home, if it's ok with you that she comes." Charming…yet again.

"I think that's a great idea. It'll give you a chance to make some more friends before school starts, Layla." With that, Claire takes out $50 in cash from her wallet and insists I take it. I tell her it's too much, but there's no arguing. I've never even seen a $50 bill in person. "Find any books you'd like to get? I found three that I'm sure will be added to the 'I'll get around to it one day' shelf. Luke will be so pleased!" she giggles.

"Thanks," I say as I put the cash in my back pocket. "I didn't find anything."

Will says the movie is starting soon so I thank Claire for the money, shopping, and lunch, and promise not to be home too late. There's a theater in this shopping center, too. Will and I walk the five minutes from the bookstore.

"How was your first adventure away from home?" he asks, holding the door for me as we exit the store.

"Um…it was fine. Shopping, lunch, girl stuff. What movie are we seeing?" I ask changing the subject from me.

"I think it's some parody movie. It should be stupid enough. Is that ok?"

"Yeah, that's perfect actually." I could use something I don't have to get emotionally involved in. My emotions are on enough of a roller coaster as it is being around Will right now. "How's the project going with Luke? Making any headway? He won't let me look down there, so don't give me any details of the project."

"It's going pretty well. He has a lot he wants to do, so it's going to take a while. Guess that means I'll be in your way for a while." He smiles at me for what seems like eternity and I feel my heart in my throat. Why does he look at me that way? I'm sure he'd stop if he knew the effect he was having.

"Guess so," I chuckle awkwardly. There is no way Will Meyer could ever be in my way.

"Can I ask you something?" he asks.

"Sure." I can feel his eyes on me but don't turn my head to meet his gaze. Walking and talking with Will takes a heightened measure of concentration.

"Mr. and Mrs. Weston, they're your uncle and aunt, right?"

"Yes…that's right."

"So…um…why do you call them Luke and Claire?" He's certain to have picked up on this considering the amount of time he's at the house. His question leads me to believe he thinks I'm being rude, which I can't stand.

"Hmmm…well…" I'm not sure how to explain the rift that had been the only relationship I knew between the adults in my family, which led to the estrangement of my uncle and aunt.

"I know you didn't really know them until you came here, but, they're still your family," he qualifies. There's a conviction in his voice that confirms my suspicion that he thinks I've been rude to Luke and Claire. There's no way to explain without opening myself up to him. I don't think I can do that. I don't think he really wants me to open up either. He's probably just correcting me so my etiquette will be more appropriate for my new surroundings. I *have* heard that people in the South place a higher level of importance on proper etiquette.

"It's complicated," is my best first answer.

"I'm sorry," he says, turning his head. I can't tell if he thinks he's been intrusive or is giving up.

"It's ok…really." I want to be able to tell him, to form the words, but I don't even know myself. The more time I spend with Luke and Claire the more I'm utterly confused as to why my parents didn't have a relationship with them. It makes me wonder what they would think about me living with them now.

I don't say anything else about it and Will doesn't ask.

We arrive at the theater and get our tickets. We're the first ones there, which makes me glad. Standing there with Will makes me feel like his friends are joining *us* somehow and I don't feel like a complete outsider.

We're settled into our waiting for just a few minutes when I see Will's friends from the Village Green concert approaching. They meet us and the introductions begin.

Chapter 6

I am immediately and uncomfortably aware that we are equally paired off, three boys and three girls. Will smiles at me, but then I think he must notice my discomfort and his smile fades. He turns his attention back to his friends awkwardly.

Oh, god. What if Will thinks I think this is a date?

I have a fleeting thought of trying to telepathically tell Will I have not made that presumption; to tell him that logically I know that if he hadn't run into me in the bookstore it would have been the five of them, and there's no way that was any kind of date. Even more logically that I know there's no way on God's green Earth that Will Meyer would ever be interested in me like that.

It doesn't appear that the other two couples are really couples either – no hand holding, no closer than necessary proximity – so I'm feeling a bit more at ease. Yes. As the banter and introductions begin it's clear that no one here is anyone's boy- or girlfriend. *You're being ridiculous*, I tell myself. *Since when do you even pay attention to things like that?* The tension in my body releases and Will's smile is back. Maybe I *am* telepathic.

What I am not at ease about is the fact that I am wearing a plain white t-shirt, denim shorts, and sandals, and have my hair in its usual ponytail. The four who are now standing in front of me are perfectly put together from head to toe. All I can think is that I'm totally and completely out of place. I am, once again, utterly plain.

Caroline introduces herself first. Her hair is cut short like a pixie, but slicked to the side with a decorative bobby pin. She is absolutely and undeniably adorable.

"I'm Caroline, and this is Gwen. It's so great to meet you!" she says giving me a hug. The embrace catches me off guard, but I reciprocate out of not wanting to be rude. It's quick, but…nice. As she releases me her eyes catch mine. They are stunningly bright green.

"So, you're Layla. It's great to meet you. Will has told us all about you!" Gwen is so…perky, but not in a dumb kind of way, which is good because she is a knock out: blonde hair, blue eyes and all.

Wait. Did she just say that Will told them about me? What could he possibly tell them?

I'm lost in the thought for a moment and stumble my way back into the conversation. "Um…it's really nice to meet you, too. Thanks for letting me intrude on your movie night."

Caroline cheers, "Oh my gosh! You're not intruding! We're just glad we're getting to meet you before school starts. Will went on about how great you are, so we've been dying to meet you!"

"Well, I don't know how great I am. Will doesn't know me very well yet, so, we'll see." I say trying to downplay whatever he's told them. My head is going through the catalog of conversations I've had with Will, the various, and generic, chats we've had around the kitchen table with Claire, discarding anything that I know is not interesting enough to pass along to anyone. By the time I'm finished I still have no idea.

Chris and Tyler take a breather from their conversation with Will and introduce themselves to me. They are both very good-looking. Chris' short, blonde hair reminds me of Justin Timberlake back in the day. Both he and Tyler are built like Will: strong and fit.

"Nice to finally meet you," Chris says. *Finally?* So Will has talked about me to Chris and Tyler, too. *Why?* Then it occurs to me and the tension that was making an encore performance begins to release. Luke probably asked him to introduce me to some people and make sure I didn't have to sit alone at lunch when school starts. Will and I are becoming friends, and he's a genuinely nice guy, so of course he wouldn't refuse. It makes perfect sense. I can stop wracking my brain now and enjoy the rest of the evening.

"Well…it's really nice to meet all of you. I'll have to find out what Will's been telling you so I can dispel any myths," I say with a small laugh.

"Ok, ok, you guys! Let's get inside and find a good seat before we have to sit in the front row." Will says ushering us all in.

I sit next to Will in the middle of our group, with the girls next to me and the guys next to him. As promised, the movie is completely stupid, but exactly what I needed. I laugh and am happy to not get emotionally involved with any of the characters. I've needed the break. Maybe that's why I haven't picked a new book yet. The stories have been an escape for me, but my life here is so opposite of the one I left. I don't need to escape now. I don't want to either.

We leave the theater and walk to the restaurant, which isn't far. I really like this place. We didn't have anything like it in Orlando. People went to the mall to get out of the heat. They weren't going to walk around outside like this, that's for sure. Now that I think about it, I really don't know if Orlando had anything like this. We were regulars at three places: Wal Mart, Publix, and Denny's. Orlando could be booming with places like this, but I never got the chance to see them.

I walk with Gwen and Caroline who are not at a loss for conversation.

"Will told us your grandfather just passed. I'm so sorry. Were you very close with him?" Gwen asks.

"Thanks. Yeah, we were…close. My grandmother passed away three years ago…it was just us since then and I took care of him." I'm trying to answer honestly. I'll let them attach their own definition of *close*. I can tell by their silence and averting eyes that they aren't sure how to respond to my answer to so I bail them out and change the subject. "So…what do you do for fun?" It's a lame question, but it takes the focus off me, which I prefer, and gets them talking again.

Gwen responds quickly, grateful for the save. "Well, sometimes we walk the trail at the nature preserve, and there's this really great park not far from here. Caroline and I go watch these guys play whatever sport they're in the mood to play. We get some sun and the boys play soccer, football, Frisbee…whatever. Will's parents won't let him play organized sports so-"

"Hey! Let's not bore Layla with the details of my complicated family. Who's hungry?" Will says, cutting her off.

I can't imagine Will's family being *complicated.* He's got to have everything he could ever want. They probably just don't want him to mess up his beautiful face. I don't blame them.

Dinner's good at another local place. The only local restaurants I knew of back home were Chinese holes-in-the-wall and mom and pop diners that are dives. The places here are classy and have style and charm. I sit at dinner with my new friends for over two hours and can't believe I'm actually enjoying myself. I can count on one hand the number of times I just hung out with friends over the last five years.

My nerves are dissipating and I find myself engaged in normal conversation. It's been so long since I've related to people my age that I don't think I was sure I would know what to do. It makes me nervous and I find myself fidgeting. A few deep breaths and I'm settled. Not that much better, but settled. Will is never short of conversation topics, and the others never mind adding their two cents. They make it easy to feel normal that I almost forget how out of place I am.

We prepare to leave and the girls insist on hugs before Will escorts me to his car. If I'm going to be friends with these girls for any length of time, I'm going to have to get used to that. I'm not really a hugger, but I have to admit it was nice feeling connected to them.

As we approach Will's car I'm surprised to see that he doesn't drive something flashy or extravagant, like a BMW or Mercedes. Instead, he unlocks and opens the passenger side door of a simple red Prius. I really don't care what kind of car he drives. I'm just surprised.

We drive the fifteen minutes back to Luke and Claire's and talk about the movie and Will's friends. He asks what I think about them but I'm cautious to give any details beyond that I like them. I'm afraid what I say won't come out the right way.

It's still early when we pull up to the house. I reach for the handle to the door and begin to thank Will for inviting me tonight, introducing me to his friends, and for the ride home. Before I can speak a sound he instructs me to wait and he's out of the car, on his way to my door – again with the gentlemanly behavior.

I step out of the car and say thank you. Will immediately asks, "Have you been down to the lake…at night…I mean…yet? It's really…beautiful." He's uncharacteristically stumbling over his words, which makes me smile a little because it's cute.

"No, actually, I haven't. I hadn't even thought of going down there at night. I'm not the best swimmer, so I figured I'd only go near water when there was some hope of rescue." I laugh nervously. My heart is beating so fast that I'm sure he can hear it.

He smiles that perfect smile and says, "I'd rescue you…again."

I smile nervously and step away from the car so Will can close the door. We walk around the side of the house and go through the gate there. I'm bubbling with curiosity with every step.

What is he doing?

The lights are on in the back of the house, both inside and out, and I can see Luke and Claire in the kitchen.

"Hold on a sec…I just want to let them know I'm home." I tap on the back door and open it quickly. Popping my head inside I say, "I'm back. I'm just going to walk down to the dock for a few minutes...with Will." Claire grins and tells me its fine.

"Don't stay out there too late, Layla. The outside lights are on a timer and will go off at eleven." Luke gives me a look that I can't decipher, but he seems like he enjoyed giving some parental direction, so I just smile.

I close the door and join Will. "Everything ok?" he asks.

"Yeah." I put my purse down on the patio table and lead the way to the dock.

The path seems longer tonight and the farther we get from the house, the darker it becomes. Then suddenly, as if by magic, everything in front of me begins to glow. It's angelic. I stop at the end of the path in total and complete awe. There are small lights glowing from each of the posts along the dock. They aren't bright, but are just enough to light the way. I've almost forgotten Will is with me until I hear him say, "I told you."

"You were *so* right," is all I can say. I thought I had been in awe at the daytime view, but this... this is beyond words. "You've...been down here a lot?" I ask.

"Not a lot. But enough to know it's a view not to be missed," he says staring out onto the glowing water. How does he do that? He's too smooth and eloquent in his speech to be a typical 18-year-old boy. Maybe that's just it. Will is anything but typical.

At that moment, I am unexpectedly intrigued by him. It's more than his face or stature, or even the hospitality he's shown me. A switch has flipped and all I know is that I want to know him. I've never wanted to know someone like this before. There's depth to him, more than I had initially given him credit for having. Tonight, and over the past few weeks, Will has shown himself to be the opposite of who I assumed he would be. Now...now I'm in trouble. I've spent so much time trying to push every thought of him out of my mind only to find myself now completely spellbound.

I sit down on the dock, removing my shoes as I always do so that I don't lose one…or both. Will removes his shoes, too, and sits down next to me on my left. He sits close, but not too close. We're there for a long time, just staring at the water and the moon's reflection. It's a still night, so there's no rustling of the trees, no ripples on the water. No sound but a cricket every twenty seconds.

I've never been alone like this with a boy. Will is easy to be with, but it's still foreign. A surge of nervousness shoots through me so hard that I can feel it in my teeth. A few slow, deep breaths and I'm fine again.

"I'm sorry I was so evasive earlier…when you asked about Luke and Claire," I say. "It *is* complicated, but I don't mind telling you…if you're still interested." I look up and over at him to see what his response, if any, is, wondering if my refusal earlier cut him off from caring any further about the subject, but he surprises me.

He turns his head and catches my eyes. "I am *very* interested in *everything* you have to say, Layla."

My heart leaps inside my chest. He shouldn't say such things. He clearly has no idea the effect he has on me. Being here with Will…it's the first time in a very long time that my desire to share a part of myself with someone is outweighing my fear of any consequences. My heart begins to race again. I take a few more, hopefully not-so-obvious, deep breaths and give Will the not-so-abridged version of the drama.

"Well…hmm…where to start. I was seven the first time I met Luke and Claire. We all went to Orlando to have Christmas with Gram and Gramps. Luke and Claire had been married a couple of years, I guess. We did Christmas morning at our house and then drove to Gram and Gramps' house, which was three and a half hours away. The plan was to open gifts with everyone, stay for dinner, and then drive home. Sounds nice, right?" Will nods. "Well, we did the gift thing, which was fun for me as the only kid, and then we *started* to eat dinner.

"I was only seven so I didn't completely get it, but I knew *something* was up. Luke would say something about how his job at the law firm was going, and Dad would say something like 'Well, that's great that you've decided where your loyalties are.' Then both of them would look to Gramps. It's like they were each waiting for him to show support of their point of view and reprimand the other one, but he never said anything." I take a long pause, hoping I'm not painting my dad as a terrible person. "I had three bites of turkey and one bite of mashed potatoes before Dad declared we were leaving. I gave Gram and Gramps kisses while they told me how much they loved me and were glad we had come. Then we gathered my gifts, packed up the car, and drove home. We were there for two and a half hours."

"Wow. I don't even know what to say. That's terrible," he says but then corrects himself. "Sorry. That was rude. Here you are telling me such private things and I'm just letting anything fly out of my mouth. You don't have to tell me anything else. I'd understand. But…I'm listening, and I am interested, if you want to keep talking." His eyes are piercing in the glow of the moonlight and I'm distracted yet again.

"No…I want to tell you." The corners of my mouth lift into a small smile realizing the depth of truth to that statement. "I can't talk to Luke or Claire about any of this. Not yet at least. So it's nice to have someone to talk to. Thank you." I smile to convey my sincerity. "Looking back on it, I still don't know or understand what happened. My parents never spoke of Luke and Claire, and the next time I saw them was at my parent's funeral, five years later. My parents…they died in a car accident when I was twelve."

"Oh, my gosh, Layla. Mr. Weston said that your parents had passed away, but he didn't say anything about an accident. I'm so sorry."

"It was really hard at first, but Gram and Gramps took me in, so, I at least had somewhere to go. Luke and Claire never said a word to me then, and I didn't talk to them either. So, like I said, when Gramps died, that was the third time I'd ever laid eyes on them. I'm not sure why they didn't come to Gram's funeral. She died two years after I moved in with them.

"So…to finally answer your question…I don't call them 'uncle' or 'aunt' because that implies a relationship we just don't have. I'm getting to know them and I'm hopeful it will change one day." I feel surprisingly relieved. I've never talked to anyone about this. I was so used to keeping it to myself that I'm almost shocked at my ability to share so freely, but that's what Will does to me.

Maybe it's the way he looks me square in the eyes, or the way he turns his whole body to give me his full attention, but my heart wants to be an open book to him. I just have to get my head on the same page. Gram laid the foundation for my inability to trust and I have to force myself to not put everyone in her boat. If I hadn't had Gramps to show me the only kindness I received in that home, I'm sure I wouldn't have come here. It was because of him that I was able to retain some softness in my heart.

"Thank you," he says quietly.

"For what?"

"For your trust. I asked you a personal question earlier today, when I had no right to. I appreciate you trusting me…because you can." He shifts his weight and his right hand moves from his lap to the dock and for a split second I think that he might try to hold my hand or put his arm around me, but it rests there on a single plank. It was a silly thought and I chastise myself for having it. *Silly girl.*

I'm quiet. I want to change the subject. I really don't like talking about me, and this is the most I ever have, so I break the silence and ask, "Do you mind if I ask *you* a question?" I hope the trust goes both ways, but I have no guarantees.

"Of course. You can ask me anything." I believe him. He has a way of answering with just the right words and expression on his face to not make me doubt a single syllable that leaves his beautiful mouth.

"Gwen said something earlier today about your parents not wanting you to play sports. What's that about? Isn't this supposed to be a big high school football town?"

"Oh, that. Well, it's not really that big a deal. My parents just don't want me to put all my extra time toward something that doesn't have 'long term potential.'" He makes air quotation marks and rolls his eyes slightly. "I'm slated to go to Princeton like my dad. He had a wing of the library named after him or something, so…" He doesn't sound as enthusiastic as someone who is guaranteed a spot at one of the most prestigious schools in the country should. He sounds…embarrassed. Maybe it's because he didn't get in on his own. I suppose if his dad made a donation large enough to have a building named after him, he can demand that his kid be accepted.

"So if you're guaranteed a spot, what difference should it make whether you play sports or not?" I ask.

"It shouldn't. But…my father and I disagree about a lot of things. Going to Princeton is just the tip of the iceberg," he says.

"What do you mean?" I'm trying to make sense of it. Why would he *not* want to go to Princeton?

"Well, that's the complicated part. You see…" He doesn't get to finish because it is at that moment that all of the outside lights shut off both at the back of the house and at the dock where we are sitting. It's eleven o'clock already?

"Oh, no, the light!" I say, now fearful of how to make it back up to the house without breaking my leg. Right now the moon is bright enough to cast all the light we need to see each other here on the dock, and we'll be fine about halfway up the flagstone path, but after that it'll be difficult to see. "Well, this should be interesting," I think out loud.

"Oh, c'mon...it won't be so bad. You've walked this path at least 50 times already. You know your way. And…I'll be with you. I do have a little experience in catching you, should you fall." He smiles playfully and I can't help but mirror him.

We put our shoes back on and stand up. When we reach the edge of the dock I revisit where we left off in our conversation. "So…you were about to tell me why things with your parents are complicated." I hope he hasn't changed his mind about sharing with me.

"You don't let things go, do you?" He chuckles as I shake my head. "Well, I was going to say that I just don't have the same aspirations as my father. He sees success and wealth as the greatest things someone can achieve."

"And you don't see it that way." This isn't a question, but a pleasant observation on my part.

"No, I don't. I…uh…I actually really enjoy the work I'm doing with your uncle. My dad knows that and hates it. He thinks that kind of work is for people who don't have any other options. He only lets me come here because he won't let me get a real job." He shakes his head. "The real issue is that I only have a few months to figure out what I'm going to do," he says almost to himself. He doesn't sound like he has a clue what his answer might be.

I feel bad for him and I don't know what to say. My parents never had an issue with anything I did. Even if they were still alive today, I don't think they would have cared all that much if I chose to go to college or not.

By this time we're in almost complete darkness trying to follow the flagstone path back to the house. I stumble and Will catches me, for the second time today. "Here, give me your hand, just in case you stumble again. I'd hate to miss catching you." I take his hand without a word or hesitation. It's just as I remember it – strong, but gentle.

He holds my hand with such assurance, and I know he won't let me fall.

The same surge of nervousness that I felt earlier rushes through me again. My heart races so fast I can barely breathe, but with each step we take it subsides because holding Will's hand feels strangely normal. Like our hands were meant to fit together.

We make it back to the patio unscathed where there is a little bit of light coming from the kitchen. I grab my purse off the patio table and try the door. It's unlocked. Will walks in behind me, and I walk him to the front door as an easier, better-lit course to his car. I open the front door and stand with him on the porch.

"Thank you…for today. I mean…for introducing me to your friends. They're really great. And…for tonight. It was nice… I had a really nice time." I feel the blood rushing to my cheeks as I think about how it felt to hold Will's hand and wish I could tell him that *nice* doesn't begin to describe how I really feel about the evening.

"I had a great time today, too. I'm glad I ran into you. Or rather, that you ran into me." We chuckle and Will starts to move toward the steps. "Um…I gotta go," he says, his voice uncharacteristically shaky. I thank him again and say good-bye, but then in a moment he turns quickly and says, "Are you free tomorrow? We're all going to Grandfather Mountain to go hiking. Would you like to come?"

I'm taken off guard both by his physical one eighty and the idea of me on mountain terrain. "Hiking? Hmm. I'm not sure. You know it's completely flat in Florida, right? I'm not sure if I even have the right shoes for that." He just stares, convincing me with his eyes. Now that I am intrigued by everything about him, how can I deny him anything. "But…I guess I should give it a try…seeing as I live here now." I can't help but smile looking at him looking at me.

"Great! Tell you what, I'll text Caroline and Gwen tonight and see if they have an extra pair of hiking shoes you can borrow. If not, sneakers will be fine. I'll pick you up at nine."

"That sounds great. Thanks for including me. It'll be great to see the girls again." It really is going to be great to see them again. I like them very much, and I think they like me. It's nice being around people my own age. "Oh, and Tyler and Chris, too!"

I feel awkward as we stand there. I don't know if I should extend my hand to shake his, or if I should initiate a hug. I'm not really one for hugs, but I've already held his hand, even if it was just for my stability. It seems to be an appropriate display of friendship among Will and my new friends, so I step forward with my arms extended.

"Well…thank you, again," I say as I lift myself onto my toes and wrap my arms around his neck.

He hugs me back, holding me close with his arms around my waist and says, "Thank *you.*" I'm overwhelmed by how good it feels to be in his arms, how safe I feel. It's a feeling I am getting reacquainted with, first with Luke and Claire, and now with Will.

We linger in the moment longer than I anticipate. When we let go, Will steps back and looks at me for one intense second and abruptly says, "Ok! I'll…see you in the morning then. Nine AM, and my goal is for you to have a better than *nice* time." Stepping backward, he finds the porch steps and walks down to his car. I stand in the doorway and watch him make his way out of the circle driveway and onto the street. I sigh as I close the door behind me. Leaning against it for a moment I can't help but smile. I did a lot of that tonight.

Chapter 7

Will picks me up nine o'clock sharp. Instead of his Prius he has his mom's Denali. It's the same model as Luke's, only in white. It seats seven so we'll all be able to ride together. We pick the others up at their equally beautiful and huge homes in the neighborhood and get on the highway.

I'm halfway turned around in the front seat most of the way there so I can talk with the girls. The rest of the time I'm taking in the exquisite beauty of our scenic drive. Caroline brought an extra pair of hiking boots for me so I won't be stumbling on the trail in my sneakers. Since we'll be in the car almost two hours, I decide to wait and put them on when we get there.

The drive up the Blue Ridge Parkway is stunning. I can only imagine how striking it will be in the fall when the leaves change color. I've only seen that spectacle in books. It feels odd to now live in a place with four actual seasons. Where I'm from, we were good to get two distinguishable ones. Will must have noticed the awed look on my face and read my thoughts.

"You should see it in October. There's no green, only shades of red, orange, and gold," he says.

"It's beautiful," I say, not breaking my stare out the window. In my mind I compare the commercialized streets of Orlando to the peaceful nature of my current surroundings. There are no neon signs, no pink flamingo mascots. There is no one standing on a corner waving a sign for discount theme park tickets. No, with the exception of the asphalt, here there is only the perfection of what has been here since the beginning of time. I think about the time it has taken these trees to mature and become the steadfast pillars they are and wonder if nature thought it took too long, as I feel it is taking me too long to become comfortable in this bark of mine.

We arrive at the gate into Grandfather Mountain right at eleven o'clock.

Will failed to tell me that there is an admission fee. I tell him I'll pay him back when he drops me off but he says I'm not allowed.

"I would have brought money had you told me!" I protest.

"It's not a big deal. Consider it your 'Welcome to North Carolina' present." He gives me the same you're-not-going-to-win-this-debate look that Luke did, so I let it go. I have a feeling I need to learn that it's pointless to argue points of chivalry with him. He makes me so nervous sometimes. I just need to calm down and go with the flow.

Tyler taunts me and says that as part of my "initiation" I'll have to cross the Mile High Bridge. It's funny because he says it like a dare. He has no idea that the prospect of being that high up is exhilarating for me. We climb the 50 steps to reach the bridge and I pause to take in the view.

"I guess they don't have this kind of view in Florida, huh?" Gwen is right next to me taking in the vision as well.

"Uh, no. We've got the ocean, which is pretty spectacular, but this is so different. Oh! Caroline's boots! I left them in the car." I turn around to look for Will so I can run down and grab the boots out of the car but Caroline stops me.

"Don't worry! I've got them!" she says.

I swap out my shoes for the boots and put them in the backpack Tyler is wearing, along with a few bottles of water stashed in there for each of us. We decide to do the bridge after our hike, so the boys pick a trail they say they think will lead to less whining from Gwen, Caroline, and me and I begin my first real encounter with nature.

We hike the trail for about two hours before we turn around and make our way back to the famous bridge. I spend most of the time walking with Gwen and Caroline. They talk about their excitement for senior year, and general girl stuff like clothes and boys. I add my two cents every now and then, but mostly just listen and answer questions they have for me.

"So, Layla, did you leave a heartbroken boy back in Florida?" Caroline asks. I have decided that it is impossible for her *not* to be cute. She could make Jules Vern's *Mysterious Island* sound adorable.

"No, no one. I didn't really have time for boys. Not that I was interested in any of them anyway. They were…not my type. Of the guys I knew, I'm pretty sure their dream vacation is going to Comic Con dressed as obscure Star Wars characters." A few boys come to mind and the thought of anything romantic with them makes me shudder. "What about you two? Are you dating anyone?" I ask. Anything to get the conversation off of me.

Gwen answers for both of them, "We're not dating anyone right now. We both have been totally into Will. I mean, who wouldn't, right? But nothing ever came of it. Tyler and I went out a few times but found out we were better suited as friends. Caroline and Chris actually dated for a year before it ended. Can you believe they're still friends?"

I'm impressed. I would never have known they had been an item. I always figured people broke up under awful circumstances, which meant they *couldn't* be friends.

"Gwen! You make it sound like it was a terrible break-up!" Caroline squeals. "It was just like you and Tyler, only you realized early on. Neither of us wanted to be a quitter, so we held out longer. When our feelings finally came out we were both so relieved. That's why we're still friends."

"What about the guys? Chris, Tyler…Will? Are any of them…you know…seeing anyone?" My attempt at sounding nonchalant is weak, but I have an unyielding need to know what Will's story is. He spent a lot of time with me yesterday, more than a guy with a girlfriend should. Twenty-four hours ago I wouldn't have cared, but after being on the dock with Will last night I have to know.

"No. Chris and Tyler aren't dating anyone, not that they aren't teaming with choices," Gwen answers. "And Will…" She smiles as she catches me snapping my head up and I know I'm busted. "…he's not seeing anyone either."

"Oh." What else was I going to say? I quickly change the subject. "So…I've got a little bit of Will's take on it, but what's the scoop on Heyward?"

"Heyward is, well, it's interesting. The entire school is made up entirely of our own little neighborhood community, and *only* our neighborhood community. It's a bit incestuous, really. Anyway, 95% of the people there are absolutely obsessed with how wealthy they are. They talk and talk and talk about their cars, clothes, trips to Aspen…blah, blah, blah. It drives us crazy, especially Will. Don't get me wrong, I *love* being rich. Actually, I love the opportunities that being rich brings me, but it's not everything." Gwen answers. "That's what binds the five…"

"Six!" Caroline corrects.

"…yes, *six* of us together. We like the advantages of wealth, just not the annoying, pretentious part. Had we not met *now*, there are any number of vultures who would have tried to take you under their wing."

"Yeah, we're glad you're here, Layla!" Caroline giggles, "Now Gwen and I aren't outnumbered!"

Gwen and Caroline give each other a look and then put their arms over my shoulder and around my waist from either side. I feel incredible emotional warmth from them followed by the sting of tears coming to my eyes. I fight the tears back and relish in the realization that I have just been inducted into their sisterhood and I couldn't be more honored. I'm pleased at how easy I seem to be adapting to life with people my age. It gives me hope that all is not lost. My friendship with them is less than 24 hours old and already it is the most satisfying friendship I've had in five years.

When I talk with Chris and Tyler they mainly quiz me about how daring I am. It was like interviewing for Fear Factor. Will and I chat generally about how I'm settling in. Some of it is repetitive conversation we've had before around the lunch table with Claire. Since he's careful not to bring up any personal conversation we started last night there isn't a whole lot more to talk about. Everyone also does their best to begin preparing me for fall and winter weather: two seasons that Central and South Florida don't really have, at least not like it is here.

As we approach the bridge, Will, Tyler and Chris pretend they're going to push each other off the side of the mountain. *Boys.* Caroline and Gwen are by my side making sure I really am ok to cross the swinging bridge. It had apparently taken them several trips to the bridge before either one was willing to cross it. They have no idea what a daredevil I can be…used to be. I haven't accessed my daring side for a long time. It used to be that the faster and higher I could go the better.

Adrenaline pumps through me as I approach the bridge. It's definitely high, and it's definitely swaying in the high-altitude wind. It's not the most daring thing I've ever done, but it's the first time in five years that I've done anything really and truly exciting. There aren't a lot of people on the bridge, so I take my first steps without anyone in my way. I stop halfway across and stare out at the cloud-covered mountains. I thought everyone had passed by me to reach the other side of the bridge, but I feel someone standing next to me and realize it is Will.

"I'm really glad you came today," he says staring out at the view with me. "The girls are smitten with you, and Tyler and Chris already consider you a little sister."

"I really like them, too, and I'm really glad I came. Thanks for inviting me. I had a nice time," I say.

"That's too bad. My goal was for you to have a better than *nice* time." Will smiles and locks his blue eyes on me, but the moment turns awkward when his smile fades like it did at the movie theater. "I'm gonna catch up with the others," he says as he releases his gaze and crosses the remaining length of the bridge.

Did I do something wrong? I wonder if he thinks he's giving me the wrong impression. I want to tell him not to worry, that I don't have any ideas of grandeur, but how do I put his mind at ease without sounding ridiculously presumptuous?

It's 3:30 and really hot, even for this Florida girl. Gwen and Caroline beg for an early release from the heat and ask if we can head back. The boys agree, although I'm sure they would have played outside until the sun went down. Gwen gets Will's keys from him so we can get a head start to the car and put the air on. I take Caroline's borrowed hiking shoes off and wait for Tyler to return with the backpack containing my sneakers and the water our throats are craving. I slip my sneakers on just as Will is getting in the car. I had considered that maybe I should not sit up front with him, that he doesn't want me to sit next to him, but it's too late as he is quick to start the car and pull out of the parking lot.

All in all, it was a good day. Despite the awkwardness that seems to keep showing up between me and Will, I bonded with girls my age, which is something I haven't been able to do for so long, and I got to see some of the amazing scenery of the state I now call home.

We make good time getting home. It was four o'clock when we left Grandfather Mountain and 5:30 as we arrive at Caroline's house first. We drop Tyler off next, followed by Gwen and Chris who live three houses apart from each other. At first I'm a little surprised that none of them suggested we get something to eat, but then think that they probably already had plans.

With my handle on the door of the car I take a breath with the intention of thanking Will for the great day, and apologizing if I had done anything to upset him earlier. I wracked my brain all the way home, replaying the day, but still could not think of what I could have done to make his demeanor change so quickly on the bridge. When I open my mouth something entirely different comes out.

"Do you want to come in? Get something to eat…or something?" I ask, immediately regretting every syllable. What was I thinking? If he's unhappy with me, I've now put him in the even more awkward position of having to politely bail out when all he was most likely hoping for was to drop me off and end this day.

"Um…yeah," Will replies hesitantly. He must still be upset, but doesn't want to be rude. He is one of the most polite guys I've ever met.

"It's no big deal...you don't have to. I was just thinking…"

"No, I want to. I mean…I *am* hungry." He smiles and makes everything better.

It's astonishing to me how with one small gesture, Will can completely turn my thoughts and feelings around. I feel silly for having spent so much time trying to figure out what I had done to upset him. I'm just so used to being the core of someone's sadness. It is quite a learning curve to exist in a space that doesn't revolve around my transgressions.

Will sits at the counter while I make chicken salad sandwiches. Claire always has one of those rotisserie chickens from the grocery store deli on hand. He's quiet and stares while I tear the poor chicken to shreds. It's in this very ordinary moment that my nervousness at being alone with Will begins to slowly dissipate for what I feel hopeful will be forever.

"Are you ok?" I ask, noticing the in-thought look on his face.

"Yeah, I'm fine. I was just wondering something…about your parents," he says.

"Oh."

"I'm sorry. I shouldn't have brought them up."

"No, it's ok. What did you want to ask?" I brace myself and pray he isn't going to ask about the accident. Everyone always asked about the accident. I continue to chop and dice the ingredients without looking at him.

"Well…I was wondering what your favorite thing about them was," he says.

"What?" I look up at him mid chop, surprised.

"I'm sorry, was that too personal?"

"No, not at all. It's just…no one's…ever asked me that before. It's a nice change." I pause to think for a moment because there were so many things that I loved about my parents. I reflect for a few short moments on my childhood. It's nice to spend some time focusing on the joy instead of the tragedy. "I think the thing that I loved most about them was also the thing that drove me the craziest. They were structured, but let me do almost anything I wanted. I don't mean I was allowed to stay up until three in the morning. I mean that whatever I wanted to do or try, they let me. It was great because it made me feel like they loved me enough to understand I was my own person. It was terrible at the same time because sometimes, after I failed miserably, I wished they would have shown some parental insight and protected me from getting hurt. But…they were always there to celebrate or pick up the pieces."

"Hmmm. That's really interesting," he says thoughtfully. "Most of the people I know don't want their parents involved in their lives at all. They prefer to keep their distance, being allowed to do whatever they want. Your perspective is…refreshing," he answers.

"Well, isn't that what parents are for? Aren't they supposed to protect us?"

"Yes. But what happens when they want to protect you from something you don't need protection from? What if they *think* they're protecting you, but in reality they're keeping you from being the person you're supposed to be?"

"Well…maybe you have to respectfully stand up and make your case, and take responsibility if whatever it is you want to do blows up in your face."

I know from our earlier conversation that Will is talking about his dad. Will has dreams that are nightmares to his father. I don't think it's fair. It's clear that Will is not a suit and tie kind of guy, and the idea of being forced into corporate America is slowly killing him.

"Yeah. That'd be nice." Will shakes himself and changes the expression on his face from deep in thought to ready to eat so I put his sandwich on a plate and hand it to him. "This looks really good. Thanks."

"You're welcome. I'll share my secret tips for a perfect chicken salad sandwich with you someday. I have to know I can trust you and that you won't steal my recipe and create a chicken salad sandwich empire!" We laugh and it makes me happy to see him smile again.

"You can definitely trust me, Layla." He smiles at me and I know he means it.

Chapter 8

School is starting soon and I still haven't been to see the campus. I'm already registered so it's just a formality for me to visit before classes start. Formality, or not, I've got to get the lay of the land before I set foot onto the battleground. Claire insists that today is the day for me to see Heyward Washington Preparatory Academy and I can't argue any longer.

Claire tells me the school isn't too far from home. We turn off the main road and down a secluded, wooded drive. Pulling up the drive I'm sure Claire is running an errand on the way to the school, dropping off some legal documents at a high profile client's office. The building I'm staring at looks like the White House. Its architecture is startling in the middle of what I would call the woods. Tall columns stretch the height of the three-story building, with two two-story wings jetting out from either side. It's so out of place.

"Are you coming?" Claire asks as she gets out of the car.

"Um…ok," I say getting out with her. I'm really not interested in the awkwardness of meeting one of Claire's clients, but this building is so amazing, I almost can't take my eyes off of it.

"Welcome to Heyward Prep, Layla." Claire smiles as my jaw drops.

The woman in the front office greets us pleasantly and addresses Claire by name. She's a tall, thin woman, older, with short graying blonde hair. She speaks with a sweet southern accent, reminding me of Paula Dean, warm and sugary sweet. She's calmly thumbing through a stack of papers as Claire introduces her as Mrs. Whitman and informs me that without her the school would have crumbled years ago.

"Oh, Claire, sugar, you're too sweet! It's such a pleasure to meet you, Layla. I hope you'll enjoy your time here. If you need anything, don't hesitate to come see me. Ok? I've got your schedule right here, dear. You can find your classrooms today if that'd be helpful." She pulls a small, rectangular piece of paper from the stack she's handling and gives it to me, along with a map of the school. The map is quite intricate – color-coded and arranged by grade.

"Yes, that would be great. Thank you," I say as I accept the papers. I look at the map more closely and see that all my classes are on the east wing because that's where all the senior classrooms are. The rest of the administrative offices are on the third floor of the main building, which I somehow already know is a place I never want to go. According to the map, it's a floor filled with conference rooms and the offices of school officials who hold my academic future in their hands. A closer examination of my schedule reveals that all my classes are honors and to say I am thoroughly panicked is an understatement.

"I'm sorry, Mrs. Whitman, there seems to be a mistake. I'm not qualified to take honors chemistry or trig," I tell her with cool concern in my voice. I'll be here a lifetime if they expect me to pass those in order to graduate. I try to hand my mistake of a schedule back to her but she holds up her hands in refusal.

"There's no mistake, sugar. All the senior classes here are honors. Don't worry, though. We have some brilliant students who are able to tutor you, and there are some students at the college who help us out with that, too. We'll make sure you're taken care of, dear," she says nonchalantly, as if a tutor is going to somehow magically make me understand complicated math and science. This is going to be a very long year.

"Um…ok." I sigh and purse my lips. I twirl a lock of my long ponytailed hair as I contemplate this.

Another administrator walks into the office and Claire becomes involved in an immediately heated conversation about how this year's mock trials should be coordinated. I motion to her that I'm going to go ahead and find my classrooms and excuse myself.

The main hall of the building is unlike any school I've ever seen. The floors are carpeted and the walls are painted a warm, khaki color. It's incredibly inviting. There is no linoleum flooring or fluorescent lighting, which every girl here is sure to enjoy. Fluorescent lighting never made anyone look good. Along the walls are oil paintings of the school's founders and board of directors, all in gilded frames. Of course, Gregory Meyer is at the helm of this ship. That doesn't surprise me. I have the impression that Mr. Meyer enjoys being at the center of everything. Even his portrait creeps me out. It's like the ones at the Haunted Mansion at Disney where the eyes follow you.

Further exploration down the hall leads me to the library where my schedule indicates Study Hall is held. I pass through the heavy, solid wood door and the room is instantly like a dream. There are elegant sofas and the room is filled with rich mahogany furniture. A fireplace has wingback chairs strategically placed in front of it. The room looks more like a lodge than a library. The smell of old books fills the air, and I inhale deeply several times. There are two rows of tables with green banker's lamps like the kind you see in movies. It's wonderfully overwhelming and I have to make myself leave before I find a book and a corner and am never seen again.

I find the east wing easily. Each room is marked with a simple "E" and the number of the room. There are six classrooms on each floor. The science and math rooms are on the first floor, which means my English, civics, and Spanish classes are upstairs. All the rooms are the same so I decide that I don't need to go upstairs to locate my other classrooms.

Walking back down the long hall toward the main building I see a gold-plated sign pointing to the dining hall. *Dining hall? Why don't they just call it a cafeteria?* As I come within reach of the doors I see why. This is no cafeteria.

The room is filled with large round tables covered with white linens. Each table has ten high-back chairs, and there are small floral centerpieces on each table. With four huge silver chandeliers hanging from the high ceilings, the room is more like a hotel ballroom than a high school eatery.

I don't see an entrance to where the students pass through the kitchen and receive their lunch from the industrial size pot it's held in, only a set of swinging double doors. *No…it can't…they couldn't actually have wait staff here!* I'm in shock at the mere thought. I'm used to packing my lunch and I certainly don't want to draw any more attention to myself than I already will, so I better find out from Claire if I'm absolutely crazy, or not.

"I'm sorry I didn't show you around the school. Did you find everything ok? What do you think?" Claire asks as we pull out of the parking lot.

"No problem. Yeah, I found everything just fine. It helps that all the senior classes are in one place, and the library is amazing," I say.

"Isn't it? High school wasn't like this when I was there!" Claire says.

"Speaking of that…I have a really silly question." I take a deep breath before I ask the most bizarre question I have ever asked. "Do they have…waiters…in the dining hall?" I'm astounded that I even have to ask the question for clarification.

"Yes. Ostentatious, isn't it?" Claire says.

"It just seems…weird. Doesn't *anyone* bring their lunch?" I ask, knowing full well what the answer is.

"Oh…no. There's a menu of about five or six things that rotate each week. It's never the same menu two days in a row. It's all really good food, though. Sometimes Mr. Meyer holds lunch meetings here when the entire firm is involved. There's a professional chef on staff and he runs the place like a five-star restaurant." Claire pauses. "You have to remember the lifestyle that these kids are used to, Layla. Their parents don't want them treated any other way." Claire's explanation reminds me that I have a lot to endure this year. I'm grateful for Will and my new friends, knowing they'll protect me from the pompous, dark side.

Claire and Luke's office is on Main Street in downtown Davidson, just a block up from the Village Green. Claire has to run in for a few minutes so she gives me the option of getting a tour of Meyer, Fincher and Marks and waiting in her office or doing something else. Because I really don't want to have an up-close stare down from Mr. Meyer, I opt for something else. I notice the bookstore Luke told me about and I'm sure I can fill my time there while I wait. Claire pulls up to the curb right in front of Main Street Books and as I get out I tell her I'll go to the coffee shop if I finish in the bookstore before she's done. The blue trim around the windows and the red door immediately invite me in. It looks old, which I interpret as dedicated. From the outside it seems like the kind of place that has worked hard to fight the giant booksellers, but always prevails. It's the kind of place that remembers you and what your reading preferences are by your face, not your frequent buyer card.

It isn't a huge store, but the warm brown wood floors and white shelves draw me in and I feel right at home. After seeing my class schedule I think I better get a jump on the help I am certainly going to need in trigonometry and chemistry. I've never been a member of the "nerdery", but I'm also not one to wait until I'm utterly and completely lost before I ask for help. I pass the racks with Davidson College apparel and browse the aisles until I find the section that should hold math tutorials. After looking for a few minutes I find one book that I think might have what I'm looking for so I pick it up and begin flipping through the pages.

"Trig, huh? If you've got Professor Donavan be sure to bring him Cowtails and caramel crèmes; they're his favorite," a young man says. His Main Street Books nametag reads Marcus.

"Oh, I'm not a student at the college." I say.

"So your idea of fun on a Thursday summer afternoon is brushing up on your trigonometry?" he quips.

"No. I just got my schedule for this year and if I don't get a head start on this I'm going to be a senior next year, too," I say trying to sound casual about my deficiencies.

"Well, you're in luck. I'm a math major at Davidson. I'd be happy to help," he says extending his hand. "I'm Marcus…Reynolds."

"I'm Layla…Weston. It's nice to meet you." I shake his hand and smile. "That actually would be great. I've got enough to think about this year without having to go prematurely grey over math."

"What are you talking about? This is your senior year – the time of your life!" Marcus is an enthusiastic guy and very down to earth. He's my kind of people.

"Yeah, well…I just moved here and I'll be going to *Pretentious High*," I say.

"*You're* a student a Heyward Washington Prep?" he says, his eyebrows shooting up in surprise.

"Yes. Is there a problem with that?" I don't like the way he said it. It's ok for me to mock the school with my friends, but I find Marcus' remark insulting.

"Oh, uh, no. You just don't strike me as the type to go there. First of all, you're in *this* store looking at *academic* books. Second, well…you're polite. Sorry, you threw me off."

"I'll…let it slide this time," I smile, easing up. "So you could really tutor me?"

"Yeah, definitely. In fact, I'm on the list of tutors for your school through the college. Just sign up and put my name down. They'll call me and get us connected."

"Then I suppose I don't need this book today," I say putting it back on the shelf.

"I was just getting off work. Do you want to go next door and get a Coke, or something? It'll save us the introduction time when we start tutoring." Marcus says taking off his nametag.

"Sure. I was going there anyway to wait for my aunt," I say.

We leave the bookstore and walk to the coffee shop next door. It's the same place I first met Will and I blush a little as I remember the icy mess of his drink.

As we sit down at a table in the window I think about how lucky I am to have met Marcus. If he's on the list of tutors for the school he's certain to be a big help. They won't let just anyone near their precious students.

"So exactly how terrified of trigonometry are you?" he asks.

"About as terrified as I am of chemistry. Both are honors classes. In fact, all of my classes are honors. English, Civics, even Spanish, I'm not worried about. But these two will be the death of me."

"Well, I'll be able to help with trig more than chemistry, but I'll do my best to get you through both," he says.

Marcus has dark brown hair and light green eyes. He's attractive by anyone's standards. He's tall, but not as tall as Will. Will seems to have become my benchmark, which really isn't fair to Marcus, or any guy for that matter. It doesn't really matter anyway. I'm buying my time until I graduate and I can go back to Florida. If things continue to go well with Luke and Claire, I'll at least have family to visit for holidays, and friends to see while I'm here.

"That's great. Have you tutored a lot of Heyward students?" He obviously has an opinion of them, so I wonder what his experience with them has been.

"Not a lot, but I've had enough experiences with their kind of people to know that I don't need to have any more. *You* were a surprise." He takes a sip of his drink. "Just be sure to be on guard. There are some people associated with that school who are like vultures. If you don't protect yourself, they'll eat you alive."

Claire walks by and spots us in the window of the coffee shop as she comes in.

"Did you find what you were looking for? You haven't been sitting here long, have you?" Claire asks.

"No, not long, just a few minutes. I found a book that I thought would help, but then I met Marcus. He works in the bookstore and goes to Davidson. He's on the tutor list for Heyward. Marcus, this is my aunt, Claire." I say.

"It's very nice to meet you Mrs. Weston," Marcus says, standing to shake Claire's hand.

"It's nice to meet you, too, Marcus. You're smart to get a head start on this, Layla, especially since Luke and I will be zero help in trig or chemistry. I'm very glad Layla found you, Marcus. Do you want anything, Layla," Claire asks as she moves to the counter.

"No thanks," I say quickly.

"I'm glad she found me, too," Marcus says. He smiles right at me and it occurs to me that he might actually be flirting. The possibility that Marcus could be interested in me isn't nearly as preposterous as the idea that Will ever could be. I dismiss it still because I need Marcus' help to get me through trig and I can't cloud my interaction with him with the vain ideas of a silly schoolgirl.

Claire buys herself a drink and I join her at the door to leave. "It was nice to meet you, Marcus. You're welcome at the house anytime for tutoring," Claire says as she exits.

"Nice meeting you, too, Mrs. Weston," Marcus says.

"I'll fill out the tutor request when school starts. So…I guess I'll see you soon," I say.

"I look forward to it." He raises his hand in a brief wave as I make my way through the door.

Chapter 9

I spend the rest of the afternoon with my iPod and ear buds at the edge of the dock. Will has been giving me some Music 101 lessons. Last week's homework was to check out the classics like Miles Davis. We listened to a couple of them in the car to and from Grandfather Mountain and I have to admit that I was pleasantly surprised. I'm bobbing my head up and down embarrassingly to the music when Will appears behind me, poking me in the shoulder.

"I hope that's *old* music you're listening to," he says, startling me so much that I jump a little.

"Oh, my gosh, Will! I almost fell in the water!" I jump up quickly and playfully punch him in the arm. I take a quick step back as I've startled myself with this behavior. It was the move of a girl completely comfortable and at ease with not only Will, but also herself. I'm shocked, and pleasantly surprised. *Could that really be me?* I ask myself.

"I already told you that I was here to rescue you." He smiles that perfect smile and I realize that the answer to my question is *yes*. "So you checked out the school today. What'd ya think?"

"Gosh! Word travels fast around here. Well…it's the nicest school I've ever set foot in, and I understand it'll be the best food I've ever eaten as well. I'm mostly looking forward to spending time in the library. It was spectacular."

"Listen, I've got an errand to run for Luke. Do you want to come with me, along for the ride?"

"Sure, sounds fun." It sounds like more than just fun. It's a chance for me spend time with Will. It is a perfect opportunity in my quest to know him.

Will needs to get nails, screws, and plywood – items that reveal nothing of my unmerited surprise – at the hardware store. While Will gets the things he needs, I look around the store and think of my dad. I'm obviously quiet and by the time we leave the store I haven't said more than ten words.

"Hey, are you ok?" Will asks.

"Yeah. I was just remembering my dad. When I was a little girl I used to go to the hardware store with him. He was really handy and *always* had a project going. One of my favorite things was to help him, and by help I mean I kept him company while he worked. Being in there just…it reminded me of him." Talking about my dad is hard, but easier since Luke has engaged me in such normal conversation about him, but as the words leave my mouth I realize that sharing my feelings with Will is surprisingly easy. He makes it that way. Everything in me wants to trust him. When I talk, he looks at me with unwavering attention. He fixes his eyes on me and I can see he's listening. It's comforting to be heard.

"That's good. It's important that you have those memories. It keeps him with you. I think that's a special thing, Layla, and you should never lose it," Will says smiling softly, his voice smooth and reassuring.

We get back to the house and Will takes his purchases down to the basement. He and Luke emerge a few hours later as Claire and I are fixing dinner.

"Thanks for your work today, Will. You've got a good eye. I'm glad I've got you around to help me with this. I'll see you tomorrow?" I'm still confused as to what the basement project has to do with me, but have to admit that I'm becoming curious to see what they're doing down there.

"You're welcome, Mr. Weston. I appreciate the opportunity. I really love the work." He pauses before he hesitantly addresses me. "So…I *was* going to hang out with Tyler tonight, but…" As he stares at me I somehow feel like that's my cue.

"Would you like to stay for dinner?" I ask without knowing if it's all right with Luke and Claire. "Is it ok with you?" I ask Claire, remedying my error. She smiles softly and nods and I turn to Will and wait for his reply.

"Yeah, that sounds great. Thank you," he answers, smiling heavenly. As he pulls out his phone and presumably texts Tyler that he won't be meeting up with him, my heart leaps. Just as quickly as it leaped, it falls flat as I recall Will's propensity for quick mood changes. I could be on the receiving end of his smile all day, but I don't know how much more of the swings I can take. After the night at the movies and then on the bridge, I have no clue where I stand with him. One minute he's making a point to be with me, but in the next he's doing everything he can to get away. Do I say something to him? Where is this in the rulebook of how to be friends with a guy? I don't want him to go, so I decide to walk cautiously through the evening waiting for Will's smiles to turn to frowns. For now I'm happy that Will is here. He could be anywhere else but right now he's choosing to be here with me. I need him. I need his friendship. I'll just have to be especially careful so I don't give him any impression that I have the wrong idea about our friendship. I can't lose him.

Claire and I make chicken divan and salad. It's so fattening, but delicious. We decide that the salad balances it all out, though. During dinner I teasingly beg for clues as to what Will and Luke are doing in the basement, but get quickly shut down each time. I'm lowering my guard with Luke and Claire a little bit every day. They make it so easy to feel at home here. We ebb and flow together so well that it's scary. It's like we've known each other forever, which is a feeling I never expected to have with them. Will fits in perfectly with us, as well. His sense of humor is as twistedly funny as Luke's and mine. I've discovered that is something Luke and my father *did* have in common. They both could make me laugh to the point of tears.

After dinner Will helps me with the dishes. Most of it went in the dishwasher, but Claire has a few pieces that need to be washed by hand so I wash and Will dries. The pot we cooked the chicken in is cumbersome and the water sloshes everywhere with each swish of the sponge. By the time we're done the bottom half of my shirt is soaked. Will follows me upstairs to the loft and waits while I change.

"This room is amazing," he says as I re-enter the loft, refreshed and dry with a new shirt. I'm surprised at his comment. I've always imagined his house being majestic and more impressive than ours.

"You haven't been up here before?" I ask.

"No. I bet the view from here is almost as good as the one from the dock," he says.

"Yeah, you get a better picture of the whole scene from here. This is my favorite spot in the house. It has the best view of the lake," I say as I sit in my oversized chair.

"Really? I think I'll have to judge that for myself." He smiles and sits in the chair with me, squishing his body next to mine. I feel a rush of nervousness come over me and my body temperature begins to rise. "Hmm, you might have something there." The moonlight is shining through the trees, which makes the scene very dramatic with the shades of dark blue and gray it casts on everything. "But I still think the view is better from the dock."

"Oh, really? Well, I guess we'll have to do a comparison tonight, then, won't we?" I realize I'm flirting – something I don't do well at all – and stop myself immediately. As much as I like him, Will is my friend and I don't want to do anything to tarnish that. I don't want to give the impression that I think there's more going on here than there is. I'm having too much of a good time with him tonight to watch his smile fade again and have him disappear.

Will stands up and immediately grabs my hand and pulls me out of the chair. I'm thrust into his arms and his eyes lock onto mine as he steadies me. It seems like he's holding me for an eternity and I can't breathe. My heart is beating so hard that he's just got to feel it. I break his gaze and quickly move to the stairs. We pass through the kitchen, each grabbing a bottle of soda before making our way to the dock. We stand there, silent, for a few minutes when I concede.

"Ok. You win. This view *is* the better of the two. But you have to admit, it's a close race," I say.

"I don't know…it might be too close to say. How about we call it a tie?" he says sitting down at the edge of the dock. *He's sitting, which means he's staying!*

"Agreed," I reply, following his lead and sitting next to him.

I don't understand why Will is here. There have to be at least a dozen girls clamoring for his attention. He has his pick of any girl he wants, yet he's here…with me. Maybe he feels sorry for me, being new here and not having any friends but his. I certainly haven't painted a picture of leaving a flock of friends behind in Orlando. Maybe I just bring newness to his life. I may not know why he's here; I just know I don't want him to leave.

"So…how are you feeling about school?" Will asks.

"Nervous. I've got honors trig and chemistry. I stink at both. But, I'm feeling hopeful. I met someone today who offered to tutor me," I tell him, excited to share the news that the likelihood of me flunking my senior year diminished quite a bit today.

"Oh…well, you know I'm pretty good at both, so *I'd* be happy to tutor you," Will replies.

"That's ok. Marcus is a math major at Davidson. He's on the tutor list at Heyward already, so…" I say.

"Marcus Reynolds?" Will's voice is stiff.

"Yeah, you know him?" I ask.

"Yes." Will's demeanor changes. He's lost his shine and is distinctly darker. His body seems to slump over slightly, but even this small move changes his god-like body into something sad and defeated.

"Is there something wrong?" I ask.

"No. Marcus is a good guy," he says.

"How do you know him?" I would have asked anyway, but the change in Will's demeanor makes me especially curious.

"His dad worked for mine for a few months, but…it didn't work out." He's hesitant and vague.

"So you and Marcus were friends?" I ask, hoping to get some insight.

"I was…friends…with his sister, Holly, but they moved away last year." *Friends?* Will straightens himself like he's realized something. He pushes back from the edge of the dock, puts his shoes on. *Here it is again.* "I should go," he says as he stands to leave.

"I'm sorry. Did I do something? I didn't mean to upset you." I can't let another moment like this go by without confronting him. I put my shoes on quickly and stand to face Will. I wobble a bit in my haste and have a good three seconds where I'm genuinely afraid I'm going to fall in the water.

"You didn't do anything. I'm sorry. Like I said, Marcus is a good guy. You two will be great friends." He turns and starts walking back up the dock to the path back to the house. "It's getting late. I'll walk you back up before the lights go out."

I follow Will and we walk the flagstone path back to the house. He doesn't offer his hand of assistance this time and I'm filled with disappointment. With every step I become more and more curious as to why Will's attitude changed when I mentioned Marcus. I don't want to press him and make him upset, so I'll leave the subject alone…for now.

"Thanks for hanging out with me tonight. If it weren't for you I'd be a total hermit," I say awkwardly, searching for something to hopefully break the tension.

"I like hanging out with you, Layla. I…I can be myself around you. I want you to know how much I appreciate that," he says.

"Well…I have a confession to make. You're not exactly like I thought you were going to be. I thought you were going to be pretentious and stuck-up. But, you're nothing like that at all. You're down to earth, funny…charming. You're easy to be around. So…I like hanging out with you, too," I tell him in some vain effort to make him stay.

"That's good to know. That's *very* good to know." Will smiles softly. Tonight there are no hugs, no intensified looks. Will simply turns and is on his way.

I go to bed but have a hard time falling asleep. There's something there – tension – between Will and Marcus. I like Marcus, but I'll end any friendship with him long before it really begins if my loyalty to Will demands. The more I think about it the more interested I become. After a while of theorizing, I make a final determination. Looks like I'll be visiting my new favorite bookstore in the morning.

Chapter 10

Claire is thrilled when I ask if I can use her car. Since I've been here I haven't driven anywhere. I make my way to town and am proud of myself as I enter and exit the two roundabouts that lead to Main Street, and even more proud that I didn't get lost. The roads back home are basically in a grid, but here, they're anything but.

I find a place to park in the small lot by the library. Parking there means I'll have to walk across the Village Green and cross Main Street to reach my destination. It also means I'll have some extra time to sort through my strategy for how to get Marcus to explain why Will was so bothered at the mention of his name. With every step across the Green I do my best to figure out how to smoothly bring Will into the conversation. I'm still not sure what I'll say or do, and even more sure it will not be done smoothly, but I put my hand on the doorknob and know that I've run out of time.

It's not until I'm standing at the front door to the bookstore that it occurs to me that Marcus might not even be here. *What's wrong with me?* I'm never this impetuous. But I'm here now, so I might as well go in. I don't see anyone right away, but then he appears.

"Hey, you're back!" Marcus greets me.

"Yeah, I didn't get to look around the whole store yesterday, so I thought I'd pop in and take a look." *Casual. Be casual,* I tell myself.

"Oh, great! We've got a great selection for a small store." Marcus walks toward me. "I can show you around, if you'd like."

"Sure," I say. It'll be easier to bring Will up in casual conversation if Marcus is right there with me.

"Are you looking for anything in particular?" he asks.

"Nope. I just love a good bookstore. You never know what you're going to find," I say.

"I was thinking…if you want to get a head start on your trig, we don't have to wait until school starts. I would be happy to start tutoring you now, or whenever you want." Marcus hesitates and stumbles over his words. He reminds me of myself when I talk to Will sometimes. I remember my thinking that he had been flirting with me during our first meeting, but the thought is fleeting as I focus on my intentions. His raising the tutoring subject is my chance. I take it because I don't know if a smoother segue will ever be handed to me.

"Well, it turns out I might not need you after all. I have a friend at school who offered to help. You know him. Will Meyer." I can feel my heart pounding inside my chest as I say Will's name, not knowing what kind of a response I'm going to get. The tension could all be on Will's side, or I could be opening a huge can of worms.

"Yeah. I know Will." Marcus gives the same dead-pan look that Will gave last night.

Can. Open. Worms.

"Is there something wrong?" I ask trying to sound even more clueless than I am.

"How good of friends are you with Will?" he asks.

"Very good friends. Why?" I say.

Marcus pauses, seeming to choose his words carefully before speaking. "Will is a really nice guy, Layla, but you need to be careful. Just…make sure you stay *just* friends with him." Marcus' cautionary tone is serious and only serves to intensify my need to know what's going on. *What does he mean, stay* just *friends?* I say to myself. Asking him what he means won't answer my questions about Will's reaction last night. I need more information.

"Will told me that he was friends with your sister, but your family moved. Why didn't you go with them?" I ask.

Marcus takes a deep breath and lets it out with a heavy sigh. I can't tell if he's annoyed at my questioning or upset at the subject matter. "My parents and Holly moved early last summer. I was already registered and set to start at Davidson so I stayed." His answer is short and curt.

"Oh, well, that makes sense. Didn't your dad work at the law firm?" I'm trying so hard to sound like I'm making curious conversation rather than holding an inquisition.

"Yeah, but…Gregory Meyer is…well, he and my father had differing opinions on some issues," he says, irritation rising in his voice.

"What did your fathers disagree on?"

"They disagreed on whether Will should date my sister or not."

I stop in my tracks and turn to face Marcus. "What?"

"Will and Holly started dating and Will's dad didn't think it was a good idea." Marcus is clearly getting upset. I can see that talking about his sister is difficult.

"So he fired your dad?" I ask in disbelief. I can't believe that Mr. Meyer would even be able to do that legally.

"My dad wasn't fired," he answers defensively. "Gregory Meyer made him an offer he couldn't refuse."

"Will's dad bribed your father to quit and relocate?" I'm sure the tone in my voice speaks to how ludicrous I think that is.

"Layla, you've got to understand something. Around here, Gregory Meyer is like royalty. He's done a lot for this community, but no one has a clue who he really is. He wants things the way he wants them, and if you get in his way…well…don't get in his way." Marcus is stern in his warning.

"I don't understand what this has to do with who Will dates?" I can't wrap my brain around the idea that Will's father paid Marcus' father off to leave town *just* so Will couldn't date his daughter. "You said Will's dad didn't think it was a good idea for Will and Holly to date? Why not?" I ask.

"I really shouldn't be telling you any of this. Will is your friend and I don't want to interfere." Marcus pauses and makes a hard line with his lips. "I have a lot of respect for Will. He was really upset when Holly left. He hounded me for a long time for her phone number. It was months before he stopped. He works hard to not be like his dad. I can't imagine it's very easy, considering how influential Gregory Meyer is. You could do worse as far as friends at Heyward go. All that said, you still need to be *really* careful, Layla. Listen, I've gotta get back to work. I'd still really like to tutor you, if you'd like. If not, I'd still really like to be your friend. Just let me know."

I walk back to the car slowly. I'm even more confused by Marcus' answers than my conversation with Will that sparked this quest. Marcus put a strong emphasis on me staying *just* friends with Will. Will and I are becoming *great* friends. In fact, I'd say he's my best friend. I've spent more time with him than anyone, and shared more with him than I have with anyone since my parents. I like hanging out with Will, and he likes hanging out with me. Will and I are friends and that's never going to change.

Chapter 11

The air is filled with the smell of hamburgers and chicken being grilled to perfection for Luke and Claire's annual end-of-summer bar-b-q. Neighborhood friends and co-workers from their office are slowly trickling in and making themselves comfortable under the shade of the trees in the backyard. They saunter around the yard like they're on parade. The girls who are soon to be my classmates stand in poses that look every bit uncomfortable as they do ridiculously awkward. It's like one of those weird America's Next Top Model photo shoots.

I can't smell the deliciousness of summer or get caught in the judgmental eye of the debutants because I am watching from the window in the loft, not sure I'm ready to meet this onslaught of guests. I've almost decided what illness I'll feign when Luke finds me.

"You can't hide up here forever," he says joining me at the window. "Although, this *is* probably the best seat in the house."

"I know. I'm sorry. I'm just not the best with big crowds of people. Especially when most of them will be judging every move I make," I say.

"Layla," Luke says, turning me to face him. "I know we didn't know you very well when you came to live here, but the one thing we have known from the very beginning is that you are a strong young woman. You have persevered and endured more, and faced worse than what waits for you down there. You're Layla Michelle Weston. You can handle anything."

"Thanks, Luke." His words of encouragement and vote of confidence unearth a well of emotions that I choose not to let escape. I think of my father and know that he would have said the same thing to me, and I find myself realizing that being here with Luke and Claire, among any other options I may have had, is truly the absolute best place for me to be.

"Don't worry. If you get cornered, just tell them I said you had to check on something and you're *oh, so sorry* that you have to go." Luke smiles, takes my shoulders and gives them a gentle squeeze. "Oh, Will and his parents just arrived."

I'm suddenly nervous and excited at the same time. I want to see Will, but I'm scared to meet his father. I would blame Marcus entirely for my fear if not for the deadly stare Mr. Meyer gave me the night I met Will. I just need some time to talk to Will before I face his parents. Maybe if I have a clearer picture of what Marcus meant when he said I should stay *just friends* with him I'll know better what to do or say or how to act.

I step outside into the courtyard and find that it is absolutely too late. Standing there in front of me are Will and his parents, Gregory and Eliana Meyer.

"Layla, you're here! Of course you're here, you live here!" Will stutters. He's surprised and uncharacteristically nervous. "Um…Layla, these are my parents, Gregory and Eliana Meyer. Dad, Mom, this is…my friend, Layla."

"It's very nice to meet you both," I reply, shaking both their hands with the best, most confident handshake I can muster.

"It's nice to meet you, dear. Will was just telling us about you on the way here. We weren't aware you two had become such good friends. We're so glad you're settling in well, and we're so sorry about your grandparents." Will's mother is the most eloquent speaker I've ever heard. She's almost too well spoken. It seems forced like Audrey Hepburn in *My Fair Lady*.

"Yes, William's been keeping you secret from us…and I can see why," Mr. Meyer says, as he looks me up and down. He's clearly evaluating my worthiness, but I don't know why he's acting like he's never seen me before. The man gave me more than the once over that night on the Green. "I had no idea he was cultivating such a *friendship* while he's been working for Luke." He says the word with abnormal disdain. "Now that we know you and

William are such good friends, we *must* have you and your aunt and uncle for dinner soon," he continues in a cool and mysterious tone. I can see where Will gets his charm. There's something about Gregory Meyer that is infectious. He is definitely more than a few years older than his wife – 15, maybe 20. Their age difference makes me wonder about her and I have to pinch myself for being so nasty.

"That would be very nice, thank you." I say as politely as possible.

Will's parents excuse themselves to go schmooze with the other guests. I look at Will and my heart sinks. I hadn't expected him to tell his parents about every minute we've spent together, but I'm hurt that he's never said anything about me at all. We've spent so much time together and have shared some very personal things. I just assumed he would have at least mentioned me.

I leave Will standing on the patio and walk toward the dock, plagued by the only conclusion I can come to: Will is embarrassed to be my friend. I should have known it was too good to be true. People like me don't fit with people like Will. He's just been hospitable to me this whole time. I feel so incredibly foolish. All I want is some time to gather my thoughts but Will is a few steps behind me as I reach our place on the dock.

"Layla? What's wrong?" he asks softly.

"Nothing." I don't want to cry. "I understand. It's ok, really."

"What are you talking about?" he asks, confusion crossing his face.

"I understand why you didn't want them to know we were…friends…or whatever it is we are," I stammer.

"What does that even mean?"

"I…I feel really stupid. I thought we were friends, but it's clear that you're embarrassed by me. I know I'm not like everyone else here, and I thought the same of you. But I guess not, so…I understand." I push out this response, barely finishing the last syllable without bursting into tears.

"Layla, it's not like that. I *am* different. I'm anything *but* embarrassed of my association with you. You don't understand," he says, starting to pace, running his hands through his hair.

"Then what is it? Why didn't you want them to know we're friends?" I ask.

Will continues to pace, shaking his head as if arguing with himself. He stops, seeming to have come to a conclusion of his own. It takes him a few moments before he speaks. "It's not that I don't want them to know we're friends. It's that I don't want them to know that…I want more than that." Will says.

"What?" I'm in shock. These are the last words I expected to hear in this moment, or ever for that matter. Even in my wildest of dreams I never imagined that Will would see me as anything but a friend. My heartbeat is increasing rapidly and I can feel the blood rushing to my head. I think I might faint.

"From the moment you slammed into me that night at the concert I have loved every second of every minute that I have spent with you. I would rather spend my time with you than with anyone else." He takes my hand in both of his.

I open my mouth to speak but nothing comes out. I'm speechless.

"But…my parents can't know," he says, releasing my hand and walking to the side of the dock. He rests his elbow on a post, and his head in his hand.

"Why can't they know?" This conversation is beginning to resemble the one I had with Marcus.

"It's complicated, Layla. Trust me."

"Does this have something to do with Holly?" I hate the way the words roll off my tongue and I immediately regret saying them.

"You…spoke with Marcus." Will breathes a heavy sigh. "Of all the people for you to randomly meet, it had to be him. I'm sure he gave you *all* the details." Will looks beaten down. He's plagued by whatever happened with Holly. I want to comfort him, but am selfishly afraid I won't get any answers if I do.

I approach him and put my hand on his arm. "Will, what happened with Holly?" I ask slowly, trying to sound soft and sympathetic.

It takes him a minute to speak and when he does there's such sadness in his voice. "Holly and I dated last year. She was the first girl I had ever met whose life goal wasn't to be a socialite. So, after a couple of months I introduced her to my parents as my girlfriend. Three weeks later she was gone. Her father relocated the family. I tried to get in touch with her but…I haven't heard from her since. I had no idea what really happened until Marcus told me." Will's head is heavy and he's lost the confident posture I've come to love.

"What did Marcus say?" I ask. This is far more information than what I got from Marcus. I'm both shocked and grateful that Will is being so forthcoming with me. But with every new piece of information, I realize that my life here is going to be much more complicated than I thought.

"He said that my father came to their house to convince Holly to break up with me. When she refused he gave her two options. She and her parents could relocate with more money than they could dream of, or they could stay and find themselves penniless. Mr. Reynolds knew my father has the connections to do it, so he chose curtain number one. I knew Marcus was telling me the truth because this is one of dad's trademark moves. He calls it the *House Call.* He gets people on their own turf so their defenses are down, and then he strikes. There isn't a business deal he's made that hasn't involved a *House Call.*

"I don't blame them for taking the deal. I just hate that I put them in that position. My father has done some terrible things before, but I never thought he'd hurt someone I cared about. I mean…I'm his *son.*" Will looks up at me and speaks with more seriousness than I've ever heard one person speak. "*That* is why he *can't* know how I feel about you. I won't put you in that position."

"Oh, Will." I put my arms around him and hold him as tightly as I can. I'm so glad that I chose to hug him that night on the porch. If not, I'm not sure I'd be brave enough to do it now, no matter how badly I wanted. "I feel the same way about you."

"Layla, I couldn't be happier to hear you say that. I don't want you to go away, and I would sacrifice being with you in order to at least have you close to me," Will says softly.

"William," a voice calls and disturbs our tender moment. We turn and see Will's father approaching the dock. "Is everything alright here?" he asks.

We stand there silently stunned and I decide that I must improvise to hopefully save Will from the backlash his father may offer.

"Yes, everything is fine, Mr. Meyer. I was just having a little homesick moment. I'm still adjusting to being away from all my friends back home. Will was being a good friend," I say, hoping I'm being convincing. I look at Will. "Thanks Will. I promise not to have another meltdown anytime soon."

"No problem, Layla. That's what friends are for. We've got each other's backs," he says.

"Well, just as long as everyone here is ok. William, your mother needs you to bring something in from the car." Mr. Meyer doesn't linger. He finishes what he has to say and turns to walk back up the path, fully expecting Will to follow him.

"Yes, sir," Will replies. "Thank you for that," he whispers to me.

"We'll talk about this later," I say quietly.

Will dutifully follows his father and disappears to the other side of the trees. I stand there on the dock for a long time. I can't move. Everything I now know is overwhelming my mind. The one thing that seemed to be so much an impossibility that I repeatedly shoved it away is now staring me in the face: Will wants *me*. That must be why he was so hot and cold with me. One minute seeming to want to be with me, the next changing his demeanor all together and disappearing on me. He was just scared. I don't know what to think or how to feel. I want to be happy, but I'm torn and confused. Here is this great guy who wants to be with me, and I want to be with him, but we can't be together.

The bigger issue is that I now know what happened with Holly. If Will and I were to be together…I know I can't be bought but…Luke and Claire…I don't think they have a price tag either, but what is the alternative? Would Gregory Meyer really destroy them if I refused to stay away from Will? The only thing I know for sure is that I want to be with Will, too. I just don't know how to make that happen. Will says it's possible, but maybe…

My thought process is sporadic and wild. Whatever we do, we'll need an ally. Luke and Claire are my best bet. If I ever wanted to test their trust, now is the time.

I'm fortunate to find Claire alone in the kitchen gathering snacks to refill outside. I waste no time and tell her the whole story of what transpired from the time I stepped outside and into Greg and Eliana Meyer to now. She isn't shocked in the least.

"Yes, that sounds about right," Claire replies, shaking her head.

"You knew Mr. Meyer was like this and you didn't say anything?"

"What was I going to say, Layla? I didn't know what would happen between you and Will."

"I really care about him, Claire. What am I going to do?" I sit down at the counter and put my head in my hands.

"You're not going to do anything. If you and Will can just hold out until graduation, Luke and I can help. But if you press this, if you press *him*, it could be disastrous," Claire says.

"I don't want you and Luke to get hurt. It would kill me if you lost everything because of me." I'm starting to hyperventilate, and all that comes to mind is the role I played in the death of my parents. I couldn't stand it if I was responsible for hurting Luke and Claire, too.

Claire takes me by the shoulders. "Calm down. It's ok. Luke and I know how to handle Gregory Meyer. Anyone who's worked for him for any length of time is smart enough to know that he can turn on you in an instant. We're prepared so don't worry about us. I'll fill Luke in tonight and we'll talk about this later. Now, you can go back outside and mingle like there's nothing wrong, or you can go upstairs and I can report an illness to anyone who asks. What would you like to do?" Claire's voice calms me. She handles crisis better than anyone I've ever known; an attribute that I'm certain makes her an outstanding attorney.

I think for a moment. "I'll go back outside. Chris and Tyler just got here, and Gwen and Caroline should be here soon. Thanks, Claire." I take a cleansing breath and exit through the French doors. I find Chris, Tyler and Will sitting at a table, eating. Will looks at me with uncertainty of where he and I stand now that I know his secret. I smile at him as best I can to let him know that everything is ok. At least, I think it's going to be ok.

I spend the remainder of the afternoon with my friends trying to act like my life didn't just take a 180-degree turn. I'm so cautious about doing anything that might create suspicion about Will's feelings for me, or mine for him, that I'm vigilant to the point that even *I* think it's overkill. Now that I know how Will feels about me it's impossible to go back. Regardless of the outcome, things will never be the same.

While the boys play Frisbee and toss a football around, Gwen and Caroline introduce me to several girls who are also students at Heyward. They are all very cordial, but as soon as they're out of earshot I'm filled in on exactly why I need to stay away from them. Those exchanges make me feel at ease; they're normal conversation for us. The girls run interference with certain others who are, according to them, especially vicious. I feel like I have my own personal security team.

At the end of the night, Will tells his parents that he offered to stay and help clean up. His father says he doesn't understand why Luke and Claire never hire anyone to do that for them, but he allows Will to stay. It is, after all, good PR for the Meyer family.

We sit in the courtyard attempting to sort through the situation. I just couldn't go to the dock. I'm afraid I wouldn't be able to think clearly if I sat there with Will in what I consider to be our place.

"I didn't tell my parents we were friends because I was afraid my feelings for you would be apparent. Just the thought of you makes my whole world stop." Will clears his throat, realizing he's made quite a statement about me *to* me. "In my world, girls like you and Holly are almost non-existent. My father would love to choose the girls I date, and has, but his criteria for women are different than mine, which is putting it mildly. I want someone of substance and he chooses girls based on how photogenic they are. His ideal woman wants a guy so obsessed with his job that she can lead her own life separate from him, only to show up on his arm at the appropriate black tie event or ribbon-cutting. That's what my dad wants for me." Will sighs heavily. "That's what my mother became: this submissive *thing* bending to his every whim. Now that he's met you, he knows that you're different, you're not like the others."

"How could he possibly know that I'm not like the other debutants around here?"

"Anyone who takes half a second of time with you knows that you're brilliant and focused. You are so beautiful but you have no idea just how beautiful you are. You're opinionated and have dreams that extend beyond being someone's arm-candy." I smile and am sure I'm blushing, too. No one has ever said such amazing things about me before. "And if he meets you again as the girl that *I* have chosen, it's only going to reinforce how hard I work not to be like him. It infuriated him that I was with Holly. He considered it a slap in the face to the empire he thinks he's built for me. It'll do the same for me to be with you. Layla, I can't risk losing you. I can't risk never seeing you again."

My head is spinning. His description of me tells me that I didn't completely lose myself while living with Gram and Gramps. The real Layla has been there all along, just waiting to be unearthed. I know the surfacing has been because of him.

"If we can't be together, why tell me how you feel at all?" I ask.

"I don't know. I guess I just wanted you to know. We've spent so much time together. It was killing me not knowing if you felt the same way. And I know I've acted a little hot and cold at times. I'm sorry about that. I know it's not ideal, but we can make the most out of the time we do have together until graduation, and the summer."

Wait. He's serious about us not being together. "Will…" I sigh, not sure what I'm about to say.

"I want you to always feel safe with me, Layla, and I will do whatever it takes to make sure you do. I'll do my best to protect you. I'm never going to let anyone hurt you." Will leans forward in his chair and takes my hand.

"I do feel safe with you. I'm just…confused and…I…I wish you hadn't told me. I could have at least gone along, obliviously pining away for you like some silly schoolgirl. Eventually I may have even given up. But now…" Not knowing what to say, I do the only thing that comes to mind. I stand, walk inside the house, and leave Will sitting there in the moonless night, alone.

Chapter 12

I've spent the last few days in seclusion in the loft, not sure what to think or how to feel. Nothing is unfolding the way I thought it would and I don't know what to do.

I tell Luke and Claire that I don't want to see or talk to anyone. Claire tells Gwen and Caroline that I'm sick when they call, and brings food up to me when Will is working with Luke, which has been every day. I avoid the lake because I know Will would look for me there. Claire also brings messages from Will. They're all the same: he wants to see me.

Sometimes I can hear him talking with Luke in the foyer. I love his voice and miss watching his lips form the words. I hear him tell Luke he just wants to talk to me for a minute; that he just wants to make sure I'm ok. Luke defends my wishes and tells Will he has to wait until I'm ready to talk to him. My heart wants me to scream out to Will and tell him that I miss him, but my mind won't allow it.

I spend hours in my favorite chair thinking…not thinking…staring. I don't want to move from this spot. I close my eyes and I can still feel Will's body against mine as we bet on the view that night. It allows me to be close to him when I'm not ready to see him yet.

I have to snap out of this and consider my options. I've wallowed long enough. I'm not about to stop being a sensible girl altogether.

I run through my options. First, I can leave. If I'm not here, I won't have to see Will and one day maybe it'll be as if I never met him. I can tell Luke and Claire that I want to go back to Florida. Maybe there's still a spot for me at that boarding school. After that I'll be at Florida State and out of everyone's hair. But, I'm growing closer to Luke and Claire every day and I don't want to leave them. They're all the family I have left and the thought of being without them is too painful.

Second, I can tell Will I want to be with him. I can throw caution to the wind, follow my heart, and let the pieces of Gregory Meyer fall where they may. If we do that, we run the risk of God only knows what. Everything I understand about Will's father tells me that he doesn't rest until he gets what he wants, and this scenario assumes that we are somehow impervious to the perils of Gregory Meyer.

My decision comes one morning as I wake from a dream that changes my perspective forever.

I'm in my room. Not my room at my parent's house, or at Gram or Gramps', but my room here with Luke and Claire. On my bed are several boxes marked with my name. Some are marked *old Layla* and some, *new Layla.* I find the boxes marked *old Layla* and put them on a high shelf in the closet. These are the boxes I brought when I moved in with Gram and Gramps. The other boxes marked *new Layla* are the ones I brought from Gram and Gramps' here to Luke and Claire's. I don't recognize all the things inside, but I accept them as mine, unpack them, and put them away.

My mother walks in and I'm so happy to see her that I stop what I'm doing immediately and run to her. She's dressed in her usual broomstick skirt, t-shirt, and sandals. My little hippy wraps her arms around me and I'm filled with oozing warmth from head to toe. I haven't felt that warmth in so long.

"What are you doing?" she asks in her sweet voice that I have missed so much.

"I'm unpacking," I say.

"Why did you put your things away in the closet?" she asks.

"Because those things belong to the old Layla. That's not me anymore."

"Why is that not you?" she says, crunching her face in confusion.

"I had to make life here easier for Gram and Gramps, so I put away everything I used to be," I say.

"But Jack and Carol aren't here. You aren't living that life anymore, are you?"

"No, I guess not," I say, my voice pitching up at the end with a tone of realization.

"When you were younger, you were the most tenacious little girl anyone had ever seen. If you wanted something, you did what you had to do to make it happen. You sacrificed so much to make things work with your grandparents. We all make sacrifices, Layla. It's part of growing up. Isn't it time you did something to make *you* happy?" She walks out of the room and I try to catch her. I reach out, try to run to her, but my arms won't stretch and my legs won't move.

And then she's gone.

I wake up, my face wet with tears, my heart aching from watching my mother vanish in front of my dreaming eyes.

Light is streaming almost blindingly through the thin line between the drawn curtains and I know it is mid-morning. Will should be here by now, working with Luke in the basement.

I stand at the top of the stairs in my pajamas, my hair in a ponytail. A shower will have to wait. I walk downstairs after several days of isolation and find Luke, Claire, and Will in the kitchen. They look up, startled by my emergence, but clearly happy to see me. They're all smiles. Will's brighter than the others.

"Layla!" Will says excitedly. He starts toward me but Luke stops him. I like Luke as a protector. It suites him well.

"It's ok, Luke." I look at Will, almost emotionless, not certain of how his feelings may have evolved over the last few days. Has he regretted telling me? Does he now feel I'm not worth his affection because of how I chastised him? But his beaming face shines a light on the probability that my refusal to see him hasn't changed anything. "We need to talk," I say as I walk outside and go to the only place I know where things somehow become clearer.

Without stopping, I walk straight to the end of the dock, not looking behind to see if or how far behind me Will might be. With every step I consider the reality that in moments I could be making the biggest fool of myself. Is Will satisfied having just made his feelings known? He made it clear that is impossible for us to be together. But since he didn't have to say anything in the first place, I resolve that he must truly care for me, and that tenacious little girl emerges once again, ready to claim what is mine.

"Layla. I'm so happy to see you." He tries to touch me but I pull away. I know it sends the wrong message, but I need to keep a clear mind. Feeling Will's skin against mine in any way is far too distracting. "I'm sorry, I shouldn't have…"

"What is it that you really want, Will?" I need to hear him say it, whatever it is. It has to be more than he *just needed me to know* before I bare my soul to him.

"I want…you," he says.

"What does that mean?"

"It means…I care about you, Layla. But…" I cut him off before he can tell me again that we can't be together.

"When I moved in with my grandparents I was dropped into a life that I didn't want. I didn't really know them and all my grandmother did for two years was prove why we never had a relationship with her to begin with. Nonetheless, I made sacrifices in order to make my grandparents happy.

"When I moved here with Luke and Claire I discovered that life didn't have to be that way. I didn't have to make sacrifices for everyone else's happiness at the expense of my own. I can make choices based on what will make me happy."

"What are you saying?" He looks at me, a bit bewildered.

"I'm saying…don't I get any say in the situation?" Will looks at me, wide eyed. "I'm saying…what if your father isn't the only one who doesn't stop until he gets what he wants? I want to be with you, Will. If you want to be with me…then maybe we can make it work," I say, fully aware that I'm doing something I haven't done since before my parents died: making my desire known, regardless of the risk of getting hurt.

"It's not safe, Layla. I…I don't know what he'll do…" he protests.

"Then he won't find out. I'm not going anywhere," I say with conviction.

"You…want to be with me…even though no one can know? Even though if my father finds out I can guarantee he'll make our lives a living hell?" Will's tone reflects both elation and disbelief.

"Will, I spent the better part of two years being reminded daily that I wasn't worthy of anything good. Then I spent three years taking care of my grandfather, both loving him and believing that I was being punished. So, with all due respect to your father, I've already been through hell. I won't let someone else determine my worth anymore. I was recently reminded that I used to be full of audacity. I'm reclaiming that."

"I…can't believe I found you," Will says brushing my cheek with his hand. "Are you sure you can do this? Hell, *I* don't even know how to do this. I've *never* defied him, Layla. But for the first time in my life, I have the uncontrollable urge to do so. I have you to thank for that." He smiles, taking my hands in his. My heart literally flutters as his skin connects with mine and I'm overwhelmed.

"Yes. I'm sure. But…the only way it's going to happen is if we have Luke and Claire on our side. I already told Claire about our conversation at the bar-b-q…and about Holly." I watch him cringe slightly and can only pray I haven't broken him a little in the process. "But maybe now that some time has passed, it'll be different with me?"

"No offense, but he's not going to be anything more than cordial to you, if that. He's certainly not going to look at you as a viable option for me."

"Why not?" I know I shouldn't be, but I'm a bit offended.

"You're inconsequential to him," Will says matter-of-factly.

"Harsh."

"It's not you. My father only gets to know people he can use to his benefit. You have nothing to offer him, so he's not going to waste his time. Personally, I think it's a tragedy *not* to get to know you." Will says the last part so sweetly I feel my heart swell. "But you need to really grasp the reality of the situation. I know now that what he pulled with Holly's family is just the tip of the ice berg of what he's capable of." I can see that Will means what he says.

"So now what?" I ask.

"Now…we talk with Luke and Claire. I agree with you. The only way this has any chance of survival is if we have their backing." His whole stance has changed. He's oozing confidence and strength and my attraction for him skyrockets. He's commanding and I feel how his protectiveness of me, of us, has becoming priority number one.

"Does anyone know? I mean, did you say anything to Gwen or Caroline, or the guys? I just wondered if anyone was safe."

"Yes. They know. Next to you, they're the people I trust most. They were here during the whole thing with Holly, so they're pretty protective of me, but they don't know the whole story. They know my father paid her dad off, but they don't know about the threat to wipe them out financially. They just think Holly's dad was a sucker. I'd like to keep it that way. I don't want them to worry any more than they already do. They think the world of you and were really supportive of whatever I decided."

"What do you mean, whatever you decided?"

"Well…I decided that I didn't want to be without you. But, I meant what I said, Layla. If I have to not be with you so that you don't disappear on me, I'll do that. I'll do whatever it takes to keep you in my life," he says, pulling me closer. "Are you still sure you really want to do this?"

"Yes. I thought about it a lot. This is what I want. *You* are what I want," I declare with joy. I love staring into Will's ocean blue eyes, and now I feel like I've been given permission to stare as long as I want. This is my time. My penance has been paid and my reward has just enveloped me in his arms. "I hope it's ok that I already told Claire."

"I would have thought it strange if you hadn't. I've had several conversations with Luke over the past few days. He knows how I feel about you. He's not completely jazzed about the idea of us being together, mainly because he knows more about my father than most. But…fortunately he likes me, and he's willing to be supportive. More than that, he loves you and wants you to be happy. Of course, he and Claire don't know what *you've* decided."

I find it romantic that Will has talked with Luke about his feelings for me. It makes me feel good to know that they're supportive. If this is the journey I think it's going to be, I may need a shoulder to cry on at some point.

Luke and Claire are still in the kitchen when we walk in. I know Claire has already talked with Luke, but I still need to explain my decision to be with Will. Luke is more concerned than Claire, but that's ok. He knows things about Gregory Meyer that no one does and I'm sure he's more scared than he's letting on.

"You need to know that this is not my first choice, Layla. I'd prefer that you not get involved with Will romantically at all. No offense, Will." Luke makes his position clear while Will nods his understanding. "But Claire and I will support you and help in any way we can. We'd rather know what's going on than have the two of you sneaking around on us. We must have full disclosure from you both."

"What do you mean *full disclosure*?" I ask.

"Don't do anything stupid. Keep us in the loop," Luke says with a deadpan look. "We can't help you if you keep *anything* from us," Luke says seriously. "It will get messy if Gregory finds out. You need to be prepared." *Messy?* What does that mean? I feel like I should be asking more questions but I don't think I can wrap my head around this fully. I'll just have to cross each bridge as we get to them.

We're lucky that Luke and Claire like Will so much. I don't think they'd have taken the risk for anyone else.

Will had already been at the house for hours helping Luke with the basement when I emerged this morning. Our conversation interrupted their progress and Luke declares it's time to get back to work. I can only imagine the conversation between the two of them as they descend into the basement.

Will gives me a sweet wink as he passes through the doorway, and Claire and I follow Luke's lead and return to a level of normalcy by doing the dishes.

"Are you certain this is what you want, Layla? You've been through so much. I just don't want you to take on anything more than you can handle," Claire says, looking and sounding more like a mother in this moment than she has before.

"I haven't had control over any part of my life since my parents died. When I came here I told myself that this was my opportunity to start over, to revive the Layla that died a slow and painful death. Deciding to be with Will is just about the biggest way I can take back control. I'm so glad we have your support because there is nothing that is going to keep me away from Will. I would hate to lose you and Luke now, just when I got you." I've shocked myself in the assertion of my position. Being that bold is not something that I thought came naturally to me anymore. And while I truly hope I haven't offended Claire, I am pleased with myself that I didn't falter.

"There's the Weston passion I was looking for." Claire smiles approvingly, joining us in allegiance.

I smile back at Claire knowing that I have shown both my resiliency and my heart. I held in so much for so long, any expression like this feels like emotional vomiting. Claire didn't silence me, or even flinch. I have a feeling she has given her support much more freely than Luke has.

"You've got a few calls to return," Claire tells me moving us forward into normalcy. "Gwen and Caroline called every day. So did Marcus Reynolds."

How I had forgotten about Marcus is beyond me. He's partly the reason all this came to a head in the first place. I need to talk to him. I was pretty rude to him and I need to apologize.

"Did he say anything?" I wonder.

"He said he was sorry and asked you to please call him." She just looks at me, probably wondering what I'm doing to these poor boys.

"Did he leave a number?" I ask.

"He said you could call him at the bookstore…or come by anytime," Claire says, handing me the keys to her car. Clearly she thinks I need to talk to him in person. The guys are going to be in the basement for a while so I take the keys and decide to go see him after a quick change out of my pajamas. I'll feel better about apologizing in person anyway.

I walk into the bookstore and look for Marcus. There's no one up front and I carry a twinge of hope that he's not there as I walk in, but about halfway through the store I find him.

"The security here is a little lax, you know," I say smiling, trying to make peace.

"Hey," Marcus replies, quietly surprised to see me. "I'm glad you came. Layla, I'm so sorry. I got carried away with the information the other day. It's still painful to think about the whole thing. But like I said, Will's a good guy. Just be careful, ok?"

"No, I'm sorry. To be honest with you, I came here looking for answers and it all just blew up in my face. Will told me about Holly and I…well, I guess I just wanted to hear both sides. I'd still like you to tutor me…and I'd still like to be your friend, if the offers still stand," I smile hopefully.

"Of course." Marcus sticks out his hand to shake mine. "Friends?"

"Friends."

"You know, you have a knack of showing up here when I'm getting ready to leave. I'm headed out on a break, you wanna join me?"

"Um…I don't have a lot of time, but, sure." I walk with Marcus to the Soda Shop where we sit outside while he eats lunch.

"You sure you don't want anything?" he asks.

"No, thanks." I pause, thinking if I should tell Marcus about Will and me or not. He has given such a stern warning about staying *just friends* with Will that I don't see him responding well. I decide it isn't a good idea, and to let Will determine who can and can't know about us. So I continue to smooth things over with Marcus instead. "I'm really glad things are good between us. I didn't like how we left things last week," I say.

"Me, too. I like you, Layla. I'm looking forward to getting to know you better," he says.

"Well there will be plenty of time to get to know me while you spend countless hours saving me from death-by-trigonometry," I laugh. "I like you, too, Marcus. You know, Will had nothing but nice things to say about you and your family."

"Really," Marcus says, not as a surprised question, but with a tone full of nothing but skepticism.

"Yeah. He still feels terrible about the whole thing," I say, cursing myself for not thinking before speaking.

"Good. He should. He knew his father would flip but he didn't care," he says sharply, his demeanor quickly morphing into defensiveness.

"C'mon, Marcus! Who could predict that his father would do what he did?" I feel myself getting upset. I'm not defending *just a friend* anymore, and I fully recognize that we can absolutely count on Will's father flipping on us.

"You're right. I'm sorry," he says, calming himself. "How about we agree not to talk about Will Meyer? We'll just take any conversation about him completely off the table. Ok?"

"I think that is an excellent idea," I answer, relieved. Will is off limits so I won't have any reason to tell Marcus anything.

"When does school start? We can get a jump on that trig…if you want," he offers.

"Three weeks, I think. I'll give you a call and get something set up. Or you can call me…whichever." I stand up and grab my keys. "I've gotta go. Thanks for letting me stop by, Marcus. It means a lot to me that you called, too."

"Thanks for coming by. I was afraid I wouldn't see you again. Don't be a stranger. You know where to find me," he says.

"Bye, Marcus," I say.

I walk back to the car and get in. I sit there for a few minutes thinking about Marcus. Everything is going to be ok. I can be friends with him and more with Will. I feel like things are beginning to settle down and fall into place. I have to take Will's father out of the equation totally. If I focus on him I'll completely fall apart. With that, I realize that for the first time in a really long time, I'm happy.

I pull out of the parking lot and get completely twisted around and find myself on a side street somewhere behind the library. As I sit getting my bearings I see that I'm sitting directly in front of the Law Offices of Meyer, Fincher and Marks.

It's a beautiful old house that has been converted into an office. There is a round, gazebo-like covered porch, complete with a porch swing, and wooden slats that remind me of fish scales.

Staring at the house-turned-office space I think about the deals made and the lives torn apart within its walls. As I bring myself back into the moment, I catch movement in my periphery. To the side, near the back of the house I can see the back of Gregory Meyer. He's directing someone, or thing. He moves just enough to his left to conceal half of his body behind the building, and enough to reveal two men holding another man between them, shuffling mostly into view. That knot in my stomach has returned and I'm frighteningly aware that if I look any longer I may be witness to something no one is supposed to see.

I want to move, but I can't. My foot won't leave the brake. *Drive, Layla, drive! Just turn the wheel and get the hell out of here.* It's no use because what happens next happens all too fast. The two men reveal themselves as thugs and begin taking turns punching the slumped mess of a man between them in the gut. It seems to be going on and on and on. *Oh my god!* Finally the man begins to vomit and the hoods release him into a crumpled mess on the ground, landing in his own sickness. Not that I can hear anything, but I turn the radio up in some attempt to tune out what I'm seeing. I can't even begin to imagine what this man did or didn't do to deserve this beating, but whatever it was, it surely was a betrayal that Gregory Meyer was not going to let go unpunished. Perhaps this is what happens when you refuse the *House Call* offer.

My heart beats faster and my foot has finally decided to obey the command I've been screaming at it. I turn the wheel and move as quickly around the corner and down Main Street as fast as I can without drawing attention to myself. *I'm a girl*, I think. *He wouldn't do that to me…would he? And there's no way he'd physically hurt his own son, right?* I spend the drive home telling myself that Will and I are different. Surely a father wouldn't do anything so outrageous to his own son.

It's after four o'clock by the time I get into the shower. It had been a long day already and I let the hot water rush over me longer than I usually do as I consider the scene I just witnessed. It feels wonderfully cleansing, baptismal. I spend the time rationalizing and convincing myself that while Gregory Meyer is a ruthless man, he would never physically hurt his own son.

I step out of the shower, wrap a towel around me, and wipe the steamy condensation off the mirror. I'm looking at a girl who's been missing for quite some time. This is a girl who is finally experiencing life and excited about it. I'm taking control and deciding what *I* want…finally. Will is the best reward I could have received for having endured the last five years as I did. Having Luke and Claire is the bonus.

I did it. My penance is paid and I am…mostly free. Gregory Meyer is the last thing standing in the way of my total and complete freedom. I'm not going to let him ruin this for me. If I can adapt to handle the last five years, I can do anything now knowing that Will is my prize at the end.

Chapter 13

I walk out into the loft and am pleasantly surprised to find Will there, waiting patiently for me on the couch. My heart skips a beat as he stands and greets me with that brilliant smile of his. He's sweetly nervous and it makes me smile even brighter.

"Hi," he says, taking three perfect steps toward me. He has obviously gone home, showered and changed because he's anything but sweaty and dirty. He's perfect. Who am I kidding? Even sweaty and dirty Will is perfect.

"Hi! What's up?" I ask full of joy.

"Well, I wanted to ask you something," he says a bit sheepishly.

"Ok. Ask away." I bite my lower lip to keep from grinning like a fool.

"Layla, would you please do me the honor of letting me to take you out…on a date…officially…tonight?" He looks at me with a sweet intensity that leaves me breathless.

For a moment I'm speechless. I run through every acceptable answer in my head, from cute to coy to mimicking his intensity. I go for simple honesty and say, "Absolutely."

Since Will was alone in the loft, I assume he's already spoken to Luke and Claire about tonight. He'd have to explain why he wanted to wait for me there rather than anywhere else.

It must have been a weird experience for them. I'm sure they expected it at some point, but perhaps not this soon, and certainly not like this. I blame Luke. If he didn't have Will come to work on the house with him, I wouldn't have met him again until school started and my plan of pretending to have never met Will Meyer would have gone undisturbed. Not blame, thank.

"Mr. and Mrs. Weston, we're just going to get some dinner. We won't be back late, but is there a particular time you'd like Layla home?" Wow. I never thought about this scenario in my whole life. Not the date part, but the old-fashioned chivalry that Will exercises so freely. It fills me with a feeling I'm having difficulty describing. Perhaps this is what being made to feel special feels like.

"As long as she's home by midnight, I think that'll be fine." Luke sounds so parental. I think he likes it. I can tell his caution about my being with Will is not going to wane any time soon, but that's ok with me. It's nice being the one taken care of instead of the other way around.

"Thank you…for everything." I'm so grateful to Luke and Claire for how understanding and supportive they're being. It is the most important element in my ability to move on with my life. I felt stunted for so many years, and now it's like the chains have been released. I'm free to give and receive love, and to reclaim myself.

Will unlocks and holds the passenger side door open of his car for me and I get in. I watch him walk in front of the car, making his way to the driver's door. As if in slow motion, I see every movement he makes. One arm swings at his side while he runs his other hand through his hair. He smiles and I wonder what just ran across his mind. As his seatbelt clicks into place he looks at me with his irresistible blue eyes and I'm gone.

We drive down the tree-lined streets of the neighborhood and I can't help but be nervous. This isn't just *our* first date, it's *my* first date, and here I am with Will. He's more than I could have ever dreamed of for myself, and he wants to be with *me*. I'm certain I don't deserve him, but I'll ride this out as long as I possibly can.

We get to a light and Will turns to me. "You look beautiful, by the way. I like your hair down like that."

I smile and say thank you as I realize he's never seen me with my hair down. I wanted this to be special, so I put some actual effort into how I looked and changed my clothes and did my hair before we left. My pride in having achieved my goal is shoved aside when the awareness of what is happening occurs to me. It makes me so nervous that I consider shielding my face from the window.

"Will, aren't people going to see us out together? I mean, if someone sees us, and tells your father…"

"We don't need to worry about that where we're going. I have an idea for tonight that I think you'll like." He glances at me once to see my reaction, but quickly put his eyes back on the road.

"I'm sure whatever you have planned will be great." I mean it. I really don't care what we do. I don't have anything to compare it to anyway. I just want to be there, with him. If Will thinks we'll be ok, then I trust him. "Am I…dressed ok?" I stutter out.

"You look perfect. Beautiful." He looks at me for a long time and I can feel the blood rushing to my cheeks and my body temperature rising. There's something about being alone with Will that makes me know that I am being forever changed. I can feel the warmth of his body, and smell his cologne. It's comforting, natural.

Will reaches over and quietly takes my hand in his. "Is this…ok?" he asks.

"Always," I tell him. I can't imagine a time when I wouldn't want Will to hold my hand.

We pull into the parking lot of a small shopping center. It isn't new and trendy like the one I went to with Claire. This one is definitely older. There's a department store, a hair salon, and a hole in the wall bar, among some other odds and ends places. Will opens my door, as I am learning to allow, and we walk to the sidewalk in front of the stores. He leads us to a grocery store and as we walk in I immediately think, *we're going grocery shopping?*

He stops my thought process in its tracks. "We're not going grocery shopping." If he can really read my mind, I'm going to be in big trouble. He picks up a shopping basket and takes us through the store. He obviously knows where he's going, so I just follow.

"I'm going to give you one tiny glimpse into my plan. This place makes great gourmet sandwiches. Pick out anything you want. They're all really good." Whatever his idea is, he is so pleased with himself. He's grinning from ear to ear and I can see he really wants to make this special.

He points out the ready-made sandwiches and I pick chicken salad with tarragon mayo. I'm not sure if I'll like it, but it sounds good. Will chooses some kind of ham and cheese. He also puts a big bag of Baked Lays, and fork/knife/napkin packets in the basket.

"Do you like coleslaw, or maybe potato salad? Or maybe just some of these olives?" His coolness is leaving him and he's starting to act nervous. It makes me nervous, too, so I look around to see if anyone has spotted us. There are only few people in the store, and no one I recognize, of course. No one seems to be looking at us, so I guess we're in the clear.

Then I realize he's nervous because he wants this to be so special for me that it's making him worried. I make it my goal to spend every minute of my time with Will letting him know that everything he does makes me feel special. I never want him to worry about that.

"Uh…coleslaw is good. And I like olives, so…whatever you want is great."

"I'll get both. What would you like to drink?" He directs me to the cooler next to the deli section where I don't recognize any of the soda brands. I choose cream soda because, well, you can't go wrong with cream soda.

As we walk back to the car Will's nervousness is dissolving. He lets me in on my side and then puts our dinner in the trunk. When he gets back in the car he's smiling again. His confidence is returning and I feel a wave of peace come over me.

We've mixed in with the traffic already when I ask, "So, can I have a clue as to what we're doing because so far we just ran an errand." I giggle.

"No clues. You'll see soon enough. I think you're going to love it." We're at a red light already so he holds his piercing blue eyes on me a moment longer. Waves of emotion wash over me every time his eyes meet mine. I live for these moments. It's in these moments that the rest of the world vanishes into nothing, and all I see is Will and myself. The pain of my past is gone and I see a future ahead of me, filled with joy. "You know, that's become my favorite sound in the whole world."

"What sound?"

"Your laugh. The first time I really heard it was the night I stayed for dinner. We sat on the dock together and that was the night that I knew I wanted to be with you." His tone is smooth and confident, and I am, again, overwhelmed with joy that this is my life now.

"Well…I have a feeling you'll be hearing a lot of it." I can't control my smile. I've come undone and Will Meyer is the source. I want to feel this way forever.

The light turns green and we're headed back in the direction of home. We take the exit off the highway and then turn into our neighborhood. We're clearly going back to Luke and Claire's. I'm confused. Are we going to watch a movie or just hang out? If so, why all the fuss to go pick up food? We could have ordered in.

We pull into the circular driveway and Will parks parallel to the front door. As I get out of the car, Will retrieves our dinner from the trunk along with a backpack. Closing the trunk he looks me square in the eyes and says, "Ready?"

What I want to tell him is that I'm ready for anything as long as it's with him. I sum up my feelings and say, "Absolutely."

Will grabs my hand and I follow him around the side of the house wondering why we aren't using the front door. It's beginning to get dark, but there is plenty of light in the backyard. We walk across the patio and follow the flagstone path to the dock, both silent every step of the way. The only sound I hear is the occasional snapping twig and my excited heartbeat. Will stops when we get to where the path ends and the dock begins.

He pauses a moment and then says, "Wait here for a sec."

I'd wait an eternity for you.

He hands me the bag with our dinner and walks out onto the dock. Taking the backpack off, he crouches down and opens it. From it he pulls a huge red blanket and spreads it out. The deep color against the white painted dock is striking in the light orange hues of the sunset. He sets out two plates, which look like they're made of glass so I'm impressed they didn't break in the bag. He takes the food and gestures for me to sit on the blanket.

My heart is racing and my mouth is dry. As I sit down and crisscross my legs, I'm very glad I wore shorts. My first option was a skirt, which would have increased my nervousness by a million percent in this moment. The sun is setting behind the trees and the sky is filled with orange and purple hues. It's my favorite time of day.

The water is still with the exception of the occasional fish coming up to kiss the underside of its home. Will sits at an angle next to me so that we can face both each other and the lake. I can smell his cologne again. It's a clean scent that suits him well and only adds to the physical part of my attraction to him.

"Oh, I almost forgot!" Will reaches into the backpack and fishes out a flashlight. He switches it on and off to show me that it works. "For later. I can't have you stumbling all over the place," he jests.

"Oh, are we going to be here that long?" I tease him back.

"You don't have to be back until midnight. The lights go out at eleven so I've got an hour with you in the dark." There's passion in his eyes and I have to catch my breath. This can't be real. I want to pinch myself and wake up. I'm certain if this dream goes on any longer I'll somehow mess it up completely. I drop my head in awe and embarrassment, focusing my attention on unwrapping my sandwich. My heart and mind are at war. It feels so natural and right to be with Will like this, but I have no point of reference, no words of wisdom passed down to me to know what to do. I don't want to look like a fool.

"So…is this ok?" He's slow in his speech and cautious with his words. He can tell I'm feeling overwhelmed.

"It's wonderful. Thank you," I say. "You're really working on making this *better than nice*, aren't you?"

"Is it working?" he says.

"It's definitely better than nice. It's perfect, Will." I can feel the rush of heat to my cheeks and I bite my lip again to keep the Cheshire grin I'm fighting from revealing itself.

"Layla, I know that us being together isn't going to be the smoothest thing. But I want you to know that in every moment, no matter what happens, *you* are where my heart is." He sighs, frustrated, hesitant to say what's on his mind. "My father…he corners me into doing a lot of things I don't want to do. I need you to understand that I don't want to be with anyone else. I want to be with you."

Corners him into doing what? I think, but don't dare ask aloud. "I understand, Will. I don't want anyone else either." Will brushes my cheek with his hand and I feel warm all over.

That's enough intensity for now so I awkwardly change the subject. "So…we never really talked about our hiking adventure to Grandfather Mountain. I'm glad I went. And I didn't fall once!" We both chuckle. "I felt like an idiot though. Every time I turned around, someone was catching me staring in awe with my mouth gaping open."

"We don't do that enough. We're so used to the scenery that we take it for granted. Having you around is refreshing…in a lot of ways." His silky voice makes it hard to concentrate. He could recite the Gettysburg Address and I would still be smitten. "Gwen and Caroline are crazy about you, you know. They're happy to have another girl in the group so they're not outnumbered. The guys think you're pretty great, too. Like I said before, you're refreshing."

"That's great, because I like them, too. I didn't really have a lot of friends back home."

"I find that very hard to believe," he says.

I want to be honest with him, but I'm afraid. Afraid I'll say too much and then the dream will be over before I've fully enjoyed it. I'm afraid of telling him that what little leisure time I had consisted of puzzles, game shows, and homework. How I longed for excitement but stifled it for my overbearing and resentful grandmother. I mostly stifled myself because of my guilt. I was utterly and completely boring and no one wanted to be friends with a geriatric baby sitter. I want to tell him all these things and more, but I can't. I don't want to be that girl anymore. I want to be different and create a new life here. He's risking so much to be with me. How can I tell him that I'm really not worth it?

"Well…I was really focused on taking care of my grandparents…so…not a lot of time for friends." I take a bite of my sandwich and wait for his response. I haven't given what I would consider a satisfactory response, but it will have to do for now.

"I think that's really admirable, Layla. Not a lot of people, let alone someone our age, would give up so much to take care of someone else. We're all so…self-absorbed, so consumed with ourselves." His eyes turn serious and introspective. "You should always be proud of what you did and who you are, and anyone who didn't take the opportunity to know you when they could is a fool."

"You give me too much credit. I…thanks." I can't tell him. It's too soon. I change the subject to the first thing about him that comes to mind. "So, tell me more about your non-ivy league dreams. If you don't want to follow in your father's footsteps, what *do* you want to do?"

He hesitates. "It's not that I don't want to follow in his footsteps...necessarily. I want to be successful like him, just in my own way. You know, without threatening and manipulating people? I love my dad because he's my dad. But…he's a very, *very* determined individual. When he sets his mind to something, it happens, which is why we have to be careful. He's like a rocket – completely unstoppable. It makes it hard to have a reasonable conversation with him, because if you don't agree with *him*, you're being unreasonable. He can't grasp the idea that money isn't the most important thing to some people."

"Why *isn't* money important to you?"

"Why *should* it be?" His question is hard. He doesn't understand my meaning and his immediate reaction tells me I hurt his feelings.

"I…I don't know. I'm sorry. I didn't mean to upset you." I didn't mean it the way it came out. I'm genuinely curious why someone with more money than I can fathom isn't interested in a single dime of it, but I should have known better than to ask. Will has done nothing but prove his disdain for the kind of wealth his father propagates and I disregarded that in six little words.

"I'm sorry. I get worked up when it comes to my dad. And…I'm nervous. You make me nervous," he says shyly.

"I make you nervous?" I ask in astonishment. This makes me smile and I relish in this moment before Will speaks again.

"Layla, this is a big deal, how I feel about you. I don't want to mess it up."

"How I feel about you is a big deal, too. But…I have to warn you, I don't have a clue what I'm doing." I turn away from him, embarrassed.

"Don't worry. We're in this together. I promise," he says lifting my chin with his hand.

"But your dad…"

"Layla, it's not about you. Don't take this the wrong way, but…you could be anyone. He doesn't understand me, or *any* of the choices I make. I told you before that I really like the work I'm doing with your uncle. My dad thinks I'm too smart for *that kind of work*. He doesn't understand the satisfaction it brings me, and he certainly won't understand what I see in you." His eyes are suddenly brighter – confirmation that his passion is deeper than the number of zeros in his bank account. He quickly changes directions, "Ok. This is decidedly the worst first-date conversation ever! I promise not to be so deep and depressing next time."

"You think there's going to be a next time?" I say, teasing him and helping to lighten the mood.

"What? You're not impressed with my moonlight picnic?" He spreads his arms out to feature his handy work.

"I'm *very* impressed. You've ruined it for any other guy," I say, laughing with him.

"I don't plan on giving any other guy a chance to outdo me." His passionate stare makes me nervously excited. "I'm…drawn to you, Layla. I've never felt that way before. I'm with you and it's like…lightening in a bottle. I'm sorry that it took tragedy to bring you here, but I am *so* glad you're here."

I'm filled with so much joy that my whole body tingles. "You make me happy, Will. It's been a long time since I felt truly happy, so…thank you."

"No, thank *you*. I can't believe you're braving so much to be with me."

"That's what you do when you care about someone as much as I care about you." I smile knowing that my mom would be proud.

Will picks up his bottle of soda and clanks mine in a toast. We spend the next hours laughing and talking about the important *un*important things in life like favorite colors and foods. We compare embarrassing childhood stories and share the woes and thrills of being only children. It's hard to talk about my childhood without saying too much about my parents. I'm not ready to tell him everything, and not sure I could get through talking about them without breaking down. But with every moment that passes, I'm thrust into a place of connectivity I didn't know existed. I hang on every word Will says. I feel wanted with every question he asks, but inadequate with every answer I give. He deserves more than my boring life but doesn't hesitate once during his inquiry of the details of my life. He wants to know me just as much as I want to know him. There isn't a second of silence in those hours.

We eventually pack up the picnic, take our shoes off, and sit at the edge of the dock. He sits so close I can hear his breathing and feel the warmth of his body. It's intoxicating and I never want to move from his side. I am so completely comfortable in his presence. It's like this moment was ordained since the beginning of time. I can't imagine there being anyone better than Will, nor can I imagine anything better than sitting next to him in this very spot at this very moment.

The moon is brilliant and bright and I'm so in awe of it that I don't think about what I do next. Without a word, I lay back on the dock to get a fuller, more comfortable view of the moon. Will follows my lead and lies next to me. Then, eyes staring at the incomprehensible glow, he reaches over and quietly slips his hand in mind. This moment is different than in the car. We've connected in a deeper, more passionate way since then. A shock surges through my body and I take one solitary deep breath to savor the moment.

It's only a few minutes before I am completely overwhelmed. The emotions of everything I've been through in the past weeks and months are coming to a head and I can't stop it from pouring out. I try to fight the tears back, but it's too much.

"Layla, are you crying?" He sits up and effortlessly pulls me upright with him. I hate that he's seeing me cry. I need to be stronger than this.

"No." I lie, although I don't know why since the tears streaming down my face are evident.

"Did I do something to upset you? I'm sorry," he says. He's the only good thing in my life and he thinks *he* upset me. Impossible.

"You didn't do anything, Will. I just…it's been an overwhelming time in my life. You've come to me at just the right moment." In one smooth motion Will puts his arm around me and draws me to him. I lean against his shoulder and bury my face into his chest finding comfort. His arms wrap around me like a warm blanket and I realize it's the safest I've felt in years. It's at this exact moment that no matter what happens I know my heart will forever belong to Will Meyer.

I don't know how long we've been sitting here…me nestled in Will's embrace. It doesn't matter. I could rest here forever. At some point it occurs to me that Luke said I needed to be home by midnight. I *am* home, and I can stay out here with Will, in his arms, all night if I want to, but reality strikes when Will releases me and asks if I'm ok.

I take a deep breath. "I'm ok. My emotions just got the best of me. I'm so sorry. Who cries on their first date? Seriously! So embarrassing!" I wipe my face and hope my eyes aren't too puffy.

Will gently brushes the hair out of my face. "Layla, you can cry, laugh, scream at the top of your lungs, or sit silently with me anytime. If you need to cry, I'm going to catch every tear, and I promise to do my best to never be the cause of a single one."

I take a cleansing breath and soak up the compassion in his voice. Its calm tenor penetrates my heart and I feel immediately at ease.

"It's pretty late. I should get home," he sighs, checking his watch. "Wow. It's 12:30. It's a good thing I told Luke what I had planned for tonight."

"You told him?" I say in surprise.

"Yes. I felt like if Luke was going to trust me with you I had to be honest with him about everything. We can't do anything to lose their support," he says, taking me by the shoulders.

"I agree." I sigh, partially from crying, but mainly from simply being in Will's presence.

We stand up and put our shoes on and start walking back to the house. We're halfway up the path when Will needs to turn the flashlight on because the moonlight is no longer enough to sustain our vision. As we walk he takes my hand again, instinctively. It's magical. We walk around the side of the house and back through the gate, our path lit only by the beam of the flashlight. Will releases my hand only as long as it takes to unlatch the gate and let me through. I don't hear the crash of metal before our hands are entwined again.

We reach Will's car and I stand next to him while he puts the backpack in the passenger seat. I'm waiting to begin our good-byes when Will puts his hand on the small of my back and guides me up the porch steps to the front door. Forever a gentleman.

He faces me and takes both my hands in his. "I had a really great time with you tonight, Layla. Actually, every moment I spend with you is amazing. I meant what I said. I'm not going anywhere." He's intense and holds my gaze while the earth stands still. The wind blows through the trees and crickets chirp, all in a serenade. He pauses and takes a deep breath. "I'm sorry. I don't mean to scare you. This is happening kind of fast, huh?" It's adorable to see Will nervous, as if he has any reason to be anxious. He has no idea that I'm already completely and irrevocably his.

I hesitate only a moment before I respond because I've decided that I'm *not* going to be scared. I'm not going to hold back on my feelings anymore. "Everything was perfect, Will." I smile knowing that there isn't one ounce of nervousness in me. "And, I'm not going anywhere either."

Will has done what I didn't think was possible. He has delivered me to a place of peace. A place where, with him, I don't have to be afraid to embrace who I am and what I want. I'm delighted to see him show the smile that has become a ray of hope for me. Hope that I can go on after so much pain. Hope that this girl, who knows more about death than life, can find an existence beyond tragedy. Hope that my penance has been paid and I'm free to live again.

Will lets go of my hands and wraps his arms around my waist. I intuitively lift my hands up his arms to his shoulders, and in one flawless, fluid motion Will presses his lips to mine. It's not passionate, but sweet, like a first kiss should be. His lips are soft and smooth and his kiss is gentle. It isn't awkward, but comfortable, like our lips were made to fit so perfectly together. We linger there for a long moment, which allows me to savor in the perfection of my first kiss.

Always the gentleman, Will pulls away first. He stares into my eyes and digs a hole into my soul with his gaze. I'm sure he can read my every thought and knows my every emotion. I wish he could. That would mean I wouldn't have to speak the words that might change how he feels about me. The truth of how I'm responsible for my parents' death. He'll need to know, but I can't tell him yet. I don't want to wake up from this miraculous dream he has fashioned for me. I'm being selfish, I know, but I don't care. I just want to stay right here and relish in sharing this amazing moment with him.

Will shines a satisfied grin and clears his throat, forcing himself to change the subject. "I promised Mr. Weston I'd come by tomorrow to work on the basement."

"Oh, yeah, my surprise." I have to think of something to say even though I'm still lost in the moment of our kiss, still feeling his lips on mine.

"I really can't wait to show it to you. Speaking of…how about I start showing you around the city tomorrow when I'm done? This town is crazy with street names, and it's really easy to get lost if you don't know where you're going." Will still has me by the waist, and we're still close enough to kiss. Oh how I want to kiss him again.

"I think Claire wants to show me around, but I'm sure there's plenty of town to see, so, yeah, that sounds great. But, are you sure it'll be ok? I mean, what if someone sees us?" I ask nervously. I don't want anything ruined when things have barely started. He's being awfully free with the suggestions of us spending time away from the seclusion of the house.

"I think it'll be ok. We just can't have any of *this* out in the open." he says, giving my waist a little squeeze. "You're still new enough here to pass our little tour off as an act of good will on my part. We'll have some time together and then we'll get Tyler, Chris and the girls. Sound nice?"

"It sounds better than nice," I say. A grin emerges and covers what I feel is the entirety of my face.

Without releasing my eyes, Will reaches one hand over to open the door for me before letting me go. I take one step toward the door when he stops me. "Thank you, Layla. You have no idea how you've changed my life." He kisses me sweetly on the cheek and walks back to his car. I stand in the doorway and watch him drive away. I miss him already.

I lock the door behind me and close my eyes, doing my best to relive the last few hours, but more importantly, the last ten minutes. I reluctantly come back to reality and decide I should make sure the back door is locked, too. Luke may have thought we'd come back through the kitchen. I push open the swinging door and startle Luke. We both jump at the sight of each other.

Luke has the freezer drawer open. Seeing it's me, he holds up two cartons of ice cream and bribes me. "I'll give you a scoop if you don't tell Claire!"

I walk over to a cabinet and reach down two bowls. "Deal."

Chapter 14

In my weeks of knowing Luke and Claire, I've watched them closely. They make a great team, like Mom and Dad, and, if I'm honest, Gram and Gramps. Despite Gram's propensity for highlighting my eternal punishment, she and Gramps were good together. They adored each other. It was me Gram hated. I see the way Luke looks at Claire, like the way Dad looked at Mom, and Gramps looked at Gram. It makes me wonder if the problem was that the Weston men were too much alike. Whatever the reasons, I don't need to know them. All that is in the past and Luke has earned my trust. I'm moving forward.

"How's your bribery ice cream?" Luke asks.

"It's great. Although I might need some chocolate syrup if I'm going to keep this totally 'hush-hush'," I say with a smirk.

Luke drizzles my ice cream with syrup and sits back down. "How was your night?"

"It was…great. Will told me he filled you in on his plan."

"Yeah, Will…he's a nice kid." He pauses, choosing his words. Am I about to get the 'birds and the bees' talk? *Oh, no!* I try to think of something to say to change the subject but I'm too late and Luke continues. "Did you know his father has been an attorney for 35 years, and in that time, he has *never* lost a case?"

"Impressive." Random, but at least it isn't the sex talk.

"Yes, it is. Do you know *why* he's never lost a case?" I shake my head. "He's never lost a case because Gregory Meyer *always* wins. He's an aggressively powerful man who does whatever, and I do mean *whatever,* it takes to get what he wants." Luke's face is serious and his eyes work hard to pierce mine.

My brow furrows. "Why are you telling me what I already know?" I ask.

"Apples and trees, Layla," he says.

"You know Will isn't like that, Luke," my jaw is set. I am immediately angry. "Is there something you're trying to tell me about Will?"

"No, but I've worked for Gregory Meyer for a long time and I want you to be really clear about the kind of family Will comes from. What Gregory did to Holly's family is just the tip of the iceberg of what that man is capable of doing. Don't get me wrong, Layla, I *like* Will. You wouldn't be seeing him if I didn't. I just want you to be careful. It might be more than you're emotionally ready to handle right now. That's all I'm saying."

My mind races back to the images of the man having his lunch involuntarily removed via a swift beating outside the law firm. I remember how Mr. Meyer stood there as, what I can only assume was his directive, was carried out in front of him. From that, I know that Luke and Will aren't sugarcoating it in what they're telling me about Mr. Meyer. Yes, they have all done a thorough job at making sure I'm completely terrified of this man. I *know* that Will isn't like that. He does everything to keep himself from being like his father in any way, shape, and form. Luke has spent all this time with Will and somehow doesn't know that? I'm furious and at a loss for words.

"Yeah, well…you don't know anything about Will, and you don't know anything about me," I toss my bowl of unfinished ice cream in the sink and am afraid for a split second that it may have been hard enough to break the bowl. When I'm confident that it's still in one piece I go upstairs, straight to my room.

I throw myself on my bed, fuming. *Why? Why is he doing this to me?* I chant in my head. They've already given us their support. Haven't I suffered enough? Don't I deserve *one* good thing in my life? Will is the happiness I've been waiting for; the happiness I paid for. He is the only thing that has brought me pure joy since before Mom and Dad died.

I begin to wish that my parents were here so I could ask them what to do. Then I experience the most horrid thought I've ever had in my life: I *don't* really wish they were here. If they weren't dead, I wouldn't be here, and I wouldn't have Will. Then the most disgusting part emerges. I'm glad they're all gone because I want Will more than anything else in the world.

I think I'm going to throw up so I run to the bathroom. I try to heave it out, to get the ugliness of my inner most thoughts out of me, but nothing happens. I take off my clothes in a furious rage and turn on the shower as hot as I can stand it, and then some. I get in and just stand there, letting the steaming hot water rush over my body. Maybe it will cleanse me somehow. I try to tell myself that it isn't true; that I would take my parents back in a heartbeat, even if it meant losing Will. But it isn't true. I want Will and I wouldn't trade anything that brought me to him. I feel repulsive, like a monster. Maybe my penance hasn't really been paid. Perhaps this is an extension of my hell. I get to be with Will, but have to live with the knowledge that the ones I loved had to die in order for me to have him.

The heat begins to dissipate from the water. My skin is red and my fingers are wrinkled. I turn the water off before it becomes too cold and wrap a towel around me. I shake my head to its senses. *I am not a monster,* I tell myself. I don't know yet how I will reconcile these feelings, but I am sure of that one thing. I have to believe that my parents would want me to move on. It's still a revolting thought that I wish I could scrub from my brain. Then I remember what Will said to me just a few short hours ago on the dock. *I'm sorry it took a tragedy to get you here, but I'm so glad you're here.*

What do I do about Luke? I was terrible to him. He's only trying to protect me. I'm just not used to being protected. Being protected means someone giving you the God's honest truth because they care more about what happens to you in the long run than what happens in that moment; even if in that moment you are among those most hated in the world. Gram gave me the God's honest truth, but that was because she wanted me to pay. If there's one thing I'm clear on, it's that Luke is not trying to make me pay.

Luke made it clear he was nervous about me seeing Will, so why did his caution set me off the way it did? He didn't go back on his support; he just tried to give a clearer picture to what they've already been telling me. If Will is working hard to not be like his father, having a better understanding of Gregory Meyer will be important. *Right?*

I feel so foolish. I wish I hadn't responded so emotionally. This is such a strange place for me. I've never been able to be so free with my feelings. I can't begin to imagine the fall-out if I had ever yelled at Gram that way. There were so many times I just wanted to scream, *I said I was sorry!* But I didn't…couldn't. Now I've emotionally vomited all over Luke. I took out the aggression I pent up for Gram and covered him in it like a bucket of mud.

I decide the best thing for me to do right now is go to bed. Things will look clearer in the morning.

*****

I wake up and stretch, having gotten my first solid night of sleep since moving here. My head is clearer and as I lay in bed my mind filters through the events of the past few weeks. It's hard to believe I've been here as long as I have. What's harder to believe is that I'm really and truly happy here. What started out as a destination to pass the time until college has grown into a place that holds more love than I thought possible.

I think about my new friends whom I am already closer to than anyone I knew in Florida. I already see that our closeness will be long lasting, especially with Caroline. I hope to spend more time with them and learn to trust them as deeply as Will does. The very thought of them brings a smile to my face and a joy I can feel deep within.

I hesitate, but ponder my conversations with Marcus, too. He may be a good ally…if I ever tell him about my relationship with Will. If he sees how Will is fighting for us to be together, he'll know that Will isn't like his father. He'd see what Holly saw in him. Aside from his current contempt for the one who holds my heart, I think Marcus and I could be good friends.

I feel shaky as I recall the moment Mr. Meyer found Will and me on the dock, and am even more creeped out recalling the stare down I got from him on the Green. I'm nervous at the thought that he may have caught Will in the lie, so I quickly turn my thoughts to something more pleasant. I feel my face blush and my heart flutter the instant I focus my feelings on Will. I close my eyes and try to recall everything from last night. The heat from his body as he sat close to me on the dock, the way his skin felt as he slipped his hand into mine. Mostly I remember the way his lips felt pressed against mine. I smile with anticipation as I remember that I will see him again today, and hope for a repeat of last night's goodbye kiss.

Determined to stay in my current frame of mind I stop my thoughts before I recall my conversation with Luke. I treated him so terribly; I have to make amends. There's no reason to stay mad at Luke. In fact, I really should thank him. He and Claire have done more for me in the time I've been here than I ever thought possible. They've proven their commitment to me, and a simple *I'm sorry* won't suffice. I need to *thank* them. I think about it for a few moments and then it occurs to me. I'll give him the one thing I've held back.

I think through what I'm going to say to him and wonder if he's told Claire about our exchange last night. While I hope what I have to say to him this morning will change our relationship forever, I feel a twinge of fear that he and Claire may have changed their minds about how supportive they're willing to be. Even though I'm confident in their acceptance of me, I have to entertain the possibility that I may have destroyed any support of my relationship with Will in one silly, childlike fit. I take a quick shower – last night's doesn't count – and get dressed. I leave my hair damp so I can get downstairs faster. As I approach the kitchen I hear Luke and Claire talking. Recalling the last time I eavesdropped, I really should back away…but I don't. I step forward gingerly and slow my breathing so I can hear them.

"Well someone had to warn her! You know how he is, Claire!" Luke says with a strong passion in his voice I hadn't yet heard from him. Even in last night's warning his tone was tender.

Claire seems to be the gentle voice of reason. "We've already been through this with them, Luke. They care about each other. You can't change that with threatening stories about his father. The best we can do is to be there for them, and protect them from Greg."

"What if she gets hurt? What if she gets her heart broken? I just couldn't bare it." His voice is soft, defeated now. "I thought I was doing the right thing, but what if *I* hurt her? What if *I* broke her heart? I'm trying, Claire. I want to do right by them…but I feel like I'm already failing."

I realize even more in this moment that last night's warning was more than Luke just asserting some newly found parental right. He feels an obligation to my parents to take care of me…to protect me. I hadn't considered this until now, and am relieved that I came to my senses last night. There's a connection there between Luke and me, and that space, that canyon that had been between him and my father seems absolutely irrelevant now. Luke and Claire are my family, all I have left, and…I love them. Yes, I love them. How could I not? They have recreated a life for me that I should have been living but was denied by my own grandmother's unforgiveness. I have been given a life more full in this last month than I ever thought I'd have. I am so incredibly grateful that tears begin to sting my eyes. I take a deep breath and become more determined with my choice that will hopefully solidify our family bond forever.

I take a few steps back and call to them. I want to give Luke time to collect himself if need be. I put on my *I just had my first kiss* voice and call, "Good morning!"

"Good morning to you! You sure are happy!" Claire greets me as I walk through the door. She's patting Luke's back in an effort to comfort him as he pulls himself together. I can see he's been crying. The slightly puffy eyes are a Weston trait.

I smile at Claire as I pass, making a beeline for Luke. I stand facing him, firm and purposeful, and say without hesitation, "Good morning, Uncle Luke." He catches my gaze and smiles, pleasantly surprised and relieved at the same time. I throw my arms around his neck and give my *uncle* the first hug I've ever given him. He hugs me back and holds me tight. It's warm and natural. We fit together like family. This is all I need to do. No explanations about the past and no conversation to smooth anything over. It's a step, the first of many. I know I can trust Luke and Claire, and, really, that's all I need.

Luke looks at me with what I can only describe as pure love in his eyes. The only other person who has ever looked at me in this exact same way is my father. Then Luke makes one request, "Layla, just promise me one thing, please? Promise me that you won't keep anything from us. We can't help you if we don't know what's going on."

"Uncle Luke, I…" I sigh to gain my composure. "I promise." How can I deny him? He and Claire are putting themselves at risk to protect my wish to be with Will. Will has already made the first step by keeping Luke in the loop, and who knows what other conversations have transpired in the pit of the basement. While I'm confident there will be nothing to share, I have decided that I truly trust Luke and Claire, so I will make and keep this promise to him.

There's a knock at the back door and Will lets himself in. "Hey Westons!" he says cheerfully. His tone changes when he recognizes that there's more going on this morning than breakfast. "Oh, am I interrupting something? I can wait outside, or come back later." His backpedalling is so cute that I can't help but giggle just a bit.

"No, no, no. You're not interrupting anything." Luke's tone is serious, but brightens after he has a second to think. "Come in! There's still a lot to do in the basement, so I hope your calendar is clear today." Luke gives Will a hefty pat on the back.

"Yeah, I'm available pretty much all day. The only thing I have planned is to show Layla around. I promised her I'd help her try to decipher the lack of logic to the street names around here. Is that ok?"

"Claire?" I defer to her because she initially called dibs on giving me a tour.

"Yes, of course." Claire is, once again, very accommodating and I feel embarrassed that I've rejected her kindness. It took weeks for me to allow her to take me shopping and have time to connect with me. I feel like I've slapped her in the face and I know I need to plan a night to be at home. Although I stayed holed up in the house my first weeks here, I spent most of that time with my head in a book or staring out at the lake.

"Thanks, Claire. I was thinking that maybe we could have a movie night, or something, this week. We could order in?" I say eager to inspire hope in Luke and Claire that I haven't already gone off the deep end with Will.

Luke is the first to respond. "That sounds great! I'm looking forward to it." He motions to Will and they head to the door to the basement. "Let's get going, Will. That basement isn't going to finish itself."

Will moves toward the door but stops directly in front of me. "Hi. How are you?" he says, our conversation from last night clearly still on his mind, too.

"I'm great. Really great," I smile and Will gives me a quick kiss on the cheek before he follows Luke through the door and down to the basement. I press my lips into a hard line in an effort to keep from grinning like a Cheshire cat but fail epically.

Claire and I are alone in the kitchen now. She hasn't said much since we greeted each other earlier. I don't want to mention what I overheard her and Luke talking about. It wasn't meant for my ears and I don't want to intrude on their private moment, even though what I really want to do is thank them. Thank them for not giving up. Thank them for making it their mission to love and protect me. Luke would never have broken down like that had he known I was right there, listening to every word. He's doing his best to protect me and that's all that matters. It also seems that he's doing his best to rectify whatever happened between him and Dad. I don't care about the issues that caused the lack of communication between them. That was their problem, not mine. I'm ready to move on with my life. Luke is a real, solid part of my life now and I don't want to ruin that by digging into his relationship with two people who are dead. I just want to move on with my life. I have Will and I want to spend as much time with him as possible. I want to know him deeply, and I want him to know me. I'm ready to trust and want to be an open book to him like he's been with me. I held back that first night on the dock because I just didn't know how to tell him about the burden I will forever carry. I've never been allowed to talk about it before, so I'm not even sure I can form the words.

I can feel Claire's stare. She wants to say something, and I'm afraid of where the conversation might go. I want to leave the room for fear Luke has assigned her the duty of giving me the "birds and the bees" talk but, to be honest, I'm hungry and want to eat. I reach for the bread to make toast when Claire finally breaks the silence.

"So…are you going to tell me about your date, or not?" She's giddy! I can't believe I didn't see that coming! I imagine that this is what Caroline would be like if she knew about Will and me. *Does* she know about Will and me? "Well?"

"Oh, um, yeah." I run through my mind everything I can tell her without spilling all the details. I want to keep most of them for myself. They're far too special to just throw out there like ordinary experiences. Will isn't ordinary, and neither are my feelings for him, so I'll hold on to most of the details for safekeeping. They'd be too difficult to fully explain anyway.

"Will said you were going to the dock last night. Do you want to tell me what happened?" she says with a playful smile.

"Well…it was really…wonderful," I sigh. "We got dinner and then came back here for a picnic. He brought a big blanket to sit on and a flashlight so we could see our way back to the house. It was really sweet."

"And…" Claire prompts.

"And…we had a great time." I am intentionally evasive. I don't want to give too much away, and I'm not going to offer details that haven't been solicited.

"Well, I'm guessing that this morning's kiss wasn't the first one?" Her tone has turned motherly, but not so much so that I think I'm in danger of a speech or lecture, or God forbid the sex talk. Not like Luke's last night. No, she's fishing for all the girly details that I imagine the mother of a teen would want. *So this is what it feels like.*

"You would guess correctly." I'm blushing now.

"That's so sweet, Layla." I can see that even knowing what she knows about Will's father and the situation we are in, Claire is still a hopeless romantic.

"Are you going to go back to the office this week? You know, you don't have to stay with me. I'm ok." I have to change the subject before Claire meshes her mom voice with her cross-examining expertise and flushes the details out of me.

"Yes, actually. I have to meet with some clients this week. I have a case coming up and there are some depositions I need to be present for. Luke will be in the office sporadically this week, too. Are you sure you'll be ok? I can work half-days if you need me to."

"I'm fine, really. I was thinking of calling Gwen and Caroline. Is it ok if they come over for…a movie day…or something?" I just think of this and haven't formulated a plan quite yet, but am sure Claire will be delighted that I'm reaching out to my new friends.

"Definitely! That'll make me feel better for you to not be here all by yourself. And then maybe you girls can go out; shopping, lunch, movie…these are the last weeks of summer, you know."

"That sounds great but…shopping…uh…I'm a little low on funds," I say. I've still got the money Gramps gave me tucked away, but want to save it for something special. I haven't a clue what that something is yet, so I'll probably just add it to my college fund. I knew my being totally and utterly broke would come up eventually. "I was going to ask about getting a job. Is there any place close to here that you think might be hiring?" I hadn't paid attention to what was around when I was driving nearby with Will. I was too focused on him. I'm only slightly familiar with some of the shops on Main Street in town. I think about asking Marcus if they're hiring at the bookstore, but somehow I don't think that would go over too well with Will. Maybe the coffee shop?

"You're not getting a job, Layla." *What?* "Luke and I knew you would ask and we've already decided." She's sweetly serious now, very motherly. "You carried a lot of responsibility while you were with your grandparents. This is your senior year and we want you to enjoy it fully. Consider us your bank. Whatever you need, we're here to help you. If you ask for a million dollars or a brand new car, we'll have to talk, but I'm confident we can cover most everything else."

Consider them my bank? That's the craziest thing anyone has ever said to me. I don't know what to say. I try to think of a solid argument to give her. I think about Will and how his father won't let him get a job, but immediately recognize the differences in his reasoning compared to Claire's. I know they just want me to have a different life here. It's hard to swallow sometimes. I never imagined that it would be so hard to be taken care of again. Claire isn't going to back down so I comply. "Thank you, Claire. You really don't have to do that, but, thanks. I won't take advantage of you, I promise."

"We know," she smiles and hugs me without hesitation. I thought it might have just been Luke, but I'm just as happy in Claire's embrace as his.

Luke and Claire have taken over a place in my heart that was starving. It had once been alive, but over the last five years it fell into a slow and painful place on the brink of death. In such a short period of time Luke and Claire have gone from strangers…to parents. I shudder internally at that thought. It brings back my nightmarish experience from last night. My mind is racing and I do my best to release myself from Claire naturally, not forced like my body is screaming to do. I'm comfortable in her arms, but I've got to move fast if I'm going to fight off the onslaught of tormenting thoughts infiltrating my brain. I excuse myself, grab a Pop Tart in lieu of making toast, and make my way to the lake.

I sit in my usual spot on the dock and become lost in my thoughts. I still feel awful about where my mind went last night and begin to wonder if I got over Gramps' death too easily. *Should it take me longer? Should I still be mourning?* I try to remember how long I mourned when mom and dad died only because I think that might give me a point of reference. It seems that it would be different mourning the loss of one's parents compared to grandparents, but I was a caretaker for Gramps, more like a parent than a grandchild, and that confuses me even more.

I replay all the painful scenes of my parents' death in my head: the accident, the hospital, therapeutic evaluations, the judge, the funeral, and finally moving in with my grandparents. The more I think about each event, only one thing stands out to me. One thing that I've never thought of before:

my stone, cold silence. I had been in shock and almost completely shut down immediately after the accident, but with each passing moment now, it occurs to me that much of silence was not my choice.

I remember the first night Gram and Gramps came to stay with me after the accident. I had been so happy that they were there with me. It didn't matter that I barely knew them…I wasn't alone. Gram sat on my bed with me while I told her everything that happened the night of the accident. Then, she held me while I cried myself to sleep. She never said anything. She stroked my hair and was gentle and comforting.

I spent days in bed, and when I was out of bed I walked around like a zombie. I didn't eat and found pleasure in nothing. It was almost a month before I was ready to talk about Mom and Dad again. To do that, I went to the one person alive who I thought I could trust most. Gram sat with me on my bed like she had every night since she arrived.

"I miss them so much, Gram," I said through my tears; the first time my 12-year-old self put actual words to my pain.

I tried to continue, but Gram cut me off, "Hush, dear. We're not going to talk about it. You made a mistake. You didn't mean to kill them. It's over now."

When I tried to talk, she quickly hushed me again and that was it. That was the last time I ever spoke a word to my grandparents about my parents death.

It's a hard thing to remember. Those five years seemed like an eternity. Grandparents are supposed to take you for an afternoon or weekend, spoil you, and then send you home sugared up with noisy toys. While you're with them you tolerate the game shows, puzzles, 4:30 p.m. dinners, and 8:00 p.m. bed times, but I had five years of it. No friends or parties, no sleepovers; nothing that resembled the life of a teenager. I took it like the sour medicine that it was, as my punishment for taking their son away from them.

I shake my head to clear it. I have to get off this dock. It's a strange contradiction that in order to clear my head, I need to leave the place that helps me do just that. I go back inside and find Luke and Will taking a break.

"There she is!" Luke says excitedly.

"I was down at the lake…on the dock." My reply is forced. I really just want to find Claire. She emerges from the living room with Gwen and Caroline behind her. *Even better!* Time with them will be an even better way to distract me. "Hey, what are you doing here?" I ask in an almost squeal.

"We came to kidnap you! We decided that we haven't had enough time with you, so we're here to whisk you away! And you can't say no." Caroline's attempt at forceful is ridiculously cute.

"No way! I mean…I was *just* thinking I needed to get out, so it's really great that you're here." I've barely acknowledged Will since I walked in and he looks at me quizzically. "Let me change really quick and I'll be ready to go." I turn to Will to say good-bye, but it just comes out as a weak smile and a wave. I'm not sure if I should try to kiss or hug him. I've never initiated that kind of physical contact before and this isn't the time or place to test the waters of my comfort level. I can't worry right now if I've hurt or offended him. If I have, I'll smooth things over with him later.

Gwen and Caroline follow me upstairs. They show no signs of being in awe of the library loft like I am every time I see it. I suppose if my house had been as enormous as this one I'd have little to be impressed with, too. It's just eleven o'clock so the girls think we should do some shopping and then lunch. I change into something more fitting for my company and we're quickly back in the kitchen to say our good-byes.

Claire insists on giving me her credit card in case I find something I just can't resist. I doubt that will happen, but I take the card because it will make her happy. I'll need it for lunch anyway. As I turn to leave Will grabs my hand and pulls me to him. He wraps his arms around me and gives me one sweet kiss. I can't help but kiss him back. He smells like wood, and Will and his closeness makes everything I'm struggling with in this moment so much better. He releases me and I avoid making eye contact with anyone in the room. My face begins to fill with heat and I know if I don't leave now I won't be able to hide it.

Chapter 15

Caroline drives us to the same outdoor shopping mall where I first met them. We wander the stores, not really finding anything. I've already browsed the racks of a few of the stores with Claire and know there isn't anything of interest to me in them. Even if there was, I can't bring myself to pay the exorbitant prices.

We've been shopping and chatting for about an hour when Caroline and Gwen give each other a knowing glance – the same one I saw on the hike – and then stare at me until I can't take it anymore.

"What?" I say, looking at both of them. "Ok…if you're about to do some kind of ambush makeover…"

"Are you going to tell us about your date with Will last night or not?" Caroline is busting at the seams.

"You know about that?" I say with surprise.

"Hello! We knew before you did! We knew before we *met* you! Will's been talking non-stop about you for weeks. It was inevitable," Gwen says. "Besides, that little kiss in the kitchen was telling enough."

Oh, yeah, the kiss. That was right there in front of everyone, wasn't it? "Wow. I…don't know what to say," I stumble. I'm not being elusive; I *really* don't know what to say. "What did Will say?" I ask slowly, wanting to know what they already know.

"Will has never talked about anyone the way he talks about you, Layla. To be honest, it was starting to get on my nerves. I'm glad we met you when we did otherwise I would have had to hate you on principle," Gwen says, with a bit of a wink. "He's seen a couple of girls, mainly ones his dad set him up with, but Will never liked any of them, not like this. Even when he was with Holly it wasn't like this." My stomach churns at the mention of Holly's name. I'm momentarily filled with fear knowing that a *House Call* is in my future if Will's father finds out about us.

"Well…are you going to fill us in or not?" Caroline asks eagerly.

"Oh, um, ok. Well, it was really great" I say nervously. I'm not sure how much to divulge so I tell them as much as I did Claire and hope that they don't push for more.

"This is so great, Layla," Caroline says hooking her arm through mine. "Will needs a girl like you. The choice of girls for someone like Will is slimmer than slim. You'll understand better once school starts, but, well, we're sort of the outcasts of the school. Chris, Tyler, Caroline, and me…we're buying our time until we're out from inside the Heyward bubble. We play the game and make nice as much as possible, but not Will. His family is literally the wealthiest of all the families at Heyward and Will doesn't hide his hatred of it. It baffles the rest of the school. But Layla…you're one of us. You're exactly what Will needs."

My time with the girls has definitely changed and lightened my mood. I'm feeling much better now. I don't know how to thank Gwen and Caroline for their encouragement and support. I'm not sure that they fully grasp the risk Will and I are taking. I have a feeling they know better than to broadcast my and Will's relationship until he gives them the go-ahead, but I'll leave it to him to dispense any instructions on the topic.

Throughout the afternoon both Gwen and Caroline continue to quiz me on minor details of my date with Will, and I answer as vaguely as I can. While I'm warming up to the idea of having girlfriends with whom to share all of my new found *girly-ness* with, I really want to keep the details to myself as my personal treasure, just as I did with Claire. I was forced to keep my feelings inside for so long, so it's nice to know it's *my* choice now.

We shop for another hour or so, with Gwen finding a pair of boots she can't live without. We stop for lunch and are back at Luke and Claire's by four. Caroline has a hair appointment and Gwen a fitting for her cousin's wedding, so they drop me off with a promise to call me tomorrow. I walk into the kitchen and find Luke, Claire, and Will exactly where we left them. I wonder if Will knew what Gwen and Caroline's hidden agenda had been today. I'm sure he did and most likely saw it as my initiation into their sisterhood.

"You're back! They weren't too terrible to you, were they?" Will says as he locks his arms around my waist. He's quite free with expressing his feelings for me around Luke and Claire. I take it as a good sign that he feels as safe around them as I do. This is the only place we can be ourselves like this.

"No, I had a really great time with them," I say.

"Well, good. Are you still up for a tour today?" Will asks.

"Actually…would it be ok with you if we didn't go today? Could we hang out here?" I'm thinking that my staying in night needs to come sooner than later for Luke and Claire. They obliged me this morning, as they usually do, and I'm beginning to feel badly about that. I hope they won't mind me asking Will to stay. On second thought, they're probably happy to have us somewhere they can keep an eye on me.

"Yeah, sure, whatever you want to do is great with me," Will replies, giving me a little squeeze.

"Is that ok with you, Aunt Claire?" I ask. I've called her *aunt* and it makes her teary eyed. I feel a flutter in my stomach at the thought that something I did could evoke emotion in someone like that.

"I think that's a great idea, Layla. Why don't you two check out what movies we have up in the loft, or we can go get one, and then we can order in," she says joyfully.

Will and I head upstairs to the loft to see what our choices are. Having not watched a movie since I've been here, it takes me a few minutes to figure out which beautiful piece of furniture houses the DVD's. I finally find the exquisite piece. It's a tall, dark wooden case with stunning scrolled engravings on the doors. There are hundreds of movies inside. I'm scanning the titles when Will comes from behind and puts his hands on my hips, making my heart skip a beat.

"What changed?" he asks.

"What do you mean?" I reply.

"You called her *Aunt* Claire. What changed?" His voice is like velvet, soft and smooth.

"Well…" I pause. How do I tell him that Luke's warning about his tyrannical father was the catalyst to my embracing them as family? I don't. "The time that I've been here has proven to be good…better than expected, actually. They've been really wonderful and so incredibly supportive. They're my only family. It just didn't make sense for me to pretend like they weren't."

"I think it's nice," Will says and leaves it at that.

*****

Over the next weeks Will and I spend as much time together as we can. Whether it's while he works on the house with Luke, spending time with our friends, or the moments we can sneak away and be alone, I enjoy every minute of being with him. My favorite times with Will are simple. We walk the campus of Davidson College where no one knows us. It's a beautiful campus right in the middle of town. I only got nervous once or twice that we would run into Marcus.

Will never hesitates to hold my hand or put his arm around my waist while we're with our friends or even with Luke and Claire. With the exception of when I went shopping with the girls, he always kisses me on the cheek, never the lips, in front of anyone. In fact, he continues to be a perfect gentleman in private as well. We've shared a few beautiful kisses by the lake but nothing passionate. I receive one single soft and gentle kiss before he leaves me at the end of our time together. I'm probably over thinking it, but I can't help but wonder if I'm doing something wrong. Aren't I supposed to be beating my boyfriend off with a stick and telling him we should wait? But, in all honesty, I wouldn't have it any other way. Will provides the safety and security that I have longed for and I can't imagine anything better.

We've just ended one of our long walks and I'm making dinner. I'm experimenting with some southwestern seasoning and Claire is making what she makes best, salad.

"I thought I'd mix salsa and the seasoning together, coat the chicken with it, and grill it like that. How does that sound?" I wasn't asking anyone directly, just taking a poll.

"That sounds delicious! I'll get the corn started," Claire says. She pulls the corncobs from the freezer and sets them in the sink. They thud and clank loudly as they hit the huge stainless bowl.

Luke enters the kitchen, dread painting his face almost white. All three of us notice but Claire is the first to say something. "Luke, honey, what's wrong?" she says.

"I just got off the phone with your father, Will. He's invited us all to dinner tonight. He said he's especially interested in getting to know Layla," he says. Gregory Meyer's invitation isn't really an invitation. Invitations are something you have the option to decline. No, this *invitation* is an expectation of our presence.

No one is saying anything until I frantically ask, "What does that mean?"

"It means he's not stupid. Can I talk to you outside?" Will says as he walks out the back door to the patio.

Luke steps forward to intervene but I hold my hand up and tell him it's ok with my eyes and follow Will outside. The sun is setting and a red evening glow hovers around us. It's such a beautiful sky. I'm afraid it's about to be ruined.

Will is pacing and breathing deeply. He's fuming. It's worse than the day of the bar-b-q.

"Will?" I try to get his attention. "Will!" I say louder and he finally stops. "Talk to me."

"Layla…this is…this isn't good. He knows. There's no other reason for him to express such an interest in you." Will is visibly shaken.

"Maybe he's just testing the waters. Maybe he *thinks* something is going on, but he's not sure. We don't have to tell him anything." I'm not confident in my theory at all, but want to be hopeful.

"He's not testing the waters, he's testing us. We can say nothing or tell him whatever we want about our relationship but he's still going to know. All he has to do is spend five minutes with you and he'll know you're everything he detests about women. You're smart, independent, and ambitious. He'll put it all together and know that I'm in love with you." Will is pacing again and doesn't realize what he just said.

"What?" I ask needing to clarify the words I can't believe my ears just heard him utter.

Will stops pacing and looks at me realizing he's just declared his love for me. He steps forward and puts his hands on my hips. "I love you, Layla. This isn't exactly how I had hoped to tell you. I actually had this whole plan, but…there it is. I love you. Say something. Please."

I stare at Will in disbelief. All I can think is that I'm going to pass out in this surreal moment. "I love you, too. More than anything and with all my heart, I love you." My mouth is moving and I hope that sound is coming out. This is the moment I've been waiting for – my moment of redemption when I'm finally allowed to have something good, something so wonderful as Will's love.

The words have barely left my lips when Will is kissing them.

He kisses me like never before. He's more passionate this time, like he's driving home a point. Our lips moved together and I can feel the heat from his breath mingled with mine. His right hand holds the back of my head while his left arm pulls me closer to him by my waist. My heart races and my breathing becomes deeper as my arms reach behind him and up his back and I'm kissing him just as passionately.

Will pulls away just as forcefully as he embraced me and it's over all too soon. "I'm so sorry. I shouldn't have done that, not like that," he says, catching his breath.

"Why are you sorry?" I'm only sorry he stopped.

"I just don't want…I can't get carried away," he says.

"Is it me? Did I do something wrong?"

"Oh my gosh, Layla! It *is* you, but not the way you think. You do everything right. It would be far too easy for me to get carried away with you. I don't want our relationship to turn into *that.* I love you too much to let anything, even how much I want you, ruin this."

"Oh…ok. I see." I understand, but it doesn't seem to make me feel much better. It's a strange feeling to want Will the way I do. I want to be as close to him as I possibly can. I want to feel his hands on my body pulling me to him. It's in those moments that everything, every tragedy of my life, slips away. My past is gone and Will is my future.

"I think you should fake an illness," Will says turning our conversation back to the issue at hand.

"Will, we can't hide from him forever. I can do this. Let me help, please." I look into Will's eyes and fall into them immediately. I start to think of a strategy and wonder if there isn't any kind of pleasant resolve to this. "Isn't there any reason he would like me?"

"My dear, sweet, Layla," Will says, his words penetrating my heart. "There are infinite reasons for him to like you. Unfortunately, the only reason he cares about is absent from your profile. You lack the shallowness necessary to live a life obsessed with money and power."

"Oh…well, is there anything I can do or change? Don't you think I could *make* him like me?" I'm good at adapting to meet the need of the circumstance. I did it for five years with my grandparents, and I'm willing to do anything if it will make things easier for us.

"Are you kidding me?" he smiles and takes my face in his hands. "Layla, there is nothing about you that should ever, *ever* change. You are perfectly desirable just the way you are."

"So what are we going to do?" I ask, realizing all my hopefulness isn't going to make this situation anything other than what it is.

Will takes a deep breath and says, "We're going to face him. We don't have a choice. We'll be as elusive as possible. Lie if you have to, but know that he's going to question you without you even knowing it's happening. Choose your words carefully. Luke and Claire will jump in where they can and I'll do as much of the talking as I can. I'm here to rescue you, remember." Will's smile at the end of his instructions only partially works in relieving my fears.

While I agree to his terms of how to handle our dinner with his father, my mind can't help but continue to run wild. Maybe if I pretended to be the airy, indifferent girl he prefers he'll back off and let Will and I be together. I know that won't work. I can't do indifferent, and I'm certain I can't pull off airy. Then I think that maybe what Mr. Meyer would like is if I lay the adoration of him on thick. *This is crazy!* I tell myself. I decide that my best approach is to trust Will and follow his lead.

I run upstairs to my room and make an attempt at finding something suitable to wear to an interrogation. I don't have a lot to choose from, so I put on my light blue dress, the one I wore to Gramps' funeral. It seems appropriate. Claire is dressed in a casual floral skirt that hits just above her knee and pink top, so I don't feel out of place.

The four of us stand in the living room, silent for a few long minutes. No one has anything to say. There is no way to know exactly how tonight will go. We just know that we are unified in our front, which is the best thing we have going for us.

"Thank you, Mr. Weston. Your support means a lot to us," Will says as he shakes Luke's hand.

"There's no need for the formalities anymore, Will. You can call me Luke. We're allies with the same purpose. We both love Layla and will do whatever we have to do to protect her," Luke says.

We let out a collective sigh and walk out the door.

I ride with Luke and Claire just to be on the safe side. When we pull up to the house I see where the inspiration for the Heyward Prep building came from. The Meyer's home is a small scale of the White House. Tall pillars flank the steps, and the black shutters pop against the bright white exterior. Will opens the front door of his house for us, but before he does, he gives me one long, hopeful look.

We walk into the foyer and I'm speechless. It is just as majestic as I imagined it would be. The floor and stairs are vanilla colored marble, and there are two large pillars of the same material on either side of the doorway. The dual staircase curves around to meet at an adjoining center of the exposed hallway on the second floor. Champagne floral curtains swag from all the windows. The house oozes elegance.

Will leads us to the back of the house where the formal living room is next to the dining room. The cherry wood table is set with what I'm certain is fine china and enough forks and spoons to make my head spin. Test number one will surely be seeing if I pick the right fork for my salad. There are wonderful smells coming from the kitchen that make my mouth water. I forget for a moment that the purpose of me being here is not to enjoy a delicious meal, but to be cross-examined by the winningest attorney in the state.

I'm brought back to reality when Mr. and Mrs. Meyer enter the living room, greeting us with subtle cheers. My body stiffens and I desperately wish I could hold onto Will for stability. Claire is right next to me and steadies me as I side step to maintain my balance.

"Oh, good, you're here. Welcome! We're sorry for the short notice, but so glad you could join us," Will's mother says in her overly rehearsed speech. "Gregory just *insisted* that we have you for dinner tonight." She is a beautiful woman. Her dark auburn hair is pulled back into a bun at the nape of her neck and I can't remember if it is long or short. She wears black pants and a silver flowing top. She is stunning, everything her husband requires her to be.

"Don't crowd them Eliana. Give our guests some room." Mr. Meyer makes his way to toward us and shakes Luke's hand in greeting. With that formality over, he addresses me. "Hello, again, Layla. We're so happy you could come tonight. We didn't get a chance to chat at the bar-b-q, but we're *very* interested in getting to know you." He smells like leather and cigarettes. I choke a little at the aroma. I hadn't noticed the pungent odor at the bar-b-q so I'm a little taken off guard. I shake his hand politely, but he holds it longer than necessary, along with the gaze he has on my eyes. I'd say he makes me uncomfortable, but that would be an understatement. He absolutely makes my skin crawl.

He makes me nervous, but I'm not going to show it. I'm not a witness to be cross-examined so I pull myself to a self-assured posture and smile. "It's a pleasure to see you again, Mr. Meyer. Thank you so much for your invitation. I've heard so much about you from Will and my aunt and uncle," I say with as much confidence as I can portray. "I'm equally as interested in getting to know you, too." Will shoots me a look like I'm saying too much. I make a mental note to stop trying so hard and hope that I can follow through.

We sit down to dinner, Claire and I on one side, Luke and Will on the other, and Mr. and Mrs. Meyer at the heads. Our hosts make small talk with all of us through the first and second courses, and Luke and Mr. Meyer talk vaguely about a case for a few minutes. I do my best not to look at Will too many times. I compliment Mrs. Meyer on the menu and ask her all sorts of questions about the meal. While she didn't prepare the meal herself, she shares that she loves to cook and wishes she could do so more often. She oversees everything in the kitchen, so she keeps her hand in the pot a little.

Dessert is about to be served when Mr. Meyer makes us wait no more for his true intentions to manifest and begins his questioning.

"So, Layla, William says you two have become great friends. Exactly *how* great of friends are you?" Here it is. It's not the subtle approach we thought it would be. In fact, it's downright blatant. I'm immediately struck by Mr. Meyer using the exact same phrasing that Marcus used when he cautioned me in my friendship with Will.

"Dad," Will begins, but he's cut off quickly by his father.

"Now, William, I'm just asking her a question. You've been spending a lot of time at the Weston home. I think I have a right to know what this young lady's intentions are." His tone is smooth, but not at all calming the way Will's is. It's cunning, creepy, and manipulative. He makes it sound like he's asking simple questions, but in reality a plan is forming with each question he poses.

"Dad!" Will raises his voice to his father, which gains the man's attention. It's clear that Will has never done this before by the look Mr. Meyer gives him. "Dad," he says in a more suitable tone. "I already told you that Layla and I are friends. What more is there to know?" Will says in our defense. I'm afraid he's doing more harm than good by being so passionate in his defense, but since his father has decided on a cannon ball approach, what choice does he have?

"I don't see the harm in the kids being friends, Greg. Layla's new here and Will's done a great job at introducing her to his friends, helping her get settled," Luke says, working to diffuse the situation and focus on Will's efforts to get me connected. Luke's speech is slow, concentrated, and deliberate. He knows exactly how to speak to *the* Gregory Meyer.

"I don't mind them being friends, Luke, *if* that were all there was to it." Mr. Meyer locks his gaze on me and I feel a shiver run down my spine. "And that's exactly what I need to determine."

"It's ok, Will, Uncle Luke. I understand. If I had a son like Will I'd want to make sure that every aspect of his life was on track," I say calmly and slowly while I try to formulate a plan of what to do next. I only know that my one and only goal is to diffuse Mr. Meyer's passive-aggressive assault, and make him believe that Will and I are not in love. "Will's right, Mr. Meyer, we've become great friends. When he comes to work at the house he eats lunch with Claire and me so we've had a chance to talk a lot. He's been great to fill me in on the ins and outs of Heyward so I don't get lost in the shuffle. He introduced me to Chris, Tyler, Gwen and Caroline, so I've made some new friends through him. It's been great getting to know Will and I've really enjoyed spending time with him." I take a slow, deep breath. "Will is really wonderful…" I say, pausing as my mind races through scenarios, none of which seem plausible. Then it hits me. I know what to say. I look at Will and see his eyes get big and his anxiety level rises. "…but I'm actually sort of seeing someone."

"Really?" Mr. Meyer says skeptically. "Who might the lucky young man be?" He's not moving an inch from his position or believing me for one second. *Who? He wants to know who? What difference does it make? C'mon, Layla! You can do this!* I scream to myself. Then it hits me. It's the lesser of two evils but it's the only thing I can think of.

"He's actually my trigonometry tutor. I've already been meeting with him and…well, we've really hit it off." I smile, saying the last part with a tone to hopefully indicate that there is a spark of romance there.

"That's too bad for Will, but it sounds like it is good news for this fellow." Mr. Meyer softens his posture and takes the last swallow of his wine in one gulp. "Does this tutor of yours have a name?"

I see the blood drain from Will's face as he puts it together. Of all the people I could have named! I look at Will apologetically and hope the next words out of my mouth won't be the nail in anyone's coffin. "Yes, sir. His name is Marcus Reynolds." I wait.

Mr. Meyer is silent and considers our conversation. He motions to the server for more wine before he speaks. "The Reynolds' are a fine family. *You'll* fit in perfectly with them."

That's it. The judgment has been passed. I'm a "them" and not an "us." I've officially been rejected by association, not that I would have been accepted in any way. But…he seems to believe me, which means no dodging bribes or worrying about financial ruin for Luke and Claire. Will and I will be able to spend the next several months doing our best to enjoy being together while avoiding being caught.

Mr. Meyer eyes me a few times, but doesn't say anything else to me during the rest of our meal. He doesn't even look at Will, but that doesn't seem strange. He barely let Will speak tonight, which only added to my Things That Make Me Hate Gregory Meyer list.

Mrs. Meyer tries to engage me in more friendly conversation about my cooking prowess but I'm not very talkative now. I answer in short, polite sentences. Mr. and Mrs. Meyer walk us to the door after dessert and coffee, and Will walks us out to the car. I'm insanely nervous to hear what Will's take on the evening is. I think we are all in shock at Mr. Meyer's approach. It was the complete opposite any of us were expecting.

"Well that was interesting," Will says. Not exactly the response I was expecting. He's lost in his thoughts, looking in my direction, but not at me.

"Interesting, how?" I ask curiously.

"Marcus? Really?" He's upset and staring at me now. I didn't mean to hurt him but have done just that.

"Did you want me to tell him the truth? Will, c'mon, I wasn't expecting him to ask me so point blank like that," I say in my defense. "What happened to 'he's going to question you and you won't even know it'?"

"Playing the Marcus card was risky, Layla. It could have ended badly. He could have looked at you and seen Holly." Will's anxiety is higher than it was earlier when he blurted out his love for me and all I can think is that *I'm* the one who did more harm than good.

"Maybe he didn't," I say, trying to convince both of us that my improvisation worked.

"All in all I think it went well. Claire and I have Marcus to use in any conversation where it might look like Gregory is suspicious. Layla, you'll need to fill Marcus in soon, but we still need to be careful," Luke says stepping in.

Luke and Claire get in the car while I say good-bye to Will. We're standing on the driver's side, shielded from view. Will hugs me but is still distant in thought.

"Will, everything is ok. He thinks I'm with Marcus," I say. I'm not sure who I'm trying to convince more.

"Maybe. Something just doesn't feel right, though," Will says slowly. "He dropped it too easily. He didn't ask for any proof. We're not out of the woods yet."

Will kisses me quickly, puts me in the car and shuts the door. As we drive away I watch Will stand in the driveway, still contemplating the night. I hope he's wrong. I hope that I've been convincing enough. In order to make this work, I'm going to have to break my deal with Marcus.

Chapter 16

I've spent all morning attempting to coordinate clothes for school. I have every piece of wardrobe a person could need, but nothing looks right. It doesn't help that I'm distracted thinking about the evening at the Meyer's. I replay everything from which fork I used for what to my interrogation. Then all I can think is that I'm not going to school with normal people anymore. I'm going to school with the law firm of Meyer, Fincher and Marks. Every shirt or pair of shorts I try on makes me look and feel completely inadequate. I've tried to make it work but it's just not happening. I hate to do this, but I'm going to have to ask Claire to take me shopping. I hate even more that I feel like I'm compromising myself. Since when do I care what other people think of my style, or lack thereof? But, lately I'm caring about a lot of things I never have before.

When I ask Claire if she'll take me shopping, I swear she lets out a little squeal. She doesn't waste any time and grabs her keys. I barely have time to put my shoes on before she's hustling me out the door and she's is absolutely giddy the entire time it takes us to get to the mall. She takes me to a different outdoor mall than our first shopping excursion. *Doesn't this place have any traditional indoor malls where old people walk for exercise?*

When we get there I immediately recognize several of the stores, which puts me at ease. I can shop without worry because I know there won't be any $250 shirts at Old Navy. We shop and try on clothes for hours. I'm learning to enjoy this time with Claire. It's becoming almost effortless, and shopping with her is actually pretty fun. I remember this part of what having a mother is like and I realize how much I have missed it. My heart is full of joy and gratitude that Claire didn't give up on me during my season of sequestering when I arrived here.

We go from store to store, trying on shoes and clothes, with Claire making me promise to try on things I wouldn't normally. Her theory proves correct when I end up loving most of the things I hated on the hanger. By the time we're done I have six new pairs of shorts, four dresses, three pairs of jeans, and ten tops. I lost count of everything Claire got. It was a shopping frenzy and she loved every minute of it.

It's Sunday, but Luke is working from home to wrap some things up before a heavy work week, so Claire decides that she and I get a break from cooking and we go out for dinner. As we sit there discussing our victorious shopping conquest, I can't keep my mind from going back to our dinner with Will's parents. Even though I don't believe Will could ever be like his father, I also can't help but consider Luke's warnings.

"I have a confession to make," I say to Claire. "The morning after my date with Will, I overheard you and Luke in the kitchen."

"Oh?" she replies.

"I'm really sorry that I listened. I didn't plan on it. I just heard Luke talking when I came to the door, but I should have backed away." I feel badly and I want her to know that I don't normally do that sort of thing. I suppose I don't feel badly enough to confess to overhearing their exchange the night I arrived in Davidson. I'm causing such a mess right now, I don't want to remind her of the uncertainty she had about me living with them.

"It's alright, Layla. So you heard Luke's concerns…," she says, trailing off at the end inviting me to fill in the blanks.

"Yes, and I appreciate them. Really, I do. I just…" I'm not sure where to take this conversation now that I've started it. I don't want to freak Claire out and tell her about the beating I saw outside the firm, not that she's unaware of Mr. Meyer's dealings. I decide to do a little fishing and let her do the filling in. "What is it about Gregory Meyer that has both Luke and Will trying to keep me away from him? Besides, I thought I handled myself pretty well the other night," I say.

"First, to be clear, it's the other way around. We're trying to keep *him* away from *you.* But…it's hard to explain. I'm not really sure how much I should tell you," she says.

"Please, Aunt Claire?" I softly plead.

Claire breathes a heavy sign and relinquishes what she knows. "I'm sure you noticed that Gregory's wife, Will's mother, is much younger than him," Claire says. I nod, remembering my judgment of her and how badly I felt. "Well, Eliana is Gregory's fourth wife."

My jaw drops. I've never known anyone who had been married that many times. I had a few friends back in Florida whose parents were divorced and remarried, but that's almost expected these days. But married *four* times? Wow!

"The first three Mrs. Meyers lasted four, three, and then two years when they were swiftly divorced with a small settlement as agreed to in their pre-nup. Then they vanished. No one has seen or heard from them since. Eliana and Gregory had been married a year when she got pregnant with Will. Apparently she was about to get her walking papers, too, but Gregory decided to keep her around because he thought the baby would soften his image. The sad part is the rumor at one point was that wife number three was pregnant but Gregory didn't know."

"Why did he divorce them?" I ask, still in shock.

"They wanted him to be a husband. You know, surprise lunches on a Wednesday, weekend getaways, flowers and romance, conversation, relationship. That's more than what Gregory Meyer wants. He wants to do his job, make a ludicrous amount of money, and come home to a trophy wife who shopped, played tennis, and had martinis with her girlfriends in the middle of the day. When important events come around, he wants to waltz in with her on his arm for photo-ops." Claire's speech is filled with disgust. I can see why she appreciates Luke the way she does. He's nothing like that.

"Will said that this *trophy wife* is what his mom had become. She wasn't always *the* Eliana Meyer?" I ask.

"No, not at all. She was probably the most down to earth, real one of them all…and the most beautiful. Even after Will was born she bucked Greg's system for a long time, but eventually gave in when he threatened to take Will from her," Claire says speaking in a hushed tone.

"So Will's dad really just kept her around because of him? And he kept Will around because he thought it would be good PR?" I've transitioned from shock to disgust.

"Yes, and I think Will knows the whole story, which is why he works so hard to not be like his dad. It's one of the reasons Luke and I like him so much. Will loves his mom a lot and would do anything for her. I think it makes him sad to know that she compromised herself for him." Claire's tone is sad and filled with compassion for Will.

My discussion with Will on the patio after the bar-b-q is making more sense, but there are still some gaps. Had I not witnessed an instance of what Gregory Meyer will do to prove a point, the main gap might be why they haven't pried themselves free from underneath his thumb. I have a feeling there are gaps I'm not even aware of yet. My initial instinct is to want to try and reason with Mr. Meyer, but I quickly nix that as an option as I realize that both Luke and Will are proficiently reasonable people and still can't seem to do it.

"Luke and I are still concerned about you seeing Will. We really like him, Layla – the Will we all know now, but he's young and Gregory still has time to manipulate him into who he wants him to be. Gregory is incredibly persuasive and not to be underestimated," Claire says. "Luke and I almost didn't break free ourselves, and we nearly lost everything," she continues, closing her eyes tightly as she recalls the pain associated with this memory.

"What do you mean?" I ask.

"Luke and I were at the peak of our careers. Luke was up for partner and I was being considered for a junior partner position. We were both working day and night so that we could grab the brass ring Gregory Meyer held out for us. He flashed dollar signs and bonuses and perks in front of us and we got completely sucked in. We hardly saw each other and barely spoke when we did. We didn't plan for it to happen. When Luke and I met we were both starry-eyed law students who wanted to change the world. We were focused on right and wrong and upholding justice even when everyone didn't agree with us. Everything just happened so fast after the promotions were proposed. We were the youngest attorneys to ever be considered in the history of the firm.

"Obsessed, we closed ourselves off to anything that didn't have to do with the firm. We didn't even answer the phone if it wasn't from an associate," Claire pauses and takes a deep breath. "Then your grandmother died, and, Layla, I am so ashamed to admit this…but…we weren't at Carol's funeral because we didn't receive the message that she had passed until three days after the service." There's the answer I'd been looking for, and it's sadder than I ever imagined it would be. "Luke was devastated and vowed then and there that his relationship with his family was more important. He had already lost your parents and his mother, so we withdrew our names from the partnership committee. Luke was bound and determined not to let another day go by without reconnecting with his father and he wasn't going to let anything stand in the way."

"What? How? I was there! Gramps never said anything about Luke ever." I'm perplexed. If Luke had been reaching out to Gramps, why didn't he tell me?

"He talked to Jack a few times a month, usually during the day while you were at school. Jack asked that if Luke was going to call, to call then. They were typically short calls. They talked about the weather and sometimes about Jack's health," Claire tells me, sounding sadder with every word. "Luke wanted to come down, help Jack get some things fixed around the house, spend some time with him, with you, but Jack wouldn't have it."

"Luke…asked about me?" I ask hesitantly.

"He did, and Jack would brag about your grades and what great care you were giving him," Claire answers hesitantly. "But, I really think you should talk about that with Luke. I think he'd rather explain."

Explain? What is he going to explain? Why would Gramps keep me from Luke? Is it because of the rift between him and Dad? Dad had been dead for over two years by then! Why are all the men in this family determined to keep me from knowing the truth? I'm screaming in my head, calling out for someone to answer me, but there is no answer. There isn't going to be an opportunity to talk with Luke anytime soon. My sentence at Heyward starts in a few days and I have to survive that first. I've waited this long, I can wait another week. Besides, I have plenty to navigate through with Will and his family.

"What did Mr. Meyer say when you turned down the promotions?" At this point I'm surprised they're still alive.

"Well, that's where things get interesting. He wasn't happy. The golden rule around here is *don't cross Gregory Meyer*, but Luke has worked very closely with Gregory since his internship during law school. He had Luke working on some things that were a little hazy in the legal department, and while there's a confidentiality agreement in place, Luke still knows enough to make things very messy for Gregory. Greg knows that, so he leaves Luke and me to do our jobs. Plus, Luke is an excellent attorney so Gregory keeps him around to keep the firm's winning ratio up. Gregory would have gotten rid of me had Luke not told him we were a package deal. If not for the cards that Luke holds, he would have fired us when we turned down the promotion. You don't say 'no' to Gregory Meyer."

After what I witnessed outside the firm, and every creepy meeting I've had with Gregory Meyer, I believe every word Claire has just told me. The only reason Gregory Meyer keeps anyone in his life is if they're of use to him. Will already made that clear. "Wow," I say still in shock from the entire conversation.

"As for Will," Claire says, bringing the subject back around. "We're happy for you to see him. We know how much he means to you, and Luke certainly has gotten an earful from Will about you. You need to know that if we see any signs of Gregory Meyer manifesting in him, we're going to pull the plug on the relationship. We love you, Layla, and we won't stand by and watch you get hurt."

"Aunt Claire…I appreciate your concern but Will isn't…" I've softened my tone so as not to sound like a belligerent teen, but Claire isn't falling for it and cuts me off.

"Layla, I agree with you that today, right now, Will is *not* like his father. He's every parent's dream boyfriend, but we can't see the future. I'm telling you that as much as Luke and I like Will, we are watching him closely. We know Gregory Meyer and know what we're looking for. If we see it in Will, it's over. I pray to God that Will never changes, but we have no guarantees," she says. "Now that I've said all that…please, *please* don't keep anything from us. We can't protect you if you don't tell us what's going on. Promise me that you'll tell us if anything ever happens with Will that worries you," Claire says, looking at me with the same deep, penetrating love Luke gave me when he made me promise to tell him if things got serious with Will, only this time I'm reminded of my mother.

"I promise," I tell her, and mean it.

After a few long moments we silently agree that everything had been said that needed to be said and go back to our dinner. We review our purchases and Claire decides that now we need new shoes. I'm not sure if I'm up to more shopping, but I know it'll make Claire feel better after laying such heavy information on me that I agree without hesitation.

We get home around eight and Luke is just emerging from his office. He wouldn't have known we hadn't been home all day if we weren't carrying a dozen bags.

"I see you two have had quite a day!" he says, chuckling at the sight of the two of us totting in like two pack mules.

"Layla and I needed new clothes for school," Claire says cozying up to Luke, pretending to need to butter him up about our purchases when in reality Luke would give Claire the moon if he could. He kisses her on the cheek and relieves her from the burden of her heavy bags.

"*You* needed new school clothes?" he asks Claire with a wink "Did you have fun? I'm assuming you've had dinner."

"Yes, but I can heat up some leftovers if you'd like," I offer, but Luke opts for peanut butter and jelly. "Ok, I'm just going to take my things upstairs. Thanks, Aunt Claire. I had a lot of fun today." I search for something meaningful to say. "You're…bringing out the girl in me," I say smiling. It's the biggest smile I've given them since I moved here. It wasn't forced, but real and honest. It's the best indication I can give her that despite the intensity of our conversation earlier, I am really and truly happy.

I lay my new clothes out on my bed and line up my new shoes on the floor in front of my dresser. I pull a few of my old clothes out but just can't seem to make the old and new coordinate. I throw in the towel and decide I'll wear only new clothes to school. After all, that was the point of today, wasn't it, to make me blend in, at least exteriorly, with the flock at school? To make it so I don't stick out like the sore thumb I am.

I look at my old clothes lying messily next to my new ones. *That's me,* I think. I'm something old and used and disheveled next to Will like a mismatched pair of socks to his tuxedo looks and charm and character.

My conversation with Claire is ringing in my head. Visions of Gregory Meyer having bodyguards carry bride after crying bride away are floating through my mind; them begging and pleading for his love and attention.

I shake my head to rid myself of the unnerving daydream and begin gathering my clothes when I see it: my favorite blue shirt and a pair of my new jeans, both simple pieces. This modest shirt is the nicest one I brought with me when I came to live here. It's nothing special but is my go-to piece because of how accommodating it can be to coordinate with almost anything. The jeans are new and sturdy. They're built to last. When I lay the shirt with them, they make the shirt something a little special. The jeans…bring out the best of it and make it more than just a t-shirt. The blue is brighter and its structure more pronounced. Separate them and it's just a shirt…just a pair of jeans. But together…they make something so much more.

I see it now more clearly than I had before. The old and the new *aren't* mutually exclusive. What Will and I do is make each other better. Without Will I'm just an old shirt, but I'm done being just an old shirt.

I stand in the shower for a while after I'm technically done, lost in thought. Knowing what happened to Marcus' family, I know what I need to do. I can't let Gregory Meyer destroy Luke and Claire. I can't let him infiltrate the only family I have left. I will do whatever I have to do to protect the ones I love. Whatever the game Gregory Meyer wants to play, not only can I play it, I can beat him at it.

I get ready for bed and decide to watch a movie instead of my normal reading. Tonight I need something mindless to help me wind down. Luke and Claire are in the loft already watching something I've never seen before and I join them.

It feels good just being in the same room as them. It's impossible to be around them and not feel how much they love me. The smallest glance, the way Claire pats the side of my leg as I pass her on the couch…gestures that make my heart warm with love and acceptance. It's been a long time since I've felt that. It's the kind of love that is willing to move mountains for you. The kind of love that is willing to stick around even when they don't agree with your decision, just so they can pick up any pieces that might fall. It's been a long time since I've felt that unconditional love.

I know that somewhere, deep down Gram loved me, but her love came with strings attached. It didn't take long after hearing phrases like, "I'm doing this as a favor to you," and "That's ok, it's just one of the most important things in my life" before I cut myself off from my own feelings and surrendered to making up for how I had broken her heart. My job was to make her happy. Period. It wasn't hard because I really loved both Gram and Gramps, and I know I owed them. I just wish I hadn't owed them so much.

I climb in bed and pull the covers up to my chin, satisfied that the movie did its job. Will is going to be over in the morning and my first objective is to find out how he's doing. I've been troubled since we left him standing in his driveway deep in his own concern. For now, I'll sleep well knowing that I'm going to do whatever I need to do to protect everyone from Gregory Meyer's wrath, whatever that looks like.

Chapter 17

I'm in my usual spot in the loft staring out the window trying my best not to be shaken by Will's worry. I'm jostled from my stare when I hear someone coming up the stairs and turn to see Will standing at the railing looking solemn.

"Hey," I say to him. "You're here earlier than I was expecting."

"We need to talk." Will approaches me at the window and takes my hand and leads me to our place by the lake. With every swift and silent step I search for reasons for Will's despair. I run through scenarios of backlash from his father ranging from childish time-outs to death threats.

"Will, are you ok? Did something happen?" I ask.

"Yes," he says.

"What happened?" My stomach begins to churn as my mind exaggerates scenarios that terrify me. Has his father already begun to wage threats against me, or worse, Luke and Claire? Or have the threats been directly aimed at Will? What more could he do to Will that he hasn't already done?

"What happened is…I fell completely and helplessly in love with you." Will is focused and determined, but rattled.

"What's going on, Will?" As much as I want to, this isn't a moment to respond sweetly to his profession of love. Something has happened and my gut tells me it isn't good.

"Watching you drive away the other night… The idea of you leaving forever is the most terrifying thought." He rakes his fingers through his hair and breathes a heavy sigh. "I have an idea, and I just want you to hear me out, ok?" I nod and wait for him to speak. When he does, he blurts out the last words I expected to hear from him. "Run away with me. We can go…away…down to Florida maybe. There's an account that I have access to.

I can drain it and we'll be gone before anyone ever knows. We can live off the cash so he won't be able to track us. We don't have to live like this, Layla. We don't have to live in fear."

I want to tell him that nothing would make me happier than to leave everything behind and follow him to the ends of the earth, but I can't do that. I just got Luke and Claire and they just got me. It would break their hearts, and mine, if I left them. I can't shake the knowledge that running away would only trap us in this prison of hiding forever.

"Will, as romantic as running away with you sounds, it's just not realistic."

"Layla, if he finds out…" Will is distraught. He puts his hands on his head and begins to pace. "This isn't like other times I dated girls he didn't approve of just to piss him off. With the exception of Holly, I didn't care what happened to any of those other girls. He could say or do whatever he wanted because I didn't have feelings for them. You're different, Layla, and he knows it. I won't let him take you away from me. I'm not going to let him destroy us." He stares at me, waiting for my response. This is the most nervous I've ever seen him.

"Will, this isn't only about me. You may be trying to protect me, but I want to do whatever I can to protect you, too." I reach up and rest my hand on his cheek. Looking into his eyes I see everything that I've been waiting for. The whole of my future lies in the depths of these ocean blue eyes. "If your father knows we're together he's going to make your life a living hell. I want to be with you. I already made it perfectly clear that I'm willing to do whatever I have to do not to lose you. I can do this. Please."

"Layla, love, I'm not concerned about me. I would take a thousand of my father's tongue-lashings, sanctions, and acts of retaliation before I let him do anything to hurt you," Will says caressing my cheek with his thumb. "I have spent every minute since dinner with them going back and forth between what is the *best* thing and what seems like the *cowardly* thing. Part of me feels like not giving him reason to come after us is best because then he wouldn't have what his twisted mind would consider cause. The other part of me wonders what kind of man am I not to stand up and tell my father that I'm in love with you, regardless of what the fallout might be?" This visibly disturbs him. I hate seeing him having lost his confidence.

I take Will by the shoulders and look up into his eyes with as much intensity as I can assemble. "What kind of man are you? You're a man who is willing to risk everything for someone like me. You're a man whose passion is leading him straight into greatness. You're the best man I know." Will throws his arms around me and holds me closer to him than I thought was possible. "We cannot make everything about your father. If we do, then *that's* what will destroy us…and then he wins anyway."

Will's breathing eases and he pulls back to look at me. "How did you do that?"

"Do what?"

"Talk me down off the ledge. I have a suitcase packed in the car. I was ready to leave, Layla. I'd still go if you changed your mind."

"I'm too logical sometimes. Trust me – I want to pack a bag, too, but we would never be free, Will. We'd constantly be running. I don't want to do that. At least we have this place. We have someplace where we don't have to hide. Someone once told me that we should make the most out of our time together. Let's just do that."

Will holds me in his arms for a long time and whispers "I love you" to me over and over again. I rest my head on his chest, blanketed by his strong arms. I will never tire of hearing those words from him, and hope he never stops saying them.

"How do you feel about doing a lot of nothing with me today?" he asks sweetly.

"I would love to do nothing with you," I answer. I pull my head from his chest and kiss his chin without thinking. It's the first time I've initiated any physical touch with him like that. He doesn't flinch but tilts his face to mine and kisses me.

Will and I spend the day in the loft in the perfect do nothing afternoon. We choose books at random from the wall and read. Will creates a game where we each pick an excerpt and try to carry the dialogue between the two books. It's like a sophisticated version of MadLibs, but even more hilarious because we're reading from *The Wizard of Oz* and *Gone with the Wind.* Visualizing Rhett Butler and the Lollypop Guild together has me laughing so hard I'm crying.

We talk and watch movies and nap on the oversized couch. It's just the right size for us to lie next to each other, me cradled in Will's arms, my head nestled into his chest. This has officially become my absolute favorite place to be.

"What's it like?" I ask as we lay together, our breathing synchronized.

"What's what like?" he replies.

"What's it like being so rich?"

"Really? You have free reign to ask me anything in the world and *that's* what you want to know?" His tone is humored chastisement.

"Seriously! I've never been wealthy, or known anyone who was. I just wondered what it was like. I mean, why do some people love it and others hate it?" I've always thought this was an interesting phenomenon, and there is definitely a polarized dichotomy on the subject at Heyward, even if it is among only a few.

"First, let's get one thing straight: my *father* is wealthy, I have nothing. He gives me money because he thinks it solves everything." He pauses and thinks a moment before answering. "I guess *I* hate it because I see what it does to people. I see what it did to my mom.

"I remember being little, like six, and she would take me places, play with me. She was a regular mom. She wore jeans and t-shirts, but dressed up when she needed to. She was always so beautiful. But…then…it was weird." Will's voice stumbles and I can tell this is difficult, even painful, for him to talk about. "She literally changed overnight. I remember having been at the park all day with her one day, and the next day the jeans were in the trash and she was interviewing nannies." His head rests heavier on the cushion above my head, his whole body heavy with the sad emotions this recollection conjures. "It wasn't the money that got to her. I mean she wasn't scared of being poor. She came from a blue collar, working class family that had to scrimp and save for even the smallest luxuries in life. It was the power that my dad wielded with it. I didn't understand then, but I know now that he was unyielding and relentless."

"I don't understand. Why would your dad choose your mom, having come from the class he hates so much?"

"She was beautiful. She *is* beautiful. My dad saw her and wanted her. Gregory Meyer gets what Gregory Meyer wants, remember?" Will answers with sadness saturating each word. "So, he groomed her into the woman he wanted her to be. He changed what she wore, what she ate, what type of music she listened to; he showered her with money and taught her how to live the life that he wanted her accustomed to."

I can see that it's hard for him to talk about his mom. He doesn't want to paint her in a negative light and I understand what that feels like. A memory from my own childhood floods my mind and before I know it I'm sharing every detail I can remember.

"My parents were big activists. I called them my little hippies. Before one cause had run its course they were doing research on the next up and coming one. They were passionate, sometimes a little too much, about their causes.

"I was eight when my parents got involved with a group that was protesting Taiwanese sweatshops. We drove down to Miami to a rally in front of some famous designer's gated neighborhood. We had been there for a while and I was getting bored. I held a sign and chanted with them for a while, but I didn't *really* understand what was going on. I'm pretty sure I was there for visual effect. There weren't any other kids there, not that it mattered. Half the time I think my parents forgot that *I* was kid.

"I had brought a book with me but left it in the car. When I tried to find where we parked I got lost, and when I tried to find my way back, I got even more lost. I wandered around for over an hour before I found them. I had been gone almost two hours and they didn't have a clue.

"I've never told anyone that. I never wanted anyone to think they weren't good parents. Sometimes they made mistakes. Sometimes they were just doing what they thought was right. Sometimes those two were one in the same."

Without a word Will takes my face in his hand and kisses me. I'm prepared for the bliss to end as quickly as it started, but it doesn't. Will becomes more passionate, pulling me tighter to him. His hand moves down my back to my hip and down my leg to the back of my knee. He pulls my leg up to his hip and I feel his hand on the back of my thigh. I reach my hand under his shirt and feet his bare chest. His skin is hot and smooth. I move my hand to his back and pull myself even closer to him. With every second that passes Will is kissing me harder and with more passion than I knew was humanly possible. He lifts my shirt and I feel his hand on the skin of my back. I want him more than I ever thought one person could want another. My heart is beating fast and hard, and my breathing is labored in the exhaustion our passion is producing. My body is hot and I'm filled with elation.

I never want it to stop.

But it does.

Will pulls himself away from me and I cut him off before he can even begin to speak.

"Don't you dare say that you're sorry!"

"Layla…" he says, catching his breath.

"No, Will." I protest.

"The only thing I'm sorry about is that we're not a year into the future and away from here. I want you, Layla. Words can't express how much. You are *everything* I have ever hoped for," he says, and then kisses my forehead. "But we can't…I mean…if anything ever happened…"

"I understand. It's just…difficult. I feel safe and at home with you. It feels so natural to be close to you." I bury my face in his chest.

"It's ok, Layla," he says, lifting my face to meet his. "I feel the same with you, and when you opened up like that…I just felt so…at one with you. All I wanted was to be as close to you as possible."

"This time alone together is the only time I get to really show you how much I love you." Here, I can be with Will in every way possible. Well, every way he'll allow us to be. Once school starts I'm afraid the pressure will be too much and Will is going to give up on us. I know that I'm not enough for him. The thought of not being close to Will is too much and I start to cry.

"I promised I wouldn't be responsible for one of these," he says as he wipes a tear from my cheek. "I'm so sorry." He pulls me close and I feel warm all over again. "We're in this together. We're going to make this work."

"I'll be ok. It just hit me all at once. And today…being with you…" I say sitting up. I take a deep breath and regain my senses, removing the evidence of my breakdown from my face. "I'm going to do whatever I have to do to keep you," I say seriously.

"What does that mean, Layla?"

"I'll change. I'll be more like the kind of girl he wants you to be with."

"No! I don't want that!" Will says darting up to face me. "I want *you*, just as you are! I don't want some Gregory Meyer Stepford. I want you. Just you!" Will brushes the hair from my eyes and kisses me sweetly. I feel warm and soothed, like hot chocolate. "Please, Layla. Don't say that again. It scares me to think of you not being you. I couldn't bear it."

"Ok. I'm sorry." I lay my head on his chest and concentrate on his breathing.

He sighs. "Let's get out of here. Do you want to get something to eat? There's an Italian place in town."

"That'd be great."

Will holds my hand in the car all the way to the restaurant and I cherish every second. I hold his hand and cup my right hand around our entwined fingers, stretching to his wrist. The silence in the car allows me to concentrate on his pulse. Every throbbing beat reminds me that I'm not dreaming. Being here with Will is real.

We enter the quaint, family owned restaurant and the hostess seats us right away at a quiet table in a slightly darker corner. "Thanks, Michelle," Will says politely to the hostess. She isn't wearing a name tag so he must know her. She smiles at him and I immediately feel a twinge of jealousy. *Back off! You have no idea what I'm going through to be with this guy!* This sentiment is swiftly followed by feelings of foolishness. Will barely gave her a second glace. I don't know where my head was.

After a few minutes of reviewing the menu, I order the chicken piccata and Will orders veal saltimbocca. We eat and talk and try to act like we're not in love. This isn't the kind of place that Heyward families frequent, so it'll be good practice for when school starts. For now, while we sit here, everything seems…normal.

"I'm curious about something," I say in between bites, trying to make small talk. "Why Heyward Washington? Why don't you all go to the local high school where you can be a big deal? Doesn't everyone being at Heyward mean they're all vying for supreme superiority?"

"Well, about five years ago my dad realized that I was about to enter high school. He didn't like the options so, him being him, he built his own school," Will says.

"But, isn't he all about showing the masses how wealthy he is?"

"Yes, but…he's more interested in keeping us away from the masses and letting them adore us from a distance. He thinks that if we mingle too much with the commoner that we'll become like them – happy with the intangible things of life. He went to the state about starting a charter school. He had his core founding group assembled in less than a month. Within six months Heyward was built and ready for business."

"Where'd the name come from?" I ask.

"The Heyward Washington building in Charleston is one of dad's favorite places. He's a real history buff. He swears he's related to George Washington." Will rolls his eyes having heard his father's declaration of impressive genealogy one too many times.

"I'm nervous about my first day, Will. They're going to eat me alive…in their fancy *dining hall*," I say with both fear and contempt.

"You're going to be fine. I've got it all under control." His mischievous smile stretches across his face, telling me he has used his family name to his benefit.

"What did you do?" I say smiling back, curiously worried.

"You've got three classes with me, one of those with me *and* Chris, two with Tyler, and study hall with Gwen and Caroline."

"You fixed my schedule? I don't need a babysitter, Will," I protest.

"Heyward students aren't like us, Layla. Tyler calls them *the others*. There will be three camps of people. The first will reject and be rude to you, making a point to turn you into the center of their ridicule. Did you see *Mean Girls*?" I nod. "It's worse than that."

"The second group won't care either way about you. The third, and most dangerous, will try to take you under their wing and to turn you into one of them. Tyler, Chris, and the girls know who they are so I asked them to make sure you didn't find yourself alone with any of them," Will explains.

"How did you change my schedule?" I ask a little more appreciative of Will's looking out for me. I forget that I have to let him show me he loves me in deed and action and not just with his amazing kisses.

"Mrs. Whitman loves me," he says with a wink and a twinkle in his distractingly blue eyes. "I promised I would protect you, Layla. Overconfident socialites are still the least of our worries." Will's tone changes. He's still worried about his father.

"You don't think he bought it, do you?" I say.

"I don't think you would have been invited to dinner if he hadn't already made up his mind. Like I told you before, my father doesn't waste his time with people that mean nothing to him. The only reason he has to involve himself with you is if he suspects in the least that you're going to tamper with his plan for my life."

"So what do you think he's going to do?" The confidence I had in my performance has more than dwindled and I again begin to think I've done more harm than good.

"Honestly, I don't know. This isn't like it was with Holly. Her dad had a gambling problem that caused them some serious financial issues, so accepting my dad's deal was sort of a no-brainer for them. He doesn't have the same kind of easy leverage with you or Luke and Claire. That's really bothering him. We'll just have to burn that bridge when we get to it. For now, we'll stick with the plan. That means we're going to have to give him proof."

"Marcus," I whisper. "I'm so sorry about that, Will."

"It's ok. He took us all off guard and you had to think faster on your feet than we thought you would. I don't like it, but we're going to have to involve him."

"Can it wait until I get through my first week at Heyward?" I plead. I've got too much to think about with school to start strategizing with Marcus.

"Yeah…but we'll need to arrange some public appearances for you two. The Concert on the Green is the best option to start." Will is incredibly calm for a guy who's talking about coordinating fake dates for his girlfriend and another guy.

"Ok," I say, not really knowing how to respond. "So…why doesn't your dad just cut you off and leave you to fend for yourself? Isn't that what rich people do with their *slacker* kids?"

"Because he knows that's exactly what I want. I would love nothing more than to take my mom and just walk away. I could take care of us." He speaks like a warrior, prepared to defend against an oncoming enemy. "We don't need him like he needs us. We complete the picture for him so he looks good to the community and clients. If we walk, he's just a lonely old man and that doesn't sell as well."

"If he doesn't have any leverage, then what's there to worry about?" I ask, tearing apart a roll and buttering it. The last syllable has left my mouth when my memory is answering my question with a question. *Would he try to literally knock sense into Will, or Luke, like that poor guy a few weeks ago?* I wonder.

"Leverage or not, he won't rest until he gets what he wants. Right now he's counting on intimidating you into backing off. That little stunt he pulled at dinner, questioning you outright, is one he only pulls when he's either got absolutely nothing or so much that it's not worth the time it takes to play his game. With you, he's got nothing to work with, and if you don't back down… Well, I can promise you that it will drive him crazy to not have anything to work with, which in turn will make him even more furious with both of us."

It's the first time I've really begun to understand the severity of the situation. Just because Will's his son doesn't mean he won't do what he thinks is necessary, even if it is extreme. Will's father is not going to give up. He's not going to see how in love we are and magically be swept up in the romantics of it all. In any other circumstance he might like me, but because Will loves me, and I love him, I am now Gregory Meyer's enemy.

After dinner we walk off the tiramisu we shared. We've put away the worry for now and do all we can to simply enjoy being with each other. We pass the law firm without a word and cross the street. I don't even look at it except to acknowledge its presence in my periphery. I'm glad when we find ourselves in front of the coffee shop where we first met. We look at each other knowingly and begin to laugh. It's the first jovial moment in the night. I open the door to the shop and Will asks where I'm going.

"I still owe you a Coke, remember?" We laugh some more and Will follows me in.

The mood, however, quickly turns awkward when we see Marcus sitting in the corner, drinking coffee and reading a book. It's more than awkward. I'm terrified. I just solidified the plan to tell him about Will and me after I made it through the first week of school, but…we're here now and it seems there's no time like the present.

"Hi Marcus," I say, greeting him cautiously.

"Hey Layla." Marcus is very obviously ignoring Will.

"Hello, Marcus. It's good to see you. It's been a while." Will extends his hand to shake, but Marcus hesitates, leaving Will's hand waiting in mid-air for what seems like minutes before reaching out to reciprocate. We've caught each other off guard and no one seems sure of what to say or do. "I'm glad we ran into you. Layla has something she would like to talk with you about." Will's tone is calm and easy as he leaves me standing there with Marcus. I don't know where to start so I just sit down, hoping to buy some time. The first thing I need to do is decide if I'm mad at Will for throwing me under the bus here to spill the beans to Marcus, but it takes only seconds to know that Will is right. I have to tell him what's going on not just because we need him on board, but out of respect for Marcus.

"You don't need to say anything, Layla. It's clear what's going on. He gets the money and the girl. I just hope you know what you're doing," Marcus says with disdain in his voice. He's struggling with the memory of what Mr. Meyer did to tear his family apart, all because his sister wanted Will.

"Marcus, we…I…need your help," I blurt out clumsily.

"How could you and money bags possibly need my help?" He's already skeptical and I have no reason to think he'll be on board with any plan that makes anything easier for Will.

"I told Mr. Meyer that you and I might be…romantically involved. He was questioning me as to my feelings for Will and you were the first person that came to mind." This is *so* not going the way I hoped it would, but in my own defense, it's not like I had time to prepare.

"Why would you do that? I don't want to have anything to do with that family. You know that, Layla." His brow furrows and he is *not* happy with me.

"I had to make him think that I wasn't interested in Will. I did it to protect him." I hesitate, knowing what he'll say. "I love him, Marcus."

"I told you this was going to happen. I warned you," he says, his volume rising slightly. He's more upset than I had expected.

"I know, and you have every right to say no, but…"

"But what?" he drops his book on the table and it lands with a thud that makes me jump.

"Don't you wish someone had been there to help Holly?" It's an unfair play, but it's the best card I've got.

He stares at me for a long minute. "That's a really crappy move, Layla." Shaking his head he finally says, "Fine. What is it that I'm supposed to do exactly? If it involves keeping you away from Will Meyer, I'm totally in."

"Thank you, Marcus. You have no idea what this means to us…to me." I reach over and squeezed his hand in a show of gratitude.

Will arrives with drinks for all three of us when he sees that Marcus and I have come to an agreement. "Thank you, Marcus. I'm sure Layla has expressed our gratitude for your help."

"I'm not doing this for you. I'm doing this for Layla. I won't let her go through what you put Holly through." His posture changes in a move to defend me. I know it's a move he wishes he had been able to make to protect Holly.

"Well, then you and I are on the same page." Will's reply is smooth and completely unaggressive. He knows the pain Holly experienced having faced and been threatened by his father and couldn't be more tormented about it. He and Marcus *are* on the same page – they both want to protect me. "So let's talk ground rules."

Chapter 18

Will's scheduling plan is working perfectly. I'm never alone and I get to see him in two of my classes. I'm pleased to find that most of the Heyward students really don't care either way about me, although some of them make rude comments about me going "from rags to riches." It's annoying, but not anything that I can't handle. I'm approached a dozen times in the first few weeks of school by people who want to take me on as their own Eliza Doolittle, but Gwen and Caroline are swift to come to my rescue. After a few body guard barricades by Chris and Tyler, it's a safe bet that no one is going to risk personal injury just to get to me.

I'm in a groove with my classes, doing as well as I expected in all of them. Honors English Lit is a breeze as we're studying one of my favorites, *Beowolf*. Trig and chemistry are the thorns in my side I had anticipated. I'm meeting with Marcus once or twice a week for tutoring. He mainly comes to the house, but sometimes we meet in the school library so the Heyward elite can see us, but only when Will is studying there, too. Will hasn't said as much, but I think he'd prefer that we meet at the house all the time so he or Luke and Claire can keep an eye on me. Tutoring is going well. I get it a little bit more every day and my anxiety about being an eternal senior is beginning to dissipate.

Marcus and I made a public appearance at the last concert of the summer on the Green as Will suggested. The Davidson College Symphony was closing out the summer concert series and it seemed like it was even more crowded than usual. It was especially thick with college students, most of whom Marcus knew. As we stopped and chatted with people, Marcus was sure to introduce me as his girlfriend. While we were on display for everyone my main objective was to be seen by Will's father. Marcus made a point to hold my hand or put his arm around me, which was hard for Will to see but exactly what Will's father needed. Gregory Meyer is at every one of the concerts and this one was no exception.

It's not easy for my heart to belong to Will and not be able to be with him. It's proving to be a more difficult undertaking than I thought. It's especially hard when I'm with Marcus and Will is right there, being forced to watch every moment. I wish there were an easier way to do this.

*****

The weather is turning cold and I'm experiencing my first real fall. Its 55 degrees during the day and I'm freezing. It's not that it doesn't get cold in Florida, but it's just that fifty-five here and fifty-five there are two different temperatures. Will thinks it's hysterical, but he doesn't mind holding me closer to warm me up, and neither do I.

Claire enjoys another shopping trip with me after she asked me to put on my warmest sweater and I pulled out a lightweight button-up cardigan. It's so different from what I'm used to, but I'm really enjoying the crisp air and the crunch of the leaves. It's nice to live in a place with four whole seasons. It helps me focus on this being a new chapter in my life.

It's already the end of October and Will and I have successfully evaded being caught by anyone who might reveal us to his father. We spend most of our time together at my house, and sometimes with our friends. They cover for us quite a bit, allowing us to have time alone together away from my house. We take day trips to quaint mountain towns, and sometimes drive into Charlotte.

When we're home, Luke and Claire are great about giving us enough privacy that we don't feel like we're being watched all the time. Will also does a great job of making our dates creative. He's taking his job of making our relationship as normal as possible very seriously. We've had a picnic on the floor of the loft when it was pouring rain outside. One day he pretended he was a great artist and sketched me. It was the best stick figure rendition of me I had ever seen. Another time Will tried to teach me how to fish off the dock. For a Florida girl, I am awful at fishing. I caught nothing, but Will was patient. We laughed a lot that day.

There's a buzz in the air about the New Year's Eve Gala even though we haven't even crossed the threshold into November. The school doesn't have a sports program and so there are no homecoming games or dances like at normal schools. In order for all the girls at the school to have a chance at practicing their formal arm-candy stance Mr. Meyer throws a huge party on New Year's Eve.

It's like planning for a wedding the way the girls at school talk about it. There are dresses to be designed and fittings to attend, and under no circumstance will there be an off-the-rack dress worn by any of them. I already don't want to go, but I know I'll have to attend. Will is obligated to go and I hate the idea of him going and not being there, too. I can only imagine how handsome he's going to look in his tuxedo. While I won't be able to do anything about it, I'd at least like to see which prima donna witch tries to dig her claws into him, and I suppose I secretly want an opportunity to look beautiful for him.

Halloween is apparently a big deal in Davidson. The town has organized another stellar affair. I've grown to appreciate their events. They are always done so well and end up being a lot of fun. Besides, I feel a lot less like an outsider when I'm out of the Hayward bubble and out milling about with the whole town.

The Halloween parade and trick-or-treating party meet my every expectation of the hometown greatness I've come to love about Davidson. Merchants have set up tables outside so kids can come and show off their costumes and get candy. I laugh to myself as I remember Halloween with my parents. Ours was *that house* – the one that gave out Scarrots and other healthy "treats." There is none of that here, just pure, unadulterated sugar.

I stand on the side of the Green watching the kids march up and down the sidewalk in search of the merchant who is giving out the best candy. I love watching the kids for whom this is their first Halloween. They're easy to spot. They're the kids who, when the candy is dropped in their bag, start shaking in disbelief that they just got more free candy. They're even cuter because they're usually around three years old.

As I stand watching the sidewalk festivities Will nonchalantly positions himself next to me among the scattered passing crowd and we enjoy the view together for a few minutes.

"Where are you parents?" I ask without turning to look at him. I'm probably being overly cautious, but I don't want to seem too interested in him, as there are several people from school around.

"They're getting coffee, but they've got a charity dinner to go to tonight. What are you doing later? I thought I could come over," Will says.

"That sounds great. I think Luke and Claire are going to the same thing." I smile, probably a little too big, but the idea of being totally and completely alone with Will for a few hours makes me happier than I'm allowed to fully express.

"I'll pick up Chinese on my way over. By the way…I love you." Will grins knowing that we're sharing a moment right there in front of everyone and no one has a clue.

We see Mr. and Mrs. Meyer exit the coffee shop and scan through the crowd looking for Will. They cross the street and make their way toward us, heads held high in the confidence that they've located their son. I'm nervous, even though Will and I haven't as much as glanced at each other, and I can't imagine that they would see this as anything but two friends having run into each other at a town event. Before they can reach us, Marcus jaywalks right to where we are and puts his arm around my waist. Will stiffens and takes a step back. Then, as if the timing were rehearsed, Marcus kisses me on the cheek and says, "Hey babe," just as Will's parents reach us.

"Hello Marcus," Mr. Meyer says as he hands Will his coffee. "It's nice to see you. How's your family doing?" His tenor is so obviously passive-aggressive. I'm impressed that Marcus doesn't punch him right then and there.

"Hello, sir. My family is doing well, thank you." Marcus' reply shows that he's the better man. From what I understand, this is the first time Marcus has had any exchange with Mr. Meyer since his parents picked up with his sister and left town to only he knows where. He's smooth and calm in his response, but squeezes me just a bit tighter in what I assume is an effort to maintain his coolness.

"I understand you've snatched up our newest resident. You two look very happy together. Don't they look happy together, William?" Mr. Meyer says. Will is right. His father doesn't believe us for a second, and he's taking his chance to rub our futile charade in Will's face.

"Yes…so happy it's almost distasteful," Will replies, relaying his disapproval.

"Yes, well, Layla is one in a million. Any guy would be lucky to have her choose him. I consider myself incredibly fortunate to have her." Marcus pulls me closer to him, as if that were possible, and I see Will's nostrils flare.

"William, we're ready to leave," his father says directly.

"I'd be happy to give Will a ride home if he wants to stay and hang out with us. Layla and I are going out later but I can take him home on our way. It's no trouble," Marcus offers in a lie.

Will nods silently in acceptance of Marcus' suggestion, and Mr. and Mrs. Meyer leave without saying much more. We're not there much longer before it's clear that Will can't take watching Marcus with me anymore. I have to admit that Marcus' commitment to this charade is a bit much. I'm not sure that an actual boyfriend touches his actual girlfriend quite this much in public. Marcus has either held my hand or had his arm around me the entire time. I hate to think that he's doing it to get back at Will, but it's hard not to entertain that possibility. I can't take watching Will suffer any longer so I tell them both I'm tired and ready to go home.

The drive home is humiliating for Will as he squishes into the back seat of Marcus' two-door hatch back. I barely have time to give Will a quick hug before he's bolted and I see his front door closing. It only takes a few minutes and Marcus is pulling into my driveway.

"Thanks, Marcus, for stepping in back there. We really appreciate it," I say as we walk to the porch.

"I'm not sure that Will appreciated it too much," he says.

"Well, you might want to tone it down a bit. It's just hard for him to see me with you…like that." I should be more forceful with him about his behavior, but I don't want to lose his support. There may come a day soon when we need him to really be there.

"Well…it's not easy for me to see you with him." Marcus takes my hand.

"Marcus…" I pull away.

"I just don't want to see you get hurt, Layla." Marcus takes a step closer and for a moment I think he's going to try to kiss me. I feel a twist in my stomach and I don't know what to do.

"Marcus. I…" I'm cut off by a sound that takes me back to the most horrific night of my life. The screeching of Will's tires brings him to a rapid stop in the driveway. As he flies out of the car I can see the fury on his face and know that this is not good.

"What do you think you were doing back there? I trusted you and then you've got your hands all over her!" Will shouts as he charges at Marcus.

"I was just doing what you asked me to do!" Marcus matches Will's volume.

"Pawing her in public was NEVER part of the deal," Will barks as he pushes Marcus, making him stumble backward. Marcus gains his footing and charges back at Will. Before I know it, they've each gotten more than one punch in and are both bleeding.

"Will! Stop! What are you doing?" I yell, stepping in between them with no regard to the risk of getting punched myself.

"Me? You're ok with having his hands all over you like that, and kissing you?" he says half charging at me now. He's so angry. His face is red and he's yelling at me. I back up with every step he takes toward me.

"No, Will! It's not like that and you know it! Why are you acting like this?"

"Haven't you considered why he agreed to help us? This is his chance, his opportunity to make my life a living hell as vengeance for what happened with Holly. And you…you're falling right into his plan aren't you?" I have considered it. I feel the sharp sting of every word and tears well up in my eyes. I tilt my head back to keep them from streaming down my face. "Or maybe there's another reason why *his* was the first name that came to mind." I don't even have time to gather my thoughts to express a coherent statement of defense before Marcus intervenes.

"Back off, Will!" Marcus stands in between us. "You're scaring her." Will stops in his tracks, panting, with his chest heaving.

"Just keep your hands off of her." Will wipes the blood from his lip as he moves his dagger-filled stare from Marcus to a less deadly glower at me. He holds his gaze on me for few long seconds. "I'll deal with you later." I struggle to look beyond his rage, but it's difficult. He gets back into his car, tires screeching out of the driveway the same way he entered.

It takes another few minutes before I'm confident I can speak without bursting into tears. "I'm so sorry, Marcus. I'll talk to him and get him to apologize," I say examining the cut by his eye.

"You're *staying* with him? Layla…*that* was Gregory Meyer. You can't seriously still want to be with him?" Marcus tries to furrow his brow but it aggravates his cut and he winces.

"Just because things are…complicated…doesn't mean they can't work." I realize as I'm saying this that I'm not sure who I'm trying to convince. I spent years in a complicated situation with my grandparents. It wasn't what I wanted but I made it work for their sake. If I could do it then when I didn't even want to, I can do it now…for me, can't I?

We don't talk about it anymore, and I decide not to address his lack of respect for my personal space. If it happens again I'll be forced to, but I'm hoping he had a momentary lapse in judgment and it won't be an issue. I take him in the house, tend to his wound and send him home.

Over the next days at school it isn't difficult for me to pretend to not be with Will. I'm confused. Part of me understands Will's anger. I can't imagine how I would feel to see him with another girl, but another part of me, a part that I don't want to admit is really there, is afraid that Marcus is right. I witnessed the fury that boils inside the Meyer men. His last words to me ring in my ears. *I'll deal with you later.* Now I'm something to be dealt with?

Will tries to talk to me in the covert way we learned to communicate in front of others, but I can't respond. I'm not sure what to say, but more afraid that I'll cry if I start to talk. He comes to the house, but I don't want to see him…not yet. I just need some time to figure things out.

"Do you want to talk about it?" Claire asks, finding me in my favorite spot in the loft again. She didn't have to look hard. I come home from school every day and sit here, staring out the window until dinner. I can see the lake even better now that the leaves have fallen from the trees. It's a perfect picture of the changing season in so many ways.

"This…it's just harder than I thought it was going to be. I thought it would be romantic. You know…clandestine love and all. It just makes me feel…alone. I can't be myself because myself loves Will. I don't know what to do." I feel more confused now that I'm verbalizing the garbled mess of my emotions. It's like when you cut a pan of brownies but haven't waited long enough for them to cool. They crumble and fall apart and there's no way to piece it back together so that it remotely resembles a square.

"Layla, you're not obligated to any*thing* or any*one*. If you're not sure what you want, you're allowed to take a step back and reevaluate. You're still *so* young and so much is going to change for you over the next few years of your life." Claire always has a way of letting me off the hook and making me feel empowered at the same time.

"I love him, Claire. But…" I don't want to tell her about Will's rage. She'll pull the plug for sure and then it won't be my decision. I need her help, and I did promise that I would tell her if anything happened. "Will kind of freaked me out the other night."

"What do you mean?" Claire tilts her head in suspicion.

"Marcus stepped in at Halloween and covered for us in front of Will's parents. He was a little touchy-feely and Will didn't like it. He and Marcus got in a fight and then Will…well…he got really angry and yelled at me because he thought I was taking Marcus' side."

"Layla…" Claire starts.

"He was just hurt because he didn't like seeing me with Marcus that way. I didn't like it either," I say in Will's defense.

"This is what I was talking about." Claire's eyes get bigger and I can see that she's upset. It's the first time I've seen this expression. Usually Claire is soft and tender, but right now she looks like she could fight a lion and win.

Luke interrupts us to tell me that Will is there and wants to see me. Luke never answers for me. He always asks in case my decision has changed.

"Tell him I'll be there in a minute," I answer Luke. "Claire, I'm willing to understand what happened. I really can't blame him for being upset. Marcus went overboard, but the whole thing made me realize that I don't think I can do this until graduation…or indefinitely. I don't think I can pretend anymore. I mean, I thought everything was going great, but…after what happened I realize that as long as we have to pretend, Will is going to be faced with seeing me with someone else. It just doesn't seem fair to either one of us." I'm devastated at the idea of telling Will. We've promised so much to each other. I don't like going back on my word.

"The most important thing is that you're true to yourself. Even though we love someone, sometimes we have to let go because loving them compromises who we are. I'm proud of you, Layla." Claire gives me a hug of support before I go downstairs and break Will's heart.

I meet Will in the living room. He looks sad and it breaks my heart to add to his pain.

"Hey," I say as I reach the bottom of the stairs.

"Hey. Thanks for seeing me." He embraces me and I get emotional at the thought that this could be the last time I feel Will's arms around me like this. "Layla, I can't tell you how sorry I am. It just drove me crazy to see his hands on you. The way he looked at me while he was doing it…it was like he was punishing me."

"Will…he may have gone a little over board, but we asked him to help us make it look like he and I were together. You can't punch him when he does it. What happens when we go away to school? Are you going to hire bodyguards to keep an eye on me? There might actually be guys that hit on me. You have to trust me to handle myself, but that's not what bothers me the most." I'm serious now; intent on making sure he knows what he did.

"I know, and I'm even sorrier about that. I…I can't believe I yelled at you like that." He reaches out to touch me but I pull away. "Baby, I'm sorry. I really am." My pulling away has hurt him deeply. I hate that, but once I get to thinking about that moment, his touch is the last thing I want.

"As long as we have to pretend that I'm with someone other than you, this is going to happen again. I don't want to walk on eggshells for the next seven months, Will." I can't look him in the eye. I know if I do I'll be drawn in and will go back on what I know I need to do. "I was wrong to think that we could pull this off anyway. Your dad doesn't buy it and it's only a matter of time before it all comes crumbling down around us."

"No, you were *right*! We *can* do this. Layla, before I met you I thought I'd never get close enough to anyone to feel this way. I was too scared to even try, but you make me want to be brave. You make me realize that love is real and worth every risk just to have it."

"Will…"

"Layla, please. We can do this. It won't happen again. I can deal with Marcus, I promise. I'll even apologize to him if you want. You don't understand what this is doing to me," he pleads. The tone in his voice is new. It's full of pain; pain that I can take away if I change my mind. The whites of his ocean blue eyes are now red and watery. He's holding back tears and I have to look away.

"No, Will, *you* don't understand. For five years I *pretended* that I was ok living with my grandparents. I *pretended* that game shows and puzzles was sufficient entertainment; I *pretended* to be ok with having dinner at 4:30 and going to bed at eight. I *pretended* that having friends and doing things girls are supposed to love doing wasn't important to me. I gave up everything I loved about me because I had to, and I don't want to do that anymore. The only silver lining to moving here was feeling like I had a chance to start over; feeling like I didn't have to spend the another five years waiting for the next important person in my life to die."

"I didn't know. Why didn't you tell me?" Will's demeanor is softer now, like the Will I fell in love with.

"I didn't want to be the girl with baggage at 17. I just wanted to start over. Look, if we're meant to be together, then, we will." It's a lame response and I hate giving it. "Right now, your dad makes *us* an impossibility. Standing up to him isn't an option, so what else are we going to do, Will? I don't want to be with you and pretend to not love you. It's not so easy turning my feelings on and off. I thought I could do it for the sake of keeping you safe, but it's only hurting us." I can't take it anymore. I walk to the front door and open it. "You should go."

Will steps to the door and stands as close as he possibly can in front of me. I can feel the warmth of his breath and the heat from his body.

"I understand better than you think I do. You're not the only one who's spent their life pretending to be someone they're not." He moves a quarter step closer, taking my face in his left hand. "I am *never* letting go of you. If I have to wait a hundred years, I will. I love you, Layla. We belong together and you know it." He puts his other arm around my waist, leans down and kisses me like he did the first time on the porch that amazing summer night. I force myself to be still so I don't wrap my arms around him and melt into him.

I close the door behind him, not watching him leave as I usually do. Then I drop to the floor and cry like never before. It is in this moment that I realize my season of punishment had not been those five years in Orlando. My season of punishment is now.

Chapter 19

The days move slowly and I find myself in automatic mode. I go to school every day, come home and do my homework. Then after that I either read or stare out the window of the loft from my favorite chair, except for the days I meet with Marcus for tutoring. He's asked me what happened with Will a few times, but I don't answer, changing the subject. He eventually stops asking and I assume he's either finally put two and two together, or just plain gave up.

I don't feel completely alone, as Gwen and Caroline haven't abandoned me. They did their best to talk me through things in the days that followed, but I wouldn't say anything about Will or what happened. I don't want to paint any kind of picture of him. Everything they know about the break up comes from Will. I feel bad for being so mute about the whole thing but I just don't know how to express myself without looking or feeling stupid. So they press on, making things as normal as possible.

I sit next to Tyler and Chris in the classes we have together, and with the girls in study hall. The hardest part is the two classes I have with Will. We're seated alphabetically, so I don't normally sit with him, but now that seems to be more awkward. He skips class a lot, and when he is there, he isn't really. He leaves notes for me in my locker, and sometimes Chris and Tyler will deliver them. Each one reads the same: *I will never stop loving you.* If I didn't still love him deeply I would consider a restraining order. By the time Thanksgiving break arrives I have 84 notes from Will.

I keep every single one of them in my nightstand.

Though the days drag on, Thanksgiving eventually arrives. Luke and Claire spent the holidays with some other couples from the firm at the Meyer's house over the last few years. Had Will and I not split I would have looked forward to the chance to be together on the holiday, but this year they told Mr. Meyer that they'd be celebrating the holidays with me at home. Not surprisingly, he didn't mind at all.

I thought it would be weird having a holiday without any of the family I grew up with. I'm a little sad, but it isn't like I thought it would be. I've been with Luke and Claire for almost six months now, but with everything that's gone on it feels like so much longer, like we've always been a family.

Claire and I brave the Black Friday sales, standing in line at Target at four in the morning. Later at the mall she swears she'll eventually get something for Luke, but I ultimately have to tear her away from the shoe department and we settle on some things we think Luke will love.

Shopping for Claire with Luke is an entirely different experience, and takes a fraction of the time. All we have to do is walk up to the counter of Claire's favorite stores – Tiffany's and Neiman-Marcus – where she has set aside the items Luke and I can choose from. Luke says he learned a long time ago that this is the safest way to shop for Claire.

As I scan the cases at Tiffany's, something catches my eye – something I think Claire will love – and I know what I'm going to do with some of the money I saved from Gramps.

The whole weekend we decorate the house for Christmas, play holiday music, and eat more than we should. I end the weekend feeling closer to Luke and Claire than ever.

I have a big trigonometry test the Friday after we get back from Thanksgiving break on verifying identities. My tutoring with Marcus is paying off – I'm only moderately lost instead of completely lost – but I'm still nervous. I ask Marcus to come to the house for all of our tutoring now. Luke makes sure Will isn't there working on the basement, and I don't want to risk running into Will in town or at school. God only knows what he'd do if he saw Marcus and me together.

"So that's how we use Euler's formula to show sine times x plus y equals sine times x times cosine times y plus sine times y times cosine times x. Make sense?"

"I...think so...no." I toss my pencil down in frustration.

"Hey...it's ok. We'll just start over again," Marcus says trying to calm my irritation.

"We've been going over this section for over an hour. How I'm passing this class at all is a mystery to me. Can we just pick this up next time?" I have a headache. My brain is fried and I'm sure it is making plans to crack open my skull and make a run for it any minute now. I don't blame it.

"Sure. I'll come by on Thursday. Sound good?"

"Yeah, thanks, Marcus. I appreciate it." I close my books with a furious and thundering clap and shove them across the table. I wish there were some way out of this class altogether. Not only is it ridiculously difficult for me, this is one of the classes I have with Will. His being there makes it hard to concentrate, which only adds to my deficiencies in this subject.

"So...I wanted to ask how you were doing. You've ignored me every other time I've brought it up." Marcus isn't one to give up easily. It's been several weeks and I can finally think about it without crying, so I appease him, but only slightly. He's been patient, and considering he shed some blood over the issue, I feel like he's earned it somehow.

"There's not much to tell, Marcus. Will and I broke up." Maybe I'm not going to appease him completely, but at least I'm not ignoring him altogether.

"I know you broke up, Layla. I want to know how you're feeling about it. I remember how Holly felt. It was really hard for her. Despite my feelings about Will, he's apparently a good guy and one a girl would hate to lose. So..." he presses.

"It sucks. I hate it. I wish I could take it back, but I can't. Does that answer your question?" I answer with frustration.

"You could take it back if you wanted to. I'm sure Will would be happy for you to. I know I would be." Marcus is tender and caring, but I don't like it when he inserts himself into the scenario.

"Don't say things like that," I say.

"It's true. But…I'm sorry if I made you uncomfortable."

"I know I could take it back, Marcus. That doesn't mean it's a good idea."

"Listen, Layla…do you know what the most upsetting part about what went down with Holly was? It was that they let Gregory Meyer decide for them. As furious as I was with the Meyers, I was equally disappointed in my family. Love can't be ruled with an iron fist. Meyer does whatever he wants because no one tells him he can't. When does it end? One day the Meyers are going to pay."

Marcus leaves and I sit there silently. *Could* I *stand up to Will's dad?* I think about this seriously for a full minute before I come to my senses and realize that it would be pointless. I would simply be a silly little girl trying to *distract* his son. No. This is for the best.

Miraculously I pass my trig exam and coast through the weeks until Christmas. Luke and Claire make it a really special day. We get up early and make breakfast together. I make mom's ham and cheese brunch squares while we listen to Christmas music. Then, we all sit on the floor in front of the tree and eat. Before we open gifts we take turns guessing what we think the others got us. Luke and I are totally off base. Claire already picked out the gifts we could choose from, so she has an unfair advantage.

Luke loves the cufflinks Claire gave him. He very *un*subtly dropped hints for weeks about wanting a charging station for his various and sundry electronic devices, so that's what I got for him. The earrings and iPod Luke selected from his choices are a hit with Claire.

Before my trip to the jewelry store with Luke I had been at a total loss as what to get Claire. I knew that just any gift wouldn't do, not because she wouldn't love whatever I gave her, but because it needed to be meaningful. I hand her the Tiffany Blue wrapped box with my gift inside and hope it means as much to her as it does to me.

"Oh, Layla," she says as she raises the lid of the jewelry box. Inside is a silver necklace with three tubular charms. The charms hold the birthstones of Luke, Claire and me. In the center is a pearl for me, with a sapphire and amethyst on either side for Claire and Luke. "This is so beautiful. Thank you…so much." Claire leans across the torn paper and empty boxes and hugs me tightly and then immediately puts the necklace on.

"I'm glad you like it. I know I didn't pick from what you chose, but I wanted to get you something that…well…that meant something. It's our little family." Tears start to fill my eyes, but I choke them back.

"I love it, Layla. I love you. It means more to me than you'll ever know." Claire hugs me again, giving an extra squeeze before she lets go. "Ok, you've waited long enough. It's time for you to open your gifts," Claire says, shifting the attention onto me, which I don't particularly love, but am learning to tolerate much better.

I open a few boxes with clothes that Claire knew I needed. The weather will be getting colder and I still don't have enough warm clothes to get me through. Luke got me a new iPod, which is great because I'm running out of space on the one I already have. Then, Claire and Luke give each other a smile and hand me the last gift under the tree. I open the slender box and gasp. I cannot hold back the tears now.

It's a Kindle Reader.

"We already downloaded all the classics and we set up an account online so you can download anything else you want whenever you want." Luke's eyes are wide and as excited mine.

"Thank you so much! It's perfect!" I hug them tighter than I ever have before. I'm so happy. It isn't the gift, but what it represents. They know me, really *know* me. After years of feeling like a lonely island, of being looked at and not seen, Luke and Claire have seen who I am, and it's an incredible feeling.

We spend the afternoon playing with our new toys, and Claire talks me into doing a fashion show for Luke. She paid perfect attention on our shopping excursions. Every outfit she got me is both the right size and my exact style. Then we cook and eat more food than three people need in one sitting and it's after midnight before we all go to bed.

It was the best day I'd had in a long time.

*****

Luke and Claire ask me for the hundredth time if I'm sure I want to skip the New Year's Gala as they ready themselves for their annual New Year's date. With a bottle of soda in one hand and a bowl of popcorn in the other, I confirm that I'm fine and send them on their way. They wish me a happy New Year as they leave to meet Caroline's parents, who are Luke and Claire's closest friends. I close the door behind them and settle in for a night of junk food and movie watching. If I spend too much time thinking about the fact that this could have been the first year I would have had someone to kiss at midnight I may get depressed, so I focus on the gratuitous humor that awaits me.

I've just started the first movie when the doorbell rings. I think Claire may have come back for something so I run down to get the door as quickly as I can. I hate the idea of their date being delayed at all. When I open the door I'm shocked to see Caroline standing there in her pajamas, pillow in one hand, a stack of movies in the other.

"What are you doing here? I thought you were going to the New Year's

Gala!" I can't hide my excitement at her presence on my doorstep.

"Your aunt told me what you had planned for tonight and I decided it was going to be way more fun than the Gala. So are you going to let me in? It's freezing out here!" she says.

"Yes! Yes! Get in here!" I close the door behind Caroline and give her a huge hug. I'm really happy that she's here. Caroline and I march upstairs and settle in to ring in the New Year together.

I love having Caroline here with me, but I can't deny that her presence is a reminder of Will and everything I'm missing now that we're no longer together. The more I think about him, the more I think about Caroline and Gwen. It seems unfair that Will's father would hate *me* so much and accept them.

"Caroline? Why me?" That's all I have to say and Caroline knows exactly what I'm talking about.

"It's not you, Layla. It's anything that reinforces Will's rejection of his father's supreme authority, power, and control," she says. It sounds a bit rehearsed and I wonder if this is what the conversation revealed when the smoke cleared after Holly.

"Don't you and Gwen do the same thing? I mean, Will could have just as easily fallen for you. You feel the same way about things as he does."

"We've known Will practically our whole lives. Mr. Meyer has had time to get used to us. He sees us as one of them. We're *in* this counterfeit world he treasures so much."

"So am I, technically," I say defiantly.

"Technically, yes, but it's not the same. You just got here and haven't had time to conform yet. Trust me, I know. I almost didn't make it on his good list," she says.

"What do you mean?" I'm curious. How could anyone not like Caroline? She's absolutely the sweetest, most agreeable person I've ever known. To not like her would make you the devil himself. Oh, that answers my question.

"I'm adopted. My parents got me when I was six," she says without hesitation. She's so matter of fact.

"I didn't know that. But…what would that have to do with whether Mr. Meyer accepted you or not?"

"My birth mom was a prostitute and a drug addict. I don't know who my father was; I don't think she knew either. When Mr. Meyer found out he was concerned that it was too late for me to understand how things work around here – that I had already been corrupted beyond reform. When Will and I would play together as kids, he watched us like a hawk. I don't know what he was expecting me to do. I was six. I wasn't exactly hiding a dime bag of pot in my lunch box. But, I guess when he saw that I wasn't going to damage his son he eased up. I remember those years well."

"Years?" It's going to take years for Will's dad to approve of me? And even then there is no guarantee!

"Yeah, from six until about eight. My parents were great about it though. They're a lot like your aunt and uncle. As I got older, they were really open with me and explained why my friend's dad was so weird around me. It never really mattered to me. Will was my friend and treated me like a friend should be treated."

"So what am I supposed to do?" I feel so defeated.

"You can't do anything. It's not the same, Layla. Will doesn't want to just be your friend. He's in love with you. You're the one."

"If I'm the one and he's in love with me, why can't we be together?" I'm emotional now.

"You *can* be together. *You* broke up with *him*, remember?" Caroline challenges.

"I broke up with him because I don't want to be with him and have to pretend to not love him. How would you like it if you couldn't go out in public with the person you loved most in the world? If you had to pretend to be with someone else because if the wrong people saw you together the most evil man on the planet would destroy you? Since Will won't stand up to his dad, there's really nothing left to discuss. I just can't do it, Caroline."

"Layla, it's not that he doesn't want to, it's that he can't. I know more about what happened with Holly than Gwen or the guys. Will's afraid of what will happen to you, or your aunt and uncle. I know this has got to be terrible for you, but if it makes you feel any better at all, you've got to know that this is killing him. Will *really* loves you."

I know that Will loves me. That's what makes it so difficult. I'm torn between being grateful for his efforts to keep my family safe and angry because I want him to care more about loving me than any consequences. Now I can't help feeling like a hypocrite. If I love Will, why am I not willing to do what it takes to be with him?

I think about what my mother would say about me giving up like this. I was so tenacious as a child. Once I set my mind to something, I never gave up. The last time I did that was when I moved in with Gram and Gramps. I set my mind to not set my mind to anything else. My one and only objective was to be agreeable and make their lives as easy as possible. It meant never even attempting to fight for anything, no matter how much I wanted it.

But…maybe I *can* do this for Will, for me. Maybe I just need to be patient and wait until graduation. Or…maybe not. At this point all I want to do is start over and wipe the slate clean…again. I miss Will. I miss his arms, his body, and his lips, but more than that, I miss his company. I miss the days he came to work on the basement and we would talk non-stop over lunch. I miss his friendship. If I'm going to start over I have to get rid of everything that only serves to complicate the situation. To do that, I have to talk to Marcus.

"Thank you, Caroline." I say hugging her.

"For what? I thought for sure I was upsetting you," she says, wrapping her arms around me.

"I'm just really glad I have you. Ok, enough with the heavy, let's finish this year out right! We've only got a few minutes left." I grab Caroline's hand and run downstairs and get the sparkling apple cider Claire got for me. She made me promise that I would at least toast the New Year, even if I were by myself. Caroline and I gush over Ryan Seacrest and watch the ball drop in Time Square, toasting to a better year. The previous one left a lot to be desired. The New Year can only get better.

Chapter 20

The door to the bookstore closes noisily behind me. *Gosh! There is no sneaking into this place.* Marcus rounds the corner from behind an aisle of historical fiction books. He looks good, like he always does. I have to admit that when he and I pretended to be together, I didn't hate it. I liked when he sat close to me. I liked when he held my hand. It made me not feel so alone, but it isn't the same as how I feel when Will does it, and I know I have to say what I've come to say.

Marcus smiles when he sees me and doesn't hesitate to approach. I have to stop him before he puts his arms around me and I procrastinate.

"Are you ok?" he asks.

"I'm…fine. I need to talk to you," I say.

"Sure. Do you want to go next door, grab a coffee?"

"No. This won't take long." I pause to calm my nerves. "I just wanted to let you know that I've asked for a different tutor, and that…I can't be around you right now."

"What? Layla…why?" He's visibly upset. Surely this was the last thing he was expecting me to say. "Is this because I pushed you to talk about Will? I'm sorry. I didn't mean to upset you."

"No…not really. It's for the best, Marcus. I just can't have anything complicated in my life right now," I say.

"And I'm a complication?" He furrows his brow.

"Yes."

"You know you can never be with him," he says after considering my answer.

"Maybe not, but whenever I'm with you, all I think about is Will…and Holly. I just want to start over, Marcus, and that means that I can't be around you right now. I'm sorry. I really appreciate your friendship and everything you did to try to help us. I'm sorry that it got you hurt. I hope you can understand."

"I understand that you have no clue what you're dealing with. Gregory Meyer is more than just a power hungry guy with a chip on his shoulder. He is capable of doing things…unimaginable things. You're going to get yourself hurt if you don't stay away from them. Meyer men are relentless." Marcus' tone is fierce. His eyes are darker and his face tight with strained seriousness.

"I appreciate your concern, Marcus, but I'm fine. I'm sorry that…I'm just sorry." I don't wait for a response. I turn around and walk out of the store. I get in my car and let myself cry for the loss of the friendship with Marcus that I envisioned growing and blooming, but I cry for only a minute because I can't waste my time with any more tears.

Marcus' words ring in my head on the drive home. *Unimaginable things.* What did he mean? I think on this for a while and, even though I've witnessed my own Meyer attack, decide that Marcus was being dramatic in his efforts to keep me away from Will. If Gregory Meyer were *that* dangerous Luke and Claire would have told me.

I arrive home to find Will's car in the driveway. Luke didn't tell me he was coming today. He always does, so this must be an unexpected visit. I think about slipping upstairs unnoticed but this has gone on long enough. I have to be mature and, after all, I live here. I enter through the front door and see Luke, Claire and Will sitting in the front living room waiting for me like some kind of intervention. Will stands up immediately with a small gift-wrapped box in his hands.

"We'll leave you two to talk," Claire says giving me a nod as she and Luke leave the room. It isn't like them to ambush me like this. There has to be something to whatever Will wants to say, so I don't protest.

"Hi," I say first. It's so good to see him. My heart aches as he approaches me, standing close enough that I can feel the warmth of his body.

"Hi. I brought you something. I actually got this for you a while ago and planned on giving it to you at Christmas. It doesn't seem right for you to not have it," he says quietly, reaching out to hand me the box. His voice has lost its luster. It's still smooth, but no longer dynamic.

"That's really nice of you, Will." I reach out and take the Tiffany Blue wrapped box from him. He looks on with what I can only describe as censored anticipation as I unwrap the package. Inside the larger box is a small black velvet box. My heart flutters and I'm filled with mixed emotions. Giving me gifts doesn't exactly help with my trying to get over Will, but I can't help but relish in the flood of lovely emotions that well up in me, too. To receive an unanticipated gift from someone is the ultimate proof that they thought of you when you weren't around. I like that feeling…a lot.

I open the small box and take a short, startled breath. Inside is a shiny, silver chain with an equally brilliant silver sand dollar charm. "It's beautiful. Thank you, Will," I say softly in a preemptive move to thwart any tears that may erupt.

"I know you had been missing the ocean. This seemed fitting. I'm glad you like it. Can I help you put it on?" I hand Will the box and lift my hair. His arms reach around and as he pulls the chain around my neck. His hands touch my skin and I am overwhelmed. Another flood of emotions come over me and all I can think about is how much I want him like I did that day in the loft.

"I like it very much. Thank you, again. I'm sorry, I…didn't get you anything," I say, a little embarrassed at both having nothing to give him and the thoughts that have just rushed through my mind.

"There's only one thing I want from you, Layla…your heart. You gave it to me once. I'm hoping you'll give it to me again. Before you say anything, I have a proposal for you."

I'm a little nervous. The last time Will had a proposal for me he suggested we run away together. I miss him so much and, after what I just experienced, I would actually entertain it more seriously this time. "What's your proposal?"

"I want to be with you more than anything else in this world. I know that us trying to be together wasn't the most ideal situation, and that proved to be harder for you than I ever wanted it to be. It was unbearable for me as well. My…outburst…well… These last few months of being apart from you have been the worst in my life. I didn't just lose my girlfriend, I lost my best friend – the person I trust most in this world, the one person who calls me on all my crap and encourages me beyond anything I'm worthy of. I don't want to stay away from you. I *can't* be away from you anymore. Can we sever this distance? Can we at least *try* to be *just* friends? I miss you, Layla." I can see the hope in Will's eyes and can't help but be drawn in. I want to be there, in his eyes, his heart, his soul. I have no desire to fight it, but I'm scared.

"I've hated being apart from you, too. But, I don't know, Will. What's the difference between what we'd be trying to do now and what we were doing before?" I say.

"Well, I won't get to kiss you, and believe me, that is a huge difference because I love kissing you." Will takes my hand and my heart races.

"Will." I force myself to pull my hand away. It's distracting.

"Sorry." He takes a step back, but thankfully not a too far. "So, what do you think? We can hang out together with our friends again…interact at school. We can be friends and we won't be lying to anyone."

Except ourselves, I think.

"It would be great to see you again, and I *have* missed being with everyone." I take a deep breath to buy a moment of thinking. This is the *new* clean slate that I wanted, a do-over of sorts. Will has offered me a release from the new prison I found myself locked in. A sweet release back into the life I longed for. "Ok. Yes. I think it's worth a try."

Will throws his arms around me and lifts me off the ground as he hugs me. "Oh, Layla! You just made me the happiest guy on the planet! I've missed you so much!"

"I missed you, too!" I hug him back with as much enthusiasm, squeezing my arms tightly around his neck. It feels so good to be close to him again. I don't know how we're going to do it – we may fail miserably with one of us being declared insane – but we're going to try being *just* friends. I'm reminded of my conversation with Marcus and his strict warning that I should be nothing more than friends with Will, and then the look on his face that night in the coffee shop when I asked him to help us. Having just released Marcus from any obligation to me makes this moment completely stress-free.

Will puts me down and we take a long look at one another and smile, making up for all the moments we lost while we were apart. I'm staring so closely into his eyes that I find myself intentionally memorizing every detail of them. The way the blue of his eyes starts out just a hair of a shade lighter at the pupil and gradually becomes darker, finally becoming a deep ocean blue at the outer rim of color. It's just the slightest shift in color, but it's there.

The doorbell rings, interrupting our gaze. I answer it and can't believe the worse timing as Marcus stands before me.

"Are you kidding me?" Will says from behind me.

"Hey Layla. What's he doing here?" Marcus' tone is rude.

"What can I do for you, Marcus," I say, ignoring both of them.

"You left so quickly, I wanted to finish our conversation." He's looking at Will out of the corner of his eye.

"Our conversation was through. What more is there to say?" I offer.

"You didn't give me a chance to say anything. You just left."

"She said the conversation was over." Will steps forward in a territorial stance.

"I don't recall you being there, so how about you back off." Marcus matches Will's posture, stepping over the threshold.

"How about I finish kicking your ass?" Will retorts.

"How about the two of you stop acting like little boys. Will, go in the kitchen." Will does as he's told but not without giving Marcus the stare-down of all stare-downs. Marcus grins like I just crowned him the winner of their pissing match.

"Wipe that smug look off your face, Marcus. What do you want?" I ask.

"I told you. You didn't give me a chance to argue my case," he says.

"You made yourself pretty clear. There's nothing to argue, Marcus." I'm exasperated at his persistence, but have to admit that I'm tempted to ask him what he meant when he said that Mr. Meyer was capable of doing *unimaginable things*. It doesn't matter now because Will and I are going to just be friends so his father will have no reason to do anything unimaginable or otherwise to me or my family.

"What's Will doing here? Glutton for punishment?" he says obnoxiously.

"*What* is your problem?" I snap.

"*He's* my problem. All he does is cause pain and you're letting him back into your life. Here I am standing in front of you…you don't have to hide with me, Layla." He moves closer, taking my hand in his. "Admit it. You liked it when we were together. You felt something. You weren't always pretending with me."

"No, Marcus, I didn't…don't…feel that way about you." I can never admit to him that it made me feel good to be close to him. It wasn't the same as when I was close to Will, but Marcus would never hear that part.

"You've tried this once, Layla, it's not going to work." My rejection has sparked something in Marcus. His eyes are fiery hot and his body stiffens. He releases my hand, almost tossing it down, and takes one half step forward. He speaks slowly and with purpose, not like when you talk to a five-year-old, or try to communicate with someone who speaks another language. No, this is anger…almost evil. "Trust me. No matter how hard you try, you will *never* be good enough for them."

I don't know what comes over me, but before I've even considered my action I slap Marcus across his face as hard as I can.

"I am *not* Holly. You can't make up with me what you weren't able to do for her. Now I think you should leave before Luke and Will escort you out." I can see Claire and the guys standing on this side of the kitchen door, with Luke *literally* holding Will back.

Marcus leaves, and even though I told him to, I'm sad to see him go. I hoped one day we'd be able to be friends again. I don't think that's going to be possible now, and that's disappointing.

Chapter 21

The frozen chill in the air has turned beautifully crisp. The trees and flowers in the backyard begin to sprout and my view of the lake from the loft becomes obstructed once again. Will resumes his work with Luke in the basement after a hiatus during winter seeing as the basement isn't heated yet. It's nice seeing Will on a more regular basis again. We're doing well at the "friend" thing, although we have to be more intentional at certain times. If we go to a movie with our friends we can't sit next to each other. The first time we did, we realized three quarters of the way through the movie that we had been holding hands.

Along with the new season comes the anticipation of spring break, prom, and graduation. We're days away from spring break and I'm giddy with anticipation at tearing through a good book with a blanket and a chair by the lake. It's been months since I've been able to enjoy my favorite place, and now that Will and I have made amends it isn't going to be so painful to go down there.

"Oh, Layla, Luke and I have a surprise for you!" Claire says as Will and I clear the breakfast dishes. It's Saturday and Will is readying himself for a day of work in the basement. He always arrives an hour before he needs to so we have some time to hang out. Luke and Claire are always with us, so there's no danger of any conversation that might convince us that we should get back together. I'm glad for their supervision because there are many moments when I look at Will and want to take him up on his first offer to run away together.

Luke walks into the kitchen as he hears Claire prep me for their news. "I thought we were going to tell her together?"

"You're here now, aren't you?" She winks at him, and Luke grabs her by the waist and kisses her hard on the neck. I love that Luke is so free in showing his affection for Claire.

"Ok…I'm in suspense. What's the surprise?" I look at Will to see if he's giving any hints, but he looks just as clueless as I am.

"We're all leaving on Monday for week in Asheville. It's the firm's annual spring retreat. Mr. Meyer reserves part of a resort and the whole office shuts down for spring break. What do you think?" Luke says joyfully.

"It sounds great. Oh, my gosh, that's in two days! You'll be there, too, right Will?" I look at Will but his expression is altogether opposite of mine. He isn't excited at all. In fact, he looks scared.

"Um, yeah, I'll be there," he says.

"What's wrong? You don't seem excited at all?" I ask.

Luke and Claire can see that this conversation is not going to be lighthearted. Claire looks at me and I mouth the words *it's ok* so she knows that if they leave they won't return to find Will and me in a passionate embrace.

"Ok…clearly there's more to this than you're letting on," I prompt after Luke and Claire exit the kitchen.

"I don't think you should go," he says as a matter of fact.

"Why?" I ask.

"You wouldn't like it there. It's just a bunch of attorneys talking shop for a week. It's lame. You shouldn't go. Let's stay here. Stay here with me." He's getting anxious. This is a side of Will I immediately do not like, not because it makes me afraid that I'm going to see the Will from Halloween, but because I can see that he's hiding something.

"Will, if we're going to be friends, you can't lie to me," I say.

"It's nothing. I guess I'm just nervous about you being around my father again. My feelings for you haven't changed, Layla, and he'll see that," he says.

"Mine haven't changed for you either, Will, but we won't be lying when we tell him that we're not romantically involved. Ok? It'll be ok." I stand behind Will as he sits at the island and put my hands on his shoulders in a show of comfort and support.

"Yeah, you're right. I'm sorry I was being ridiculous. It's going to be fine. Chris and Ty will be there, so we'll just all hang out. It'll be great," he says working to convince both of us.

"It'll be great. You'll see!"

*****

The drive to Asheville is as stunning as the drive to Grandfather Mountain. I'm glad I'm not behind the wheel because I can't take my eyes off the view. Around each bend in the road is a new perspective that rivals the one before. It feels like I'm opening an endless present.

The resort is nestled in the mountains and surrounded by trees as far as I can see. The décor of the lobby is beautifully rustic with wood-carved lamps topped with parchment shades ornamented with silhouettes of cowboys, bears, fish, and maple trees. There's a fireplace in the lobby big enough for five people to stand in. The red and orange flames licking the underside of the thick mantel are mesmerizing.

Luke, Claire and I step off the elevator and walk the long, low-lit corridor to our rooms. It takes a long time to reach our doors as we have been assigned to the farthest end of the hall. I think that it must be a move on Gregory Meyer's part in his efforts to ensure I'm kept as far away from Will as possible.

"Layla, how about you take this room?" Luke says pointing to the door next to theirs. Our rooms are adjoining, but Luke gives me the key and motions for me to enter through the main door in the hall. "I think you're going to like this room a lot." I open the door and discover the most perfect room I have ever seen in my life. There's a double four-poster bed made of rich wood caddy-corner in the room, a small dresser, and skinny French doors that open to a private balcony. The most perfect piece of all is a rocking chair that sits waiting for me on the balcony, a warm blanket folded neatly over one arm.

"Thank you, Uncle Luke. It's perfect," I say smiling at him. He smiles back and leaves me to soak in the beauty and perfection of this room.

After taking in the view from the rocking chair for a few minutes, I unpack my things and go to find Luke and Claire in the dining room. It is here that Luke introduces me to two attorneys and a paralegal and their families. Their kids are a few years younger than me, and I can already see what Will has been talking about. They are so self-absorbed. One girl spent five minutes complaining because there was no one available to carry their luggage when they arrived. Another whined because one of the seven sweaters she brought is one that she wore last year. It's laughable and Claire has to help me stop before I end up in hysterics.

Each family is on their own for dinner so Luke, Claire and I eat in the hotel seated at a table by the window overlooking a meadow and the far end of a vineyard.

"So how are you and Will doing with trying out the friend thing?" Claire asks.

"I think we're doing really well, actually. It was hard at first, still hard, but not having too much time alone together has been helpful. Has he…said anything?" I ask Luke, wondering if all that time in the basement has offered much opportunity for conversation.

"Nothing that you don't already know. He's still very much in love with you," Luke replies. His delivery is interesting, like he's hoping I'll say the same thing.

"How are *you* feeling about *him*?" Claire asks directly.

"Honestly? I love him more now than I ever have. But…you were right, Claire. You said if we could just wait until graduation then you'd be able to help us. I'm sorry that I put you at risk. It would have devastated me if Mr. Meyer had done anything to the two of you," I say.

"Don't be sorry, Layla. You're our family and we would do anything for you. We love you and take joy in being there for you, regardless of what the situation is. It means more to us than you realize," Luke says reaching across the table and squeezing my hand. Claire pats my back. It's nice to feel so bonded to them. It feels like when Mom and Dad were alive.

"We just wanted to make sure you were doing ok. I know it's been difficult, but we've been watching and we think you're doing a great job," Claire says sweetly. It's nice to know that they're actively watching out for me.

After dinner we go back to our rooms and I take a shower. I can hear the obnoxious children whining across the hall as I get ready for bed. I sit with a blanket in the rocking chair on my private balcony and think about what a gift Luke has given me. It's dark and there's a chill in the air. I can't see the mountains but I can hear the rustle of the trees.

A warm rush of emotions comes over me and I am overwhelmed with the wish that Will was with me. I wonder what he's doing, if he's thinking of me, too. I sit and rock and listen to the wind blow through the trees for a long time. I listen so intently that soon the sound drowns out the annoying screeches of my young prima donna neighbors. Eventually they quiet and go to sleep, which means I can, too.

That night I dream that Will and I are walking hand in hand on the beach when his father approaches us. Will takes a physical stance to protect me when his father puts up his hands in surrender. Gregory Meyer holds his arms out to give me a hug, embraces me and says, "Welcome." Then he hands me a broom and directs me to get to work on clearing all the sand out of the beach house we are suddenly standing in. All the associates from the firm are there and I'm in a maid's uniform. I look around and see Will standing with a beautiful blonde, smiling, with his father's arm hung proudly around him.

It's still pitch black outside when I wake up very disturbed. *Why does this have to be so difficult?* I think. All I want is to be really and truly happy. More than that, I want Will to be happy. I can't help but become torn. Maybe being friends is really the extent of where our relationship is supposed to go. Perhaps my anticipation of the freedom graduation will bring is over zealous. Do I need to really sever my feelings for Will so he can find someone his father approves of? This isn't about severing my feelings for Will. It's about understanding that Will and I can never be together, no matter how much we love each other. Will is my best friend, and I'm committed to doing whatever I have to do keep him safe.

I sleep for a while longer, but not well after my disconcerting dream. When I wake the sun is just starting to rise and there's a faint orange glow outside. I get up, pull my hair into a ponytail and get dressed. I quietly brush my teeth and make my way down to the lobby. I follow a sign I noticed last night pointing to a nature trail. The trail is well marked, so I'm not too nervous about being a Florida girl alone on a hilly and twisted nature trail for the first time in my life.

The sun is rising and casting the most brilliant light through the trees. The leaves look like they're glowing. The wind whips around me and the smell of spring fills my nose. There are flowering trees and bushes all around and they smell divine. I stop and close my eyes, inhale deeply, and exhale slowly. In this moment I can be in love with Will. I can feel every emotion I have for him and not have to hide my expression. I picture his remarkable smile, remember how it felt when he kissed me, and even how he smells. I think about the first time he held my hand as he helped me along the path from the dock in the dark. I know I can't stay out here forever, so I want to enjoy the moments I have.

But my Zen moment is interrupted too soon with an unexpected visitor.

"Well, good morning!" I hear the man's voice bellow too loudly for this hour of the morning.

I turn and see Gregory Meyer approaching me, just a few yards away. I hadn't expected to see anyone, let alone him, out here so early. At least I know I can answer him honestly about my relationship with Will, should he feel the need to question me again. Despite my efforts to force mind over matter, nervousness weighs me down like a ton of bricks and I'm glued to this spot.

"Good morning, sir," I say, trying to sound strong. "It's nice to see you again, Mr. Meyer." I extend my hand to shake his. He offers his as well and I give him my best firm handshake. He holds my hand and my gaze even longer than he did the night of the dinner party inquisition and my stomach ties itself in knots.

"It's very nice to see you, too, Layla. How are you enjoying Asheville?" he asks, charming as ever. I'm on my guard, doing my best to analyze everything from the words he uses to the tone and delivery of each one.

"I like it very much. It's beautiful, and this is a wonderful resort. Thank you," I say with a smile. All I want is for him to see that I appreciate this trip, thus, appreciating him and hope that he backs off.

"Oh, you're so welcome. I'm glad you like it. Have you met any of the other children here? Oh, I'm sorry. You're *clearly* not a child." He corrects himself but his *mistake* is intentional…and creepy. He drops his eyes and lifts them up the length of my body. I literally feel dirty in that moment and have an uncontrollable compulsion to take the hottest shower I've ever had in my life.

"I did meet a few younger kids who are staying near our rooms. Everyone has been very welcoming," I say, ignoring his pedophilic stare.

"And you've had a chance to see William?"

"Not yet, sir." I reply.

"Well, just try to contain yourself," he says. "Show a little decorum."

"I'm sorry? I don't understand," I say.

"Let's not play games, Miss Weston. If you think for one second that I don't know what's going on between you and my son, you're profoundly mistaken," he says coolly.

"Mr. Meyer, there is nothing going on between Will and me. We're just friends," I say, confident in my truthful statement.

"Watch yourself, Miss Weston. I know when a witness is lying through her teeth," he says, lifting my chin with the tip of his finger. I am officially scared and have finally grasped the full reality of Gregory Meyer's ability to intimidate someone into doing exactly what he wants. I turn my head away and take an uneasy step back. His face grimaces even more at my defiance. "Stay away from my son or there will be consequences. Do you understand, Miss Weston?" I nod in acknowledgment, grateful that he isn't requiring me to speak. "Well," he continues smoothly, "I'll be on my way. I'm going to finish my morning walk and then head back to the dining room for some breakfast. I take a walk on this trail every morning. Perhaps I'll see you again out here enjoying the morning air. It certainly has been the highlight of my day," he says.

I nod again, screaming out in my head, "*There's no way in hell I'm going to be caught out here or anywhere by myself with you again!*"

"It was lovely to see you again, Miss Weston." He nods his head and continues his walk.

I stand there and close my eyes. *Breathe,* I chant to myself. My heart is racing and my hands are trembling. Oh, my god. I have seriously underestimated Gregory Meyer. What the hell have I gotten myself into?

Breathe. Breathe. Breathe. Breathe.

I make my way swiftly back through the winding trail and join everyone for breakfast. Before I have a private moment to tell them, Claire tells me the rest of the kids are meeting to go hiking later and wondered if I was planning on joining them. Of course I am. These group gatherings are my only chance to spend time with Will. There's no time to tell her about what just happened with Gregory Meyer now so I'll have to tell her later. At least the group activity will provide some relief. I look up and see Tyler waving to me. I am so happy to see him that I practically throw myself into his arms. He laughs and tells me Will asked him to come collect me. He and Chris are going to provide a sense of normalcy in the midst of all the insanity this week.

"I'm so happy to see you Ty. I'm trapped across the hall from future cast members of the Real Housewives!" I say, knowing he knows exactly what I mean.

"No problem! Will asked me and Chris to keep and eye on you," he says.

"Great! I'm glad I get to hang with you." Tyler puts his arm around my shoulder as we walk to meet up with the rest of the group. "I ran into Will's dad this morning," I tell him. I need to get it out. It's like when you have a terrifyingly real dream and you want to relay it to someone so you can prove to yourself it wasn't real.

"What? How did *that* go?" he asks, shocked.

"It was…awful…but don't tell Will. It'll just freak him out. I couldn't sleep and was up early, so I got up and took a walk on the nature trail. I was just standing there and he came right up to me. He was so creepy, Ty." I think about telling Tyler the disgusting once over Mr. Meyer gave me but decide it's too embarrassing. Since Will said the others didn't know about the threats his dad made to Holly's family, I decide I shouldn't tell Ty about this morning's intimidation.

"I'm so sorry, Layla. Chris and I will make sure you're never alone with him…or any of *the others*," he says, making a spooky voice. We laugh. "We'll rescue you should you get cornered," Tyler says, giving me a nudge.

I'm used to Will being the one to rescue me, but will gladly take Tyler as a hero any day.

Will and Chris are already there and join us. "Hey Layla," Chris says. I haven't seen him for a while, so I'm glad he's here.

"Hey, Will," I say. I'm nervous and afraid to tell him about my encounter with his father. I'm taken off guard when he comes close and hugs me and whispers in my ear, "I'm happy to see you."

"Me, too," I whisper back as I scour the crowd for informants.

Another group suddenly surrounds us. We break our hug and work to make small talk about getting settled into our respective rooms, and how I like the mountains. The four of us hike together, with Will insisting that I walk between him and Tyler. He razzes me about my two left feet and says that I'll have a lower risk of injury if he and Tyler both kept watch. Plus, he doesn't want anyone having easy access to me. He's still determined to protect me from as much as he can. If only he had been there this morning.

"Did you tell him yet?" Tyler asks.

"Tell me what?" Will says.

"About this morning…" Ty continues.

"What part of, *don't tell Will* did you not understand, Ty?" I say, shooting Tyler a deadly stare. "I ran into your father this morning."

"What? How did that happen? I've been with him all morning? Are you ok?" Will is in shock and almost trips on a rock.

"I'm fine! I woke up super early and couldn't go back to sleep, so I went out to take a walk. I was just standing there and he came right up to me." I try to mimic Claire's calming tone. It always soothes whatever the message is.

Will grimaces. "How…did it go?" He speaks slowly.

"Actually, I think it went fine," I lie. "He asked how I was enjoying Asheville. I told him it was great and thanked him for being a gracious host,"

I say, trying to sound very matter-of-fact, without emotion. I don't want to tell him the details of what scared me to death and made me realize that I'm in much deeper than I realized.

"Oh, ok. Well…it sounds like it went…well." Will says breathing a sigh of relief.

"It did, so, no worries, ok," I say. I don't like lying to Will, but now is not the time to go into just how right Will was about his father not buying our story. Now I don't even have Marcus as a backup. I give Tyler another deadly stare and he just shrugs. I'll take issue with him on this later.

Will makes a hard-lined smile and we leave the conversation there. There will be little chance of me running into Mr. Meyer alone again, so I'm not worried about a repeat of this morning. I'll just do my best to enjoy these days I have in the mountains. The four of us hike along watching the rest of the group blatantly work hard to prove which one of them spent the most on their high-end outerwear. It's sad really. They don't have a clue what real happiness is. I do. I'm experiencing it at this very moment as I walk between my best friend and our trusted confidants.

Chapter 22

By Friday there have been only a few opportunities for me to exchange words with Mr. Meyer – mainly *hello*, *good-bye*, *please* and *thank you* – and someone was always with me, usually Luke or Claire. I only feel slightly as scared and creeped out as I had been on the trail. I don't spend any time alone with Will because I don't want to add fuel to Gregory Meyer's fire. My imagination goes wild any time I think about what *consequences* means to him, so I do my best to keep myself distracted.

I told Claire what happened on the trail and she told me not to be too worried. "He's just trying to make sure your feathers are sufficiently ruffled so that you stay scared."

Mission accomplished.

I'm spending quite a bit of time with Tyler though. He retrieves me from my room in the morning before anyone else has a chance to intercept my day. While Will is entertaining others at his father's instruction, it's Tyler who keeps me company.

Today is one of those days. Mr. Meyer is meeting with a prospective client whom he invited to bring his family to the resort for the day and it's Will's job to make sure the client's kids are occupied.

When we're not with everyone else for the few organized activities Tyler plays cards with me in the common room, picks pine cones with me on the nature trail, and makes sure I'm never left alone. Luke and Claire are going to dinner with Mr. Meyer and the other partners and their wives, so Tyler and I sneak away and fend for ourselves. We find a great little local place where I try fried pickles for the first time…and love them.

"Why did you rat me out to Will?" I ask, shoving his arm in disapproval.

"Wouldn't it have been worse had his father told him? Layla, you can only protect Will so much. You have to be honest and up front with him." Tyler puts his arm around me and gives me a squeeze.

"You're right. I just don't want him to worry."

"He loves you. He's always going to worry."

When we get back to the resort we pop into the game room so I can crush Tyler in another game of hearts. It's quiet when we approach so we assume the room is empty, but when we enter we discover that isn't the case. Will is there with the person he's been entertaining all day. I'm caught off guard but ok for the first five seconds. The remaining seconds that drag out like hours are another story.

The catalyst to my spiraling decent into an emotional wreck is sitting unreasonably close to Will. The blonde he's been entertaining all day is the same girl from my dream.

I gasp and they both turn to see Tyler and me entering the room. Will's head actually makes a snapping sound from the jerk of motion he makes. He jumps up, but before he does I take better note of how he and the mystery girl are sitting: facing each other, close enough for their bodies to touch, his arm resting on the couch around her, her hand on his knee. I try to be reasonable, logical, but I can't. My mind is racing and I don't know what to say or do.

"Hey…guys! What are you doing here?" Will asks nervously, only this time his nervousness is not cute.

I'm speechless. My eyes dart between Will and the mystery girl and all I want is for this to be a dream too. It's not a dream, it's a nightmare; the kind where you want to scream as loud as you can but when you open your mouth nothing will come out. You try to move, but your feet are like blocks of cement.

"Uh…hey Will. Who's your friend?" Tyler asks, seeing I am going to be no help in the conversation department.

"This is Carrie. Carrie, this is Tyler...and Layla," Will says gesturing between the three of us.

"It's very nice to meet you. You two look like you're on your way back from a date that I'm sure you don't want to end, so don't let us interrupt you." She stands up and slides her arm through Will's. With her perfectly coiffed blond locks, beautiful facial features, and a killer body, she is exactly Gregory Meyer's type. There she stands, next to Will, the perfect picture of arm candy.

My mind is flooded with questions. *Are they together? Is this why Will didn't want me to come? How long has this been going on? What exactly* is *going on? How could I have been so stupid?*

Tyler puts his arm around me and kisses my cheek. "Yep, that's us! We both love long walks on the beach and moonlit nights. We were just on our way back out. See you later!" Tyler is a smart-ass, but sometimes it works. Keeping his arm around me he takes me out of the room and to the garden that leads to the vineyard. When we reach the trail I'm still shaken. Tyler takes my hand in both of his and tells me it'll be ok.

As we walk, I let Tyler keep my hand. It's comforting. We walk to the far end of the vineyard, within the boundary of the light posts, and sit in silence for a long time. My mind is still racing, and now I'm crying.

"Layla, it's going to be ok. She's nobody," Tyler says, doing his best to diffuse my tears.

"Tyler, this is going to sound insane, but I've seen that girl before," I say through my sobs.

"What? Where?" Tyler puts his arm around my waist and lets me put my head on his shoulder.

"I...had a dream...and she was in it. I told you it was crazy." I say in between sobs. Tyler doesn't speak. He just listens with a furrowed brow as I continue. "I had a dream that Will's dad welcomed me to the family, but was really welcoming me as hired help. Then I was standing in a beach house, in a maid's uniform, with everyone looking at me. I looked up and saw Will standing there…with Carrie…his father's arm around him in a show of approval. And now she's here!"

"Layla, it was just a dream. She's a generic blonde who probably has a hundred doppelgangers out there. You don't have anything to worry about." Tyler's tone is sweet and comforting as he strokes my hair. "I've known Will a long time and I can tell you without reservation that he is as loyal as they come. I know how he feels about you and he would never do anything to hurt you."

"Thanks, Ty. But…" I say, laying my head back on his shoulder. This is so silly. Will doesn't belong to me anymore. "There's no reason for me to act like this. Will and I aren't even together. He can see whoever he wants. Right?" I say solely in an effort to convince myself.

Tyler kisses the top of my head. "It's going to be ok, Layla. Technically together, or not, Will loves you. I've never seen him love someone like he loves you."

"Ty!" a voice calls out.

It's Will, and he's approaching quickly. Before I know it he's right up on us, looking distressed.

"Will," Tyler says, jumping to his feet.

"I need to talk to Layla, alone, please," he says looking at me intensely. "Can you go up the lodge and watch out for us?"

"Layla?" Tyler says, asking me for permission to leave.

"It's ok. Thanks, Ty," I say. I wipe my face and try not to look as upset as I am.

"I just wanted to tell you how sorry I am," he says.

"For what? I have no rights to you anymore, so there's no reason for you to apologize."

"You looked pretty upset when you found Carrie and me. I…I'm under orders to entertain her, remember?" Will reminds me. His eyes are wide and hopeful.

"It's ok, Will. We're not together. You can be with whoever you want," I say.

"Really?" He sounds surprised, and maybe a little disappointed.

"Really. You…want me to be jealous?"

"Well, I guess I thought it would bother you," he says.

"Of course it bothers me, Will, but I have no right to be bothered by it. You don't belong to me."

"Yes, I do, and you belong to me." He hangs his head and paces slowly. "I …hate that you witnessed one of these."

"*One of these*? What does that mean?"

"Whenever my dad has prospective clients he…he makes me *entertain* their daughters until the deal is done," he explains. I can't believe what I'm hearing.

"Excuse me? Are you telling me that your father whores you out to solidify his business deals? Is this why you didn't want me to come?" I'm flabbergasted. Never in my wildest imagination did I ever dream that Gregory Meyer would stoop to something so disgusting, but maybe this is what Marcus meant by *unimaginable things*. More than that, how could Will put up with this? It's one thing to be forced into going to a college you don't want to. This is entirely different.

"I wouldn't put it like that." Will says. I can see this isn't exactly the response he thought he was going to get.

"How would you put it, Will?" I retaliate. If he wants *bothered*, I'll give him *bothered*.

"If she doesn't go back and tell her parents that she had a good time, the whole deal with my father could be over," Will says actually trying to rationalize the situation. "You have no idea how things like this work."

"Enlighten me! What constitutes a good time? What does *entertaining* these girls entail exactly? I'm sorry, did we spoil the moment you were about to kiss her? Or maybe you were on your way back up to your room!"

"My god, Layla!" Will is pacing again. "You don't get it! You don't understand what it's like to have a father…" Will starts but I cut him off before he's barely uttered the last syllable.

"You're right," I snap. "I *don't* know what it's like to have a father." I'm still. "Do you know *why* I'm17-years-old and don't have a father, Will? Do you?" I say the last part louder and with more aggression.

"Yes," Will answers quietly. He's calm now, realizing his words.

"Why?" I demand.

"Because your parents are dead," he replies slowly.

"And why are they dead, Will?"

"Because…there was an accident. Layla, I'm sorry…" I cut him off again.

"My parents are dead because of me. The accident was *my* fault. So, no, I don't have a father…and I never will again."

I leave him standing there in the vineyard and walk, almost run, to the path that will lead me to the lodge and the safety of my private room. I enter the lobby and dash past Luke and Claire. I can hear Will yelling for me in the distance but I don't yield as I rush to my room. Claire calls to me as I shut the door behind me. There's commotion in the hall and I hear Will tell Luke that he needs to talk to me but Luke denies him access to my room. I feel fortunate to have Luke here. He's my shield, protecting me from getting hurt any more than I already am.

As I listen to Luke's voice through the door I think that maybe I do know what it's like to have a father again. There's a knock at the door that connects my room to Luke and Claire's. It's Luke asking if he can come in. I allow it, as long as he's alone. He promises he is and enters gingerly.

"Do you want to tell me what happened?" he asks quietly.

I don't answer.

"Will said there was a misunderstanding. Do you want to tell me what that means?" he continues. Claire is rubbing off on him because his tone is soothing and brings me down from my emotional ledge.

"No. Yes. I don't even know. This whole thing was a huge mistake, Uncle Luke. I don't know why I ever thought that Will and I could be just friends. I…I can't be with him. I can't be with anyone," I say.

"What are you talking about?" Luke asks, his brow furrowed.

"I have to be alone, to pay for what I did, for the rest of my life," I choke out.

"What is it you think you did, Layla?" Luke positions himself on the bed so he can face me. He is focused and intent on our conversation.

I sit there for a few moments wondering how to tell my uncle that it's my fault his brother is dead. Things can't get worse, so I swallow hard and just say it.

"The accident was my fault," I whisper slowly.

"Oh." Luke replies, looking down for a quick moment before snapping his head back up. "You really think that your parent's death was your fault?"

"I know it was," I say.

"Layla, sweetheart, that couldn't be farther from the truth," Luke takes my hand in his.

"It *is* the truth. Mom and Dad promised that we would go out to dinner that night, but there was a bad storm so Mom said we would have to go another time. I should have just left it alone." I take a few deep breaths to gain my composure. I can feel the start of hysterics coming on. I've never told anyone this and I'm scared of what Luke's response will be. "But I didn't leave it alone. I begged and begged. I wouldn't give up until they gave in. It's my fault they're dead." The deep breaths don't work and I start to sob. I can't stop. My body is heaving from the heavy cries. I slide from the side of the bed to the floor and curl into a ball.

Luke wraps his arms around me and won't let me go. I try to break free but he won't budge. "It wasn't your fault, Layla! It wasn't your fault!" Luke repeats this over and over again while he rocks with me there on the floor.

"It *IS* my fault! Gram said so!"

"Wait, what? What did she say?" Luke takes me by the shoulders.

"She said that it was an accident and that I didn't mean to kill them. Don't you see! That's why I had to give up everything. I had to sacrifice *my* life for the son I took from them. And now…it was stupid…I thought I paid my penance and could have something as wonderful as being loved by Will, but I can't. She said that I didn't deserve anything good after what I had done, and she was right. My punishment will never be over," I say, trying to make Luke understand.

"Oh, god. Layla, that woman… You punished yourself for five years for something that you had nothing to do with. Layla, look at me." Luke takes my face in his hands and looks me straight in the eye. "Your parents died because another car hydroplaned into them going sixty miles an hour, not because of anything that you did or didn't do. You're lucky to be alive. *We* are lucky that you're alive. You have no idea how you have changed our lives. We were so lost before you came." Luke sighs, taking both my hands in his.

"Did you know that we had a daughter? No, probably not. She'd be ten this year. She died when she was two. I told you we used to have a boat. We got rid of it after Penny died. We had just come in from our last day on the lake. The weather was getting cooler and we knew we wouldn't be able to go back out until the next spring. Claire and I were busy unpacking the boat. We had been inside long enough to take Penny's life jacket off and set her at the table to color. Claire helped me take the deck box we kept on the boat into the garage before we put the boat in storage. We were gone maybe five minutes. When we got back to the kitchen Penny wasn't there. We checked her room and the playroom; there was no sign of her. Then Claire ran outside and started calling for her. By the time we got to the water it was too late. We think she tried to get back on the boat and…well…

"I understand about guilt; about blaming yourself. Accidents are tragic, senseless things, but at some point life has to go on. You have to stop punishing yourself and start living again. Your being here has revitalized us. Layla, you bring an immense amount of joy to our lives; joy we thought we'd never have again after Penny died." Luke's eyes are filled with hope, and tears. "So, you see, if your parents, and Gram and Gramps were still here, Claire and I might never have known this joy again. I…I would never pretend that Claire and I could replace your parents, but I hope that you'll allow us to stand in their place for them. We love you, Layla."

I look at him and in that moment I feel a release I've never felt before. Something has changed. I've been carrying the weight of guilt for so long that I'm not even sure I know how to fully exist out from under it. Maybe I'm feeling closer to Luke because we shared something so personal with each other. All I know is that I feel lighter.

"I'm so sorry about Penny. I didn't know," I say sadly. I'm heartbroken for both of us. What a joy it would have been to know that I wasn't alone. "Is that why you didn't want me to come live with you?"

"That was my doing. I just didn't know if Claire could handle having you around, but you being with us has provided the most incredible healing we could have ever imagined. I don't know what we'd do without you." Luke embraces me and holds me tight. I feel the love he's pouring out to me, and begin experiencing my own healing through it.

"Uncle Luke, what do I do about Will?" I ask, hoping for some wisdom.

"What do you *want* to do?" he asks, drying his tear-stained face on his sleeve.

"I don't think I'm cut out for this right now. I never thought that much about it, but when I did, I never thought I'd have to lie to myself, or anyone else, about loving someone. I can't be Will's girlfriend because then I have to lie to everyone. I can't be just his friend because then I have to lie to myself. Maybe I need to separate myself from him all together." I'm confusing myself, but somehow Luke understands.

"If that's what you think is best, then Claire and I support you in that. You know, he's down the hall wanting to talk to you. Do you want me to send him away, do you need more time?"

"No, I'll talk to him," I say. I just want to get it over with. "Is there any way we can leave early? I really want to go home," I ask.

"The reception is tomorrow night and there's no way that Claire and I can miss it. It's the only activity that everyone is required to attend. We can leave as soon as it's over, I promise," Luke says, giving me a hug. His embrace means so much more to me now. We've shared something that will forever bond us and nothing will ever change that.

Luke leaves the room and sends Will in. He reaches out to me but I pull away from his touch. I can see that hurt him, but I just can't. Once again I'm afraid if I let him touch me, hold me, that he'll never be able to let go, and neither will I.

Will speaks first. "Layla, I really am so sorry. I didn't mean to hurt you."

"I know you didn't." I say. I'm not going to get into the issue of my parents. I have to focus on the problem at hand. "Will, I can't keep doing this. There's no happy medium."

"It's just a few more weeks until graduation. We can do this," he says.

"It's not just a few more weeks, Will. It's anytime we're anywhere but at Luke and Claire's. We have to hide our relationship, even our friendship, from your dad. I finally got away from the prison of pretending to be someone I'm not. I thought I could do again here to protect you, but I just can't. The best way to protect you is for there to be nothing to hide. I was wrong to think saying we were just friends was going to change anything. The bottom line is that I love you, but we can't be together at all," I say firmly. I'm proud that I didn't cave when I looked into his beautiful eyes that are full of love and pain.

"Layla, don't do this. Please. We can figure this out. We can create our own world, just until we graduate. Please. I love you," he says emotionally. He's holding back tears again and it tears me apart.

"And what happens after graduation? You'll go off to Princeton, I'll go to Florida State and it'll be over anyway. This isn't what I want, and you deserve better than having to sneak around with me. Your father has you wrapped so tightly around his little finger that we can't be near each other without arousing suspicion. My god, Will, we can't even be friends! If it's not safe for us to even be friends, then maybe you and I aren't meant to be anything at all." I hesitate for a moment, considering if I should tell him about his father's off site *House Call*, but it isn't going to make a difference, so I decide against it.

"Layla." Will says my name and I want to take back everything I just said. I want to rush into his arms and have him hold me forever.

"Is there any way to stand up and change things with your father?" I ask, already knowing the answer.

"You know there's not." he answers, his face distressed.

"Then there's nothing left to say." I need him to leave quickly so I can let the waterfall of tears I've been holding back flow.

"I told you before, nothing will change how I feel about you," he says. He walks away and I close the door behind him, wondering how I found myself closing a door on Will Meyer for a second time.

I fall on the bed and bury my face into the pillow and cry, letting my body heave with each sob. I hear the door open and in seconds Claire is laying on the bed next me, holding me while I cry, not saying a word. She just lets me sob until I have no more tears left. I cry myself to sleep and sleep hard. I don't dream, for which I am thankful. When I wake in the morning, Claire is still there, asleep in the dress she wore to dinner the night before and I'm sure she was a wonderful mother to Penny.

Chapter 23

I spend all day Saturday in my room. I pack everything I can pack and then rearrange and pack it again before I sit on the balcony, rocking and, sort of, read for hours. I didn't think I was going to be doing any reading on this trip, but am glad I have my Kindle.

Claire knocks on the door and pops her head in. "It's almost time to leave for dinner. How are you doing?" she asks.

"I'm ok," I say. "I'll get ready and be down in a few minutes."

Claire smiles and closes the door. I brace myself and get my new black dress from the closet. I really like this dress. Claire and I both agree that it is very Audrey Hepburn, simple and elegant. I pull my hair up into a twist and feel like Audrey in *Breakfast at Tiffany's*. I'm as ready as I'm going to be. The mini-divas and their families have already left, which is a relief. I worked very hard this week to avoid them as much as humanly possible.

We get in the car and make the short drive to the other side of the resort where the reception is being held.

"Are you ready?" Luke asks.

"Yes…mostly," I answer. "I'll park it at our table and pick at my food all night."

"We won't leave your side," Claire says reassuringly.

"Oh, no, please don't do that. You two need to have a good time. Mr. Meyer needs to see you having a good time, right? If anyone asks, just tell them that I'm not feeling well," I say.

We give each other one last look of solidarity and walk into the reception. There's a band playing and the music is louder than I would have expected, but the female singer is pretty good. Everyone is dancing, adults and kids, and it looks like some kind of weird second-chance prom.

The room is decorated simply with white tablecloths and centerpieces with candles and flowers. There are three sets of French doors that lead out to a courtyard. I can see Tyler and Chris across the room talking with some people I met briefly earlier in the week but can't remember their names. In all honesty, I never tried. I make eye contact with both of them and we each give a nod of acknowledgement.

After we find our table, the wait staff promptly brings us our dinner. We have a choice between baked chicken and prime rib. I opt for the baked chicken. I guess everyone's already eaten because we're the only ones at our table. I eat slowly so that I really will have food to pick at all night. Luke and Claire finish and I insist that they enjoy themselves. Watching them dance together makes me smile. Whether it's a slow song or a fast one, they move together perfectly. They smile at each other and steal an occasional kiss. It's beautiful.

I continue to pick at my chicken when I feel a tap on my shoulder.

"Hey…how are you?" Tyler asks as he sits in the empty seat next to me.

"I'm good. How about you? Have…you talked to Will?" I ask hesitantly.

"Yeah, I talked to him," he answers. "I'm sorry. I know this has got to be a weird situation; not one that anyone would think of as typical, but I meant what I said about how Will feels about you."

"I know. It's just not meant to be. Thanks for your shoulder. You're good friend. I appreciate all you've done for me this week. I would have been a pretty lonely girl if you hadn't kept me company." I tell him.

The band starts to play a song that Tyler and I simultaneously say we love. That's all it takes for him to insist I dance with him. I give in quickly and we walk to the dance floor. It's a slow song and one of the guys in the band starts singing. Tyler puts his arm around my waist and holds my hand in his to his chest. It feels good to know that I didn't lose his friendship.

About halfway through the song I see Will walking toward us from across the dance floor. I'm not nervous because I know he won't make a scene here. But my body must be tensing up in Tyler's arms because he whispers in my ear not to worry and that everything will be ok.

"May I cut in?" Will asks.

"Layla?" Tyler defers to me again as he did in the vineyard.

"Ok." It's the only response I can give.

Will takes me in his arms and I feel the rush of warmth run through my body that I had worked so hard to avoid last night. I don't want to like it so much but I miss his touch terribly. I want to cut off all my feelings so I can move on but I allow myself this one last encounter. I allow myself to love and be loved because in about two minutes that's all going to end forever.

"Hi," he says, pulling me close to him.

"Hi."

"Layla," he says.

"Will…don't."

"Just listen to me. I know I have screwed up more than once, and I couldn't be sorrier. Is there nothing I can do to make it up to you? How many times do I have to apologize before you forgive me? I will again and again, if I have to. I'm not giving up, Layla. We belong together," Will declares.

"What am I supposed to say to that?"

"Tell me you love me. Tell me you're not going to push me away." His eyes are intense as he speaks.

"Why are you doing this, Will? This is already difficult," I say.

"It doesn't have to be. I love you. You love me. We want to be together. We *can* be together," he says, trying to make his case.

"Will, we can't be together. Every warning you ever gave me about us being together is true. Your father will make both our lives a living hell, and possibly get my aunt and uncle disbarred, sending them into financial ruin. Tempting as that sounds, I'm going to have to pass." *Not to mention the beating I witnessed and the warning I got on the trail earlier in the week.*

"I've never wanted to break his rules more in my life. I've let him regulate me out of fear and I'm done living like that. I'm stronger now. I'm stronger now because of you." Will is serious and passionate. I can tell this is a turning point for him.

"Why would you want to be with someone like me anyway? I don't fit into your world, and your world doesn't even want me." Even if Will's father loved me, why should Will? Between the baggage I carry and my inability to fit in here, I only complicate things.

"So this is what it's come to? Fine," Will says as he releases me and walks away.

Frustrated, I walk off in the opposite direction, toward the exit. I need to get some air but I don't want to walk through the crowd to the courtyard. *This is…good*, I think. He needed to just give up and let me go. Yes, this is for the best.

I don't get far before the music stops and I hear Will's voice booming in the speaker. I slow my pace, not believing what I'm hearing. "Layla Michelle Weston, where do you think you're going?"

I turn around to a sea of heads bobbing back and forth; looking for the girl Will has disrupted their festivities for. *What is he doing?*

"Your presence is requested on the dance floor…please," he says.

I'm frozen in my tracks. I have to decide whether I'm going to fulfill his request or make a scene and run. I comply and make my way back to the dance floor. As I retrace my steps I see Luke and Claire watching, waiting to see if I'm going to cue them to rescue me. Then I see Will's father. Like a tennis match, he's alternating between looking at me and looking at Will. His face is flat, unreadable with the trait of a skilled lawyer. The last person I see is Tyler. He smiles at me and nods having been in on this from the start.

As I approach the stage, Will steps down and I whisper, "What are you doing?"

"Standing up," he says.

Putting the microphone to his mouth, Will begins to speak. "May I have your attention please? I'm Will Meyer, and for those of you who don't know her, this beautiful girl is Layla Weston. A moment ago she asked me why I would want to be with someone like her." He turns to face me. "You asked me a question, and I'm going to answer you," he says. His face is smooth and relaxed. For what he's doing right now in this moment, that doesn't make sense. His father is just feet from us. Then I see it. I look into his eyes and see something I haven't seen before: absolute and unwavering peace.

"Let me just get the obvious out there first: she's beautiful. It's not a matter of opinion; she *is* beautiful. That's not why I love her. In the time that I've known Layla I can say without a shadow of a doubt that she is the most amazing person I've ever met. She has character and integrity – traits I find missing in most people I know. She cares more about others than she does herself and is the kind of person who would sacrifice her own happiness for someone else's. She doesn't come from money, and that's ok because she understands that wealth…well…wealth is nothing. Wealth is just a status symbol that gives you power. She knows that life is more than power. She understands that when you love someone you want to tell the world, regardless of what anyone else thinks. She showed me that that kind of love really does exist, and she showed me what it means to love someone completely." Will turns back to me again. "Layla, I never knew that I could love someone the way that I love you. You have changed my life in ways I never thought possible. *That* is why I want to be with you. *That* is why I am totally and irrevocably in love with you."

His words are still lingering in the air when he drops the microphone and kisses me. Right there, in the middle of the room with everyone looking, Will kisses me with total abandon. His lips are warm, soft, and gentle and move with mine with precision and perfection. His arms wrap around me tightly, and my hands lift to grab the back of his neck. We kiss for just a moment when, for the first time, I'm the one to pull away.

The room is silent and I don't know what will happen next. I scan the staring faces to see the response. It's a mixture of unreadable expressions and those of disbelief, including mine. The wait staff is in awe and smiling. They have no idea the dangerous place Will has just dared to tread.

My eyes find Tyler and he is beaming. Behind him I see Luke and Claire who look both pleased and nervous. There are several girls in the room who look disgusted, because, I'm sure, they have had their sights set on Will, and probably believe they're entitled to first dibs. Carrie appears to be the most appalled. I don't even want to imagine what Will had to tell her or, at the very least, lead her to believe, last night. The deal between her father and Will's father is sure to be destroyed now. Will stands next to me now with his arm firmly around my waist. I feel his hold tighten and turn to see the reason why.

Will's father is walking slowly toward us. His gait is steady and purposeful. This can go one of several ways. There's a good chance he's going to disown Will right there, which would be fine with Will. Then he'll put a hit out on me for influencing his son to defect. I have a short vision of his two favorite hit men shuffling me out back of the law firm. Or, without any reason to believe this could actually happen, part of me hopes that Will's passion inspired Mr. Meyer and softened his heart; that he sees how much I mean to Will and wants Will to be happy. The third, and more probable option, is exactly what begins to unfold.

"Well, well, well! Isn't this wonderful! It appears my son has been bit by the love bug," Mr. Meyer says, sauntering toward us, stopping to face us less than an arm's length away. Only after he gives his sign of approval does the rest of the room visibly react. Some applaud, and I hear some female voices saying, "That was so sweet."

It's creepy, really, the way they held their collective breath, waiting for his lead on how to respond. I guess that's what happens when you drink Gregory Meyer's Kool-Aid.

He puts a hand on each of our shoulders and quietly says, "You just made the biggest mistake of you lives." His tone is eerie, and the look in his eye is evil and determined. I have messed with the wrong family and I'm going to pay for it. Then he smiles at the band and motions them to play. He turns and walks out into the courtyard with the band playing him out.

I look at Will and ask, "What does that mean?"

"It means he's going to do his homework. He never enters a courtroom unprepared. He's not prepared to argue his case now, so he won't say anything," Will speaks with the same seriousness as he did after dinner with his parents.

"That was a risky move there, Will," Luke says approaching us. "Are you sure you know what you're doing? Your father isn't going to give up."

"I love her, Luke, and I can't live like this anymore. Do we have your support?" Will asks, extending his hand to Luke.

"Of course." Luke shakes Will's hand firmly, while Claire hugs me tightly.

"Will said his father would do his homework…on me. What does that mean?" I ask, puzzled.

"Layla, honey, Gregory Meyer is very good at what he does. Luke and I will run through some scenarios of what he might try and…I'll have something prepared if he comes at you too hard," Claire says, trying hard to reassure me. "You're not alone, Layla. Remember that."

"Way to go, man!" Tyler says giving Will a strong, manly hug. Then he hugs me, picking me up in the process. "I told you," he whispers into my ear. He puts me down and I give him a smile of thanks.

"Ok, that's enough, everyone. I'm going to take my *girlfriend* to get some fresh air." Will takes my hand and leads me outside and down a short flight of steps that takes us to a trail through the vineyard. It's peaceful…for now.

"I didn't get a chance to tell you how beautiful you look tonight," Will says. "You look amazing."

"I can't believe you just did that," I say, still astonished.

"It was time, and you showed me that. He's not going to control every minute detail of my life anymore. If we're in this together, then we can take whatever he throws at us."

"What do you think he's going to do?" I'm concerned more about Luke and Claire than I am about me.

"He's going to dig up anything he can on you, Luke, Claire, the rest of your family. He'll first try to shame or embarrass *you* into leaving. Is there anything you think I should know about?" He looks at me intently, but reassuringly.

"No, there's nothing." I feel better after talking to Luke about my guilt over the accident. Now that he knows how I feel, I'm sure I can withstand any lashings on it.

"What about Luke and Claire?" he asks.

"I don't know. I guess I should find out, but they seemed pretty secure in the dirt they've got on your dad, no offense."

"None taken," Will replies with a smirk. "What about…" He stops himself short.

"What?"

"What about your parents?"

"No, nothing. They were peace-loving hippies."

"Ok, then. If he doesn't have anything on you or your family, he'll have to work harder. That's going to frustrate him. He's not used to it being difficult. Most people have skeletons in their closets that they want kept there," he says.

"What about you? Do you think he'll pull out some of your skeletons? You know, to divide us." I don't really think there's anything there, but want to know if there's more to the demands of dating client's daughters.

"Well…he might, but the one I was most ashamed for you to know about already came to light."

"I'm sorry about that. I was crass and shouldn't have reacted that way." I take his hand in both of mine. Knowing what I know about his father I should have been more understanding.

"It's ok. I should have told you. I was embarrassed. I didn't want you to think of me that way," he says.

"I want to ask you something about that, and I hope it doesn't hurt you," I say.

Will nods, giving me permission and saying, "I'm an open book to you, Layla. There's nothing you don't have access to."

"Have you…*been with* any of them?" I give him some privacy as I ask by not looking him in the eyes. If he needs a moment to think, I want to give it to him.

He lifts my chin up so our eyes meet. "No, *never*. Call me old fashioned, but I've never seen the point in giving away to just anybody what was meant for just one."

"How do you do that?" I ask smiling.

"I'm ridiculously charming, remember?" he says grinning.

"Oh, yes, that's right," I say mirroring his grin.

We stroll through the vineyard, enjoying our new freedom, however short-lived it might be.

Chapter 24

It goes without saying that Will isn't allowed to drive back to Davidson with us. It's ok because it gives Luke, Claire, and me a chance to debrief. Claire tries to engage me in girly conversation about my sweet moments with Will, but Luke won't have it. He begs us to wait to gush until he isn't present, and says we need us to be levelheaded. We still have no idea how this is going to play out.

There is a lot of silence on the ride home. My mind runs through everything I can think of that Mr. Meyer might try to use to destroy me. I'm 17-years-old, what can he do? Then my imagination begins to get the best of me and all I hear is Marcus' warning about *unimaginable things*.

"What do you think he's going to do?" I ask about the man who seems to hold my fate in his hands. "I mean…he's not going to…hurt me, like, physically, is he?"

"He's more of a break-you-down-until-you-can't-take-it-anymore kind of guy. He usually doesn't have to get too nasty because the financial payoff is enough to make whatever, or whoever, go away," Luke answers.

"Well…I'm not going anywhere. What does he expect me to do?" I'm annoyed.

"He expects you to leave," Claire offers.

"Well…that's just…I mean…that's not going to happen," I say flustered. I don't know how I'm going to do it, but I will stand my ground and take whatever Gregory Meyer throws at me. I've been to hell and back in my life already, so I'm sure I can handle the Devil himself.

Luke and Claire carry a lot of hushed conversation on the drive home. I turn up the volume on my iPod, letting their conversation remain as private as possible. I don't want to focus on the potential terror. I want to enjoy having

Will and his love. I want to enjoy not having to pretend anymore. I want to enjoy the freedom…however fleeting it may be.

*****

It's been months since Will and I took our usual seats at the end of the dock. It's nice to sit here with him knowing that we aren't hiding. The moon is full again, the way it had been so many times during our first evenings here, but the mood is different. Will is distant, and deep in thought.

"He's right, you know," he says, breaking the silence.

"Who's right?"

"Luke. He's right about my father. He's not going to give up, Layla. He's never going to make this easy, and if it looks like it is, it's a trap. We can't be too careful," he says putting his arm around me protectively. It makes the moment feel somewhat normal. Being close to Will always makes things feel better, but there's something different about it this time.

"Well, we'll just have to do what we can until graduation, right? I've already been accepted to Florida State, and with your grades I'm sure you can still get in. We'll go to Tallahassee and start over." I'm hopeful, thinking this is a good idea.

"That's great idea, in theory, but he'll never allow it. He'll block my acceptance into every other college or university *except* Princeton. With his connections, I won't be able to audit a class at community college. He'd rather see me dead than let me do anything that might taint the perfect picture he's painted of himself.

"But I'll figure this out, Layla. I promise. I'm not going to let him hurt you or your family. You are everything to me and I would lay down my life to protect you." Will holds me tighter and I lay my head on his shoulder. We sit there in the moonlit glow and listen to the water ripple and the leaves of the trees rustle in the wind. This is my happy place, but it's being tainted by Gregory Meyer. I hate him. I hate what he's done to Will. I hate how he's made my personal renaissance his personal fight.

By midweek word has gotten out at school about Will's very public profession of his feelings for me. There are mixed reviews. Some don't care any more or less about me than they did before. They happily ignore me as equally as they have from the start. Some are even more disgusted with me and make rude comments as Will and I pass by them. "Slumming it, Will?" some say as we walk through the halls hand-in-hand. But, shockingly enough, some are actually happy for us, although they never make it public knowledge. By the end of the day on Friday I have fifteen notes stuffed into my locker, all with sweet sentiments and praises for our bravery.

"So happy for you and Will. He's a real catch!"

"I wish I was a brave as you. Well done!"

"You two make a perfect couple. I hope I have as much courage as you one day."

I'm thrilled to know that my circle of supporters, however silent they may be, extends beyond Will and our four friends. It's still a weird feeling, though. It doesn't seem fair that it took an act of heroism for two people to be together. If there's one thing I've learned it's that life isn't fair.

*****

"I have a surprise for you," Luke says as he knocks on the open door of my room.

"A surprise?" I ask.

"Today is your birthday, or did you forget?" he says.

"I didn't forget. You just didn't have to do anything," I say sheepishly.

"It's your eighteenth birthday and it's a big deal. Just get over here!" Luke grins and takes me by the hand and leads me into the kitchen where

Will and Claire are waiting.

"What's going on?" They're all smiling, indicating that I'm the only one out of the loop. Will pulls a sleep-mask out of his pocket and instructs me to put it on.

"Are we taking naps, because that actually sounds like a great idea," I jest.

Will smirks and hands me the mask. I do as I'm told and Will takes me by the hand. Even without looking, I know the soft strength of Will's hand. He leads me downstairs and I realize that today I will finally see the project he and Luke have been working on since I arrived in this life-changing town. I can't imagine what they could have done down there that would be for me. Whatever it is, I'm already grateful because I know I certainly don't deserve it.

We reach the bottom of the stairs and Will takes me five more steps ahead and turns me around. It smells fresh and new. The scent of fresh paint and new upholstery fills the room. I feel the tight weaving of Berber carpet under my bare feet. The room is silent except for the excited breaths of Will, Luke, and Claire.

"Before you take your blindfold off, I want you to know how much you mean to Claire and me. This room is just one small way that we can express how much we love you. We know it was a big adjustment coming to live here, and we couldn't be happier that you did. We hope you love this room as much as we do," Luke says, starting to get a little choked up near the end.

I take my mask off and am astonished by what I see, so much so that I feel the trembling that precedes a gush of emotions. I take a deep breath and push it down until I can at least take in the whole of my gift.

The huge room has been painted a subtle shade of khaki. There's a plush couch and chair in light blue plaid with a captain's wheel coffee table and a wicker rug under it. Starfish, sand dollars, and blown sand glass spot the walls and decorative tables. The whole room has been designed in a beach theme…just for me. It's overwhelming.

One small wall moves me more than the anything else. On it hang pictures of my parents and grandparents; both of their wedding pictures, and pictures of me with each of them. I trace my fingers around the frames in an attempt to connect with them. I remember how beautiful my mother was. My father used to say her smile was like an all-day sunrise. I see how my father is holding my mother and it makes me think of Will. He holds me the same way and in that moment I'm reassured that we'll share that same kind of love forever, too.

An old fashioned chest is situated below the pictures. I look at Luke for permission to enter it and he nods. I lift the lid and start exploring. Inside are photos and letters. As I file through them I realize that the letters are between my grandfather and Luke, all postmarked after my grandmother's death. He really did reach out to Gramps. Beneath them is a discovery that I never dreamed about. My mother's wedding dress has been preserved in a box with a window in the lid. It's beautiful, and so her. I always thought so every time I looked at their wedding album. Next to her dress is a small, black velvet box. I open it and the emotions I've been waiting to unleash cannot be held back any longer as I stare at my parents' wedding rings.

"This is…more than wonderful. Thank you so much." I wrap my arms around Luke tightly. Tears are streaming down my face and I don't try to wipe even one of them. "You did all this for me and I'll be away at school in just a few months."

"You couldn't be more welcome. Every second spent working on this for you filled me with more joy than you can imagine," he says, holding back tears of his own. "Don't forget Will," he says, diverting the attention from himself to Will.

"Thank you," I say to Will, throwing my arms around his neck. "It means so much to me that you were a part of this."

"My real gift to you is on its way," he says stroking my hair. "But I'm glad you love it."

"This is real gift enough. It's so wonderful!" I say. "Claire! Where's Claire?" I spin around to find her sitting on the stairs wiping tears from her face. "Claire. Thank you." I sit next to her and hold her close.

"What are you thanking me for? I just picked out some furniture and paint," she says wiping the tears that are spilling over her eyes.

"Why shouldn't I thank you? You're part of everything that has made my life here beautiful. You're such a great mom. I'm so glad I have you." Yes, Claire has become a mother to me. I accept and embrace that now without guilt or shame. I need parents, a mother and a father, and Luke and Claire have filled that position. Claire's tears come harder now, and so does my hold on her.

We hold our embrace for a long time, neither of us wanting to let go. As we release, we look at each other, knowing that our lives will never be the same. Claire and I stand up, wipe our faces, and try to become presentable. Will takes my hand, and Luke takes Claire's. We walk, as a family, up the stairs and into the kitchen.

Since it's my birthday I decide that it'll be a Chinese take-out and movie night. We call Chris, Tyler, Gwen, and Caroline and they are there within the hour to celebrate with us. It's a normal night when nothing in the world is out of sync, and everything is wonderful.

*****

Will and I spend a lot of time in this more-than-just-a-basement. I tell him more and more about my parents and grandparents, and I can see that he understands me even better. It's a release to tell him things, good and bad, that I've held back. I'm nervous to tell him about Gram and Gramps…Gram, really. I'm incredibly grateful to them for taking me in, but how do I explain that she didn't let me grieve the loss of my parents; that, in fact, my grandmother blamed me for their death? I do tell him, and he shares in my sadness, wiping my tears as I explain every heartbreaking detail. He tells me I gave up too much and that now is my time to live. He, of course, understands that perfectly.

I'm both excited and nervous to tell Will about my parents. I can't wait to tell him all the glorious details of how wonderful they were, but I'm afraid I won't do them justice. They were imperfect people, but perfect parents to me. Once again, Will shows that he is able to understand me in ways no one ever will.

We look through old pictures that Luke made sure were in the chest with the letters and my mother's wedding dress. With each photo I build the story of my life as a child and how absolutely wonderful my life was.

After my talk with Luke about the accident, I feel more confident in sharing that most hidden part of my past with Will. I tell him about that rainy night and the guilt I carried, even without the insensitive help of my grandmother. I tell him that I'm working through it and it's not as overwhelming as it once was. And, again, he catches every tear.

Every day it gets better. Every day I take a step farther away from tragedy and closer to a life of sweet freedom.

Chapter 25

Claire and I just returned from picking up my prom dress from the seamstress and are starting dinner when the doorbell rings. I'm expecting Will so I run to the door to let him in. I open it and see Will standing there looking solemn…his father next to him.

Oh, my god. House Call.

"Hello, Miss Weston. I'd say it's nice to see you again, but our last meeting left a bit of a sour taste in my mouth." Mr. Meyer is sinister in his tone, and still finds a way to give me his creepy head to toe once-over. "Don't be rude, dear, invite us in."

I hold my composure and reply, "Won't you please come in." I look at Will for some indication of what is going on but get nothing.

We enter the kitchen and Claire is so startled at Mr. Meyer's presence that she drops the glass she's holding. It breaks into five easy pieces on the hardwood floor and I rush to help pick them up and throw them away.

"Gregory? This is a surprise. What can we do for you?" Claire has a cadence in her tone that I immediately recognize is reserved solely for him. It's slow, steady, and full of reverence. She looks at me and then at the kitchen door and I know she's telling me to get Luke from the office. I leave without hesitation and return in less than a minute with Luke leading the way.

"Hello, Luke. Well now that we're all here, we can begin," Mr. Meyer says coolly.

"What's this about, Gregory?" Luke asks, knowing the answer, but he doesn't answer Luke. He just stares at us and begins his closing argument.

"That was quite a show you gave, William. I didn't realize you hated me enough to embarrass me in a room full of my associates, and a potential client," he says with contempt. If this is the first Will is getting of this, I can't imagine the tension that has been building at home.

"I don't I hate you, Dad. I love Layla, and *she* is who I want. Is it so impossible for you to want me to be happy?" Will pleads.

He ignores Will and addresses me directly now. His complete and total disregard for Will makes my blood boil and only fuels my determination to not let him win.

"Miss Weston, do you have any idea the kind of young man my son is? No…he's much too modest. You see William has an I.Q. of 185. He's what's considered *profoundly gifted.* At age 13 he turned down early acceptance to Princeton's Civil and Environmental Engineering program. I was disappointed, but tried to understand. He wanted to live a normal life – go to school, have friends his own age. William promised to be diligent in his studies throughout high school, not slacking off because it was all so remedial to him. Then, when he graduated with the rest of his class, he would take his rightful place at Princeton. In the last year or so William has indicated he doesn't intend to keep his promise, and I can't allow that. So, what I need to know from you is what it's going to take for you to leave William alone."

"She's not going anywhere," Will says in my defense.

"Greg, all this is really unnecessary. They're just kids." Claire says. She's calm but her stance is territorial. She's a lion fighting for her cub.

"I'm sure Layla can answer for herself. Surely there's something Layla wants. Perhaps she'd like the balance of her current, *measly* college fund doubled, or tripled. I understand it's barely enough to cover a year or two at a state school. Or maybe it would mean more to her if I gave her aunt and uncle substantial increases to their salaries, or paid off their mortgage. I know…how about I pay for an indefinite amount of therapy so she can come to terms with the death of her parents."

"STOP!" Will yells, but his father is unflinching. "Your problem is with me, not her!"

"Wrong," Mr. Meyer corrects Will sharply. "Anything, including a girl as delicious as Miss Weston, that might distract you from your destiny *is* my problem, and I'm a problem-solver. I've solved this problem before, haven't I, William?"

Holly.

"I don't understand what Will and I being together has to do with whether he goes to Princeton or not. Even if Will *wanted* to go, I wouldn't stop him." I'm trying, in vain, to be reasonable even though I know that I'm failing with every breath.

"Miss Weston, what was your father like? Did he meet his full potential, or was he always reaching for more?" *How dare you bring up my father!* I scream in my head. He better make his discussion of my father brief or that could be the end of everything. "My father was a brilliant man, but he had one weakness: women. Well, just one woman, my mother. My parents met when they were teenagers. Their farms were next to each other in a rural town, which is to say they lived a mile apart. He was smitten with her. I can't blame him. She was beautiful in her younger days. They courted through high school and made a fine couple. When they graduated my father had the opportunity to get out of that small, going-nowhere town, and go to college. He was, as I said, a brilliant man, and could have been a brilliant doctor, but he chose to stay with my mother. They married right out of high school and I was born a year later. Growing up on the same farm my father did, I watched him grow old before his time, wasting away, working his fingers to the bone. I also watched my father grow angry and bitter. We worked hard and never had anything to show for it. He knew he had made the wrong choice. He substituted love for logic. I vowed that I would never live like that, and I'll be damned if my son is going to repeat the mistakes of my father.

"You see, Miss Weston, this isn't personal. It's not about you. I quite like you, actually. You've got moxie. But…you just don't fit into the plan for

William's success. I'll ask you again what your price is. I'm prepared to do whatever I need to for you to leave my son alone." Mr. Meyer speaks fluidly, like he does when he practices his closing argument. He knows what he wants and he isn't going to back down. The problem for him is, neither am I.

"Mr. Meyer," I start, and then clear my throat to gain my courage. "I support Will in whatever he wants to do, and the reason I support him is because I love him…for who he is. You may be able to buy others off, but I'm not for sale." I want to tell him that I've already endured hell and that there's nothing he can do to me that I can't handle, but I'm afraid any piece of personal information I give him is going to be tainted and twisted. So, I say what I can and my heart races with pride that I didn't completely back down.

"There's that moxie I do so admire, but let's not play games, Miss Weston. Name your price."

"I don't want your money. I'd *like* your approval, but I'll have your son," I reply.

"Excuse me?" he says in shock. He wasn't expecting me to turn him down because no one ever turns Gregory Meyer down.

"William?" he says. I'm nervous and my body tenses up closer to Will's side. The idea that someone would refuse his offer is unfathomable to him. I can see the fire in his eyes and am thankful beyond words that I have Luke, Claire, and Will to protect me.

"Now you want to talk to me? You heard her. She won't be bought and there's nothing you can do. You're not going to win this time." Will stands firm. I'm so proud of him.

"Well, Luke, it seems your niece doesn't have an appreciation for the way things work around here. I've advised her that it is in her best interest to stay away from Will, but she's seen fit to refuse," he says.

"Will and Layla have decided what they want *together*. She's not forced Will into anything." Luke stands firm as he defends us.

"Children don't know what they want or who they are. That's why I've come prepared to make sure Layla knows who she is, where she comes from. I had a feeling she would be valiant."

"I know exactly who I am," I say, reaching to take Will's hand. "And who I am is made better by Will."

"Really?" Will's father opens the large envelope he's carrying and pulls out a stack of papers. He thumbs through them and then returns to the top sheet and reads, "Layla Michelle Weston, born June 1, 1993 to John and Elisabeth Weston at Holy Cross Hospital in Fort Lauderdale, Florida. Your father was a science teacher and your mother, an English teacher. They died on June 19, 2005 in a horrific car accident." He looks up at me. "You were in the car, too. Aren't we lucky that you survived?"

"What's your point, Dad? I already know about the accident and more. Layla doesn't keep things from me so I don't know what you're trying to pull." Will releases my hand only to put his arm around my waist to draw me closer to him. It's a show of solidarity that makes Mr. Meyer's nostrils flare.

"Oh, I don't doubt that Layla has told you everything that she knows. I just wonder if she knows how much has been kept from her." Mr. Meyer looks at Luke and then flips through the documents in his hands again. "Somehow I don't think she's aware of the legacy left by her parents. What do you think, Luke?"

"Uncle Luke? What's he talking about?" I ask, confused.

"Get on with it, Greg," Luke says as if he knows what's coming. I look at him curiously as he shakes his head in disbelief.

"In 1998 your parents were involved in a few radical movements…"

"I'm aware of my parent's activism, Mr. Meyer," I say cutting him off.

"Activism is putting it lightly, my dear." It makes my skin crawl to hear him use any term of endearment toward me. "This one goes just a little deeper than protesting on sidewalks. No, this time they got involved with animal rights extremists – also known to the government as eccoterrorist."

"That's crazy. Uncle Luke, tell him he's crazy." Luke makes a hard line with his lips and remains silent. I stare at him in disbelief. His silence tells me that there is at least a hint of truth to what Mr. Meyer is saying and I think I might faint.

"As I was saying…" Mr. Meyer pulls several papers from the stack and lays them on the counter. They look like legal documents but they could be anything for all I know about legal paperwork. "It seems your father and a few of his radical cohorts released several dozen animals from a cosmetics lab in Miami."

"So he released some animals back into the wild." I really thought he'd come up with something better than this. It's a weak argument that holds no bearing on Will and me being together.

"If that had been the end of it, he may never have been caught. Unfortunately, it went much further than that. After the animals were released, your father and his friends blew up the building causing $2.4 million in damages…and killing three people."

"What? That's not true!" I feel my body temperature rising with fury. I take a step toward him, but Will pulls me back.

"It is true, but don't worry. Your father's not a murderer. He agreed to two years probation in exchange for his cooperation. The prosecution was more interested in the group's leader, who they suspected had been responsible for a dozen other bombings across the country."

"Luke, did you know about this?" Again, he doesn't answer.

"He more than knew about it. Your father came to him for help. Your uncle had been interning for me and your father knew what a *skilled* attorney I am. He asked Luke to see if I could pull some strings for him, but your loving uncle refused. Had he brought it to me I would have gotten him off completely." He looks at Luke who is clenching his jaw.

"Is all this true?" I ask Luke. "Was my father really involved in something that killed people?"

Luke pauses for what seems like forever before answering. "Yes."

"Did you refuse to help him?"

"Layla, you've got to understand…your dad was involved in illegal activity and…"

"Did you refuse to help him?" I shout.

"Yes."

"So that's why you two never spoke, because you wouldn't come to the defense of your *only* brother? My dad could have gone to jail!" I'm so angry that I can physically feel my body temperature rise. "How could you betray my father like that?"

I storm out the back door and run down the flagstone path to the lake. I almost don't stop when I reach the end of the dock. I drop to my knees and put my head in my hands and sob. I'm sad and angry and disappointed; I feel betrayed and lied to. *Is there anyone I can trust?* I'm not even sure I trust myself. I feel so foolish. My parents were radical extremists, my uncle refused to help, and my boyfriend's father is a manipulative, power-hungry tyrant. When is my life going to be normal?

I feel Will's arm slide around me as he sits next to me there by the water.

"What is going on, Will? My life is completely out of control!"

"Don't you see what he's trying to do? He knows you and I aren't going to budge, so he's trying to drive a wedge between you and the only family you have left. His goal is for you to leave and he'll do that by whatever means he can. You can't let him win," he says.

"They lied to me. They *all* lied to me. I grew up thinking my parents were noble and honorable, but it turns out they were crazy! My grandparents and Luke and Claire…no one told me anything! I must have looked like an idiot, just following along without one ounce of knowledge of what was really going on."

"You were a kid. What did you want them to tell you? However radical or crazy it may have been, your parents followed their convictions. How many people do that anymore? It was an accident that those people were in the building. My father made me read the testimonies. No one was supposed to be there."

"But they should have told me at some point," I say.

"When? When would have been an opportune time to bring up something like this? Layla, there are some things in life that we don't need to know because not knowing shelters us from something worse. You needed to see your parents as you did more than you needed to know about this. They needed you to see them simply as your parents. They did what they could to protect your love for them from being tainted. I know what that's like. I know you're angry, but put this fury where it belongs." Will kisses my forehead and leaves me there on the dock in contemplation.

Will is right and part of me hates that. I want to be angry with Luke for not having helped my father. I want to be angry with my father for having done something so stupid, but the deepest part of my anger is at Gregory Meyer for coming in and trying to tear me apart from the only family I have left. The more I think about it, the more Mr. Meyer's menacing smile and threat against my family enrages me. He stood there, delivering this information with evil glee; taking pleasure in trying to destroy the very thing that keeps me alive.

Will is more than right. I can't let him win. I'm not happy with Luke, but my love for him and Claire is enough to cover the pain. If I can overlook so many of my parent's infractions in parenting for the sake of whatever the cause of the week was, I can process through Luke's intentions in keeping this information from me. I'll need more answers, but right now I have to go back to the house. I know the war isn't over, but I have to at least win this battle.

I'm conflicted by the hope I have that Will's father is still here since he is literally the last person on earth I would ever hope to see. When I approach the back door I know Will and his father are still there because I clearly hear Luke's raised voice telling Mr. Meyer that he needs to watch his step before the world finds out who Gregory Meyer truly is; obviously a threat to expose the dirt Claire said Luke has collected over the years.

I walk into the kitchen, adrenalin pushing me step by step. All four of them turn and watch to see what my next move will be. Mr. Meyer still has that Cheshire grin on his face thinking he's won. I've never wanted to punch someone in the face more in my whole life, which makes me even more determined to stand my ground and not let him take one more second of my life away from me.

"Mr. Meyer," I start slowly. "I want to thank you for coming here today. You didn't teach me anything new, but you definitely reminded me about where I come from. However, I'm sure it's not exactly in the way you had hoped. You reminded me that I was taught to stand up for what I believe is right…even if you have to go to the extreme at times. I think it's interesting that your point today was to reveal my parents as terrorists when you are nothing but one yourself. You live in this ideological world of yours. You intimidate, coerce, and instill fear in anyone who refuses to live there with you, including your son. You don't have a clue what it means to really love and be loved. Take a long look at us, because this is what love looks like. I may not completely agree with it, but I know that what my parents, and aunt and uncle, did was to protect me. I guess you need to give up or move on to your next strategy, which will also fail, by the way, because there is nothing you can say or do that will destroy the love I have for my family. And I will never leave Will."

"You know, Miss Weston, if you weren't trying to destroy everything

I've built for my son, I might actually be able to use you one day. You would have made an excellent attorney. It's a shame," he says gathering his packet of evidence. I know this isn't over by a long shot. Mr. Meyer is too cool, too calm.

"Thank you for stopping by, Greg. You'll understand if I don't see you to the door," Luke says putting his arm around my shoulder. Mr. Meyer leaves the room and we hear the front door slam behind him. "Are you ok? Layla…"

I can't answer because that rush of fear that fills your body after a near death experience is overtaking me quickly and I don't know if I'm about to cry or scream.

"You need to know that it wasn't that I didn't *want* to help John. He needed to bargain with the prosecution so that he would *have* to testify against the group's leader. Otherwise, the guy would have gotten off. People died, Layla, and I couldn't ignore that." Luke feels just as strongly about his convictions as my parents did theirs. I respect that and can't blame him. It seems standing up for what one believes in is a Weston trait…one that I am proud to have.

"I understand. You did what you believed was right. It's hard to argue that." I'll never be able to erase this information from my memory, but my impression of my family is forever changed. Not in the devastating way Will's father intended it to, but changed nonetheless. My parents made choices that I didn't always understand, but they were my parents and I will always love them.

"This is getting out of hand. Luke, we've got to do something," Will says with urgency in his voice.

"You're right," Luke agrees. "We need to figure this out."

"Yes, but not here. Not now," Claire replies.

Chapter 26

It's Finals week and I'm so excited. I've never wanted to leave a place more in my life. I finish my civics final and bring my paper to Mrs. Dishowitz. It's my last exam and I couldn't be more ecstatic. We're free to leave after our last test of the day so I head straight to my car, wasting no time. Will and our friends are all coming over for a post-final celebration. Claire and I spent last night making all our favorite snack foods and picking out movies for our marathon.

I'm taking my normal route home, bobbing along happily to the playlist Will made for me. It has all our favorite songs on it, and music Will promises will grow on me. There's a detour sign blocking the main road so I follow it obediently. As I approach the next intersection a black town car begins to cross but stops, blocking my path. I wait for it to move along, thinking they're probably just lost. So I sit. And I wait.

I look behind me to check that the street is clear enough for me to back up and see an identical black town car parked behind me. My stomach begins to churn and fill with angry butterflies, and it feels like my heart is going to beat right out of my chest. So I sit. And I wait. After he has made me wait more than a sufficient amount of time, he emerges from the back seat of the vehicle behind me, so I do the only thing that could be expected of me and get out of my car.

"Hello, Miss Weston," Gregory Meyer slithers like the snake he is.

"Mr. Meyer."

"I'm sorry for the dramatics here, but I wanted to be sure I had your *full* attention." The source of his stench is smoking in his right hand, his other hand in his pocket. "We seem to be having a misunderstanding that you need to rectify. Perhaps I haven't been as clear as I possibly could have. I've tried to be nice, explaining some reasons that make you being a part of my son's life impossible. Since that hasn't worked, I'm going to be about as clear as I know how to be.

"You have until the end of June to leave town. Go back to Florida, move to Alaska for all I care. The point is, if you're not gone by then, well, it's going to be very awkward when the state troopers pull your aunt and uncle over and find that the car they're driving has been reported stolen and their ID's don't match DMV records," he says maniacally.

"You can't do that," I reply with fearful debate.

"Don't underestimate me, my dear. You have no idea what I'm capable of doing. If you're still in this town as much as one second into July first, and if you ever return here, you'll wish you died in that car accident, too."

"I'm supposed to leave and never come home to see Luke or Claire?"

"Oh, no, they're going with you."

"You wouldn't do that to them. You can't…" I begin.

"They've already cleared out their desks."

Consequences.

I stand in shock, having no cards of my own to play. Will was right when he said it would make his father even more determined if he wasn't able to pay me off or shame me into leaving. My only hope is in Claire's promise that they have enough dirt on Gregory Meyer to shut him up, so I stand silently, waiting to be dismissed.

"I'm sorry that it had to come to this. Had you heeded my earlier warnings we wouldn't be standing here. Now, you and Will can have your little fling through prom and graduation. I'll even let him help the three of you pack up your house. You have until the end of June," Mr. Meyer says so matter of fact. It's eerie the way he speaks. He has no remorse for what he's doing to us. I took a psychology class last year and I'm pretty sure that he is the definition of a sociopath. "Then you can be on your way to Tallahassee, or wherever, and my son will never see or hear from you again." He takes a drag from his cigarette and flicks it to the curb. "I hope you did well on your finals. I'd hate for there to be a glitch in the system when you go to register for your college classes." He scans my body with his eerie eyes, igniting my gag reflex. "It's a shame, really. Had you played your cards right, I could have done *so much* with you." With that, he turns and walks confidently back to his car. His thug of a driver opens and closes his door, doesn't give me so much as a glance, and drives ahead, leaving me standing in the middle of the road about as close to tears as I've ever been without crying.

The entire drive home I run though scenarios from tax evasion to sexual misconduct as I wonder what power Luke wields in his personal filing cabinet. When I walk through the door and find Will, Luke and Claire in the kitchen, I'm sure they've spent the morning strategizing. When I ask what the plan is I'm flabbergasted at the news they deliver.

"We took the deal," Luke says.

"Just to make it look like we're cooperating, right?" I clarify.

"No. We really took it." Luke replies.

"What?"

"Layla, it's for the best," Will agrees.

"Am I going crazy? Claire, c'mon, help me out here," I beg.

"They're right, Layla. It's for the best. His next move will be to erase our identities. You won't be able to go to *any* college let alone Florida State; and none of us will be able to get a job or find a place to live. It will be as if we never existed." Claire's angelic tone is not calming me this time. I'm angry and I feel alone and betrayed.

"I can't believe all of you! You're giving in *that* easily? After everything…that's it…it was all for nothing. He wins?" I'm more than flustered. Stand? Sit? Run screaming out of here? I don't even know what to do with my body. Everyone is just staring at me. "Fine."

Before I know it I'm standing at the edge of the dock, wishing, praying, hoping for some clarity. Some answer that would make sense of why I have had to endure all I have; why I have had to lose the ones I love.

"What happened in there?" I demand from Will as he approaches me.

"What were we going to do? We're not going to let him erase you, Layla. I'm going to do my best to get down there to you, but…"

"Maybe I can go up there? I know I'd never make it into Princeton, but there's got to be another college I can go to closer to you." I'm desperate. I can't believe we're giving up after all we've done to stand up and not let him win.

"You think he's going to just *let go* after you move? He's going to have both of us watched, our mail monitored, our phones bugged. We couldn't even fake a bad break up. He'd never buy it. I told you, Layla, he *never* loses."

"So that's it? We have until the end of the month? Then I have to walk away from you forever and pretend that *we* never existed? This isn't fair, Will." I start to cry and am torn between wanting the safety of Will's arms and being too mad at him to let him touch me. I decide that I'm not that mad and take shelter in his embrace.

"Layla, love…I need you to trust me. Look at me." He takes me by my shoulders and stares into my eyes with more passion and intensity than I've ever seen in him. "You need to know that no matter what happens, and I mean *no matter what happens*, I love you and nothing is going to keep me from you. I promised to protect you and that's what I'm going to do."

I stare at him blankly, trying to decipher some hidden message but come up empty.

"Do you trust me?"

"Yes," I say, believing that they must be pulling something together that's going to blow him away. Give him a taste of his own medicine. All they have done is work to protect me. Making me think we're going along with this asinine plan has to be a move for my best interest. They know me well enough to know I'd never sit still if I knew what they were doing, so until all is revealed, and I watch Gregory Meyer pay for his crimes against humanity, I choose to trust them. I stood my ground with him as much as I could and now there's nothing more I can do.

*****

It takes all three of them to convince me that going to prom is still a good idea. Will's father is chaperoning and I hate the thought of him watching us in our last moments together, relishing in his victory. I agree to go because Claire already got a dress for me, and I admittedly want nothing more than the opportunity to dance with the love of my life.

I reach the bottom of the stairs and am met by Will holding a clear box with my corsage.

"You look absolutely beautiful," he says just before kissing me. My dress is a simple knee-length black satin strapless number with an empire waist. Claire bought it for me from a small boutique in Charlotte. While it wasn't made special for me, there are only five of its kind and was tailored to fit me perfectly. I'm wearing actual high heels in black satin and I've pulled my hair up into my favorite Audrey style, which adds to the effect I was going for.

"Thanks. You look pretty great yourself." Will is wearing a classic black suit and is more handsome than I've ever seen him. I've daydreamed about marrying Will one day and wondered what he would look like as I walked down the aisle to meet him. I try to soak this moment in since, as of right now, this will be the first and last time I'll ever see him like this.

Luke and Claire take obligatory pictures of us, and when Chris, Tyler, Gwen, and Caroline arrive they're included. Against my protest, Will got a limousine for the night. As we all pile in, Will holds me back to tell me that the others don't know about what has transpired with his father. They don't know that this will be the last time we'll all be together like this. He didn't want to upset them and I agree.

We spend the evening avoiding any place in the venue where we know Will's father is. Even though our friends don't know I have just weeks left with them, steering clear of Gregory Meyer is always a part of any game plan. We dance and ignore those who continue to give Will and me dirty looks. Peppered in between the evil glances, some of our silent supporters make themselves known. They hug me and wish me well. It's sweet, but awkward considering the circumstances.

We leave the dance before it's officially over, having successfully evaded Will's father. It's about one in the morning when the limo drops us off at my house. When we get out of the car Will stops me from walking to the porch.

"I have a surprise for you," he says, taking my hand and walking me around the side of the house. As we reach the corner there's a small bag there. Will picks it up and pulls out a flashlight. I take my shoes off because I can barely walk on solid ground in them. The grass is a no-go for these heels!

We pass through the gate and follow the flagstone path to the safest place in my world. As we approach the dock I see a glowing lantern sitting in the center of a huge red blanket. There are two plates covered with silver domes, and two bottles of soda.

"Oh, Will." I cover my mouth in amazement. He's recreated our first date, every detail down to the cream soda. "This is so wonderful." Will leads me onto the blanket and helps me sit. I sit and wait for him to join me. He lifts the cover from my plate and reveals a chicken salad sandwich with tarragon mayo. "You remembered," I say, holding back my overwhelmed tears.

"Luke and Claire helped. When I told them what I wanted to do for you tonight, they were totally on board. They really love you, you know," he says.

"I know. I love them, too. Thank you for this." I drop my head to collect my thoughts. I'm overwhelmed with the finality of it all. I have only a few weeks left with the man I love more than anyone in the world. I have to choose to make these moments count or else when I look back on them, all I'll remember is the heartache. It's something I've thought a lot about with my parents. Had I known that they would be taken from me so quickly, I would have made every second with them matter more than the last.

"Hey…it's going to be ok." Will moves closer and wraps his arms around me. "I love you, Layla, and I promise that it's all going to work out."

"*How* is it going to be ok? What are you and Luke going to do to make everything ok?"

"You've just got to trust me. Please. I don't want to talk about my father, or you leaving, or anything that doesn't have to do with how immense my love for you is…ok? Tonight is all about you and me and how much we love each other." Will has a way of talking me down off my emotional ledge and making me feel better, even when I don't understand everything that's going on.

"Ok, you're right. You and me and nothing else." I agree.

"Good. Eat." Will smiles and I'm instantly at peace.

He's recreated our first date, but added some enhancements. We have a lantern this time for added light since the moon isn't nearly as full as that first night. Will also brought his iPhone and is playing the playlist he made of some of my favorite songs and new ones he thinks I need to become better acquainted with. He's done an excellent job over the past year educating me on good music. I don't doubt for one second that I will love every song he suggests tonight.

"Dance with me," Will says, standing and reaching his hand out to take mine.

We danced all night at prom but there's no way I can resist him now. I take his hand and stand to my feet. I'm much shorter than when we danced earlier since my five inch black satin heals are laying on the blanket. His arm is immediately around my waist and my hand in his being held close to his heart, where everything I am belongs.

"What if we don't leave?" I propose.

"Layla…"

"No, listen to me. He couldn't erase us if we stay here. Everyone knows us," I say.

"People may know you, but without any proof of your identity, there'd be nothing anyone could do. You'd have no birth certificate, no social security number, and no school records. You wouldn't be able to get a job or go to school. Going to Tallahassee is the best option. Luke told me you're already registered for classes. I won't let you give that up. You and I will be together, Layla. It might not happen in the way we hoped it would, but it *will* happen. I promise."

"It's just not fair."

"I know, but his reign of terror on both my mother and me is about to end. Just ride this out with me and it's going to be ok."

"Ok," I say in a conscious choice to trust him. I've done all I can do. "But you're not going to tell me what the plan is?"

"I *will* tell you that everything I have planned *tonight* was cleared through both Luke and Claire… so let's go."

"Where are we going? It's after two in the morning!"

"Don't worry your pretty little head about any of that," Will replies, packing up our picnic. He leaves it all there to be picked up by his cohorts and we start walking up the path to the house. I didn't put my shoes back on and the flagstone is hard on my feet. All it takes is one "ouch" and Will sweeps me up in his arms and carries me the rest of the way to the back door. Will carries me over the threshold into the kitchen and my daydreams flash before me once again.

I'm instructed to close my eyes as we enter the house. Will puts me down and says nothing else as he leads me quietly upstairs to the loft. When I'm expecting to stop at the top of the stairs, we don't. Will keeps walking and I know we have just entered my bedroom. He's never been in my room. I always tried to be respectful of Luke and Claire, and I never wanted them to think anything inappropriate was going on, especially since Will made sure there never was.

"Will…I don't think you should be in here," I warn as I open my eyes.

"It's ok. I told you I cleared everything with Luke." Will sits on the bed and looks a bit too comfortable there.

"You cleared *this* with Luke?" I say, pointing to the bed.

"Yes, but not in the way you're thinking." He pulls me to him and kisses me. "I asked Luke, since I don't know when I'll see you again, if it would be ok for me to spend one, non-sex-filled night with you. He agreed, as long as I didn't take anything from you that wasn't yet mine to have." He kisses me again.

"Wow." I'm astonished at the level of trust Luke has for Will…and me.

"What I didn't tell him was that having you in my arms for one night will be the greatest gift anyone has ever given me," Will says, caressing my cheek.

I'm standing in front of Will as he sits on the side of my bed. For once I don't have to stand on my toes to reach him. His arms wrap around me even more completely and I hold his beautiful face in my hands. I stare into his eyes and am lost in the swell of emotions. "I love you, Will. I will never stop loving you."

"You have no idea what it means to hear you say that." He kisses me sweetly and pulls away. "Before things get wonderfully out of hand, I need you to do something for me."

"Anything," I say, stroking his cheek.

"I need you to change your clothes."

"What?" I'm jolted out of my gaze.

"The other part of the deal was that I would make you put on something completely *un*sexy. And this dress does not fit that description. Don't worry, no double standards. I brought a change of clothes, too." That's good because Will is looking unbelievable. He's taken his tie off and has the top two buttons of his white dress shirt undone.

He has his hand on the back of my thigh, which I think is completely unfair considering the request he's making, but I agree to the terms and go into the bathroom and change.

I returned in about as unsexy a state as I can: pajama pants and a t-shirt with my hair in a ponytail. He keeps his end of the deal as well and is dressed similarly.

"Uh-oh," he remarks as soon as he see me.

"What's wrong?" I ask.

"You're still sexy," he says with a smirk.

"Oh, well! Guess you'll just have to grin and bear it!" I say landing in his arms.

Will takes my hand and leads me out of the bedroom. *Where are we going now?* As we enter the loft I am overwhelmed with emotion. The room is filled with twinkling lights around the perimeter of the ceiling, and the sound of Miles Davis swaying in the air. There are pillows and my grandfather's blanket on the couch.

"Everything as you requested?" Luke's voice appears from behind us. He and Claire are standing at the top of the stairs.

"Yes. Thank you so much," Will answers with a grateful smile on his face.

"It's beautiful. I can't believe…" I begin, but I don't think I even have the words to express how I feel in this moment.

"Considering the impending circumstances, we felt we could work with Will's request. The loft was the compromise. We're trusting you…and we're sleeping with our door open." Luke is soft in his tone but firm in his message.

"Yes, sir. Of course. Thank you. You have nothing to worry about." Will thanks Luke and Claire again, but I can tell he's nervous. He would never do anything to break their trust of him. It's a big deal that Luke would allow him to stay like this. I appreciate that they understand how difficult it will be when we move to Florida and Will is at Princeton. Come July first, we literally have no idea when we'll talk or see each other again.

Will and I settle in cozily on the couch with Will behind me and my head resting on his arm as he holds me close. The lights continue to twinkle and the music floats softly around the room.

"Have you picked a major yet? I know you have time, but I wondered what you were thinking about." Will is a master at making real conversation. He always asks questions he genuinely wants to know the answers to, and talking about school tops the list of anti-foreplay conversation.

"Well, I thought I wanted to go into teaching, like my parents, but I've recently been thinking about law."

"You're kidding, right?"

"Yes," I chuckle. "There's no way I could ever be a lawyer. I was actually thinking about psychology. I've been through so much, I'd really like to help people," I say.

"That sounds about right. I can't imagine you doing anything else," he says.

"Thanks for the vote of confidence."

"I mean it. For someone who has been through everything that you have, you see the world in a way most people don't think is possible; you're hopeful and optimistic. You've handled tragedy in the most remarkable way. I know that whatever is thrown your way you're going to be able to handle it.

You are an extraordinary woman, Layla. I could not be a luckier man to have you."

"You're so sweet to me." I reach up and rest my hand on his cheek. "What about you? What's your plan?" I ask, hoping to gain some insight into whatever plan is about to unfold.

"Well, I'm registered in the Civil and Environmental Engineering program. My classes have been picked out for five years, so… Technically, right now the plan is to go," he says.

"Will, why didn't you tell me about your…genius status?"

"It's just weird. I'm really good at math, so what. It's not what matters most in life. Every other girl who ever knew about it only saw dollar signs, assuming I'll be the guy who discovers how to close the hole in the ozone layer or something, and I knew you didn't care."

"I care because it's part of who you are. I care about every detail of your life because it's my life, too." I turn and pull myself as close to him as I possibly can and press my lips to his. I hold his head at the nape of his neck and let myself enjoy the moment as long as I can. I know he'll break the passion at any moment. He is nothing if not honorable.

Lying there, all I can think about is how much I love this man whose arms hold me in the safety of his embrace. It isn't right what's happening. How can one person do so much damage to so many people? First Holly and her family, and now Luke and Claire are giving up their lives here to protect me. And Will's mother! How many other people has Gregory Meyer destroyed for his selfish gain? Somehow, some way, he'll pay for the life he's lead and the lives he's destroyed.

Will brushes the hair from my face and caresses my cheek with his hand. I don't know how, but I know that everything will be ok. I turn back around and find my sweet spot, resting my head on Will's strong arm again. He holds me close and I fall asleep that night in the arms of the man I want to spend the rest of my life with. And no matter what happens, I know my heart will never belong to anyone else.

Chapter 27

When we wake up at noon Claire is at the top of the stairs welcoming us to the new day.

"Good afternoon you two. How was your night?" Claire asks.

"It was really great. Thanks for everything," I yawn.

"Yes, Claire, thank you. I appreciate the time you allowed me to have with Layla. It means more to me than you'll know." Will has a way with words that lets you know he means every single one of them. One can never doubt his sincerity.

"It was unconventional, but it was the least we could do, considering..." Claire isn't emotional about the situation at all. She's a rock, which I need. I have only a few short weeks before I have to say good-bye to Will for what could be forever. "We've got lunch ready. See you downstairs?"

"Yeah, definitely, thanks." I lay there and let Will hold me for a few minutes more before I make the first move. I sit up and rub my eyes. Will sits up next to me, keeping his arm around me.

"I've never slept so soundly. Thank you. The whole evening was perfect," I say to him.

"You deserve so much more than what I was able to do, but I'm glad you liked it." Will leans over and kisses my forehead and gets up. "I've got some stuff to do today and tomorrow before graduation. I'll be out of pocket for a little while, so I don't want you to worry."

"No problem. Between packing and getting ready for graduation I'm sure I'll be plenty occupied. Have you finished your speech?" Will is, of course, valedictorian. They probably should have taken him out of the running, considering his huge brainpower.

"Sort of. I've got an outline and I'll wing it from there." He's so nonchalant about the whole thing. I'm impressed and very proud of him, but he couldn't care less about the achievement.

"I'm sure whatever you say will be said with eloquence, as usual," I tell him.

We brush our teeth and meet Luke and Claire in the kitchen for lunch. Something is off between the three of them and I assume it has to do with whatever they've been plotting. They're too quiet and all alternate between looking at each other and looking at me. I've learned my lesson and don't bother asking. It's all legal stuff that Luke's been compiling, so I wouldn't understand any of it anyway. We finish lunch and Will kisses me sweetly and says good-bye.

*****

Claire is kind enough to put together an outfit special enough for graduation today. She knows I won't have a clue, or care. She chooses a black pencil skirt and royal blue top to coordinate with the royal purple cap and gown. The graduating class is small at just a hundred and eighty four. We walk alphabetically so that means I don't get to walk near any of my friends. In fact, I am second to last, followed only by Sharon Wyck, who happens to be one of the small groups of individuals who thinks Will and I make a perfect couple. Michael Walsh, who is walking in front of me, doesn't give me a solitary glance the entire time, which would be consistent with the preceding nine months we were in the same civics class.

Will's speech is strong and to the point. He talks about seizing the moments of our lives, regardless of what the consequences may be. "The opportunity of a lifetime must be seized in the lifetime of the opportunity," he says. The depth of its meaning is lost on everyone in the room but me and my family. I watch his father watching him looking proud, not of Will but of what he takes credit for in him.

"Our time here at Heyward has been interesting to say the least, but this last year has meant more to me, personally, than any other. It was the culmination of all I have worked for. As I prepare to take the first step on a path I never imagined would be before me, I am grateful for those who have touched my life. If our paths never cross again, know that you have impacted my life in incomprehensible ways.

"So as you move forward and prepare to take over the world, or your father's company, whichever is more lucrative," only this crowd would find the ironic humor in that, "remember that our lives are short. Seize every chance you have to live your life. Good luck to you…we're all going to need it."

The crowd applauds loudly and Will resumes his seat with the rest of the class. We file row by row up to the stage and cross as each of our names are read. While each person has his or her own cheering section, it isn't like graduation ceremonies I've been to back home – not nearly as rowdy. Tyler and Will lead the cheers as my name is called. I hear Chris, Caroline and Gwen, too, but it's hard to hear anything over Tyler's howls. I look out briefly and see Luke and Claire standing and applauding me and I wonder if they're thinking about Penny, thinking that they will never see their daughter cross this stage, that Luke will never walk her down an aisle...hoping that I can one day truly fill that hole in their hearts.

For one solid moment everything is right in the world, and I'm happy, but that feeling is crushed as I exit the stage and pass directly in front of Gregory Meyer. I give him the strongest look I can, knowing that he's close to being taken down.

The group resumes its dignity and the final proclamation of our graduation is spoken. We move our tassels from one side to the other and it is official. We've all finished a crucial chapter in our lives and are being set free like wild animals into the chaos of the real world. We stand to our feet and begin looking for our loved ones. Luke and Claire find me first and hug me so tight I almost can't breathe.

"Congratulations! We're so proud of you!" Claire says as she squeezes me.

"There you are!" Caroline shouts above the crowd.

"Hey!" I say wrapping my arms around her tiny frame. "Where are the guys, and Gwen?"

"They're coming. I gotta find my parents. We'll see you soon!" Caroline hugs me again and then darts in and out of the crowd in search of her parents. Everyone is coming to our house for a graduation dinner party that Claire insisted upon. It didn't take much twisting of my arm. I really want to see my friends before we have to leave for Florida. It isn't that critical that I see them before I leave since *they* are allowed to visit me any time they want. It's having all of us together, Will included, for the last time that is going to be difficult.

"Layla!" I hear Will's strong voice over the crowd and turn to find him. It takes just seconds before his arms are around me and we're locked together. Will gives me a hard, excited kiss. He's so happy and I love it. He's been in deep thought lately and it's so wonderful to see him this way. "Congratulations, baby!" he shouts.

"You, too! Your speech was great! I loved it." I yell above noise.

"It was lame, but thanks! I've gotta go to this thing my dad is doing to show me off," he says rolling his eyes. "But I'll be at your place as soon as I can, ok?"

I tell him its fine as he kisses me and leaves. The rest of the afternoon is like a blur before everyone gets there. Caroline's were the only parents to accept our invitation. Claire and I make all the food and I wrap the little token gifts I bought my friends before everyone arrives. It might be a long time before I see them again and I want them to have something that will remind them of me. I got Gwen and Caroline each a silver bracelet with a starfish charm. I was stumped on what to get Chris and Tyler so I went for the obvious: money clips with their initials engraved on them.

"Very cool! Thanks, Layla!" Chris hugs me, tossing the wrapping onto the kitchen counter.

"Thanks, Lay! Now I won't have to walk around with wads of cash rolled into my sock!" Tyler's humor is one of the things I appreciate about him and our relationship. I'm going to miss him terribly.

Gwen and Caroline open their gifts and squeal.

"Oh! I love it!" Gwen screams. I'm especially glad she likes it since Gwen is very particular about her clothes and accessories.

"It's perfect, Layla. Thank you so much for thinking of us." Caroline hugs and holds me tight. "So…what did you get Will?" she asks with an inquisitive smile.

"Well, let's just say it's something very personal." It is *very* personal. I don't want to ruin it by telling anyone ahead of time. I got the ok from Luke and Claire and that's all I need.

Will doesn't arrive until about six o'clock. Everyone shows him their gifts from me, but he doesn't once ask where his is, knowing I'll give it to him when we're alone. Chris, Tyler, and Gwen leave around seven because they have family in town and their parents have festivities of their own planned. Caroline and her parents stay just a little longer and then leave for the night. Before everyone leaves they promise to see me as much as possible before we go to Florida. It means a lot to me. I don't like not telling them about what is really happening. I could really use the girls' support especially.

Will and I help Luke and Claire clean up and I do my best to not bring up the tragedy that awaits us at the end of the month. It's June twelfth and we have exactly 18 days until we evacuate the place I have come to know as my home. That's just eighteen days left with the person I want to be with for the rest of my life.

Living on the lake has its benefits. One of them is that even though it's the middle of June, the air is comfortable by the water. Will and I say goodnight to Luke and Claire and go to the dock. We sit facing each other and Will takes my hands in his. It's a perfect moonlit night and I can't help but stare into Will's breathtaking eyes. There is safety there, knowing that through those eyes I'm seen as complete, and not some damaged little girl, and that I don't have to pay for my imperfections.

"I've got some things going on over the next few days, so I won't be around much," he says calmly.

"Oh, um, that's ok. There's still so much packing to do," I say, doing my best to hide my disappointment. I have so little time left with him. I really can't bear to be away from Will.

"I don't want you to think that I don't want to be here with you. God knows I do. I…I just have to do something with my mom. My dad will be in Raleigh the day after tomorrow and my mom's family would really like to see me before I ship off to college, so that's our only chance. It won't shock you to know my dad doesn't like us to see them." Will is uncharacteristically fidgety – his breathing is short and his heart is about to beat out of his chest.

"Are you ok? What's wrong?" I'm scared. I'm afraid he's found out something that is going to put a kink in their plan.

"I'm sorry, yes, I'm fine. I…have something for you. I wanted to have it in time for your birthday," he says reaching into his pocket. "But it wasn't ready until yesterday."

"That's good, because I have something for you, too," I smile in anticipation of giving Will his gift. I'm nervously excited and can't wait.

"I'd really like to do this first, if that's ok with you." I smile and nod. Will takes a deep breath and closes his eyes for a moment before he speaks.

"Layla, there has never been anyone who has touched my life more deeply than you have. You have taught me how to love so completely, and what it means to be willing to sacrifice your life to preserve that love. There will never be another moment like this, and I'm going to seize as much of this opportunity as I can, because *you* are the opportunity of my lifetime. I can't promise that I know when we'll see each other again, but I can promise that when we do I won't be letting go of you ever again. Until that time, I want you to have this. It was my grandmother's." Will pulls out a ring box and opens it. Inside is the most beautiful white gold ring with a small square diamond set in the center. The diamonds on either side are set in a leaf shape and it is the most stunning ring I've ever seen. It isn't huge or gaudy like something someone would buy now. Its antique design is simple and understated. "I'd be honored if you would wear it as a symbol of my promise to you. I love you, Layla. Nothing, absolutely *nothing*, will ever change that."

"I love you, too." I'm crying and that's all I can get out as Will takes the ring from the box and places it on the ring finger of my left hand. I can't imagine how the actual proposal could be any more beautiful than this but I will spend every moment until then in glorious anticipation.

Will holds my face in his hands and kisses me. "I swear to you, Layla, I *will* keep my promise. Just promise me that no matter what happens you'll never give up."

"I promise. I'll never give up on us." I kiss him back and hold him close. I take a deep breath and say, "Now it's my turn. I'm not sure I can follow that, but I'll try." I pull a small velvet bag from my pocket and hold it out in front of me. I'm not as good with words as Will is, but I do my best to speak from my heart. "Because you mean more to me than anyone else in the world, I want to give you something that means the same." I hand Will the pouch. He opens it carefully and pulls out a white gold band. "It was my father's wedding ring. I want you to have it…my promise ring to you. You don't have to, you know, wear it, if you don't want to…or if you think it'll cause problems with you father. I just want you to have it. It's engraved." He turns the ring and catches the engraving in the light. It reads *forever*.

"Oh, Layla. Baby, this is amazing. That you would entrust me with something so precious means more to me than you'll ever know. Yes, of course I'm going to wear it." I help him put the ring on, as he did with me. I force myself to be aware of everything. The way we hold our hands together, how it feels to slide the ring on his finger, the look in his eyes as the ring reaches its resting place. This may be the only time that we exchange rings like this and I don't want to forget a millisecond of it.

We sit for a while longer resting in each other's arms and watch the lake glow from the light of the moon. It's an exceptionally beautiful night and I don't want it to end. I can't take my eyes off my ring. It is the most beautiful thing I've ever seen and it will never leave my hand.

As I walk Will to his car he seems to have a slower gait. He's never been one for rushing, but it's obvious that he is intentionally walking more slowly. We stand next to his car and he holds me for a long time. When we can't stand there any longer, Will kisses me deliberately. It's so beautiful that I start to cry. I'm overwhelmed with the love I feel in this one kiss. Will finally breaks away and I can see that it was emotional for him, too.

"We've still got a few weeks left," I say brushing his cheek with my hand. It's unusual for me to be the one consoling him. He's so good at that with me. I want to do the same for him.

"I know…It's just…I want you to know beyond a shadow of a doubt that I love you. I need you to know that, Layla. Promise me you know that, please," Will demands. I've never seen him this emotional before.

"I know that, Will. I promise," I say in my best effort to comfort him. I don't like seeing him upset like this. My anger for his father begins to surface, but I push it down to keep my focus on Will. I'm not going to let Gregory

Meyer interrupt this moment.

"Ok…good. I guess…I need to go now. Tell Luke and Claire I said thank you for everything." Will gets in his car and rolls his window down. I lean my head inside and kiss him again.

"I'll see you soon, right? When you're back from your grandparents'?" I ask.

"I love you, Layla," he says, still holding back tears.

"I love you, too, Will."

Will pulls onto the street and I watch him drive away, looking forward to seeing him back on my doorstep in a few days.

Chapter 28

The time until Will comes back is occupied with packing, packing, and more packing. It's only going to be a couple of days, but any time away from him feels like an eternity. Caroline and Gwen are here to help keep me company and make sure they see me before I leave. They're glad Will's gone for a few days so they don't have to fight for time with me. I have to admit that I've neglected them a bit lately. I became the girl who is so in love with her boyfriend that the rest of the world no longer seems to exist. In all honesty, I wouldn't change a thing. They haven't seemed to mind, but if they knew everything that was going on, they'd be even more understanding.

Everything, except my clothes, has already been boxed up and stored in the garage. Claire has errands to run so Caroline's mother is there to help. She's a psychiatrist at the hospital in Charlotte and said she welcomed the day off. I think about picking her brain since I'm considering psychology as a major, but I don't really want to think about school. I want to stay right here with Gwen and Caroline and enjoy the last few weeks I have with them.

"All of this stuff is going with you?" Gwen asks in amazement. "The last time we moved, my mom dumped a truck load at Goodwill and bought new stuff to outfit the new house." This isn't surprising. Gwen's mom is everything Mr. Meyer wishes I would be. She's superficial and gorgeous and knows her place on the arm of Gwen's father. I'm surprised Gwen turned out as wonderful as she did.

"Claire said we don't have enough time to sort through everything before we leave. Luke's position at the firm in Tallahassee starts July fifth. I'm sure she'll do a purge as we sort through everything at the new place." The story we all agreed was most plausible is that Luke accepted a position at a law firm in Tallahassee both because it was a move to advance his career and so that they could be close to me while I'm at college. The reality is that Luke and Claire have squirreled away enough money for us to live on for more years than I thought possible. Luke and Claire will take the bar exam in Florida and join a law firm down there in time because early retirement would drive both of the crazy.

"When's Will getting back? Shouldn't he be helping with some heavy lifting or something?" Caroline asks.

"They should be back sometime tonight. It'll be late so I'll just see him tomorrow. You know, I never asked where his mom's family lived," I say. "Do you know?"

"They're up in Hickory. Will's dad is weird about him seeing that side of the family," Gwen answers.

"Yeah, that's what he said." I reply.

"They're worker bees, you know. They make furniture. That's where Will gets it. Mr. Meyer doesn't like to socialize with people like that. He just wants to hire them," Gwen continues with her typical side commentary on the subject.

"I want to ask you two for a favor. It's going to sound silly but…can you keep an eye on Will? I'll be gone and I just want to know that you guys are looking after him. Not to sound weird or anything, but he might take it kind of hard." I hope I haven't said too much, but I really need them to pay special attention to him after I'm gone. I hate leaving him here with his father to gloat his victory over him.

"Gosh, Layla! It's not like Will isn't going to take every chance he can to sneak down and see you! But, I suppose being in love will make you a little over protective." I'm going to miss Caroline's sweet southern accent. I'm going to miss everything about Caroline. I want to take her with me. Maybe I'll be able to tell her what really happened when she visits. I don't think any of our friends will be surprised to hear that Gregory Meyer ran us out of town.

I'll miss all my friends here. I feel a bit guilty for having not missed anyone when I moved from Florida. I never made enough of an effort to stay in touch with anyone like I should have, so I take responsibility for the distance. I will not let that happen between me and Gwen and Caroline. They embraced me and introduced me to a love I could have only received from them. Knowing I have just a few weeks left here makes me want to pack in as much time with friends as I can.

I didn't spend nearly enough time with Chris or Gwen. Will they come to see me in Florida or will the absence of their visits be a casualty of not investing enough in them while I was here? I need them all to come to visit as much as possible; they're my only link to Will.

I'm sure I'll call them more frequently than they'll like, but I'll die every day that I don't know how Will is doing. None of them are going to Princeton so I'll demand that Will communicate with them every day, following each phone call or email with a report to me.

"Oh, my gosh! What is *this*? I can't believe we didn't see this earlier!" Caroline squeals. She grabs my hand and examines the ring on my finger. "Did you and Will get engaged?"

"No…not really…it's a promise ring. It was his grandmother's." I'm shy for a moment, not sure how to explain the beautiful moment Will and I shared just a few nights ago.

"Layla, it's gorgeous." Gwen's tone is sweet and sentimental, not typically like her. She's holding back tears. "I'm so happy for you."

"Gwen?" I prompt. "Are you crying?"

"It's just…you have to know how incredibly lucky you are. There isn't a better guy out there than Will." Gwen has shocked me. She's usually so tough, but it's nice to see this side of her.

"She's a sucker for true love!" Caroline chimes. "I can't believe you didn't tell us about this! If I weren't so happy for you, I'd be furious. So what's the plan?"

"There isn't one really. We just have to be patient. We don't know how long it could be, but we're both in it for the long haul I guess. I…gave him something, too – my dad's wedding band." I hesitate to tell them, but they'll see it later tonight when Will gets here anyway.

"Wow. All you two need is a cake and some flowers and you're on your way." There's the Gwen I know and love.

The doorbell rings and Caroline's mom calls to us that she ordered pizza. I sit in the half-packed kitchen with my two best girlfriends eating pizza, talking and laughing until my sides hurt. I relish every syllable that leaves their mouths and try to etch it into my mind forever. Even when they come to visit me in Tallahassee, it won't be the same as being here in Davidson. My heart is here and I'm so angry with Gregory Meyer for forcing me to abandon it.

"Did you save some for us?" Luke calls as he and Claire breeze into the kitchen.

"Of course!" I reply mid-laugh.

"Great! How's the packing coming?" Claire asks, changing my mood almost immediately.

"It's coming." I don't really want to talk about the impending tragedy of leaving almost everyone I love behind. Claire can see that and doesn't discuss the move anymore.

We abandon packing for the rest of the night and talk about college. Caroline is going to design school in California and Gwen is headed to Clemson for business. I love how unassumingly brilliant Gwen is. She's got Kate Hudson's beauty and Steve Jobs' brain.

Talking about going away to college seems normal. The girls assume that we'll all get together for holidays and random visits, but they have no idea just how permanent my move is; that Gregory Meyer will have to be six feet under before we're all together again.

*****

I wake with my alarm at 8:00 am and smile as I wait to hear the voice that has followed that morning ping almost every weekend for the last few months. It's Will's voice that makes everything we're going through bearable. I've waited longer than usual when I figure Will probably got home later than he expected and is enjoying a well-deserved morning of sleeping in, so I reach for my phone and send him a quick text.

Layla Weston: Good morning, sleepyhead! Can't wait to see you soon!

I put the phone down and take a shower. In lieu of taking the time to dry my too-thick hair I opt for a single French braid. Will said he liked how wavy my hair was after an overnight braid once so I'll take it out when we go out tonight.

It's an hour before I check my phone again. No text from Will. *He must really be out of it. He never sleeps this late.* I expected Will to reply by now. I hope his father didn't given him and his mom a hard time when they got home. He didn't say they had been *forbidden* from seeing his mother's family, just that his father didn't like it. Besides, he's getting what he wants in just a few weeks. I'll be in Florida and Will will be on his way to Princeton, but with Mr. Meyer you never know just how evil his mood is.

I walk into the kitchen half-expecting to see Will there, but he's not. There's no one in the kitchen or on the patio. Luke and Claire are early risers so they're probably out tying up loose ends with clients at the firm. I grab a bowl and pour myself some Frosted Cheerios and eat.

We're just a couple of weeks away from the Meyer-imposed deadline. I remember when Gramps died realizing that my final days in that house were coming to a close. Those were my happiest moments in the midst of the sadness of losing Gramps. It's quite the opposite now. I was never really home with Gram and Gramps, but here…this is the most home I've known since Mom and Dad. And now, because one man can't let his son choose his own path, I have to give up the life I have earned.

I hate Gregory Meyer.

Luke and Claire enter the kitchen as I'm cleaning my breakfast dishes. Gregory Meyer is with them.

"What's he doing here?" I say with intended rudeness.

"He's looking for Will," Luke answers.

"What do you mean he's looking for Will? He and his mom were coming home last night from Hickory." I grab my phone. Still no text from Will.

"Miss Weston, I really don't have time for your games. I gave you and my son a measure of latitude and I don't appreciate you taking advantage of it. Now, if you'll retrieve my son we can get on with our day..." Gregory Meyer's face is expressionless but his tone is full of contempt. His mere presence makes me sick to my stomach.

"Will isn't here. Are you telling me Will is missing?" I look at my phone again, refreshing the text screen in some attempt to force Will's reply.

"Layla," Claire approaches me, speaking softly. "If Will is here you need to get him."

"He's not here! I don't know where he is. I thought he was coming home last night. I haven't heard from him." This has got to be some mistake. "Haven't you tried contacting Eliana's family? Maybe they stayed longer." I say frantically.

"I have contacted them and they report that Eliana and William left last night around 8:00 PM. If you know where my son is, Miss Weston, I suggest you tell me now. You know what I'm capable of. Don't think that you can play games with me." Gregory Meyer takes a step toward me in attempted intimidation but Luke intervenes.

"She doesn't know where he is, but if we hear from him we'll encourage him to contact you. There's a lot going on, Greg. He probably just needs some time," Luke says calmly. "You should go home. They may be there already."

Mr. Meyer gives me a threatening look that reminds me of our ill-fated meeting on the trail in the mountains. "Don't think you're buying yourself any more time, Miss Weston. You still have a deadline." With that he excuses himself and leaves.

"Ok, Layla. What's going on?" Luke asks directly.

"I told you, I don't know," I reiterate slowly. Luke and Claire look at each other in that knowing way and then back to me. "Do *you* know what's going on?"

"We don't know where he is either," Claire says. Her tone is soft and tender, and full of fear.

"Mr. Meyer has something to do with this and he's trying to blame me! Did you notice how he didn't ask where his own wife was? He doesn't even care about her!" I'm furious from fear. Will is nowhere to be found and he hasn't contacted me at all. "Ok, ok, ok…" I say in an attempt to calm myself. I try to practice being like Claire in a tense situation in hopes that I'll achieve her level of coolness one day. "Let's be reasonable. Will is probably just taking some extra time with his mom. He's leaving her here with *him* and that worries Will. I don't like that he hasn't contacted me, but I'm sure I'll hear from him tonight."

"I'm sure you're right, Layla," Claire says, this time matching *my* calming tone. "There's still quite a bit to get done. We've got plenty to pass the time.

We'll hear from Will before we know it."

*****

It's been two days and no one has seen or heard from Will or his mother. Mr. Meyer has launched an all-out search across the state sparing no expense on private investigators. It's about time he used his money for something worthwhile. There haven't been any solid leads and I'm doing my best not to lose my mind. Gwen and Caroline have been over continuing to help pack the house. Despite the insanity of what's going on, Luke and Claire have insisted we continue to pack. After all, we still have a deadline.

The doorbell rings and I open the door to find Marcus. Without hesitation I put my arms around him and hug him tightly. Regardless of the words we last shared, Marcus had been a good friend. He stepped in to help when we needed him and I will always be grateful.

"I'm really sorry, Layla," he says. "He's gonna turn up. Nothing is going to keep him from getting to you…you know that."

"Thank you, Marcus. I appreciate you coming. It means a lot to me. I'm so sorry about the way we left things…"

"Water under the bridge. Let's just move forward, ok?" He smiles and I'm comforted to know he is still my friend. "Any word, yet?

"No, nothing. It's crazy, Marcus. At first I really thought they just stayed another night with his mom's family, but when he didn't contact me at all by that first night, I knew something was wrong. I can't believe he would be somewhere and not contact me."

"Do you think Mr. Meyer had something to do with their disappearance?"

"I don't know. I can't imagine that he would actually do something to his own family. Whether he had something to do with it or not, I wouldn't put it past him to fake this whole search and rescue effort just to make himself look good. I just hope they turn up before we leave."

"You're still leaving?" Marcus asks with a bit of shock.

"Have to. Luke and Claire start their jobs and they aren't going to let me stay by myself," I tell him, maintaining the illusion that we're leaving of our own volition.

"You'd think their boss would cut them some slack."

"Yeah, well, you know how some lawyers can be, right? You'll come visit me, won't you?" I ask.

"You think I'm going to miss out on a free place to stay near a Florida beach? I'll head down when the weather starts getting chilly around here," he says.

"Sounds like a plan. Thanks again for coming, Marcus. It means a lot to me." I hug him again and open the door.

"Don't worry. They're going to turn up, Layla." Marcus kisses my cheek and walks to his car. As I watch him drive away all I can think is that I hope he's right.

"Layla, was that Marcus?" Claire asks as I close the door behind me.

"Yeah…he wanted to see how I was doing. I guess everyone knows Will is missing."

"That was nice of him to come by," she says. "Sounds like you two made up."

"We did. I'm glad. I really didn't like the way we left things. With us leaving next week, I don't think I could bear having things unsettled with him." I sit down on the couch, lean over, and put my head in my hands. "Will's out there…somewhere. Why hasn't he called me, or you, or anyone? It's been three days since they were supposed to be back. We're leaving in a week! What if he's out there and hurt? What if…what if they don't find him? What if we're not here when he comes back? Oh, Aunt Claire!" I go from nothing to the ugly cry in seconds. I can't take it anymore. How did my life become so doomed?

"Oh, Layla. I'm so sorry this is happening. You deserve so much better than all this. I know it's not what you want to hear, but…maybe this move back to Florida is really the best thing for you. You can start over." Claire embraces me, stroking my hair back as she consoles me.

"I'm tired of starting over. How many do-overs can one person have?"

"Look at me," Claire says, but I hesitate. "Look at me, Layla." She's more commanding now so I know she's serious. "You can have as many do-overs as you need. Life is imperfect and so are we. We are never going to make all the right choices. We're never going to be in every ideal situation. All we have in life is our ability to control our actions. We can change our part of any outcome at any point.

"After Penny died I thought my life was over, but Luke held me and gave me this same speech. Knowing he was right by my side made me believe I could move on with my life. Because I did, I was gifted with you. We're right beside you, Layla."

I don't say anything. I just lean in harder and let Claire hold me while I drain myself of all the tears I'd been holding in.

*****

It's June thirtieth and there is still no sign of Will or his mother. Luke said that since it's been more than ten days Mr. Meyer wants to call off the search. He's assuming they're dead. I can't accept that. I'm going to need more than Gregory Meyer's unwillingness to be relentless in his search to make me back down.

The house is packed and so are we. Since our deadline has arrived, we really don't have a choice in leaving. Chris and Tyler arrived before 7:00 AM to help get the truck packed, and Gwen and Caroline come around 9:00 AM for moral support. Between the three of us girls there isn't a dry eye.

"I want you two to know how much I love you both. You welcomed me into your circle and became sisters to me. Thank you…so much." I say in between soft sobs. I hug them both tightly, not wanting to let go.

"We love you, too. We're so glad you came here. Before we met you, I remember Will telling us that you were going to breathe a breath of fresh air into our lives; he was so right." Caroline says through tears.

"I know it isn't like me to, you know, get all mushy, but…Layla…you changed our lives. You showed us what it means to be true to yourself and uncompromising. I don't know what we'll do without you." Gwen hugs me fiercely and I know that my earlier fears of her not coming to visit were unmerited.

We say nothing of Will's disappearance, not wanting to make the moment any harder than it already is. The girls leave, saying they can't bear the idea of watching me drive away. After Chris and Tyler finish loading the truck I'm forced to say my goodbyes to them.

"You better not forget about us!" Chris says picking me up as he bear hugs me.

"I wouldn't think of it," I whisper in his ear. I'm afraid to talk any louder than that for fear I'll burst into tears…again.

Saying goodbye to Tyler is harder. He had come to my aid and helped me understand Will in those times when it seemed impossible. He reassured me and helped build my confidence in Will's love for me.

"I think I'm going to miss you most of all," I tell him.

"Not half as much as I'm going to miss you. If only I had seen you first, I would have made you mine." He holds my face in his hands and kisses my forehead. "You're an amazing person, Layla – a spitfire. Don't ever forget it. You had the courage to stand up to Gregory Meyer. If you can do *that*, you can do anything. That's one of the reasons Will loves you so much. You gave him courage he didn't know he had. You did that for all of us." I embrace Tyler and don't want to let go. He is as close as I will ever be to Will again. "I love you," he whispers.

"I love you, too," I tell him.

"I'm so sorry about Will. They're going to find him," Tyler whispers.

"I hope so," I say, echoing his whisper.

"Layla, it's time," Luke says softly, placing his hand on my shoulder. I pull away from Tyler and take a long look at him.

"The four of you need to come down and see me soon, ok? Road trip, right?" I try to lighten my tone in an attempt to stop the tears.

"I don't have to let Gwen drive, do I?" Tyler jokes.

"No…definitely not." We both laugh and I feel good about leaving on a high note.

We hug everyone again and say our goodbyes. Caroline's parents are still there, as are Chris and Tyler's, which I think means a lot to Luke and Claire, too. Claire and I climb into the Denali and pull out of the driveway with Luke behind us in the moving truck, towing the Lexus. I cringe as we drive past Will's house. I feel like I should be doing something to help find Will, but the reality is that there is absolutely nothing that I can do. I've not powered down my phone in almost two weeks, and kept the ringer as loud as it will go. I even set a different ring for Will's number.

It's late in the day when we leave so we stop in Savannah overnight and continue on to Tallahassee the next day. The drive is fine. It's mostly desolate, especially through South Carolina. Claire and I make small talk, but I mostly listen to my iPod. All I want to listen to is the playlist I created of my favorite songs from the bands, old and new, Will introduced me to. It's on shuffle and repeat.

We have adjoining rooms at the hotel in Savannah, which is good because Claire is close by to console me in the night as I cry in my sleep. Every night since Will disappeared it's a variation of the same dream. I'm in the back seat of my parent's car on the night of our accident. We crash and there's blood splattered on the windows and me. As I look up I see Will in the driver's seat and me in the passenger seat. Sometimes I'm me at the age I am now. Sometimes I'm twelve. Every night I wake up to Claire stroking my hair and telling me it was just a dream and that I'm ok.

When we arrive at our new house in Tallahassee, Claire gets out and meets Luke at the front door. I sit in the car for a while, soaking it all in. I can't bring my body to move. I'm having déjà vu, only I didn't feel completely dead inside the day I arrived at Luke and Claire's house in Davidson.

I force myself to open the car door and get out. Each step is labored and forced. The house is smaller but just as beautiful. I push the huge double wooden doors open and get my first glance of the place I'll live in numbed existence until Will is found. The floor plan is typically Floridian: very open and lots of windows. I walk to the back of the house and I'm immediately struck by the view, which is the first time I've felt much of anything outside of fear in days.

"We had it built for you. If you follow it, you'll find a manmade lake. It's not Lake Davidson, but, we didn't think you should have to give up everything." Claire says as we stare at the obviously new dock poking out from the thick brush of trees and vines.

"Thank you, Aunt Claire," I say quietly.

The moving truck with all the furniture and boxes arrives a few hours later and the movers work diligently to get everything set up. Nothing looks, feels, or even smells the same. I wanted to make this move just like it was planned to be, but there is no way it can. I was going to live in a constant state of hope and anticipation that Will and I would be together again one day, but now that Will is missing it's not the same. I spend my time in a contrast of fear and hope. I don't want to give up on Will being out there somewhere, but he's been missing for so long.

I've been through more than one person should be able to withstand in five short years – Mom and Dad's death, my imprisonment with Gram, and losing myself completely to care for Gramps. Now Will's gone. It's like the universe is slapping me in the face.

Sometimes I wish I had died that night with my parents – one swift death instead of several repeated slow deaths over the last years. Now the most painful thing of all: I don't want to say it out loud, but the truth is…Will may be dead, too.

I've nearly finished unpacking, breaking down boxes as I empty them. There are dozens more than when I first moved in with Luke and Claire, so it's no wonder it's taken me a week to unpack instead of hours. As I deposit a few broken-down boxes in the garage, I choose a few more marked with my name. I don't remember packing up this many things, but Gwen and Caroline were with me most of my packing days, making the mundane task more palatable, so forgetting isn't that surprising.

There's a lighter box that I think must have scarves and gloves in it so I stack it on top of one a bit heavier and continue to wear a path in the floor between the garage and my room. I've started a box of seasonal clothes so I decide to go ahead and transfer the scarf box items to the seasonal box. I cut the packing tape, breaking the seal along the edges. When I open it all I find is newspaper. Lots of newspaper. *There's nothing in here?* I think just before my heart stops.

No. There *is* something. Underneath the sheets and sheets of crumpled newspaper sits a black velvet jewelry box. I feel my brow furrow and my eyebrows tense. I didn't pack this box but it has my name on it. I pull the black box into my hand and recognize the scent that lingers from it. For a brief moment I am filled with hope. I allow my mind to stroll through hopeful places it hasn't been in quite some time. I decide to open the box while I'm visiting these not-forgotten streets, and I am not disappointed. As the box creaks open the light catches the shiny metal inside. I think my heart is going to leap from my chest as I stare at this remarkable treasure.

Will's ring.

Acknowledgements

Thank you, first of all, to you, the readers. I want you to know that I am honored that you chose *The Lake* and invested your time and emotions into Layla's story. I hope you'll stick around for the journey and see Layla through to the end. I think you'll be glad you did!

I am so incredibly thankful to my dear friend Lisa (LB!). You played a major role in the development of this story. You gave your honest feedback whenever I asked, and you never held back. Your questions challenged me, and your pure love for Will and Layla's story was, and continues to be, invaluable. Never underestimate your impact on this process. I will never have enough words of thanks to give you. I treasure our friendship. I am so glad Jason married you!

Thank you to my editor, Lisa, who fixed all my 'buts.' You were and continue to be a lifesaver! I'm glad we're discovering that we have more in common than Old Navy. I'm so grateful for you and our growing friendship!

I couldn't have been more blessed than to have author Erin Healy walk along side me through this process. From the first call to tell you I was writing a book but had no clue what I was doing, to the time you gifted me in helping me create a stronger introduction to Layla's story, you believed in me and encouraged me in my writing. Who would have thought that when we met all those years ago that God would connect us again this way? Thank you for your advice and guidance. You are truly the best thing to happen to my writing career.

To everyone who beta read the book and gave me feedback: your input made Will and Layla's story better and for that I'm truly grateful. Lisa B., Lisa S., Sarah, Erin, Jenna, Kelly, and Christi: thank you for cheering me on!

To my dear, sweet friend Dana. Thank you for keeping this baby safe from the very beginning. You have been a constant source of support and encouragement. I treasure you and our friendship, and I don't know what I'd do without you.

Thank you, Vinh, for helping to make Marcus sound like a trigonometry genius. I have and always will admire your brilliance!

I have such great respect for the authors who have gone before me, paving the way for stories like Will and Layla's to be told. Ted Dekker, Erin Healy, Colleen Hoover, Jamie McGuire, J.K. Rowling, Suzanne Collins, Kathryn Stockett, and Stephanie Meyer: you are my inspirations. You have written incredibly addicting stories that aren't easily put down. Thank you for your fearlessness in creating characters and stories that inspire us to be better friends, stand up for what is right, and love more deeply.

A huge thank you to Amazon! Thank you for making it possible for independent writers to get their work out there. You've created an outlet that fulfills the creative need in so many and I am eternally grateful!

Many thanks to my dad and mom, David and Anna, for raising a daughter who turned out to be pretty fearless. Having three older brothers helped in that process, too, I suppose. To said brothers – Glenn, Derek, and Chris - thank you for challenging me throughout life. You are all brilliant and talented, and I'd like to think I'm a good, albeit strange, mix of the three of you. I could have used fewer swirlies, but they helped shape me into the person I am today, so thanks.

To my kids who have encouraged me through this process simply by thinking it's cool that their mom wrote a book.

Last and *never* least, enormous gratitude to my husband, Donavan. Thank you for your love and support, for listening to every story line idea, letting me space out every now and then as the wheels turned in my head, and for the nights you had no idea what time I actually got into bed. Most of all, thank you for always believing in me. You are my best friend and the best partner in life a girl could ask for. I couldn't have done this without you. So much!

About the Author

The Lake is the first book in AnnaLisa Grant's Lake Series. AnnaLisa earned her Master's degree in Counseling at Gordon-Conwell Theological Seminary in Charlotte, North Carolina. She and her husband Donavan live with their two children in Matthews, North Carolina.

Other Books by AnnaLisa Grant:

The Lake Series:

The Lake

Troubled Waters

Safe Harbor

Anchored: A Lake Series Novella

As I Am

Five

Made in the USA
Lexington, KY
25 February 2016